Be Careful What You Wish For

Anne-Marie Price

This novel is entirely a work of fiction.
The names, characters and incidents portrayed in it
are the work of the author's imagination.
Any resemblance to actual persons, living or dead,
events or localities is entirely coincidental

Copyright © 2018 Anne-Marie Price

ISBN: 978-0-9942761-6-2

DEDICATION

Kathy Hood
The Best Ever Childhood Friend
I had to set you free,
So that you were not held back by me.

THANKS

The Editors Book Club
The Society of Women Writers WA

ACKNOWLEDGMENTS

MY IMMORTAL
Words and Music by BEN MOODY, DAVID HODGES and AMY
LEE
© ZOMBIES AT MY PUBLISHING and FORTHEFALLEN
PUBLISHING
All Right for Australia & New Zealand Administered by
WARNER/CHAPPELL MUSIC AUSTRALIA PTY LTD
(Publishing) and DEVIRRA GROUP (Print)
International Copyright Secured. Al Rights Reserved.
Reproduced by Permission of DEVIRRA GROUP.
Unauthorised Reproduction is Illegal

ABOUT THE AUTHOR

Anne-Marie Price is predominately a writer of fiction, to not only give voice to the stories that are given to her through her dreams; but to make it possible to be someone else.
Writing is in the blood of the Price family with Anne-Marie being the fourth generation of writers.
Anne-Marie was born and raised in Perth, Western Australia. She lives with her parents Margaret and Laurence and her three cats, Bells, Rainbow and Jackson.

Also By This Author

Hostage Of Diplomacy
The Search For The King James Bible
Stirling Trilogy
Stirling Breed
Stirling Masquerade
Stirling Conspiracy
Tiger's Eyes

Sunday 20 October

God's Errand

The wind danced amongst the magnificent autumnal array of red, orange and yellow leaves of the trees and was piercingly cold. It gave a timely reminder that winter was fast approaching. Father Michael Casey wrapped his overcoat tighter around him as he strode down the High Street of the village of Stirling just north of Bath in the south of England.

He was Father Thomas O'Brian's assistant at the Catholic Church, St Andrews, who was battling the late stages of colon cancer. Having arrived only the evening before, this was the first chance that Michael had to see something of the village in daylight for many years. The main streets of Stirling were cobbled and many of the surrounding shops retained their 19th century charm.

Not that I intend to linger as the cold wind keeps me moving, thought Michael, *but I feel like I've stepped into a time warp. I wonder, if the bus I'd arrived on is the only modern vehicle that has ever been seen in the village.*

Villagers were keen to stop Michael to talk. Some he had seen at Mass earlier that morning, most wished to pass on their thoughts and prayers for Father Thomas.

I'd like to stop to chat but I'm on an errand for Thomas. And my destination is a good half an hour's walk outside of the village centre, Michael rationalised. *A quiet and peaceful village,* he thought, and as he continued down the street, away from the church and cemetery at the top of the hill; he wondered, *Is it likely I'll become bored with too much peace?*

Michael Casey was reasonably tall, fair-haired and with a solid muscular build. At 32 he was in the prime of his life and he was considered quite handsome.

Approaching an attractive two-story thatch cottage almost hidden by an abundance of greenery, Michael felt immediately warmer, and assumed it was the energetic pace that he had set getting there. That was until he saw a tall, good looking, and dark haired 16 year old boy in only a black tee shirt and thin tracksuit pants, working industriously in the front garden. A heavenly scent wafted through the air as the teenager harvested the herb bushes.

Before Michael was a low fence with a charming gate that artistically hung upon only one hinge. Not wishing to disturb this creative display, Father Michael put his hand out to vault over the gate but it opened by itself. He felt even warmer as he stepped inside and was undoing the buttons of his overcoat as the teenager approached him.

'Merry Meet! You must be Michael Casey. Old Tom told us that you'd soon be joining our village.'

Michael looked into eyes of the deepest blue and only by instinct did he shake the hand that the teenager held out.

'I'm Ethan Tempest,' continued the teen. 'I presume you've been sent for some more of Ace's jungle juice?'

'Your Grandmother?' Michael's question caused Ethan to burst into laughter as he wiped the back of his hand across his sweaty forehead. 'Old Tom couldn't have told you that!'

Michael looked surprised. 'Is that really respectful to Father Thomas, Ethan? I obviously made a mistake in presuming that because Thomas said that Acacia Tempest was a witch, that she was old.'

Becoming serious, Ethan shook his head and a ray of sunlight gleamed off the pentagram around his neck. 'Respect isn't always evident in what we say but what we feel. Thomas likes a joke, and the nickname Old Tom is an indication of my respect as I cannot call him Father.'

Michael considered this carefully before asking, 'Do you approve of Father Thomas' wish to use herbs rather than western medicines that already exist that will ease his pain?'

Ethan's eyebrows rose in surprise at the question. 'Tom did allow western medicine to aid his fight against cancer until the words "inoperable" and "no cure" were finally used. Those pain relieving drugs can also reduce the quality of life.' The boy wiped his forehead again, only managing to add more dirt than remove sweat. 'But what I think is irrelevant. It is for each person to decide what is right for him or herself. If I'm ever in the same situation, I mightn't be able to resist the opportunity for a pain free, mind free death instead of a slow and agonising one!'

Not What I Expected

'Ethan, are you going to bore the man to death, or invite him in? Blessed Be Father Casey!' The soft, amused female voice made the two men look around at the beautiful vision that stood in the open doorway. Michael's jaw dropped in surprise as he looked upon the most beautiful young woman that he had ever met.

At 25, Acacia had a voluptuous figure and the most luscious waist length wavy black hair; but the years of raising and training Ethan had given her an added air of confidence and poise. An impish smile touched Acacia's lips as the Priest took in her attire.

The simple black dress she was wearing was above the knee in length, figure hugging, with tight long sleeves and a rounded neck, completed by a hanging gold belt around her waist and knee high boots. She was also wearing a pentagram around her neck like Ethan's.

The clearing of Ethan's throat brought Michael back to reality as he stepped up onto the verandah, his hand extended to her. As he approached, Acacia felt the shock of recognition as if they had met before. *My perfect man now stands in front of me but the Catholic Priest's collar destroys the fantasy I had clung to for many years.*

'My apologies, Miss Tempest, but... Are you really a witch?'

Acacia shook his hand as she laughed, quickly recovering from her surprise and disappointment. 'Even old witches were young once, Father Casey, and please call me Acacia.'

'Call me Michael.' As she gestured for him to follow her inside, he was puzzled by the words that had just left his mouth. *Not 'Call me Father Michael', but just 'Call me Michael'. So much more intimate an address for someone I've only just met. And yet… there is the feeling of having met before.* Ethan returned to his gardening as Acacia led the Priest down the narrow hall into a spacious and inviting kitchen.

Along one wall of shelving, were jars and bottles of herbs, oils and other objects, many of which Michael couldn't have identified even if the labels had been in English.

'That's not Latin otherwise I would recognise some of the words.' Michael pointed to the jars.

Acacia glanced over her shoulder. 'No, it is Gaelic, my grandmother's tongue.' He was invited to sit down at the dining table in the middle of the room as Acacia gathered together from the shelves the herb jars that she needed for Father Thomas' mixture and put the kettle on to boil.

Startled, Michael felt a cold wet nose press against his hand, and looking under the table, he found himself looking into the soulful eyes of an old German Shepherd. Without looking up from her work of crushing and mixing herbs with a mortar and pestle, Acacia stated, 'That's Benny. He's about ten and was Grandmama's dog.'

Michael patted the dog's head, his fingers finding an itchy spot behind Benny's ears. 'I always thought that witches kept only cats.'

Acacia poured boiling water into the mixing bowl from the kettle before placing a tea towel over it and whispered, *'With love I call upon every force I know. Water, Fire, Earth, and Air. Harness the powers within myself. And Help Thomas to fight his illness as there is still a task for him to fulfil before he is taken from this mortal plane.'*

To Michael she said, 'A witch has a variety of animals to choose from for a familiar. We have, in fact, many different animals here on our small farm. Would you like a guided tour while the herbs are being infused into the water?'

'That would be lovely, thank you.' Michael gave Benny a final pat before rising to his feet.

The farm hadn't appeared very big from the front, but as he stepped out the back door, behind Acacia, Michael realised that looks could be deceptive. The property may have been narrow, but it extended well back into the woods that formed a natural boundary for the village. A few steps beyond the house was a well-kept 18th century stable with the doors standing wide open during the day to permit Acacia's two horses to come and go as they pleased.

In an area cut off by a low picket fence, there was a worm farm that handled all the farm food waste that didn't go to the chickens that roamed free, or to the pig. Like the horses, the chickens had a night roost that protected them from the weather and foxes.

There was also a vegetable garden as well as an orchard about the same size as the herb garden, and a fence surrounded it to keep the animals out. The rest of the property was grass and magnificent, mature trees, with the occasional man-made shelter for the sheep, as well as troughs for food and water.

A Motley Crew

Acacia allowing him the opportunity to take it all in, bent down to pat the always excited Jack Russell Terrier who had raced over to greet them. There was a mixed variety of animals, all together, grazing side by side. There were the two horses, one a pretty chestnut mare, and the other a midnight black colt; half a dozen sheep, one ram, the hens, Daisy the cow, a goat, and apart from Benny and Jack, the Jack Russell, there was also a Keeshond, which was a Dutch Barge dog. What Michael noticed was the lack of felines.

'What about cats?'

Acacia's eyes twinkled mischievously as she straightened. 'We have at least ten cats, but at present I've sent them off to do some work in the village. There has been a small plague of mice in Stirling, so anyone interested in ridding their house of vermin will leave their doors open today to let the cats do their work. They'll return here by night fall.'

'You can't train cats, can you?' Michael looked even more surprised.

'To a certain extent.' A smile touched Acacia's lips, 'It depends upon your relationship with and handling of them. This place is a haven for them. People can be very cruel.'

'I believe there is good in everyone!'

Sadly, Acacia shook her head. 'Yes but not everyone utilises that good. With the exception of Benny and my own familiar, Tiger, the domestic animals on the farm are here because their previous owners abused them.'

'Don't you have a problem with all these animals having additional offspring? Surely that is just adding to the problem of homeless and unwanted animals?'

Acacia smiled. 'All the dogs and cats are sterilised. I have a deal with the local vet, where I'll look after any homeless animals that are dumped at the clinic and help to find them a good home, and he gives me a discount on sterilisation and check-ups.' They turned and headed back inside.

Potent Herbs

'Ace, you're not supposed to scare the man off! He may be a useful client!' Ethan stood in the kitchen doorway, a basket bursting with freshly cut herbs on his arm.

'I don't need any potions, thank you!' Michael looked across at him with a sudden frown. *I don't know which annoys me, the suggestion that I might actually partake of their pagan concoctions or that the intimate conversation with Acacia had been interrupted.*

'The image that history has painted of us is really quite distorted!' Acacia chuckled. 'Slowly the rest of the western world is coming to realise and accept what we have been practising since the beginning of time. I'm qualified in many areas of natural therapy and massage as well as being an herbalist.'

Father Michael was still sceptical and Ethan gave a soft laugh as he placed his basket onto the kitchen table, but remained silent as commanded telepathically by Acacia.

'Leave it Ethan!'

'So, no crystal ball or tarot cards then?' asked Michael.

'If that is what the client wants. Some people prefer more modern approaches to their future and health.' It was difficult for Acacia to keep the laughter out of her voice, but she needn't have worried, as Michael took his defeat gracefully.

'I suppose you must deal with a lot of scepticism?'

Ethan nodded. 'Scepticism, though, is natural. We can't spend our lives with blinkers on.'

'True.' Michael agreed, looking into the basket and picking out an unusual leaf. 'Is it poisonous?'

'It's quite edible,' Ethan stated and before he could protest, Michael had popped the leaf into his mouth to chew upon. A mischievous look was exchanged between Ethan and Acacia. It was Ethan who spoke as Acacia took a colander out of a drawer and began straining the liquid from the bowl on the bench into a glass jar.

'I'm not sure that you should've done that.' Ethan paused as Michael swallowed the leaf before he continued, 'You see that particular herb is rather good for increasing endurance in… night time activities. A couple of leaves and I'd want to be certain that there were a couple of lively and very willing ladies around to enjoy the results.'

A slight flush crept across Michael's cheeks. 'I see. It's just as well that I only had one leaf then. No harm done as I'm sure that I can control any resulting passion if it arises.'

Ethan's eyebrows rose as he drawled, 'Better you than me then.' With a quick glance at Acacia, he left the room, heading upstairs to wash up properly after his gardening.

'You're going to have your hands full with that one!'

An impish smile touched Acacia's lips. 'Oh, I do hope so!'

A slight choking sound told her that she had finally shocked the priest. Shaking the last drop of golden water from the strainer, Acacia placed it on top of the bowl before screwing the lid on to the jar. Finally, she turned around to face Michael.

'I apologise if I've upset you, but you see I have two major roles in Ethan's life. The first is to ensure that Ethan's powers have superseded my own. The second is to prepare him for manhood. His next mentor will have even greater powers than mine and this will mean an Elder. So it is essential that Ethan is physically as well as mentally prepared to become an adult.'

'Is Ethan not your brother?'

Acacia shook her head as she picked up the glass jar and placed it on the table in front of Michael.

'We are perhaps only very distant cousins, but in a village it is better to try to conform to some sort of normalcy.'

That caused him to laugh. 'What I've seen today definitely does not remotely resemble normal!' Picking up the jar, Michael headed down the hall to the front door, adding, 'I'm glad that I've met you and Ethan. I don't think I'll be getting bored in this village too quickly.'

Although Acacia smiled, she laid a hand gently upon his arm. 'Have patience with Thomas, his time is very near. If you need any assistance, please don't hesitate to ask for it. Merry Part.'

Michael held out his hand, which she shook, 'Thank you Acacia. I'll see you about the village then.' With the jar safely stashed in a coat pocket, he headed back up the hill towards the Catholic Church. There was so much for Michael to think about, and as he attempted to stop his thoughts wandering to Acacia's lovely red lips, or the voluptuous curves of her body; he wondered *if I'll indeed regret eating the aphrodisiac herb?*

An Exchange Between Siblings

Standing silently in the kitchen doorway, Ethan watched as Acacia scraped the herbs from the colander into a small jar before rinsing out both the strainer and the bowl. Without turning around, Acacia said, 'Well?'

A deep chuckle answered her and a mischievous smile illuminated his handsome face. 'That's a soul that needs saving, Ace, are you up to it?'

'You over rate my abilities.' Acacia drawled and shook her head as she turned around. 'Have you done your homework for Monday?'

Ethan screwed up his nose, 'Yours or theirs?' He was answered by a look of reproach but he only laughed. 'Oh Ace, how easy it is to get a rise out of you! You're going to have to learn to control that when you have your own children. You and twins? Now that I can't miss!'

'You have seen my future?' Acacia was startled. Not so much by this ability but that he had not previously shared this information with her.

An impish smile came and went. 'Oh bits and pieces, but I don't want to spoil the ending!'

'Odious boy!' Laughing, Acacia hugged him, 'Oh, how you'll break hearts!'

Ethan's arms tightened around Acacia as his eyes searched her from head to toe. Acacia waited patiently; knowing that Ethan had to make the first move. Slowly he lowered his head so that his cheek was against hers before whispering, 'Promise me...' His voice was low and husky. 'Promise me you won't wear anything as sexy as this tomorrow at the teacher/parent night!'

A choked laugh escaped from Acacia as she pulled away from him, 'Why ever not?' There was laughter in her voice and perhaps it was actually relief that nothing came from their moment of closeness.

The impish smile was back. 'For one thing, my science teacher won't be able to keep his eyes off you!'

'What about a nice tailored suit?' A sparkle of mischievousness entered her eyes.

'I was thinking of something with a lot more material.' He hesitated, becoming more serious as he continued, 'Ace, will I be forced to leave you when my next mentor comes?'

Acacia turned away to stare blindly out of the kitchen window. 'That may depend upon what he has planned for you. Although I presume the Family will allow you some say in the matter. I was led to believe that this was meant to be your home for life.

Ethan knew how hard she was trying to keep her voice even, and moved forward to place his arms around her from behind. 'Well then, he'll just have to adjust to our way of life here, won't he?'

Acacia turned, managing to smile, 'We'll see.'

A Night Time Visitation

Michael was rather non-committal when Father Thomas asked for his opinion of the Tempest siblings. *I'm confused about my visit to the pagan farm that I am unable to explain how conflicted I felt whilst there. It was alien to me and yet… somehow I felt at home. That confuses me as much as trying to fathom why Thomas is so intimate with the Tempests as we're surely from two different worlds?* debated Michael.

Marjorie, the rectory's housekeeper kept him busy with parish matters for the rest of the day, so Michael wasn't able to dwell for too long on these anomalies. That was until he was finally preparing to go to sleep. As he climbed into his bed, Michael wondered, *Are these feelings of dissatisfaction and restlessness due to the Tempests or their aphrodisiac herb?* Firmly putting all and any thoughts of a sexual nature out of his mind, Michael was asleep the moment his head hit the pillow.

'Michael?' The soft female voice and the gentle touch to his shoulder caused his eyes to fly open and to sit up abruptly in bed.

'Acacia? What on earth are you doing in my room? At this time of night?' The priest looked around him in confusion. *There's a strange, eerie glow in the room and…* 'What on earth are you wearing?' Studying Acacia, Michael vocalised his last train of thought. Amused she glanced down at the scanty attire she wore, something similar to what she had seen pictures of angels wearing in paintings, a flowing drapery of silky material but seemed to be more risqué as it was almost see through.

'You tell me, this is after all your dream. This is how you depicted me.' Acacia reached for his dressing gown that was hanging on the back of the door and slipped into it.

'This is a dream? It's not real? What have you done to me?' Michael sat up a little straighter as his anger rose at the thought, *Has Acacia put some sort of spell on me?*

'This is not my doing Michael. I'm currently tucked up in my own bed at home. Oddly enough having this same dream. Someone wants us to meet in a more intimate setting. They obviously decided that we can't truly be ourselves with each other except in the dream world.' She hesitated before she sat down on the edge of Michael's bed. *Close enough to keep our talk private but not close enough to make it appear sexual or threatening.*

'Aren't I allowed the privacy of my own dreams?'

Acacia's eyebrows rose in surprise. 'Are you able to dictate so strictly what you can or cannot dream about? Or are you ashamed that someone might actually know you're human if you have thoughts or dreams involving someone else?' Noting the rise of colour across his cheeks, she assumed that she had guessed correctly and sighed.

'If you're unhappy with this dream, then pinch yourself and you will wake up. I'm sorry if you're so threatened by me that we can't just talk. I'm curious to learn why someone has gone to all the trouble to ensure that we meet in secret like this.' Slowly she rose off the bed again and smiled ruefully. 'I suppose I should be grateful that you're not more affected by the herb you ate at my house or you probably would have been imagining me naked.'

When Michael uttered an embarrassed laugh, Acacia knew that his thoughts had been travelling along the same lines.

'Blessed Part Michael.'

'Bless…' He caught himself up as he had been about to answer in the same manner. 'Good night Acacia.' Determinedly he pinched his arm and as he awoke from the sharp pain, Acacia vanished from his dream.

In her own bed, Acacia also awoke from their shared dream. *I'm disappointed that Michael hadn't allowed us time to explore why we were sharing our inner most thoughts. I'm curious to know who had orchestrated the meeting of the minds and why they felt such a meeting was necessary.*

Monday 21 October

Teacher/Parent Night

That evening Acacia and Ethan rode their horses across to the high school. Ethan didn't normally ride his midnight black colt to school, as there was nowhere to stable a horse all day. But for the couple of hours that they would be at the teacher/parent night, their horses would stand tethered in the school courtyard, where they were protected by the library and the gymnasium from the cool autumn winds.

True to Ethan's request for something with a lot more material, Acacia wore a 19th century style riding habit, made of a very deep blue velvet with long sleeves, a tight corseted bodice and a floor length full skirt. A floor length black cape with a hood, that was her favourite cloak, covered her. Her hair tumbled free down her back.

Before Ethan could offer his assistance, he found Father Michael Casey standing beside Acacia's mare. As they exchanged greetings a mischievous smile touched Ethan's lips.

'I'll see you inside, Ace, I want to find Mary before the gym gets too crowded.' With a wave of his hand, he was gone and although Acacia understood exactly what Ethan had wanted she was not prepared to play his game. Smoothly, she swung her leg over her saddle and would have gently eased herself to the ground, but she was surprised when Michael placed his hands about her waist and easily lifted her down. Acacia silently cursed herself as she found her cheeks flushing and her pulse quickening at the touch of his hands.

'Thank you, Michael. What brings you to a teacher/parent night?' She looped her reins over a railing and they headed towards the gym together.

'Father Thomas thought that it would be a good way to meet some of the local people in a more social atmosphere.'

Acacia halted abruptly, causing Michael to look back at her in surprise. 'Perhaps it would be best if you aren't seen entering with me. You should protect your reputation,' she said.

Michael would have laughed, had he not seen the seriousness in Acacia's eyes. 'Now if I entered with my shirt tails hanging out and lipstick all over my face, then there would be cause for scandal. I didn't realise that just because you're a witch, you were also a whore!' His words stung, as Acacia knew that they would.

'People will believe whatever they want. The truth doesn't always matter.' In answer, Michael linked his arm through hers and escorted her inside.

As Acacia had predicted, the occupants of the gym were stunned by their arrival together. Trying to ignore the stares and whispers, Acacia led Michael up to the Principal, Karen Greeves. Karen was an attractive woman in her late 40s, with short red hair and a very athletic build from her many years as a sports teacher.

With introductions made, Acacia slipped away and glided across the room to speak to Ethan's science teacher, Brian White. Brian was middle aged, quite short and rather portly, what little hair he had left was grown long and pulled up and over his bald spot. She controlled a grimace as Brian's eyes swept hungrily down her body. *I had hoped that this old fashioned costume would not encourage him.*

'I do hope that Ethan isn't giving you a hard time this year?'

Brian's hungry look disappeared into a frown. Ethan's intellect far and away superseded the teacher's and the teenager was not afraid to cut the pompous ass down to size.

'Oh, we have a better understanding now dear Acacia. So long as I stay away from alchemy and metaphysics, Ethan won't openly supersede my authority. In front of the class anyway.' His laugh was a little too forced.

Acacia's lips twisted into a mocking smile as she knew the truth behind the battle that raged in the class room. 'If that is the fairy tale you tell yourself to get through your day Brian then there's no point continuing this discussion.'

The teacher frowned as he reached out to firmly grasp Acacia's arm. 'That is Mr White to you, Acacia!'

Her eyebrows rose in a supercilious manner that made her looked even more like Ethan. 'I'm thankfully not your student any more Brian. Your intimidation tactics did not work then upon me, nor will they do so now! Remove your hand or be prepared to suffer the consequences.' There was no hiding her scorn from the voice.

'You always was too hot to handle! Or should I say frigid?' He tried to wound her but Acacia only laughed.

'Whatever keeps you warm at night! But it will certainly never be me!'

'Go away Witch!' Brian White was forced to release her arm as his fingers suddenly felt like they were burning.

'Certainly, Brian, anything for you.' Acacia glided across the room to the calming influence of Ethan's English teacher.

Ethan's Warning

Ethan had joined a beautiful, tall Anglo-African girl of his own age. She was looking a little worried as they overheard the heated conversation between Acacia and their Science teacher.

'Are things all right on the farm, Ethan?' Mary's gentle concern always touched Ethan. *No matter how tough things are for her and her family, Mary always thinks of others. Money is her major worry as her father, now the sole parent with limited skills, is struggling to feed and educate Mary and her younger brother Davey.*

Ethan shrugged. 'Ace spent most of today with Old Tom. His time is near, and I know that it hurts Ace that she can't help him. Sometimes, even together, we can't change the bad things in life.'

Mary sighed. 'Heads up! Here comes the Princess!'

Ethan choked on a laugh as Claudia de Bere sauntered over to join them. Claudia was in some of their classes, but there the similarities ended. Long blonde hair was swept up in a ponytail as the teenager's beautiful face bubbled with her rich, plummy upbringing. Why she wasn't attending an exclusive school no one knew. Claudia's eyes swept over Ethan and Mary, and a false smile spread over her features.

'However do you manage to co-ordinate your wardrobe, Ethan, if everything you own is black?'

'It's easy Claw, its called poverty. You should try it!'

Claudia executed a perfect little shudder. 'No, thank you! Although with Halloween around the corner, I suppose you'll be in your element?' Giggling, Claudia flittered away again to where her mother stood talking to Father Michael. Ethan only laughed at Claudia's attempt at an insult.

'She'll get hers in the end! Halloween or Samhain as we call it, is not just a commercialised myth!'

Mary looked at him concerned. 'You won't hurt anyone will you?'

The gleam in Ethan's eyes dimmed but did not vanish. 'No, I couldn't hurt anyone, but I'm sure as hell gunna have some fun!'

Claudia's Request

Claudia waited patiently until her mother paused to introduce her to Michael Casey, giving her the opportunity to hit him with the full power of her melting green eyes.

'Father Michael,' Claudia refrained from batting her eyelids but came as close to it as she looked up with faked admiration at the priest. 'Next Saturday is Halloween and I was hoping to hold a party in the ruins of the ancient pagan temple that is situated behind St Andrew's cemetery. It would make it the coolest ever, but we don't want to disturb dear Father Thomas in any way.'

Michael was obviously surprised by Claudia's request, which had attracted the attention of all in the room.

'So long as you remain away from the Rectory, I don't see any problems.' *I hope I'm not promising more than I can deliver.*

Claudia squealed in delight. 'Oh, thank you! This will be our best party ever!'

Michael had further stipulations to make. 'No drugs or alcohol may be consumed at your party. No sexual antics and there should be some adult supervision. No damage to either the temple, or the cemetery will be excusable and all involved in the party will be forced to make amends, and not just those guilty.'

Claudia's mind was already racing off to plan the Halloween party, but she managed to reassure the priest that they would leave all as they had found it.

Mischief Awry

At one end of the gym, near the stage, was a long table with finger food and tea and coffee. Many of the students, who had been dragged along to the teacher/parent night, gathered at this end of the room. They did not wish to know what their teachers were saying about them. They didn't know why they had to be dragged along to this evening as if they were little kids unable to left on their own at home. But the fact they were 16 year old, horny teens was exactly why some of their parents did not want them to be home unsupervised. The teenagers made short work of the nibbles, but even they had their limits and there was still plenty of food left over.

Claudia rejoined her group of friends, which included Kym Lee, a pretty Singaporean girl; Cheryl Mitchell, an ultra-trendy redhead; Merelda Spano, a wafer thin brunette; and Claudia's boyfriend Nathaniel Stone, who was the school's all round best athlete and good looking into the bargain. A wicked gleam came into Claudia's eyes.

'It is such a shame that all this food shall go to waste.' She picked up an uncut sponge and cream cake, balancing it carefully on one beautifully manicured hand.

'Who wants to bet five pounds that I can't land the witch one in the face and get away with it?' Her girlfriends eagerly took up Claudia's bet, but Nathaniel was more hesitant.

'It's not wise to mess with a witch, Claudia. They have powers that you and I can never possess, let alone understand.'

Claudia sighed and shook her head. *I have to remind myself that it's Nathaniel's looks and physic and not his brains that attracts me.*

'There is no such thing as magic, Nate, just as the dead are not going to rise from their graves on Halloween!'

Slipping on her apple pie smile and innocent expression, Claudia headed over, with the cake still in her hands, to where Acacia now stood talking to Karen Greeves.

'Acacia, you must take home a plate or two. We simply can't let this food go to waste.' Claudia gushed. Karen frowned at being interrupted as she and Acacia turned to face Claudia.

'Thank you Claudia, but Ethan and I rode tonight and have no means of carrying any parcels home. Besides Ms Greeves has already made arrangements for any left-over food to be sent to Marjorie, Father Thomas' housekeeper and co-ordinator of our local homeless shelter.'

'*Ace, beware!*' From Ethan came a mental projection.

Acacia smiled as she replied, '*Watch and learn!*'

Executing a perfect and natural looking trip, Claudia's hand rose to aim the cream cake at Acacia's face. Taking a deep breath, Acacia's eyes remained locked upon Claudia's hand and brought down an invisible force upon it, making it impossible for Claudia to control her hand.

Give the enemy the power to feel the strength of the element of air around her. Bend her down, a fall from grace and bring about her well-deserved disgrace! Acacia's spell was not said aloud.

In the seconds that followed, Claudia screamed as her hand was forced downwards away from Acacia and as she hit the floor, her face fell into the sponge cake.

For a moment, the whole room held its collective breath in silence and then the tears came. Sobbing wildly, Claudia picked herself up, dripping cream and sponge cake all over the floor as she held her creamed hands out helplessly in front of her. As the giggles and whispers started, Claudia turned viciously on Acacia.

'How dare you do this to me? Have you no respect for breeding? You should be burnt at the stake like all your ancestors, Witch!'

'Claudia!' The sharp, dominant command came from Mrs de Bere and not Acacia or her Principal. With a sob, Claudia turned as her mother and father approached them. Catherine de Bere was well-dressed if perhaps a little conservatively but her husband's suit was nice and expensive; an obvious indication that he wasn't only born rich, but had also married money.

'You'll apologise to Acacia, then go and clean yourself up and wait for us in the car!' quietly ordered Mrs De Bere.

The blaze relit in Claudia's eyes. 'I won't apologise! Her kind causes nothing but trouble. As for that Devil's son, he's just waiting to get his hands on me!'

Ethan sneered in disgust. 'Oh please! Virtue and innocence from the town bike? I'm not interested in such a shallow relationship!'

'How dare you!' Under the cream, Claudia's face flamed fire engine red.

Nathaniel Stone stepped forward. 'I resent that remark! Claudia was still a virgin when we first made love!'

'Claudia!' This enraged exclamation came from Claudia's father.

'Oops!' Ethan wore a sardonic smile as his eyes twinkled.

Claudia turned on him. 'I'll see you in hell for this Ethan Tempest! You'll regret crossing me!'

Ethan applauded as Claudia stormed out of the gym. 'Who says that school can't be entertaining?' he drawled.

Acacia sighed, *I applaud Ethan's cool detachment that means he came out the winner of that round. In the future, though, he'll have to be careful as Claudia will be out for revenge, and she is not the type of girl to forget or forgive.*

Karen Greeves gently laid her hand upon Acacia's shoulder. 'I'd better see the influential woman and her family out to their car.'

Acacia smiled in understanding. 'As if they're going to have trouble finding that huge BMW of theirs!'

Karen shook her head. 'I can see where Ethan gets that wicked tongue of his.' Even before the Principal had turned away, her smile had already disappeared as she went forth to dampen the coals that Ethan had ignited.

An Amusing Sparring

'So, how did you do it?' The amused and attractive masculine voice startled Acacia and she turned around to meet Michael's laughing eyes with an innocent look.

'I don't know what you're talking about.'

Michael linked his arm through hers and guided her slightly away from the main buzzing of conversation in the room.

'I'm not so easily convinced that you have magical powers, but without laying a hand on that girl, you managed to trip her over and ensure that she fell face first into the cream cake! Chance just seems too convenient for an answer.'

Acacia gave a low laugh, as she raised mischievous eyes to meet Michael's. 'The fall was Claudia's idea, all I did was ensure that the air current weighed down her hand. Are you going to tell on me?'

Michael glanced across the gym to where the off duty Police Sergeant stood talking to one of the teachers about his teenage daughter. Shaking his head, Michael returned his gaze to Acacia's laughing eyes.

'No, but I think I'll watch you though. If an eye of newt winds up in my porridge, I'll know I'm in trouble.'

'Oh no, Michael! Acacia became very serious. 'You would never find it in your porridge!' her soft voice drawled provocatively.

Michael managed to shake his head as he laughed. 'You are a very wicked child!'

'Child?' Her eyes opened wide in surprise. 'Doth quoth thy grey beard?'

'I'm thirty-two years old, and you are what? 18? 19?'

A gurgle of laughter escaped from Acacia as she spread wide her skirts and swept into a deep curtsy. 'Monseigneur does flatter me! I am all of five and twenty years. An old maid!' Acacia ended with a sad little sigh.

Michael frowned in puzzlement. 'Surely not in this day and age?'

'More's the pity!' The smile returned to Acacia's lips. 'Oh, the Georgian and Victorian eras! How I enjoyed those elegant fashions!'

For a moment Michael was taken by surprise, but he did not allow her the satisfaction of totally taking him for a fool.

'I do know you're only teasing, although I can picture you fitting in rather well with such a setting, especially dressed as you are tonight.'

Once again Acacia curtsied. 'Merci de compliment, Monseigneur!'

A Surprise Offer

A laugh came from behind them as Mary and Ethan approached from the refreshment table.

'You're speaking the wrong language, sister, a priest may be more interested if you spoke Latin and not French.'

Michael smiled as he thought, *how well suited Mary and Ethan are to each other*. With a natural break in the conversation, Ethan turned his attention to Acacia. 'Mary's father has to go straight to work from here, so I thought I'd see Mary home. Will you be all right?'

An anxious look crossed Acacia's features. 'You trust me to go alone? I mean I could be mugged, or robbed or even ravaged!'

'You wish!' A dangerous, mischievous glint entered Ethan's eyes.

'What if I escort Acacia home?' suggested Michael, breaking in on a possibly sibling battle of wits. 'I walked here, so I'm quite prepared to be your temporary knight in shining armour.' Acacia looked at Michael stunned, but it was not his offer of an escort that surprised her.

'You actually walked all this way?'

'Of course!' Michael's eyebrows rose. 'Capital exercise!'

'Perhaps I've more need to worry about you now, Ace!' Ethan didn't even duck as Acacia punched his arm.

Mary linked her arm through Ethan's. 'I'd better take him away before you feel the inclination to strangle him.'

Not at all angry, Acacia laughed. 'Just see that Ethan is home before midnight, you both have school tomorrow. Merry Part.'

Revelations of Souls

With a brief acknowledgment to their Principal, the teenagers left the gym, and once Acacia had spoken briefly to Ethan's History teacher; she and Michael soon followed. Outside the air was quite cold, but Acacia's mare was waiting patiently, chewing the odd blade of grass that grew between the courtyard slabs. Michael surprised

Acacia by lifting her effortless onto her mare. Not until Acacia had adjusted her voluptuous skirt, did Michael venture to speak his mind.

'Does Ethan hold me in dislike?'

Acacia cast a swift but brief look at down at Michael as she turned the mare towards home and he walked alongside her.

'It's just that bordering on manhood and looking forward to his sexual freedom, it's hard for him to understand why or even how a man can deny that essential aspect of his capability. Ethan believes that you need saving.'

There was a moment of silence.

'Are you to be my saviour?' The words were calmly enough spoken but they caused Acacia to blush as she looked down into Michael's face, which was illuminated by the half moon.

'I'm sorry!'

An attractive smile spread across Michael's face. 'Why should you be?'

Acacia managed to shake her head. 'We appear to strike at odds each time we meet. I am what I am, but I do not go around seducing men. And most definitely not Catholic Priests! So you've nothing to fear from me, but if you feel uncomfortable in my company, then I'll ensure that we see little of each other.'

Acacia looked straight ahead again in her anger but Michael firmly grasped her knee and forced her to look back down at him.

'I don't remember accusing you of unbecoming behaviour, Acacia, nor do I consider you to be a danger to me. What did I say to provoke such a reaction?'

Acacia lowered her eyes as she sighed. 'It was evident in your tone of voice. Just to set the record straight, my sexual initiation at 18 was arranged by the Family as it was believed that if I was to take over as Ethan's Mentor that I needed to tap into even greater powers. He was not related to me and it was completely consensual. I have had no lover since. I… I had been led to believe that a particular man was to be my soul mate. So you could say that I have taken a vow of celibacy until it is time for me to instruct Ethan.'

Acacia uttered a nervous laugh, *I can't believe that I'm having such an intimate conversation with a virtual stranger.* 'Actually running the farm and caring for Ethan these past five years meant that I've had little time to think about sex… although truth be told offers have been made! None of them were appealing though. They weren't…' *They weren't you, I nearly said!*

Michael released Acacia's knee. 'That is a long time to devote all your time and energy into educating a boy who is only remotely related to you! Your dedication to your faith, must indeed be great.' After a moments pause, he added, 'I remember you said you've been caring for Ethan for five years. How did that come about?'

'When Ethan was born and the Family realised what potentially powerful wizard he could become; Elizabeth Tempest, a witch who lived in this village was asked to train him to control and develop his powers. Being from non-magical parents and a large number of siblings it was essential for Grandmother Tempest to take Ethan not just for several hours of training a day but at times for days or weeks at a time. Fearing and jealous of his powers, his siblings were amongst the villager's children who would tease Ethan and call him a freak. More than once Elizabeth had to literally put out the flames when Ethan's temper snapped and he fought back against the abuse.'

'Elizabeth and Ethan were actually away for a fortnight at a Family gathering in Scotland when his parents' home burnt down. No one was injured and no one thought that Ethan's powers could have possibly reached all the way from the north. Even so when his family decided not to rebuild but move away, they were more than happy to allow Elizabeth to adopt Ethan.'

Acacia sighed, 'Unfortunately Elizabeth was already quite old when she started to train Ethan and she died when he was almost eleven. The farm Ethan inherited from Elizabeth and my age and powers were thought best suited to raising Ethan after the trauma of being rejected by his biological family and then the death of Elizabeth.'

A Point Of Contention

Having digested all that information for a moment, Michael finally asked, 'Are Ethan and Mary an item?'

'Not yet.' Acacia shook her head. 'Both are kept quite busy with school, Mary's part time work, and Ethan helping me run the farm. Their friendship is slowly developing into something deeper, but neither wish to rush things. I have no concerns when Ethan is with Mary as I know that he'll talk to me before he cements their relationship in a physical sense.'

'That is the reason I may have sounded like I disapprove of you. It's not something that I can comfortably accept.'

Slowly Acacia nodded her head. 'I understand and will endeavour to never mention it in your hearing again. For some reason I believed that you may have been more open minded than the local villagers.'

'Acacia...'

'You must talk to Marjorie, Father Thomas' housekeeper, and get her to organise an evening supper to introduce you to the parishioners. Many will have stayed away from the Rectory in fear of disturbing Thomas.'

'Acacia...'

'Then there is always the theology classes that Thomas used to run before he fell ill...'

'Enough!' Michael's protest caused Acacia to break off her sentence in surprise. 'Do you honestly think that I can carry on a conversation about inconsequential matters when you have accused me of being narrow minded? I had hoped that we could be friends, but obviously we can't respect each other's differences!'

'I'm sorry!' Acacia's words were little more than a whisper and Michael would have to be a fool not to recognise the sound of tears in her voice.

'Acacia...'

Retaliation

Any further words were frozen upon his lips as a very fast sports car roared toward them and as a hand appeared out of the open window a pistol fired a shot over Acacia's head. The mare rose up on to her back legs in fright, and although Michael, grasping hold of the reins, managed to stop the mare from bolting, Acacia was thrown to the ground and landed heavily on her side.

The sports car zoomed off into the night as Michael gained control of the mare and quietened her down before he attended to Acacia's needs. Although she was dazed, Acacia was still conscious and she managed to sit up as she brushed the gravel off her palms.

'We'll have to expect retaliation after that scene in the gym. Rochester should know better, though, about playing games with me.'

'Aren't you angrier than that? He could have killed you!'

Acacia shook her head. 'His wife never lets him have access to anything but blanks.'

'But the fall alone could have killed or seriously injured you.' Michael held out his hands to assist Acacia to rise, but she momentarily hesitated before placing her hand into his. With what seemed to be little effort, he drew her to her feet. She would've moved away from him, but uttered a cry of pain when she found that her right ankle would not support her weight. Michael steadied Acacia as she bordered on passing out from the pain.

'Hold still for a minute.' Michael bent over taking the damaged ankle into his hands to determine if it was broken. *As Acacia is wearing ankle high lace up boots, I'm not able to determine if the ankle is only sprained, but if I attempt to remove the boot, she will pass out.* He straightened again before he spoke.

'I'll get you home before tending to the swelling.'

Michael placed the mare's reins into Acacia's hands as she balanced precariously on one foot. He quickly mounted the horse, getting himself settled before he bent down and held his hand out to assist Acacia up before him. But she shook her head, refusing to take his hand.

'I can't do it!' Her words were barely a whisper.

Michael shook his head. 'You're not turning into a weak and helpless female now are you?' Acacia looked up at him. *The fire in her eyes is exactly what I wanted.*

'I could turn you into a toad for a remark like that!'

Solemnly, Michael nodded. 'Well you may do so when I have you home safe.' He leant down and placed his arm around Acacia's waist and without hesitating, Michael lifted Acacia up onto the horse so that she sat sideways.

'All right?'

Acacia managed to nod, but it wasn't she who took up the reins, but Michael, which allowed her to close her eyes as she laid her cheek upon his shoulder.

Fractious Child

Arriving at the Tempest farm, even though Acacia protested that she was capable of stabling her horse, when Michael lifted her down, he sat her on a pile of hay bundles in the barn as he removed the mare's saddle and bridle. Acacia attempted to limp to the house but only got as far as the stable door. Leaning against the door frame, Acacia took a deep breath and exhaling very slowly, she cursed herself for being so weak.

'You're as stubborn as a mule, aren't you? Come on, put your arm about my neck.' Michael had scooped Acacia up into his arms before she could protest.

'No! It's not necessary! Please put me down!'

A chuckle of amusement came from the priest. 'Are you sure you're not 18?'

Once more fire flamed in Acacia's eyes. 'How dare you!' She knew exactly what he meant. 'I am not a child, nor am I acting like one!'

To prove it, she punched him very hard in the shoulder. The effect was disastrous. Michael's arm, under Acacia's legs, slipped and with her full weight on just one arm, he fell backward onto the grass, with Acacia sprawled across the top of him.

Michael did something he rarely ever did, he swore. 'If this is how you treat anyone who tries to help you, I'd hate to see what you do to an enemy!'

In a very simple move, Michael flipped Acacia onto her back and knelt over her, pinning her hands to the ground. Acacia gasped in surprise at the anger in his eyes and yet something more besides. With a sweeping motion, he lifted her up and over his shoulder and despite her protests; Michael carried Acacia inside. He hesitated at the bottom of the stairs. 'Where is your bedroom?'

'Put me down! Now!'

Michael ignored her demand. 'I have no designs upon your virtue! Now where is your bedroom?'

There was a moment of silence before she finally gave in and went completely limp. 'Upstairs, second door on the left.'

Michael's anger had cooled by the time he gently laid Acacia down upon her bed. With an exhausted sigh, he knelt down beside the bed. 'I wouldn't have thought that you were that heavy, it must be the additional weight of your costume.'

A wicked gleam entered Acacia's eyes. 'It serves you right for not putting me down like I told you to!'

Michael shook his head. 'And how, in all honesty, would you have got home, let alone up to your room? Now stop arguing with me as this next step I'll need your complete cooperation.'

He picked up a pillow and placed it into Acacia's arms. 'You might want to bite on this when I take off your boot.'

Acacia took a deep breath. 'I'm ready!'

Unlacing Acacia's boot was the easy part, glancing anxiously at her face Michael tried to make his voice sound as normal as possible. 'Who is Rochester?'

At that particular moment, Michael slipped off the boot. He had half-expected Acacia to scream or faint, but she did neither. Her breathing had quickened and tears naturally fell down her cheeks, but all in all Acacia remained composed.

Her foot is quite swollen, but nothing seems to be actually broken. Her stockings will have to be removed though, and I feel that this is beyond my duties. He rose to his feet. 'I'll get you a cold compress to bring down the swelling. It might be better if you remove your stockings while I'm out of the room.'

Michael was almost out the door when Acacia said, 'Thank you Michael.' He turned and smiled before he left the room.

What Is My Offence?

With a sigh, Acacia slipped off her cape, lay flat on her back and easing up her heavy skirt, she began to roll down the thick, warm stockings. Once they were down to her knees, Acacia sat up again to make it easier to complete the removal of the hosiery. She was carefully easing the stocking from her damaged right foot when Michael re-entered the room.

She hastily pushed her skirt down to cover her shapely thighs, the colour that tinged her cheeks also stunned him, but for the moment, he made no comment as he wrapped a cold, wet cloth about Acacia's ankle. After a moment, Michael sat down on the double bed beside her.

'Have I done something to upset you? I mean one minute you're a fire queen, the next a shy child and on rare occasions, a sensible and intelligent young woman. Does my presence here in Stirling disturb you?'

Acacia did not answer straight away, but looked away from Michael to study the wooden floor. Leaning over to open the first drawer of the chest of drawers beside her bed, Acacia removed a folded piece of A4 drawing paper and handed it to Michael. Opening it, Michael managed to stop himself from gasping but surprise was certainly reflected on his face.

'A very good likeness of me considering we had only met once.'

Acacia shook her head. 'Look at the date at the bottom.'

Doing as instructed, a frown appeared on Michael's face. 'That's seven years ago! But I only met you yesterday!'

'That was when your face, that is the face in the picture, came to me in a dream. Not just once but many times. I considered it important enough to do that drawing.' Acacia took back the sketch and folded it again, but did not immediately put it away again.

'Grandmama believed that the man illustrated would one day play a significant role in my life. I had expected that when he arrived that I would welcome him with open arms. Beginning with friendship that would end with us being lovers. But you being what you are has left me so confused. I really don't know how to behave with you. Are you the enemy, a father figure or a friend? What did the dream mean then if we were not meant to be soul mates?'

Michael stood up, paced the room, and absently noted the ambience of the room. *Although the furnishings aren't expensive or over flashy, there is a soft, feminine feel about the room, which is only heightened by the beautiful woman sitting on the bed.* Not wishing to follow that train of thought, Michael unconsciously shook his head to try to put his thoughts back on track.

'I hope that you can consider me a friend, but I understand if that will be difficult for you as in natural progression I can never be your lover.' Sitting down again, Michael asked, 'Tell me, why do you feel so uncomfortable about my profession?'

Acacia pressed her hands against her cheeks but couldn't stop them from colouring up. 'I suppose I feel confused as I've come to accept that I would love this man when he entered my life, and that he would come to love me. Seven years of waiting for Mr Right, who turns out to be Mr Wrong… I suppose I feel…' Acacia broke off not wishing to be rude, but Michael answered for her.

'Cheated?'

Acacia's hands fell down to her lap as she nodded.

Intimacy Interrupted

Michael cleared his throat, about to speak, but the words were never to be spoken as Ethan unceremoniously entered the room.

'Ace, Rochester is going to have to be taught a lesson! He…' Ethan broke off upon seeing Michael sitting on Acacia's bed.

'My apologies, Sis, perhaps I should come back later?' He turned to go, but Acacia called him back.

'It's definitely not like that, Ethan, I was thrown from Sally and sprained my ankle.'

Ethan's face hardened in anger as he stepped forward and removed the towel Michael had placed around Acacia's foot. With tenderness, that Michael didn't believe that a teenage boy could possess, Ethan examined the damaged ankle. Satisfied that nothing was seriously damaged, Ethan rewrapped the towel around it.

'Rochester?' He was answered by a nod.

'Excuse my ignorance, but who or what is Rochester?'

Ethan's frown deepened at Michaels' question. 'Rochester is a low life, double crossing, thieving son of a bitch!'

A sceptical look crossed Michael's face as Ethan's answer did little to reduce his ignorance and he looked to Acacia for a more comprehensive answer. She smiled in sympathy.

'Rochester is Mr de Bere's first name. He sees himself as an old fashioned squire and expects any woman to be honoured to share his bed. He has such a pig headed arrogance of his own appeal that he wouldn't leave me alone when I refused the honour.'

Ethan grunted in disgust. 'Honour indeed! You should have let me turn him into a skunk like I wanted to!'

Acacia sighed. 'I agree with you now, but back then I didn't think that he would actually begin a smear campaign against my standing in the community. At that time no one knew that I was a witch, most believed that I was simply a naturopath. Matters could have become very ugly if Father Thomas hadn't stood up for me.'

Ethan threw himself down upon Acacia's pillows. 'When are you going to let me deal with him?'

Acacia shook her head. 'We can't afford to alienate anyone in Stirling. Including the de Beres.'

'Maybe,' stated Ethan, 'but driving around like a mad man and firing at people even if it is only blanks must be seriously dealt with! At least report him to Sargent Boyd.'

Michael couldn't help but shake his head. 'I'd best leave you.' He rose to his feet as he spoke. 'I'm sorry if I've disappointed you, Acacia, but I am what I am, and I hope that when that becomes a little less distasteful to you, we can be friends.'

Acacia managed to nod, not trusting herself to speak. Ethan showed Michael down the stairs and out of the house. When this was done, Ethan returned to Acacia's room.

Resolution Sought

Acacia had swung her legs over the side of her bed and was attempting to undo the zipper of her dress. Ethan assisted his sister to her feet, supporting her with one arm about her waist as she stood only on one foot and Ethan used his other hand to undo her zipper.

'Are you terribly upset, Ace?' Slowly, he eased her out of her dress.

'About Michael?' Acacia sighed. 'Oh Ethan, I don't know if I should be angry or scared, but I just can't ignore or wipe away the feelings that I've accumulated for a man I didn't even know. Was it foolish to have done so?'

Ethan shook his head as he undid the hooks of her bra.

'The dreams led us to believe that Michael is to be as important to you as Mary will be to me.' With her bra removed, Ethan sat Acacia back down upon the bed before he pulled out a large, floppy jumper from under Acacia's pillow, which was her preferred nightwear. Acacia expected Ethan to either hand the jumper to her or put it on her himself, but when neither event happened, she looked up at him questioning.

The appreciative look in his eyes as he swept down her almost naked body, brought a lump in Acacia's throat as she found it impossible to swallow. When Ethan spoke, his voice was quite low and husky.

'How can any man believe or wish for heaven in another world when it is so obviously here on earth?'

A small shiver of anticipation swept over Acacia, but Ethan misinterpreting it as a shiver of cold, he quickly slipped the jumper over Acacia's head and eased her into it.

'Ethan?'

'I'd best get a proper ice pack for your ankle.' He would've left the room, but Acacia grabbed hold of his hand and drew him down on the bed beside her.

'Ethan, I've never asked you if you wished me to teach you the ultimate joy of sexual intercourse. I suppose I always figured that you'd tell me when you were ready. That is to say, I will understand if you truly wish your first time is with Mary.'

'To be honest with you I don't know exactly what I want.' Ethan placed an arm, brother like, around her shoulders. 'Yeah, I would like my first time to be with Mary, but I don't want to be a fool and ruin it for us both due to inexperience. The major problem is that I've come to consider you as a sister, and thus reluctant to get too physical. On the other hand, you're a very sexy babe, and any man would be honoured to worship at your temple. In the end, I may want coaching, but I'll pass on the full trial run. I hope that doesn't upset you?'

Acacia smiled and planted a sisterly kiss on his brow. 'Not at all! I've been reluctant to complete your training as I have come to see you as a brother and it could make things awkward between us.'

Ethan rose to his feet. 'I'll get that ice pack now.'

Acacia nodded and slipped under the sheets, wondering, *what will happen to me when Ethan acquires his new mentor soon?*

Another Midnight Meeting

'Michael?' That soft, alluring voice and again the gentle touch of a hand to his shoulder caused his eyes to fly open. An embarrassed Acacia stood beside his bed, this time clad in a dress straight out of the Regency period. 'I'm sorry but someone is determined to make us meet in our dreams. Pinch yourself and I'll be gone again.' The step she took back from his bed was a little wobbly as Acacia had a sprained ankle in the dream world as well as in reality.

'So we are dreaming again then?' Michael scrubbed a weary hand across his face and without pausing to think he reached out to take Acacia's hand. 'You feel real enough.' He was aware of the slight gasp she issued at his touch.

The tingling sensation that runs through me at such an innocent connection. She was amazed. 'Unless you're dreaming that I'm a ghost then yes, I would feel real to your touch.' Acacia reluctantly tried to draw her hand away but Michael retained a firm but insistent grip upon it.

'So everything would feel real?'

'Yes.' Acacia was unable to read from his almost brooding expression what he was actually thinking. She jumped slightly as his thumb caressed against her wrist. *It is such an intimate touch, such a lover's touch.*

'Can we be held accountable for what we do in a dream?'

'I… I don't know. If you have principles in the real world, they should be upheld in our dreams. Michael, I think you should wake up now.'

There was a fire and passion in his eyes that Acacia found impossible to resist as Michael drew her down on to the bed beside him. She hadn't been expecting it, and therefore landed a little awkwardly against him. He breathed in deeply as her hair brushed against his cheek.

'You smell divine! I bet you taste divine too!'

Before Acacia could get out any more than, 'Michael, you shouldn't…' he had tenderly laced his fingers through her hair and lowered his head so that his lips brushed lightly against hers.

A small mewling sound escaped from Acacia, neither of them were positive if that was a sound of pleasure or of protest but Michael, heedless to the disapproving voices screaming in his ears, sought a second and more substantial kiss. Acacia laid her hand against his chest, intent upon pushing him away but found that as his lips explored hers, her fingers tightened upon his pyjama top to hold him near.

'You said we could only be friends.' She managed to protest when Michael finally released her lips. 'Does your vow of celibacy not also apply to your dreams?' His hand trailed down to the column of her throat. Then after a moment of hesitation, began to caress a little lower.

'Can we honestly be masters over our dreams? Why else should someone want us to meet like this? So intimately? So temptingly?' He placed an ethereal kiss against her throat. 'You are so beautiful! Why can't we meet as lovers here even if we can't realise it in the real world?'

'Could you… would you be satisfied enough with just that?' There was so much doubt and longing in her voice, that Michael drew back a little to study the conflicting emotions that swept across Acacia's features. 'Betraying the vow you made as a servant of God and never able to seek fulfilment in the light of day.'

Michael sighed as he drew further away from the vision of splendour in front of him. 'You couldn't be satisfied with just this? It has to be reality or nothing for you?' He caressed wistfully along Acacia's shoulder before allowing his hand to drop to his side.

She sadly shook her head. 'Being with you like this would only make me want you all the more in the real world. We would have to hide any suggestion of such an illicit relationship when awake and ultimately it would break my heart to know you so intimately and even so never to actually know you at all physically.'

Dashing away a tear, Acacia dragged in a deep, shuddering breath. 'Please wake up now before I embarrass myself any further. You already know what is in my heart. Please don't make me reveal any more of my tortured soul to you.'

'I am so sorry that I cannot be what you want me to be.' His conscious began to nag him even louder and Michael began to heed its warning. 'If things were different… If I had met you sooner…' Unable to finish his apology, Michael pinched his own arm and with regret and yet with relief he woke up.

Acacia awoke to find herself crying. *There's no relief, only regret that it seems that as tempting as it would be to become Michael's lover in our dreams that it would never be enough for me. I would always want it all.* Burying her head into her pillow, she allowed herself to sob out her disappointment until a natural sleep came to claim her.

Tuesday 22 October

The Discovery Of The Century

The following afternoon, Claudia de Bere, Nathaniel Stone and Claudia's girlfriends, Cheryl, Kym and Merelda checked out the church graveyard and the pagan temple for their Halloween party. Merelda had a pen and note pad, taking notes as Claudia reeled off instructions.

'We'll need flood lights as well as a generator for electricity. A CD player, a very long table, about forty chairs and the usual Halloween decorations.' *The temple,* mused Claudia, *considering that it is very, very old, is in remarkably good condition. The four walls are still in one piece, and thankfully a roof still covers the temple. Most of the windows are long gone, but an energetic sweep through will see the removal of most of the dirt and rubble that lies upon the floor.* None of this Claudia intended to do herself, as that was what servants were for.

As the other girls picked up the brooms they had brought with them and Nathaniel carried out some of the larger rocks and fallen masonry; Claudia checked out the altar that remained standing. The altar was not dissimilar to any other altar, with the exception that it was carved out of a single rock. Stumbling on a pile of rubble Claudia fell against the altar and grazed her wrist upon the stone.

Claudia swore colourfully and Nathaniel rushed to her and although she was not bleeding badly, he wrapped his clean handkerchief around her wound. A creaking sound from behind the altar caused the teenagers to drop their tools and slowly back towards the entrance. If something horrible jumped out at them, they were ready to run.

A section of the wall slowly slid open to reveal a magnificently leather bound gold embossed book. Pulling away from Nathaniel,

Claudia took the book out of its hiding place. It was the size of an A to Z file and very heavy, Claudia laid it gently upon the altar. Doing so caused the wall to close up the hiding. The girls gathered around Claudia, none of them capable of taking their eyes off the impressive tome. It was covered with a myriad of figures, most dancing; others involved in various sexual positions. Claudia was about to open the book, when Nathaniel placed his hand firmly over the top of it.

'Don't Claudia! You don't know what repercussions will occur if you open that book! It would be safer to hand it over to Acacia or Father Michael.'

'How can you be so sensible at a time like this?' Claudia pushed his hand out of the way. 'We may be the first people to see this book in over a hundred years! This is a historic moment and I'm not going to miss the opportunity to create history!'

With her girlfriends urging her on, Claudia opened the book. A gasp of wonder came from the girls, the pages being beautifully ornate and the lettering in Roman script, with the words in Saxon English. Each page held a different spell ranging from cures for cold sores to summoning the Master of Evil. When Claudia turned to this page, she found it impossible to take her eyes away from the border of illustrations that alternated between varying sexual positions and methods of cruelty and punishment.

'Can you imagine what my Halloween party would be like if we could actually summon the Devil?' Her voice was low and husky, as her breathing quickened.

'You must be crazy! The consequences could be diabolical!' Kym protested, and the other girls nodded.

Claudia only laughed. 'Oh please! As if these spells could actually work! What I meant was that we could use this spell during the party to give it a real horror effect. Nate can even jump out at the right time dressed as Satan and give them all a good fright. What do you think?'

The girls discussed it amongst themselves. 'If it's just for show, we don't see why not!' stated Cheryl.

Claudia glanced up at Nathaniel who had remained silent. 'Well aren't you going to talk me out of this ceremony?'

Nathaniel shook his head. 'No one can ever talk you out of doing something that you've set your heart on. Besides which you've already snapped my head off three times today, so I wasn't going to try for a fourth.'

Laughing, Claudia leaned over the altar to draw Nathaniel closer to kiss him. The other girls conveniently looked the other way. On very rare occasions Claudia she could be truly affectionate. Not that this moment or feeling ever lasted long.

'The book states that we must cast the first half of the spell at midnight, at least a week before Halloween.' The girls moved closer around Claudia as excitement sent a chill of anticipation through them.

'What do we have to do?' Kym's question returned their complete attention to the book. As Claudia read, a wicked smile touched her lips.

'We have to prepare a sacrifice!'

Michael Pays A Solicitous Call

At about the time that Claudia and her friends were working in the temple, Michael had walked down to the Tempest farm to see how Acacia's sprained ankle was healing. As with his first visit to the farm, he found that he was undoing the buttons of his heavy jacket. When he reached up his hand to knock on the front door, it opened on its own. As he called out in greeting, Ethan's head popped out of the kitchen door, and Benny trotted down the hallway to see whom it was.

'Merry Meet! Come on in. You're just in time for pumpkin scones,' called out Ethan.

Stepping into the house, Michael had already realised that, as the wonderful aroma of hot scones had wafted down the hall. Pausing to say hello to Benny, Michael leant over and patted the shy old dog, which followed him back up the hallway. In the kitchen, Michael found not only Ethan but also Mary, whose nose and cheeks were liberally covered with flour. Michael's eyebrows rose in amusement.

'Have you been baking with flour or rolling in it?'

Surprised, Mary glanced into the door of the microwave to see her reflection. With a gasp of horror, she turned and slapped Ethan's arm.

'You beast! Why didn't you tell me?' Mary used a tea towel to wipe her face. Ethan just laughed.

'I wanted to see how long it would take for you to notice.' He dodged out of the way, saving himself from being slapped again.

Michael smiled at their youthful antics as he sat down at the kitchen table. 'How is Acacia today?'

The laughter in Ethan's face vanished. 'Physically she'll be fine in a day or two. Otherwise... well...' He ended with a sigh.

Mary looked hesitantly from one to the other. 'Is this is a guy thing? Where no one actually speaks in total sentences but whole conversations are said in a look? Shall I leave?'

'There's no need, Mary, as there is nothing to discuss!' Michael shook his head. 'Acacia and I settled that matter last night, so I must ask you to please drop the subject.'

Ethan shrugged in a nonchalant manner. 'Your loss my friend.' To prove that he was prepared to let the matter rest, Ethan lifted a tea towel that covered the cooling scones on the bench and brought them and the tub of butter to the table. Mary filled the kettle and put it on to boil.

'Tea or coffee, Father Michael?'

'Tea please, Mary.' The shelf of tea varieties was extensive in the Tempest kitchen.

'Any particular kind?' Mary indicated the large selection.

'Surprise me!' Michael suddenly laughed.

Mary turned back to the shelf, studying the labels for a moment before finally selecting a jar. 'This is a favourite of mine, peppermint. Shall I make a cup for Acacia?'

Ethan, having sat down opposite Michael, had started to cut open the scones and butter them, but at Mary's question, he shook his head.

'Ace is in meditation at the moment. Only a fool, or a brave man would attempt to break into her trance.'

A smile touched Michael's lips. 'I thought that Acacia said that your powers had superseded her own. Surely you're a match for anything that Acacia can dish out?'

A look of horror crossed Ethan's handsome features. 'While in meditation, if done correctly, it is possible for a witch to mentally link with other members of the Family. It might be the closest humans ever come to achieving a universal consciousness. Sort of like a witch's version of email, twitter or chat rooms. If dragged out of this state rather than properly preparing departure, for a few minutes you still have access to a hundred, up to a thousand witches' powers at your fingertips. With someone of Acacia's experience and vast mental capabilities, she could very well kill you.'

In Serious Danger

Michael had opened his mouth to reply, but the words died before they were spoken, as a terrified scream interrupted their conversation. Without considering his actions, Michael was on his feet and following Ethan, who had also jumped up, to Acacia's meditation room, from where the scream had emanated.

Mary pausing only long enough to turn off the kettle also followed. The door of the meditation room was flung open, and Acacia staggered from the room. Horror was reflected in her eyes which seemed to be a bright electric blue, and although her lips moved, no audible sound followed. Ethan placed his arms around her to support her as she began to collapse.

Even in such a state of shock, Michael could not help thinking, *Acacia is one of the most beautiful women I have ever seen.* Dressed in a maroon suit consisting of a tight fitting jacket and knee length swirling double Georgette skirt; she always appeared well dressed. Her right ankle was now professionally wrapped in a bandage. In desperation Acacia resorted to mental communication.

'Ethan, someone has tapped into our secret knowledge. Our total consciousness is under attack! The Book of the Nephilim has been violated.'

'Holy Mother!' The exclamation came not from Mary or Ethan but Michael. All looked at him in complete surprise. Mary could participate or at least receive mental communication due to the training she had received from Ethan. But without any such training, the priest had demonstrated that he too was receptive. Ethan assisted Acacia to a kitchen chair and Mary got her a glass of water. The group waited in silence as Acacia drank some of the cool, refreshing liquid.

'How much damage can this book do?' asked Michael. Ethan's eyebrows rose in question. Michael gave a rueful smile. 'I'm not so narrow minded! I know of the legends of the Nephilim otherwise known as the Fallen Angels. This may be excessively serious, yes?'

Acacia managed to nod. 'This book has been lost for centuries and we had hoped that it would remain so, but in the event that it was found, the Family attached a very fine mental tag upon it so that we would know immediately when it surfaced. That tag has just been activated.' Acacia took another swallow of water. For the moment curiosity got the better of Michael.

'This tag, is it like a door bell?'

Acacia massaged her temples. 'I wish! This tag was more like a hundred volt lightning bolt. The closer the book is, the higher the effect.'

Ethan swore. 'Then the book is here?' he demanded.

'Yes.'

'Where?'

'The pagan temple.'

Without waiting to hear anything else, Ethan strode out of the kitchen, grabbing his coat, stating as he left, 'I'll get the horses saddled. Maybe we can still catch them!'

Mary, having been closely studying Acacia, decided that she would be in good hands with Michael. 'I'll go and help Ethan. Speed is a necessity.'

Michael waited until he was alone with Acacia before he spoke, 'I don't want to appear a sceptic, but I need a boost of reality for a minute.'

To answer him, Acacia reached across and touched Michael's arm. The electrical charge that he received was enough to make him swear before he could stop himself.

'The tag?' Michael placed a hand on the back of a nearby chair to steady himself.

Acacia nodded. 'Our relationship with the Grigoris, who are the direct descendants of the Nephilim, is a tentative one. During the time of the English Inquisition, a very important book was placed in the keeping of our Family, but due to the high mortality rate of witches during those persecution centuries, the knowledge of the book's whereabouts was lost.'

'Until today?'

Acacia slowly rose to her feet, her face very serious. 'Until today!'

Michael was about to stride up the passage to shut and lock the front door but Acacia stopped him as she pulled on her cape.

'There's no need to lock up our house. It's protected by an enchantment. It is a residue of Grandmama's powers. It allows people and animals to come and go without harm, so long as their intentions are non-violent. We have never had to test the Protector against pure evil, but local hostilities are easily repelled. You may have noticed that as soon as you step onto the property it is considerably warmer than that of the village. That too is an influence of the Protector.'

Michael shook his head as they left through the back door, a slow process as Acacia still limped considerably. 'I feel like I've slipped into Alice's looking glass. Logic and reality are slowly slipping away!'

Tiger

Outside, Michael found that it was necessary to watch where he walked. *Not in fear of treading in animal manure because there isn't any, but fear of treading on a cat.* In the possibly last days of any sunshine before it began to rain and snow, cats were seeking out the sun's warmth. He now found himself surrounded by a myriad of colours and breeds. Most of the dozen or so cats were stretched out on the concrete slabbing that led from the house to the stables. Acacia looked around to see what kept Michael and a gentle smile touched her lips.

'Beautiful, but lazy after their hunting.' She glanced up briefly at the roof before returning her gaze to Michael. 'Stand very still.' She suggested. Michael fought the urge to turn around as he feared something horrendous stood behind him. Taking a deep breath, he valiantly stood his ground as he prepared for whatever awaited behind him. It took all his resolve to not swear or buckle at the knees as something very heavy landed upon his left shoulder. Claws and not talons gripped his jacket for stability upon landing and Michael turned his head to find himself nose to nose with the biggest cat he had ever seen.

30 pounds (15 kilos) of muscle covered in orange striped fur and searching green eyes met his briefly before the athletic tom cat snuffed at Michael's hair. *Is this a friend or foe?* He could almost hear the cat's thoughts and was pleased and relieved that the cat decided that Michael was not a threat and uttered a rattling purr.

Acacia had remained silent as the cat had been assessing the priest so as to not distract him but now that a decision had been made she smiled and introduced them. 'This is Tiger.'

'How appropriate!' drawled Michael as this was indeed a very large domestic cat on his shoulder.

'Yes, even as a kitten Tiger had dreams of growing into one of his wild cousins. He is my familiar.' Acacia held out her hand to the stripy cat and Michael was bemused as Tiger stepped off his shoulder and onto Acacia's hand without her showing that she was accepting anything heavier than a single feather.

'That defies the laws of physics!'

'That is magic!' A mischievous smile answered him as Tiger jumped off Acacia's hand to land elegantly onto a long concrete seat against the wall of the barn that was his favourite place to snooze. Ethan led the two horses out of the stable and Michael came forward to lift Acacia up easily onto her horse, and leant a hand to boost Mary up behind Acacia. Ethan mounted his restless colt and held the horse steady as Michael came up behind him.

Ancient Sacred Ground

The horses took them swiftly away from the peace and quiet of the farm and through the main street as they raced up the hill to the cemetery and the pagan temple. No sooner had they pulled up, Ethan then sprang down from his horse and rushed for the temple doors. He went no further than the doorway though, as he checked inside.

'Damn! We're too late!' Ethan turned to find Michael standing beside him. The priest stepped forward as if to enter the temple, but Ethan laid a hand on his arm to stop him.

'Not yet, Michael. You'll only disturb the crime scene.'

Michael frowned. 'You wouldn't call in the police, would you?' A crooked smile touched Ethan's lips as he turned, went back to the horses to assist Acacia and Mary down.

'There would be too many questions that we're not permitted to answer. We have no use for human detectives, when we have our own,' replied Ethan, allowing Acacia to lean upon his arm as she limped towards the doors.

The floor had been swept virtually clean and looking over Acacia's shoulder as she surveyed the room from the doorway; Michael wondered what she could possibly find. Without a word being said, Ethan removed a pouch from his jeans pocket and handed it to Acacia. She poured a small quantity of what looked like glitter into the palm of her hand before raising her hand to her mouth to gently blow the glitter away. A gasp of surprise was drawn from Michael as the glitter formed an outline of the five people who had opened the Book of Spells.

'Never have I seen anything like that!'

Mary nodded in understanding and smiled up at him. 'The first time is always the most spectacular.'

Acacia stepped into the room and the glitter figures separated and swept back to surround Acacia for a moment before vanishing into thin air.

'Clarification I now seek from what has just occurred. Let what was hidden now be brought into the open.'

It was a moment before Acacia moved, and Ethan held up a warning finger to Michael and Mary to remain silent. Only when a deep sigh emitted from Acacia did Ethan let the others enter the temple. Leaning upon Ethan's arm, Acacia approached the altar. Michael's jaw dropped as he watched as they dropped to their knees and kissed the ground. A mischievous smile played around Mary's mouth as she watched his reaction. Gently she pushed his chin up to close his mouth. Michael glanced down at Mary, suddenly self-conscious of being upon ancient sacred ground.

When they were once more on their feet, Ethan turned to address Mary. 'It's safe to come in now.'

Mary ran up to join them; Michael approached more slowly, giving him a chance to look around. In the walls were magnificent carvings, some still quite detailed despite the years of weathering they had suffered. *Looking at the carvings, I begin to realise that life can no longer be seen as strictly black and white, as here is a world and a lifestyle that I've always believed to be dead and buried. I'd always believed that there existed other religions and beliefs, but not until this moment had I realised the complexity of the universal spiritual experience. Today, I have learnt something, and I am humbled by it.*

Ethan pointed at the small amount of blood that stained the altar. 'It looks like the book is revealed by an offering of blood.' He took a small knife out of his pocket and swiftly ran the blade across his palm and smeared the blood onto the altar.

Acacia was studying the walls and the floor to see where it would open. The activation of the ancient mechanism awed the audience into stunned silence. As they had expected, the hiding place was empty.

'What now?' asked Michael as Acacia brushed out onto one hand the dust that remained in the wall cavity. Ethan went around the altar to join Acacia, handing her a pouch similar to the one that had contained the glitter like substance. Into this pouch Acacia scooped the dust.

'We'll have to see Claudia and try to convince her to hand the book over to us,' explained Ethan.

Mary shook her head. 'Do you know that for a fact, or is that an assumption based on the knowledge that Claudia was interested in the temple for her Halloween party next Saturday night?'

Ethan turned to re-join Mary. 'A bit of both really. When Claudia reached into the wall, she must have brushed against the stone, leaving a minute trace of perfume. As the stuff that Claudia wears is two hundred pounds a bottle, I doubt anyone else local can afford to wear the same perfume.'

A mobile phone began to chirp, startling the group, especially when Michael removed the gadget from his jacket pocket. A gentle smile touched Acacia's lips.

'Ah, the trappings of modern living.'

Michael laughed but upon reading the text message from Marjorie, the Rectory housekeeper his smile disappeared. 'I'm afraid I'll have to leave you. Something urgent has come up.'

Acacia quickly scanned his face as the priest dropped the phone back into his jacket pocket.

'Father Thomas?'

Michael nodded. 'He's all right, but Marjorie feels that she is no longer able to look after him on her own, so we contacted hospice service about home care. Someone is coming around now, so Marjorie wants me to be there.'

Acacia nodded. 'Understandable. Tell Marjorie I'll see her tomorrow with the jam and pickles she asked for.'

Michael hesitated, *I'd expected Acacia to have made some sort of protest or show disappointment about me leaving and her easy acceptance of my being called away had surprised me.* 'I'll see you later then.'

Acacia looked up, surprised that he was still there. 'Tomorrow perhaps, when I visit Father Thomas. Otherwise I'll send a text message about how we go with recovering the book. Merry Part.'

Mary and Ethan said goodbye, but it was obvious to Michael that their thoughts were already working on a strategy of how to tackle Claudia over the Book of the Nephilim. Michael left the temple with an unaccountable feeling of disappointment and rejection.

Acacia was not as unemotional about Michael as she had made him believe. As she and the teenagers left the temple to once again mount their horses, but this time Mary rode with Ethan, Acacia wondered, *How careful will I need to be in the future, if Michael is so receptive to my mental projections? The force of the electric shock may have been enough for me to broadcast to a wider audience, but even if that's true, I know that to allow the Priest unrestricted access to my thoughts would be dangerous to us both.*

'Ace?' Ethan's voice brought Acacia's attention back to the problem at hand. As they rode towards the de Bere mansion, they needed to formulate a plan, as there was no way that Claudia would be prepared to do them any favours.

'I don't know, Ethan, after last night's little effort, she can be in no doubt that we love her as much as she does us. We may have to strike some kind of deal.'

Ethan's jaw clenched tightly. *I don't like the sound of that, not one little bit.* 'We'll play it by ear.'

Acacia's Lone Hand

As to be expected the de Bere mansion was the largest and most opulent house in the shire. The gates of the property stood open but even so Acacia reined in her horse outside the property, forcing Ethan to do likewise.

'I should go alone. Your presence may only antagonise Claudia,' she said.

Ethan considered this before slowly nodding his head. 'You won't grovel, promise me that much.'

Acacia stiffened in indignation. 'You forget who I am, Ethan! If I don't succeed, then the Family will. This is the discovery of a century and a successful negotiation for its return will earn us both brownie points with the Family.'

Ethan could not help laughing at such simplistic logic. 'Just don't bargain too much away, Ace! I'll take Mary home.' Although Ethan's words had been spoken in jest, he had been very serious.

At that moment as Acacia rode up the driveway, she truly understood the dislike, for hatred was too strong a word, which Ethan and Claudia felt for each other. Acacia reined the mare and dismounting, limped severely as she led the horse up to the side of the building to offer Sally some protection from the chilling winds.

Ringing the ornate doorbell Acacia smiled. *I feel like a peasant girl at the door of the Lord's manor. I wonder if I should use the service entrance?* Prudence, the middle aged, well-rounded Asian maid, opened the door. Her smile disappeared upon the sight of Acacia.

'Miss Acacia!'

Acacia smiled. 'Merry Meet Prudence. I see you're keeping well. I would like to see Claudia please.'

'Miss Claudia has a visitor with her at the moment. I advise that you try later Miss Acacia.' Prudence's lips quivered and Acacia wondered, *is it in fear of Claudia's anger or my own?*

'I presume she has Nathaniel with her. Please inform Claudia that I am here, Prudence, it is imperative that I speak to her now.'

Words seemed to fail Prudence, so it was fortunate for her that rescue came from behind her.

'Prudence, there's a gale blowing throughout the house! Who's at the front door?' The deep masculine voice brought Rochester de Bere to the doorway. Prudence turned to face her boss.

'I was simply explaining to Miss Acacia that Miss Claudia isn't receiving any more visitors today, Sir.'

Rochester opened the front door wider so that he could quickly scan Acacia from head to toe. 'Nonsense! It is obviously important to bring Acacia out with a sprained ankle. Come in my dear.' There was a glint of a smile at the sight of Acacia's injury from his attempt to scare her off her horse.

Acacia thanked him and when Prudence stepped back, she entered the hall that opened up to a very large and spacious parlour.

'Now go and inform Claudia that she has a visitor,' ordered Rochester indicating to Acacia that she should be seated in the ornate parlour. When Prudence disappeared as ordered, de Bere leant against the fireplace as he continued to study Acacia.

Although I find his scrutiny disturbing, I must keep my composure and I'm glad that I didn't permit Ethan to accompany me inside. He would've been more than ready at this moment to punch Rochester in the eye for even daring to look at me in such a lustful manner. Let alone his behaviour the other night.

'I've been meaning to make an appointment to see you, but from one cause or another, I have never got around to it.'

Acacia's eyebrows rose in surprise. 'We witches can be quite modern today, I am listed in the telephone book. We even have a mobile, an email and a web page.' She tried to keep her tone light and friendly.

Rochester gave an indulgent laugh. 'I was more afraid that my reason for seeking your counsel would somehow be discovered and the last thing I wish is to bring scandal to my revered family.'

'Perhaps if you come and see me tomorrow, Mr de Bere. Confidentiality is guaranteed to all my clients.'

'Please Acacia, call me Rochester. My problem is that my wife is no longer interested in having any… physical relations.'

Acacia controlled a smile. *I'm not at all surprised as it is common knowledge that he has not only roving eyes, but roving hands and penis as well.*

'In truth, Mr de Bere, this isn't a matter I can assist in. Perhaps you need to seek a professional marriage counsellor.'

Rochester suddenly sat down upon the lounge beside Acacia, making her jump back in surprise.

'I'd thought that I could do it if I made Cath jealous. As yet I haven't found the woman to make her angry enough, but I think you could.'

Acacia swiftly rose and attempted to put as much distance between her them as was possible. This wasn't possible as he also rose to his feet again.

'I don't think that is a good way to cement your marriage, even if I was willing to have an affair with you, which I definitely am not! I have continued to tell you that over and over again.'

He wrapped his arms about her waist. 'I love it when a woman says no, but really means yes!'

Acacia pushed against his chest. 'When I say no, I mean no!' Despite this protest, Rochester tried to kiss her. Acacia was about to dish out her own punishment for this violation when Claudia stormed into the room.

'Daddy! How could you!' Instantly releasing Acacia, Rochester slapped Acacia hard across the face.

'You cheap harlot! I'm a happily married man!'

Claudia, unconvinced by this show of indignation, strode forward to stand between Acacia and her father. 'You're disgusting Father! I happened to hear your conversation so don't lay the blame at Acacia's door. It's no wonder that Mother is cold towards you.'

'You watch your mouth, young lady!' threatened her father, but was to get no further than that as a voice from the doorway behind them demanded their attention as Catherine de Bere entered.

'I suggest that you retire to your study, Rochester. Your presence here is not required.' She spoke quietly, but with a note of command.

Her husband looked like he wanted to retort, but one glance at the frost in his wife's eyes was enough to send him off in defeat. Mrs de Bere turned her attention to Acacia.

'I'll ensure that he doesn't disturb you again, Acacia. I would greatly appreciate it if this incident went no further.'

Acacia could feel the woman's pain and anguish as it radiated from her. 'Of course Mrs de Bere. I have no wish to add to the burden that you already carry. But he will be punished. A couple of weeks of impotence will dampen his lust and show that I will not be treated with such disrespect!'

The much tried wife inclined her head. 'Thank you Acacia.' With that she left Claudia and Acacia alone.

You Want It Back?

Claudia indicated that Acacia should be re-seated but did not immediately speak. As the teenager fought to bring her turmoil of emotions under control, Acacia was able to see beyond her rich bitch facade.

'I'm sorry that you were subjected to that Acacia. That is a private shame that Mother and I must try to deal with, and not all the money in the world can compensate for a dysfunctional family.' Claudia gave a deep sigh. 'You're here for the book I found aren't you?'

'Yes,' Acacia spoke softly but firmly.

Claudia nodded. 'I'll get it for you.'

As Claudia left the room, Acacia's eyes opened wide in surprise. *I didn't expect Claudia to give in so easily.* It wasn't long before Claudia returned with a puzzled Nathaniel carrying the Book of the Nephilim. Acacia almost wept at the sight of the rare monograph.

'Your discovery won't go unrewarded, Claudia. Although the reappearance of this book may never be made public, you'll receive recognition not only from the Family but also the Grigori. Is there anything that I may do for you in return?'

Claudia hesitated. 'Your promise to keep silent about my father is enough.'

Acacia carefully accepted the fragile and ancient volume from Nathaniel. 'Thank you Claudia.'

Claudia and Nathaniel followed Acacia as she limped outside. Claudia held the book as Nathaniel threw Acacia up into the saddle, before Claudia handed the book up to Acacia. The teenagers remained outside, and waved Acacia goodbye.

I'm Not Done Yet!

It was not until Acacia's mare had passed through the gates that Nathaniel finally spoke. 'Why did you give up without a struggle?'

A mischievous smile touched Claudia's lips. 'I have what I want. I copied that important spell for the Halloween party, so I don't need the book any longer.'

Nathaniel looked concerned. 'So you're going ahead with the ceremony?'

Claudia linked her arm through his and led him back inside. 'Was there ever any doubt?'

At What Cost?

Ethan had only just completed stabling his colt when Acacia arrived home. Surprise was written over his face as she handed the valuable book down to him.

'What happened? I didn't expect you back so soon. What were you forced to promise Claudia?' Ethan gently laid the book on the bales of straw before reaching up to assist Acacia down from her horse. Doing so, he noticed the red mark still imprinted upon her cheek.

'Only my silence over Rochester's behaviour.'

Ethan remained silent until he had removed the mare's saddle and placed Sally into her stall for the night. Then with restrained emotion, he cupped her chin in his hand and lifted her cheek to the light.

'Did Rochester hit you?'

Acacia pulled away from him, her eyes sparkling as they meet his. 'It's all right, Ethan. He'll be made to regret it! I had to allow it to soften Claudia towards me and give the book back without too much fuss.'

Ethan slowly nodded his head as he began to understand. 'It makes you wonder why Mrs de Bere doesn't leave him. Or throw him out.' Ethan picked up the book and they headed into the house, and he never mentioned the matter again.

A Third Assignation

'Michael?' That soft, alluring voice and again the gentle touch of a hand to his shoulder caused his eyes to fly open.

'Are we destined to repeat this dream for the rest of our lives?' There was a shade of annoyance in his voice. *I thought we had resolved this issue last time that we cannot be together in this realm or the real world!* He blinked twice as he finally managed to focus his gaze and took in the costume that Acacia had been clad in this time. Skin tight body suit in the colours and including the stripes of Tiger, her familiar. Along with a very impressive tail and cute little ears on top of her head.

'What is it that you want from me?' His almost angry, exasperated question brought tears to her eyes.

'Do you still think that this is somehow my doing? If I knew how to stop it I would!' Before he could reply, Acacia bent down and pinched his arm forcing them both to wake up. Rubbing his arm as he tried to settle down once more, Michael hazily wondered, *Am I going to end up bruised from all this pinching?*

Wednesday 23 October

Hiding In Plain Sight

Michael Casey didn't see Acacia the following morning. When he returned to St Andrews in the afternoon from his visit to the nearby retirement village, Acacia had already been to visit Father Thomas and left again. *I don't know whether to be sad or glad as it appears that Acacia is avoiding meeting me.*

He considered this as he shrugged himself out of his coat, hanging it in the hall and pulled off his gloves before he went to check on Father Thomas. Michael was surprised that the ailing clergy was sitting up in bed, bright and alert, with a huge book spread open across his lap. Michael pulled up the chair beside the bed and wondered, *Where's Marjorie?*

'Is that the Book of the Nephilim?' Michael's voice dropped to barely a whisper. Father Thomas looked up and smiled.

'There you are Michael, my boy. I've had such a lovely morning. Acacia, the dear child, has spent some time with me, and she left a message for you.' Father Thomas peered through his reading glasses at his bedside table. 'It's here somewhere.' An understandable statement as the table was covered with a lamp, various medications, and a glass of water as well as his bible.

Looking back at the book on his lap, Thomas gave a dry laugh. 'Silly me, I was using it as a bookmark!' He pulled the envelope out and handed it across to Michael. Closing his eyes, Thomas leant back against his pillows that supported him in a sitting upright position. *For nearly all of my eighty years, I've been in service to God. At ten, I'd become an altar boy, at twenty-one, an apprentice to the Priesthood, and although my faith is strong, there are times, like now, when the pain gets so bad that I wonder why my God is punishing me. In my heart, I know that this is not true, but as I look around the world at the pain, death and destruction that is taking place, I do wonder if this is indeed the will of God.*

With considerable effort, Thomas opened his eyes again as Michael, having read Acacia's note, folded it and placed it into his shirt pocket.

'Acacia wants us to look after the book until someone from her Family comes to collect it,' stated Michael. *I presume that Uncle Thomas already knows that.* To confirm this belief, Thomas nodded his head.

'The dear child said that most people would think that she wouldn't part with the book now that it has been found. Not that we want people to know about this book.' Thomas let out a lengthy sigh, which indicated to Michael that he was becoming very tired.

'The best hiding place is to put the book in plain view on my bookcase over there in the corner.' Thomas pointed to a three-foot high bookcase that was almost jammed packed with books.

'Wouldn't it be better to hide the book?'

Thomas chuckled. 'But it will be hidden. Bring me that large atlas on the left.'

Although bemused, Michael did as he was asked, laying the large atlas on the bed beside Thomas. The old priest removed the dust jacket and placed it over the Book of the Nephilim. It was an almost perfect fit, and once upon the shelf, no one would know the difference.

'That is ingenious!' Michael's exclamation pleased Thomas as he allowed the younger man to place both books onto the bookcase. When Michael came back to the bed, he rearranged the pillows and assisted Thomas to lie down flat.

'You look like you could do with some rest. I'll see if Marjorie will let me make some custard for supper.'

Thomas smiled. 'That would be lovely. Before you go Michael…' He pointed to the rosary beads that lay on the bedside table. Understanding, Michael picked up the beads and placed them gently into the old man's hands, pressing them reassuringly before he left Thomas to sleep.

Claudia's Ceremony

At ten minutes to midnight, Kym, Cheryl and Merelda stood in a huddled group inside the pagan temple as Nathaniel created a large circle of stones in the middle of the floor. The light of a powerful lamp aided his work. As per Claudia's instructions, the girls all wore make shift black kaftans and Nathaniel was dressed, reluctantly, in black jeans and a dark jumper. *I want nothing to do with Claudia's ceremony, but I can never say no to her.* The girls stood shivering as Nathaniel made a neat pile of dry sticks in the middle of the stone circle. He shook his head at their grumbling.

'It's not Claudia's idea that you're naked under those kaftans; that was all your own idea, so you've only got yourself to blame if you're cold.'

The girls gave a shriek of disbelief. 'How did you know? Were you spying on us?' demanded Kym.

Nathaniel sighed as he shook his head. 'You haven't stopped whispering about anything else for the last five minutes! The acoustics in this temple is very good.'

From the doorway came a laugh. 'There's such a thing as being too trustworthy, Nate! There are three nearly naked maidens and all you can think of is to scold them!' Claudia, also clad in a black kaftan, stepped into the temple. Nathaniel's cheeks flamed in embarrassment.

'Claudia, you know that you're the only girl for me! How can you even joke about that?'

Dropping a backpack down beside the fire circle, Claudia caressed her hand down his cheek. 'I feel strange tonight. As if there is a seductress inside of me trying to escape.' Claudia pulled Nathaniel against her and gave him a long and passionate kiss.

Cheryl coughed. 'It is nearly midnight.'

Nathaniel was released and he rocked on his feet as Claudia swept passed him. Kym bent down beside the circle of rocks to light the sticks and Claudia pulled out various herbs as well as six black candles. These were placed strategically around the fire and lit as the fire began to burn. While the girls took their position standing around the fire, Claudia gave them each a handful of herbs ranging from acorns, and pieces of apple, ferns, flax, heather, oak leaves and sage.

When the fire provided a sufficient glow, Nathaniel turned off the lamp and stepped out of the radiance of the fire. The girls moved slowly around the stone circle as Claudia recited the spell that she had copied.

'O Mighty Satan, I entreat thee to inspire your servant to manifest before me so that he may give me a true and faithful answer, so that I may accomplish my desired end. This I respectfully and humbly ask in Your Name, Lord Satan, may you deem me worthy, Father.'

When commanded, each girl sprinkled her handful of herbs into the fire, which made it burn higher and brighter. With their hands empty, the girls linked hands, still moving slowly around the fire as it rose to an impossible height, matching their own size.

As the girls moved faster, Claudia chanted Ethan's name and the fire began to swirl in a vortex as it reached up to the roof. The doors of the temple flew open as a strong wind swept an inhumane scream through the temple, which mingled with the fire vortex and projected the flames through the roof. There was an enormous explosion in the sky, which sucked up all the fire and wind.

For a moment, there was absolutely no sound either inside or outside of the temple. Then from the clear sky came a crash of thunder and a blinding bolt of lightning as it clouded over.

'Awesome!' exclaimed Merelda, breathless.

Claudia laughed as rain began to come through the holes in the roof. 'A pretty good rain dance if nothing else!' There was a strange brilliant light in Claudia's eyes as she turned to her friends. 'You'd best get home before your parents discover that you're missing. We'll discuss the refreshments for the party tomorrow. Nate and I will get rid of the evidence.'

The girls exchanged a significant look, there had to be an ulterior motive if Claudia promises to clean up.

Nathaniel moved for the first time since the ceremony had begun to pack away Claudia's candles back into her bag. With the other girls gone, Claudia grasped hold of Nathaniel and placed her hands up his jumper, her eyes burning with desire.

'Take me, Nate!'

Nathaniel looked around self-consciously. 'Here?'

In answer, Claudia pulled her kaftan over her head, proving to Nathaniel that she was as naked as the other girls had been. Lowering herself to the ground, Claudia drew him down with her.

'Come to me!' Her husky words were all the invitation that Nathaniel needed as he wrapped Claudia up in his arms and hastened to undo his jeans. Claudia pushed away his hands as he attempted to caress her breasts, she was in no mood for foreplay as she reached down to put him inside her. So erotically charged had the ceremony left her, that it was not long before they were both screaming in ecstasy.

A Message For Michael

Michael hadn't gone to bed when the howling scream from the fire vortex had startled him out of his chair where he had been reading. Fearing that Father Thomas was in trouble, Michael dropped the book on his chair and raced out of his room to Thomas'. The elderly priest was indeed awake, but quite calm as he watched the Book of the Nephilim jiggle about in the bookcase. As Michael stepped towards the bookcase, a white mist emanated from the book, rising to form a female transparent apparition.

'Thou have but a few risings of thy sun before He cometh. Thy church and thy people are in grave danger. Protect thy sanctity of thy faith.'

Before Michael could even open his mouth to reply, the misty figure retreated once more into the book. Father Thomas fell back against his pillows, and Michael came to him but the elderly priest waved him away.

'I'm all right. Go and check the church.'

Michael grabbed the church keys from their usual hook by the front door but no soon as his feet had stepped outside, the ground shook as Michael watched the fire leap through the temple roof. Catching his breath, Michael unconsciously crossed himself and would've headed for the temple, if he hadn't heard a loud crash inside the church. As Michael hastened to unlock the main church doors, everything went silent.

Instead of being reassuring, the silence left him with a feeling of increased anxiety, which turned to horror as he switched on the lights. As the thunder rolled and lightning flashed outside, Michael only briefly acknowledged that the statue of the Madonna had fallen from the altar. There was something more monumental that had gained his attention; the church walls were dripping with blood.

'Michael.' The softly spoken female voice made him look at the open doors behind him, but he was still alone in the church.

'Michael.' A shiver ran down his back as he looked down at the statue of the Madonna. When her lips moved, to repeat his name, he fell to his knees and with shaking hands picked up the statue.

'Your greatest trial of faith is coming, my son. You must decide whether you will stand and fight what is to come, even though it may destroy all that you believe in.' Michael swallowed hard.

I can't believe I'm talking to a statue. 'If I leave, Holy Mother?' There was a moment's pause.

'The white witch and her protégé are not strong enough to fight this evil alone. This is not the Horned God of their faith that comes, but the manifestation of Evil itself. Remember that an element of Evil exists in all of mankind. Go forth Michael and prepare thyself for the coming of the Antichrist and remember that God is with thee.'

Ethan's Counsel

'Michael?' The word this time came not from the statue but behind him. Rising to his feet, Michael carefully placed the statue once more upon the altar as Acacia and Ethan, both quite drenched, raced into the church. They were dressed in jeans and thick jumpers.

'Thomas told us you were here. Have you been to the temple yet?' Acacia was still focussed but Ethan paused as he looked up at the bleeding walls.

'Cool effects!'

Michael slowly turned around, still in a state of shock. 'No, not yet. The Madonna imparted to me a message.'

Acacia studied Michael carefully before turning to Ethan. 'Stay with him!' Without waiting for either to reply, Acacia ran as well as she could with a sprained ankle back out into the rain.

Realising that Michael needed some guidance, Ethan placing his hand on Michael's arm, led him to a pew to sit down. Ethan perched himself upon the back of the pew to face Michael.

'So what did the Holy Mother say?'

Michael looked up, expecting to find sarcasm in Ethan's words and expression, and was surprised that it was not there. Michael took a deep breath and let it out slowly.

'If Claudia has indeed called forth the Master of Evil, we're in serious trouble. The Madonna said that I could lose all that I believe in, but if I leave, you and Acacia won't be able to cope on your own.'

Ethan nodded solemnly. 'So what are you going to do?'

Michael sat up straight in indignation. 'Although I'm a pacifist, I won't run from a fight! Not for something I truly believe in.'

'Good man!' A smile touched Ethan's lips.

'You must have started out before that horrific scream, or were you already in the area?' Ethan grinned at the implications of the question.

'We weren't taking part in Claudia's ceremony if that's what you're thinking! We became aware of the ceremony as soon as it commenced. Acacia feared that something like this might happen when Claudia was too willing to give the book back, but once started, there was nothing we could do to prevent it coming into fruition.'

'This is insane!' Michael rose to his feet and strode up and down the aisle. 'I must surely wake up soon.'

Ethan leant back as he crossed his arms across his chest. 'Sure, and this blood is going to simply vanish in the morning!'

Sitting down abruptly again, Michael buried his head between his hands. 'A talking statue, an ancient book of magic, a pagan ceremony and the coming of the Antichrist. I thought that I would be in for a quiet life here!'

'You've been given the opportunity to leave, Michael, we'd understand if the coming battle with Evil frightens you. According to what Ace read in the book of the Nephilim, within a week the village will become cut off from the rest of the country and no one will be permitted to leave or arrive.'

Michael looked up, frowning, as a very wet Acacia re-entered the church. 'Does that mean your Family may not be able to assist us?'

Ethan's eyebrows rose in surprise. 'A minute ago you couldn't believe that this was even happening.'

'Ethan! The man's in shock!' warned Acacia. 'The truth is that we're expecting Ethan's new mentor any day now. He may arrive in time to help us but then again he might not. The Family will assist us if it is possible. It will be as if an invisible force field has been placed around the village.'

'What now?' Michael rose to his feet again.

Acacia led the way back to the church doors. 'Get some sleep. Store up as much reserve energy as you can before Samhain, as I doubt that any of us will sleep that night.'

Michael raised his hand to the power box to turn off the lights, but as a thought occurred to him, he paused and looked across at Ethan. 'How do we get rid of it? This Emissary of Evil?'

Ethan shrugged. 'According to the Book of Nephilim he'll go willingly at midnight on Samhain, with his sacrifice. It's the damage he'll cause between now and then that is the bigger concern.'

'Is the sacrifice random or preselected?'

Ethan glanced across at Acacia and he knew the answer by the expression on her face and he said, 'The sacrifice is me!'

Visitation Interruptus

Michael had actually been looking forward to Acacia's visit this time as he wanted to discuss the events of that evening further with her. But when she arrived, Acacia sadly shook her head.

'Sleep Michael. We must prepare for what is coming. We must be ready for the fight of our lives.'

Instead Michael reached out to grasp her hand to stall her from pinching his arm, 'That is what I want to discuss with you. Please Acacia, won't you stay the night with me?'

Again she shook her head. 'I can't… I can't think about anything else but you when I am like this with you! And right now I must think about how to save Ethan.'

Not certain if he should be disappointed or pleased at how she still felt about him, Michael pinched his own arm to wake up.

Thursday 24 October

I Won't Run!

Understandably Michael, Acacia nor Ethan slept well that night. Michael lied to Thomas, telling him that everything was all right. In the morning, as Ethan assisted Acacia to load up the cart for market, he was his usual cheerful but sarcastic self. Acacia, though, could not hide her concern.

'I wish you'd let me send you up to London until after Samhain.' This was not the first time that Acacia had said this and once again Ethan shook his head.

'I won't leave you, Ace. This is my battle too. Besides which, He may simply follow me to London, thus widening the effect of his visit to a larger area. I won't run, Ace, it's not how you and Grandmother raised me.'

'I don't mean to nag, but I worry for you.' Acacia finally conceded defeat.

Ethan hugged her as he smiled. 'I know, but you can't fight my battles for me. I must prove that the boy has become a man.'

Acacia returned his embrace. 'I just wish that your first major test wasn't such a life threatening one.'

'We'll be all right.' Releasing her, Ethan shrugged. 'Now don't you let your produce go for less than it's worth. It may be surplus but we've still got to try and make a profit.'

Acacia realised that the subject was now closed and gave a mock salute. 'Oui Mon Capitaine!' This piece of sarcasm earned her a playful slap across the backside.

'Don't be late for the school bus, Ethan.' Acacia tried to sound stern but failed as Ethan only laughed.

'I'll do my usual manure run this afternoon, so I'll muck out the stables as soon as I return from school. Try not to worry Ace.' This parting statement was flippantly said, but even so, Acacia could not help but worry.

Market Day

Every Thursday in Stirling was market day when the cottage craft industries and the home growers got together to sell off or trade their surplus goods and handicraft. During the year, except in winter, the markets were held outdoors in the Market Square, which had been used for this purpose since Saxon times. When the days were too cool, canvas sails were erected to cut down the chilling winds.

Usually I look forward to market day, but last night had certainly put a dampener upon any possible enjoyment. As only a small comfort, although my ankle still pains me it is at least well on the way to mending. Acacia managed to maintain a cheerful facade but such was her state of anxiety that sometime after one o'clock in the afternoon when a hand touched her shoulder from behind, she jumped nearly out of her skin.

Turning sharply, Acacia found herself faced by a weary Father Michael Casey. It took several minutes for Acacia's racing heart to slow back to a regular pace.

'You look as good as I feel.' Acacia tried for a light tone.

Michael managed to smile, as his eyes ran down the tight black sweater and full, heavy black pleated skirt that Acacia wore. 'I only wish I could feel how good you look.'

An involuntary gasp escaped from Acacia, as the priest's cheeks grew crimson. *The words I meant aren't how they had come out. Or was it in fact a Freudian slip?*

'What I mean is…'

He was answered by a soft understanding laugh. 'I know, Father Michael, you don't need to explain. How are the church walls looking this morning?' This question was asked as Acacia turned back to serve a customer.

Michael uttered a deep sigh. 'I did such a lousy job of cleaning up that Marjorie came to my rescue with the right products to use.'

Acacia waited until she had served the customer before answering him, 'How did you explain the blood to Marjorie?'

Michael perched himself on the edge of the table. 'I told her the truth. I've already discovered that Marjorie is one of those people who will always know when you're lying.' He hesitated before adding, 'we need to talk. A serious talk. I'd like an idea of what is going to happen.'

At that moment, the folk from the retirement village were heading back to their bus, and many called out a farewell to Acacia.

'Not here, Michael. Go and offer assistance to your elderly parishioners and then stop in at a few other stalls. I'll be loading my cart up to go home at two.'

Michael nodded before moving around Acacia's table to join the group heading up to the waiting bus. With their excited chatter about the morning's outing, it was easy for Michael to momentarily forget the major fate that loomed over them all.

A Surprise Visitor

It wasn't until Acacia was securing the last of her empty boxes onto the cart that she saw Michael again. As ordered, he had remained away from her, visiting other stalls until the appointed time. By two o'clock, Michael had acquired a few packages, so for the purpose of anyone, who may have been listening, Michael asked Acacia for a lift home. Acacia managed to smile.

'Not at all, Father Michael.'

Having hitched up the mare, Acacia waited until they were both seated, with Michael's packages in one of the boxes in the back of the cart, before setting the mare, off to walk up towards St Andrews. On the way, they talked of inconsequential matters until they reached the Rectory. Although Michael had at least a dozen questions to ask, he hesitated to articulate his thoughts. *It's as if the ordinary every day discussion keeps the unknown at bay. Keeps us safe.*

At the Rectory, Acacia assisted Michael with his packages as well as a box of fruit and vegetables that she hadn't sold. They found

Marjorie in the kitchen putting the kettle on. She greeted them both warmly, which surprised Michael.

I know Marjorie is very deeply religious and I had not expected her to be so comfortable about Acacia's way of life. Marjorie's Christian soul saw not religious differences but a common link between them to serve their fellow human beings. This was proven as Acacia placed the box of food on the table.

'For your mission, Marjorie. With winter coming the more you can stock up on now for hard times, the fewer people you'll have to turn away.'

Marjorie reached across and grasped Acacia's hand. 'Bless you child! I know what you give comes from the heart, as you have so little to simply give away.'

Colour swept across Acacia's face and Michael turned Marjorie's attention towards himself. 'Is Thomas awake?'

'Goodness yes!' Marjorie removed from the cupboard three coffee mugs and placed them on the kitchen bench. 'The good Father has a visitor. Someone I think you have been waiting for, Acacia.'

Acacia went deathly pale but Michael had already turned and almost ran through the house to Thomas' room. With an almost non-existent knock, Michael burst into the room without waiting for an answer.

Pulling up short, Michael quickly scanned the room and breathed a sigh of relief when he found that all was as it should be. Thomas was sitting up in bed, banked by pillows, and in the chair beside the bed sat, calmly, his visitor. Both men looked up at Michael's abrupt entrance and Thomas smiled in genuine pleasure.

'My boy, this is Jordan. He's come to continue Ethan's education.'

Jordan rose to his feet and extended his hand to Michael, who hesitated only briefly before accepting it. *I'd been expecting Acacia's 'Elder' to be much older than 35, which is how old Jordan looks. He's tall, much taller than me and very slender in build.* Michael continued to scan the stranger. Jordan's eyes appeared to be brown as was his long hair, which was pulled back in a ponytail. Steel-framed glasses, black trousers and a black shirt and jacket highlighted his handsome features. Michael felt a niggling of jealousy as he considered the Elder. *He is way too handsome!*

'How do you do? Acacia said that you'd be joining us soon. I hope you find our quiet little village to your liking?' Michael felt Acacia silently enter the room behind him.

Jordan smiled. 'I'm sure that I'll enjoy my stay here, but it is early days before I decide whether Ethan and I will remain here.'

A strangled cry brought Acacia to the attention of the others in the room. Michael turned slightly and taking Acacia by the elbow brought her further into the room.

'This is Ethan's new mentor, Jordan,' explained Michael.

Acacia did not release her rigid stance. 'Prove it!'

Father Thomas was shocked by Acacia's hostility. 'Acacia! That is hardly friendly!'

Jordan laughed, a deep rich sound that despite her fear sent a shiver of delight down Acacia's spine.

'It's all right Thomas. I know that Acacia is very anxious at the moment. While Marjorie makes the coffee, I'll take Acacia out into the garden so that she can verify my credentials.' Jordan rose to his feet and motioned for Acacia towards the door.

'May I come too?' Although Michael's question surprised Jordan, it did not throw him.

'Of course.'

Waiting For Proof

The wind was quite chilling outside but neither Acacia nor Jordan appear to notice the cold. Michael tried not to shiver from the cold in case it was misinterpreted as fear.

The garden was a walled enclosure, 30 feet by 15 feet with a small area of lawn surrounded by a neat, simple design of plants that were settling down for dormancy in the winter. The rose blooms had long gone and the hydrangeas had just had their dead heads snipped off, but the deciduous trees were still putting on a masterful display of yellows, oranges and reds as they slowly lost all their leaves.

This display of colour normally fascinated Acacia as a child of nature, but today it could not draw her attention away from Jordan's face. *I mistrust him, Jordan's arrival is too close following the midnight ceremony.* Acacia contained a need to scream in her desperate need for answers. There was a bench to one side of the garden, to which Jordan led them, motioning for them to be seated.

'I understand your apprehension, Acacia, your message to the Family got through and I am aware of the violation of the book. But you've no need for concern. An important element was left out of the ceremony. The resulted storm and the bleeding of the church walls were all that the teenagers managed to unleash. Ethan is, therefore, in no danger.'

Michael breathed a sigh of relief. 'What about the warning from the …ow!' He broke off as Acacia pinched his leg.

'I'm not yet satisfied. If you are the Stranger to come, you may well be lying. Why should I trust you?' asked Acacia.

Jordan chewed on his bottom lip for a moment before he turned to Michael. 'Father do you have a pocket knife handy?'

Bemused, Michael removed from his trouser pocket a Swiss army knife and hesitated before handing it across to Jordan. Opening the blade, Jordan tested the sharpness of it before running the blade swiftly across his palm. Michael jumped up in surprise as blood spurted forth from the wound.

'You fool! You may have done some serious damage!' Removing his handkerchief from his trouser pocket, Michael pressed it into Jordan's hand, forcing him to close his hand into a fist to slow the blood flow. Acacia moved Michael to one side and took the handkerchief out of Jordan's hand to examine the wound.

'*I seek the truth from this stranger but as he speaks may I not be misled.*' She dipped one finger into the blood and raised it to her lips.

'Acacia!' Michael's protest went unnoticed as she placed the handkerchief back over the wound.

'At least it is real. So I am to trust you.'

Jordan grinned. 'That is completely up to you, Sweet Angel, but my purpose is genuine.'

Acacia reserved her silence but Michael was prepared to voice his confusion. 'I don't understand any of this!'

In compassion, Jordan laid his undamaged hand upon Michael's shoulder. 'Witches can bleed, but the true Servant of Evil cannot. To prove that I'm the former and not the latter, was why Acacia had to determine whether in fact it was blood that poured forth from the wound.'

'I see.' It was obvious, though, from Michael's tone of voice that he did not see at all.

'Well Acacia?' Jordan's tone was quite forbidding now; causing her to look up at him concerned.

'Must I apologise?' Although her voice was quite small, there was a touch of defiance in her words.

A delighted chuckle answered Acacia. 'Ah, my Sweet Angel. I would've been disappointed if you had taken me at face value without checking. No apology is required.' Jordan held out both his hands towards her. 'Come, will you not greet me as a member of the Family?'

Acacia placed her hands into his and stepped forward to kiss him upon one cheek and then the other. 'Merry Meet Brother Jordan.' She would have stepped back again, but Jordan retained a firm hold of her hands and drew her firmly into his arms. Acacia managed to protest but this was smothered as Jordan's mouth suddenly covered hers in a kiss that Michael felt was far from being a Family greeting.

This was proven to be the case when Acacia managed to pull away and she spat out a word that although Michael did not understand, the meaning was quite clear. Jordan's reaction surprised Michael, as he slapped Acacia hard across the face. The blow was severe enough to bring Acacia to her knees, causing Michael to leap to her defence.

'There's no need for such violence!' Michael grasped Jordan by the lapels of his jacket and came to realise the mistake of confronting a powerful Elder. Michael cried out in pain as he felt as if his head would explode, but the gutsy priest refused to release Jordan.

'Enough!' commanded Acacia as she rose to her feet. 'Release him Michael, my punishment was justified, so don't suffer on my account.'

Michael reluctantly stepped away; his face still set in a stubborn line. Jordan straightened his jacket as he released his victim from his painful lesson. Acacia placed a soothing hand upon Michael's arm.

'I should've warned you about the intensity of Jordan's powers. Any just punishment handed out by an Elder for wrongful behaviour must not be retaliated against.'

Michael screwed up his nose in disgust. 'How barbaric! Does that mean because I interfered that you must be punished again?'

The fear in Acacia's eyes answered him, as she looked up nervously at Jordan, but this time the Elder smiled.

'I'll make the punishment a little more enjoyable this time.' He promised, drawing Acacia back into his arms.

Michael looked away as Acacia was forced to surrender her mouth to Jordan's, a feeling of irrational anger and jealously surging through him. *The knowledge that I'm responsible for this second punishment does nothing to lessen my anger, but I notice by the sparkle in Acacia's eyes, that her punishment hasn't been that unpleasant.*

Marjorie stuck her head out the back door. 'Coffee's ready. Will you be staying dear child?' Acacia cast a quick, searching glance at Jordan but he only smiled and politely inclined his head.

'Thank you, Marjorie, but I can't leave Sally standing out in the cold for much longer.' Acacia turned her gaze to Michael as Marjorie withdrew back inside. 'If what Jordan says is true, then there is no more need for you to worry Michael.'

'If? My Sweet Angel, you are becoming insolent! Beware of harsher punishment!' At the hard tone of Jordan's voice, Acacia lowered her eyes respectfully and murmured an apology.

'I'll wish to see Ethan tonight!' It was a statement from the Elder and not a request.

'You're more than welcome to join us for dinner.'

Jordan inclined his head again. 'I'll see you at six then. I'd best return to Father Thomas before he thinks that we've all deserted him.' He strode back into the house, not caring if Michael and Acacia followed or not. Michael taking Acacia's arm, led her through the garden gate and around to the front of the house, to where her horse was patiently waiting.

'You're worried still?' Michael's tone was gentle, unsure if she would confide in him. Acacia scanned his face before replying.

'Yes, but I can't explain why. Perhaps it has something to do with Jordan's reaction to you defending me. I fear… I fear that I will lose Ethan.' Acacia's hand unconsciously tightened about Michael's arm, unable to stop the tears falling from her eyes. He patted her hand sympathetically.

'Do you think that this uncomfortable start with Jordan will jeopardise Ethan's chance for staying on the farm?'

Acacia sighed and tried to wipe away her tears. 'I don't know, it may have done. Never mind, that's not your problem.' She released him to boost herself up onto the driver's seat. Acacia spread her skirts about her before taking up the reins. 'You should be able to sleep better tonight, Michael. I'm sorry to have scared you unnecessarily.'

Michael reached up to grasp one of Acacia's hands. 'That doesn't matter! If you ever find that you need assistance, please know that I am yours to command. You're not alone.'

Acacia returned the pressure of his fingers and managed to smile. 'Thank you Michael. Merry Part.'

Michael felt an overwhelming sense of loss as Acacia drove the cart away.

Mary Scores Off Claudia

The final bell had rung and heading out of school to the bus Ethan and Mary found Claudia and her entourage falling into step with them.

'That was some storm last night, wasn't it?' Claudia's tone was innocent and friendly and that made Ethan immediately suspicious.

'You should know, you caused it Claudia!'

She opened her eyes wide in surprise. 'Me? You must be mistaken. After that scene with Acacia and my father, I was grounded to my room all evening.'

Ethan uttered a harsh laugh. 'Oh please! We know it was you! You have no idea what you've unleashed! I only hope that you don't regret that night's work.'

Claudia smiled sweetly as she flicked her blonde hair off her shoulder. 'You'd have a hard time proving my involvement. Besides which Acacia had the book by the time that storm came. So how could I have cast a spell from it if I didn't have it?'

Ethan opened his mouth to retort but it was Mary who spoke, 'You don't have to have a piece of work in front of you to be able to recite it.'

By the colour that swept across Claudia's face, Mary was satisfied that her point had hit home. Claudia put her chin up in a defensive manner. 'Unfortunately I don't have your memory, dear Mary. Come on girls!' She took Nathaniel's hand and walked swiftly away from Ethan and Mary.

Ethan was more than pleased with Mary's successful handling of Claudia but his mind was upon other matters, more dangerous matters. Acacia had not been able to reach Ethan telepathically so that he was unaware of Jordan's arrival.

Although he did not feel up to doing the manure delivery, Ethan knew that he couldn't shirk his responsibilities, as they needed the additional money that they made from farm surplus. Although the farm saw to nearly all of their needs, education was not free, and Acacia and Ethan had talked about college in the future, and that too would need money.

The manure run was simple, although not exactly pleasant. Acacia and Ethan bagged up chicken, horse, and sheep manure as well as worms and sold them to keen gardeners, the village council and sometimes organisations. Reaching home, Ethan ran straight upstairs to his bedroom, dropping his school bag on his bed before changing into an old and worn tracksuit. Trotting down the stairs again, Ethan passed Acacia's mediation room, and noticing the door was closed, he figured that she was busy with a client. So Ethan moved on, grabbed a quick drink from the fridge before heading outside to hitch the mare up to the cart to begin his deliveries.

A Touch Ripe Up Wind

It was almost two hours later when Ethan drove the cart into the stables of the Freedom Inn, which was situated in the middle of Stirling's High Street. The Innkeeper, although he did not like it to get around, was an avid gardener and regularly took manure from the Tempests. Allan Macbeth, Mac to his friends, was a big man, Scottish, ex-navy, who ran a clean pub, and demanded that it stayed that way.

Voices of displeasure were raised upon Ethan's entrance into the Inn. Not only because his slightly offensive odour from handling manure and laborious toil, but also because he was an unaccompanied minor in a pub. Mac, though, liked to see children in his establishment, not drinking of course, but in activities that brought the whole family together. Coming out from behind the bar, Mac glared at the protesters from under bushy eyebrows.

'Shut y'r yaps!' He commanded, placing an arm around Ethan's shoulders and led him outside.

'They're reet though lad! Y'r a bit ripe!' laughed Mac, obviously not too worried himself about the smell. Ethan shrugged.

'Hauling shit can never be a rose garden, Mac! So how much would you like this month?' They walked round to the back of the cart, where there were four bags and a basket remaining.

'Whatcha got left?'

Ethan wrinkled his nose up. 'One chook, two sheep and one horse.'

Mac nodded. 'Fine. I'll take'm all. We'll store them in the old stables for the time and I'll get to me garden sometime this weekend.'

Ethan sprang up onto the cart. 'Are you sure it's not too much manure for you?' He was already walking the first bag down to the tail of the cart.

'Nay lad. The roses will be grateful for a wee feed before they be thinking of sleeping this winter. Come on now, I'll give ye a hand.' Mac heaved the bag onto his broad shoulder and carried it easily into the stables.

Between them, the job was done in a trice, and as Mac pulled out his wallet from his back pocket, Ethan was hauling the basket out of the cart. The teenager didn't even count the money that Mac handed him, merely slipped it into the pocket of his tracksuit pants before handing the surprised Innkeeper the hamper basket.

'Acacia thought that you might like a little vitamin tonic for your wife during her pregnancy.'

'How'd ye know?' Mac's eyebrows lowered in displeasure. 'We've not told a soul.'

Ethan shook his head. 'You of all people ask me how we know the secrets of the earth? Your secret is safe with us.' He closed his eyes for a moment, took a deep searching breath and smiled as he exhaled and opened his eyes again.

'You'll have a healthy child, Mac, your prayers have finally been answered. No more miscarriages, but Eleanor mustn't work too hard, and keep her out of stressful situations.'

A slightly trembling hand was placed upon Ethan's shoulder. 'Do ye see the child's sex?'

Ethan's smile broadened. 'Now, Mac that would be telling!'

Shrugging his shoulders as he accepted the basket, Mac took his defeat gracefully.

An Inauspicious Start

It was pouring with rain when Ethan got home, so he was absolutely soaked by the time he had unhitched the mare, rubbed her down in her stall and cleaned out the cart. His overcoat was saturated and as Ethan stepped into the house, he made pools of water with each step that he took. At the back door, he kicked off his boots and hung up the overcoat to dry before squelching his way into the kitchen.

Ethan breathed in deeply the wonderful smell of roast chicken as well as four or five vegetables. All thoughts of food fled when he noticed a stranger standing at the kitchen window looking out at the rain.

'*I mean you no harm, Ethan Tempest.*' The message was projected telepathically and not verbally.

Ethan uttered a short, disrespectful laugh. 'I knew that much!'

With eyebrows raised and a slight smile on his face, Jordan turned to look at Ethan properly. 'How could you possibly know?'

Ethan shook his head. 'The Protector would not have permitted you to enter the property if you had intended to harm Acacia or myself.'

'I wouldn't bet on that, Ethan.' Jordan's smile widened. 'There are few security systems that can keep me out, electronic or mystical. I am your new mentor.'

Ethan felt rather than heard or saw Acacia enter the room and without turning around he projected forth a message to her. *'Does he speak the truth?'*

Acacia quickly stepped forward to shield Ethan from Jordan's possible fury. Although Jordan was displeased, he didn't react to Ethan's question in a violent manner.

'You should have informed Ethan of my arrival, Acacia. Mistrust does not become either of you. Remember that, Sweet Angel, as I do not enjoy punishing you.'

When Acacia spoke her voice was barely above a whisper. 'My apologies Jordan. My attempts to contact Ethan failed and I dared not leave such delicate information lying around on a piece of paper or in a text message.'

Jordan inclined his head in acceptance. A displeased Ethan, though, was not satisfied. He turned Acacia around to face him and cupped her face to hold it up to the light. A bruise was already forming upon Acacia's cheek, which incited Ethan to rage. Turning swiftly, Ethan confronted Jordan.

'You Bastard!

'Ethan, No! Leave it be!' Acacia lay a commanding hand upon Ethan's saturated shoulder. 'Go and get changed, dinner will be ready soon.'

Glancing from Jordan to Acacia, Ethan did not immediately obey. 'Ace…'

Again Acacia cut him off. 'No Ethan. I was punished for a reason. Please go and have a shower and change into some warm clothes.' Ethan hesitated but only for a moment as the concern in Acacia's eyes warned him of the consequences of disobeying.

Would You Consider An Alternative?

Acacia uttered a sigh of relief as Ethan disappeared up the stairs. Not daring to look at Jordan, Acacia went to the oven to turn the chicken and ensure that the vegetables weren't sticking to the bottom of the pan. They rarely ate meat unless the farm provided the opportunity for it. Watching her closely, Jordan sat down at the kitchen table.

Like Michael, Jordan was surprised when he felt a wet nose pressed against his hand. Unlike Michael, when Jordan looked under the table, Benny growled and with his tail between his legs, moved cautiously to Acacia's side. Closing the oven door, Acacia bent down to pat old dog reassuringly.

'It's all right, old fellow, why don't you go and join Jack and Nell in front of the fire place?'

The dog hesitated before taking the longest route around Jordan to the parlour. To Acacia's surprise, Jordan managed a rueful smile at her.

'I'm not doing too well at making people like me, am I? It's hoped that it doesn't taint my relationship with Ethan.'

Acacia shook her head. 'You caught us by surprise, Jordan. We honestly felt that you wouldn't arrive before the village was closed off from the rest of the community. With that behind us, we can start again.' Acacia was busy getting out cutlery and crockery and missed the sparkle in Jordan's eyes.

'I don't see why not. Tell me about Michael Casey; is he your lover?'

Acacia looked up surprised, she was also annoyed that she could do nothing about the colour that streamed across her cheeks. 'Of course not! Michael is a Catholic Priest! Besides which, I only met him on Sunday.'

Jordan's lazy eyes scanned Acacia as he began to understand. His voice softened to almost a purr. 'Ah, I see! He was supposed to be, wasn't he?'

Although Acacia did not feel happy, she managed to smile. 'Oh well. These things happen. Would you like a glass of wine with dinner?'

Rising to his feet, Jordan shook his head. 'No, thank you. Would you consider an alternative?' He stood right in front of Acacia. She caught her breath, confused by the smouldering passion in his eyes and the glint that reflected off his glasses.

'An alternative what? We make our own cordials as well.'

Jordan closed the space between them. 'Alternative lover!' The sink pressed into Acacia's back and there was nowhere else for her to go.

'You don't believe in wasting time, do you? We barely know each other and already you expect me to jump into your bed. I'm afraid you're rushing things a little.' She gently pushed against his chest in an attempt to get him to back off.

Jordan did not move. 'Your libido has been dulled by your years of solitude. Educating the boy is important, but I feel that you need a real man. The Priest is useless to you.'

A laugh escaped from Acacia. 'And you think that you're that man? Well I'm flattered but it's too soon. I need more than three hours to form a lasting relationship.'

Jordan still did not move away. 'How about four hours?' This was said completely deadpan, and Acacia could not help laughing.

'No, Jordan!'

Temporarily giving in, Jordan stepped back, giving Acacia room to breathe again. *Although I am unsure that I like him, I cannot fail to be affected by his sexual magnetism.* At that moment, Ethan came bounding down the stairs.

Isn't It Good News?

Ethen came running down the stairs again once he had changed. *I don't like the idea of leaving Ace alone with that man!* But it all seemed quite calm in the kitchen as Acacia slipped on the oven gloves and began dishing up dinner. Ethan poured out their home-made lemonade.

Ethan took a plate that Acacia silently handed to him before sitting down at the table. He was frowning as he still considered his future. 'Can we count on Jordan's assistance with the coming of the Servant of Evil?'

Acacia cast Ethan an apologetic look as she handed Jordan a plate and gestured him towards the table. 'I'm sorry, Ethan. That was something else I was supposed to tell you. Jordan has ascertained that the ceremony wasn't completed properly so you have nothing more to worry about.'

Glancing briefly at Jordan, Ethan didn't say anything until Acacia had also sat down at the table with her dinner. Ethan raised his glass. 'Here's to the next five years!' Meaning Jordan's mentorship. Acacia cautiously raised her glass to her lips, wondering, *what will the next five years mean for me?*

Jordan Considers His Options

After dinner, Acacia left Jordan and Ethan alone in the parlour so that they could get to know each other, as well as discuss Ethan's future education. Jordan was adamant that he and Ethan would not remain in the village after the current school year had ended. Ethan wanted to argue this point but a quiet warning from Acacia made him bite his tongue and make a resolution that this matter would not be allowed to drop.

Ethan's loyalty and devotion to Acacia impresses me, but as Jordan walked back in the rain to the Freedom Inn, where he had booked a room, he considered, *It is necessary to quickly sever the link that has bonded them together. They're too close, and that could prove detrimental to my plans.* The bar was deserted as Jordan entered the Pub, having been closed for over an hour. *Even so, I can still hear the activities that had taken place that night. Conversations, clinking of glasses, good hearty laughter and the general feeling of comradeship.* With a sigh, Jordan realised, *that that is something I'd never truly experienced. Then again, I suppose that is not my role in life.* With this fatalistic conclusion, Jordan took his dripping wet self up the stairs to the guest quarters.

Mild Diversions

The hall was quiet, many of the lights in the bedrooms were already out, and the supposition being that everyone had gone to bed early for it was barely midnight. With a grim smile, Jordan thought, *I'll take care of that!*

From out of one of the rooms, came Jenny Connors, a housemaid in the Inn. At 29, Jenny was a good-natured woman, with a friendly smile and a cheerful word for everyone, but never anyone special in her life. This Jenny had always put down to her being overweight and her short mousy hair. Catching sight of Jordan, Jenny's eyes widened in surprise.

'Glory be, Mr Jordan! What are you doing walking about in weather like this? I'm surprised Acacia didn't arrange to transport you home. Or at least offer you a bed for the night.' Jenny spoke in a soft voice as she approached Jordan. He smiled seductively down upon her, sending butterflies fluttering through her stomach.

'Acacia isn't to blame, my dear Jenny. She did offer, but I preferred to walk. Now tell me what an idiot I am.' His tone was light and teasing.

Jenny blushed. 'Oh my, I wouldn't dare do such a thing! You should head straight for a hot shower, and I'll bring you up a nice bowl of chicken soup.'

Leading Jenny gently towards his room, Jordan shook his head. 'I was thinking of something a little more substantial,' he admitted.

Jenny screwed up her nose in thought. 'I'm afraid the kitchen is officially closed but I could make you a toasted sandwich.'

Halting outside his chambers, Jordan suddenly drew Jenny into his arms. 'I was thinking of something a little more physical.' Not allowing Jenny any time to reply, Jordan lowered his head and kissed her. This was no friendly peck, but a full on oral onslaught so that when Jenny was finally able to pull away, she was quite breathless.

'Really Mr Jordan! You must never do that again!' There was a tremor in her voice and Jordan knew that he would have to choose his words carefully. Smiling ruefully as his eyebrows rose.

'Why? Did you dislike it that much?'

This question momentarily stumped Jenny as colour flew up her cheeks. 'I, well, I… That is beside the point! You know nothing about me to warrant such familiarity.'

That was all the encouragement that Jordan needed. 'I know everything that there is to know about you Jenny. Your secret desires and dreams are known to me. You're wrong, though, being thin doesn't equate to being beautiful or happy.' His voice was low and husky. For a moment it seemed as if Jenny would give in, but with some resolution she shook her head.

'That's easy for you to say, Mr Jordan, standing there looking like a model.'

'Do you consider Acacia Tempest to be perfect in looks and figure?' Jenny immediately agreed. A smile touched Jordan's lips. 'Then you would be surprised to know that as perfect as she is, she has had no lover for seven years. Being perfect does not make you more sexually active.'

Surprise was evident in Jenny's face. 'I never believed that she could ever want for a partner! Well there you go. I've an early start in the morning, so I'd best say good night.' She turned to walk away, but Jordan grasped her hand and drew Jenny back into his arms.

'Not yet.' Without releasing Jenny, he opened his bedroom door. Although a flush of excitement flooded through Jenny, she hesitated on the threshold of the room.

'You can't possibly want to… I mean with me!'

Jordan kissed her again. The slow, lazy exploration of her mouth by his sent her thoughts into a tailspin. When Jordan released her, Jenny had to cling to his arm to prevent herself from swaying off balance.

'I want you very much, Jenny. Come and make me burn!' Jenny fell to the seductive tone in his voice and willingly stepped inside the room, shutting the door behind her. Jordan's reign of seduction had begun.

Do You Trust Him?

Michael was relieved when he was awoken in his dream by the familiar routine of Acacia touching his shoulder and he immediately sat up.

'Thank goodness you came! I really wanted to talk to you about Jordan.' He automatically scanned down her body to see what sort of outfit she had on this time. His eyes lifted swiftly back up to her face as Acacia wore black skin tight leggings and an oversized jumper. *She looks so young and vulnerable.* 'What is it? You look like a frightened child! What has Jordan done?' Without thinking Michael patted the bed, inviting her to sit down beside him. As she lowered herself onto the bed, Acacia shook her head.

'Nothing, yet, but he is still threatening to take Ethan away from me.'

'You knew that was a possibility when his new Mentor arrived didn't you?' He took her hand and was surprised that it was cold to touch.

'A remote possibility. The farm belongs to Ethan, I'm only a care taker until the Family relieve me of that duty or Ethan comes of age. It's just that... we've been through so much together that I don't know what I'm supposed to do once I have to leave here.' A shiver ran through her body.

'Are you afraid or cold?' Michael took her other hand into his and found it just as cold as the first.

'A little of both but mostly cold at the moment,' she admitted.

As if it was the most natural thing in the world, Michael pulled back his sheet and blanket and started to draw Acacia towards him to share his warmth but she hesitated.

'Michael... I don't think that...'

He shook his head. 'I'll be a true gentleman but I can't have you freezing on me. Whatever is coming Ethan and I cannot deal with it on our own.' Her last remaining resistance drained away at the thought of being able to spend a small amount of time in the arms of the man that she desperately loved.

Drawing the bedcovers back over the two of them, Michael wrapped his arms around Acacia and laid them down upon his pillows. The moment Acacia snuggled into his embrace and let out a contented sigh, Michael knew that being this close was going to be a serious test to his faith.

'Jordan said that nothing is coming. That the ceremony failed.' Acacia said, trying to not think about the warm, solid, and desirable body that lay beside her.

'Do you trust him?' He already knew the answer to that question but needed to hear her say it. *It still burns me inside the way Jordan kissed Acacia. I didn't know that such jealousy raged within me.*

'Not in the least but we have to be so careful. If he is indeed an Elder then his powers will be so much stronger than either Ethan or I combined. My only fear then is Jordan separating us. But if he is in fact the Stranger then the honest truth is that not just us but everyone in the village is in danger!'

Michael sighed. *I'm trying to not think about the delicious and wondrous things I could be doing if this delectable woman was naked and beneath me!* He cleared his throat as he tried to concentrate on the problem at hand. 'It's the blood thing that has you doubting your instincts isn't it? Jordan should not have been able to bleed if he was the Stranger.'

'Unless… I need to discover if there have been any suspicious deaths since last night. Or if any blood banks or hospitals have any stock missing. I just wish…' Acacia suddenly broke off. *I realise that I was about to reveal way too much to Michael about how I am feeling lying here in his arms. Or what I would rather that we were actually doing!*

'What do you wish?' Unconsciously Michael pressed a tender kiss against her hair.

Taking a deep breath, Acacia looked up into his eyes as she confessed, 'I wish that I was really here, lying in your arms. That I would only have to say the word and you would make love to me. That this could last forever in the real world. That we had met before you had taken holy orders.'

'I think we were meant to meet seven years ago about the time you said you did that drawing of me from your dream. I felt something powerful… mystical calling me. Uncle Thomas asked me to come and visit him. That he wanted me to meet the most remarkable girl he had ever met.'

Acacia raised her head from his shoulder to look at him in surprise. 'Hang on a minute – did you say Uncle Thomas?'

'Yes, so the mystical Witch doesn't know everything?' He teased.

'But we didn't meet!' She persisted, trying to ignore her flushed cheeks.

'I was here only half an hour when I was called back to London. There had been an… incident with a friend and it was essential that I went back to contain the damage. The next time I saw Thomas I had joined the order. I had felt that the strong mystical energy calling me had to be the religion that I had been brought up in. I never imagined that it could have ever meant someone like you.'

'So where does that leave us?' Acacia found herself quite breathless as Michael cupped her face in his hands.

'I don't know but this will do for starters…' Michael lowered his head towards Acacia, it was a now or never moment and their lips touched as soft as Angel's wings.

'Father Michael! Father Michael are you all right?' Marjorie, the housekeeper was shaking his shoulder. 'You were moaning in your sleep!'

As his eyes sprang open and he looked frantically around the room, he already knew that Acacia was not there but now awake in her own bed.

Friday 25 October

Keeping Busy

Rain continued into Friday morning but there was some hope that the weather would clear for the weekend. Despite the rain, Acacia dressed in jeans, a thick jumper, sturdy work boots and an overcoat; continued to work hard on the farm. *The animals need to be fed and in such weather, their shelters need to be reinforced to prevent them collapsing if a gale arises. Hard work also means that I do not have time to dwell upon my last dream meeting with Michael or what it will mean in the real world.*

In front of the roaring fire in the parlour, lay the dogs, while throughout the house the cats sought any comfortable and dry position that they could find. A bed, a chair, the lounge suite, a few even curled up alongside the dogs, all content to be lazy upon such a drizzling day. Tiger, though, took up a dry but cold position in the window of the barn so that he could keep a watchful eye upon Acacia.

Jordan had stated that he would be examining Ethan's present knowledge on Saturday, so he wasn't expected at the cottage until then. This gave him the opportunity to explore the village and its potential for enjoyment, his personal enjoyment.

Jordan had not walked up half the main street of the village before he was absolutely saturated. Attired like he was the day before, Jordan seemed oblivious to the rain, as his mind was working on bigger and more complex matters. Out of the corner of his eye, Jordan noticed a woman standing in the doorway of a house, watching him as he approached.

She was a good looking woman in her early thirties but the sparkle of life had dimmed with domestic drudgery. Jordan raised his hand in a genial salute. Carrie Watts hesitated as if debating her next move, before she picked up an umbrella from the stand beside the front door and rushed down her path.

'You'll catch your death, Mr Jordan, walking about in this weather. Why don't you come inside and have a hot cup of tea?' Her smile illuminated her pretty, fair face and Jordan willingly followed her inside.

Jordan's Lessons Begin

In her parlour Carrie draped a towel around Jordan's shoulders but he had a different plan to get warm and began by stripping off his jumper and shirt as Carrie protested.

'I'm a married woman!'

Jordan paused in undoing his trouser belt to look at her intently. 'And you go to sleep every night a satisfied woman?'

'No...' Her eyes lowered away from his as a single word was whispered.

Jordan gently drew Carrie into his embrace. 'Let me help you rekindle the passion.' With her hands pressed flat against his chest, Jordan slid down the zipper of her dress. He let his hair loose so that it hung down around his shoulders. Carrie raised her eyes to meet his as she nodded. That was all the encouragement that Jordan needed as he lowered Carrie to the floor for a demonstration of mad, passionate love making.

His Spell Proliferates

An hour later, Jordan was once again walking in the rain. Carrie had wanted him to stay, but with his task completed it was time for him to move on. During that day, Jordan met many women like Carrie. Some were more than willing to welcome him into their beds; others needed reassurance and coaxing.

I don't begrudge the effort that is needed to achieve my seduction, if it's too easy every time it gets stale and boring. Besides which I know that the women get more out of it than I do. At least for the moment. Retribution will soon come my way.

Jordan managed to make a hit as well with the men he met. Half an hour in his company was enough to make most men willing to swear lifelong friendship. One man who did not fall so easily under Jordan's spell was Rochester de Bere.

The Immoveable Mountain

In the late afternoon Jordan wandered over to the de Bere mansion. He found an immovable mountain blocking his access into the house. Jordan looked amused at a man who appeared to be a cross between a Sumo wrestler and a body builder.

The man grunted. 'Whatcha want?' Jordan's smile broadened.

'Ah, so it speaks! To see your boss, Neanderthal man, and unless you move, I'll be forced to hurt you.'

A roar of laughter answered him from the walking mountain. 'I'd crush ya!'

Jordan shook his head. 'I think not. Move!' The smile was now completely gone.

The mountain was only permitted one step towards Jordan. The Elder raised his left hand, holding his forefinger and thumb about an inch apart. Concentrating on his fingers, Jordan slowly closed the gap between them. As a result, the mountain clutched desperately at his throat, as he was unable to breathe.

'Enough! You've made your point. 'I'd heard of your arrival in the village, Mr Jordan. What can I do for you?' asked Rochester.

Jordan's eyebrows rose. 'You know who I am?'

'Who doesn't?' sneered de Bere as he reluctantly allowed Jordan into the drawing room. 'You're big news! The all-powerful Wizard!'

'You and I have much more in common than you think.' Rochester's protests were cut short by a wave of Jordan's hand. 'Please don't insult my intelligence! I know the dark secrets that lurk in the hearts of all men. There's nothing that is going on in Stirling that I don't know about.'

A sardonic curl appeared upon Rochester's lips as he crossed his arms over his chest. 'So this is a friendly warning to leave your witch whore alone? Or is there something else on your mind?'

Jordan nodded. 'So you have a desire for the delectable Acacia? Turned you down flat has she? Perhaps something could be arranged… for a price.'

Rochester shook his head. 'Not even you could procure what I want! This is one woman who is answerable to no man.'

Jordan's interest was tweaked. 'Makes you want her all the more right?' There was a moment of hesitation before Rochester nodded. Jordan smiled. 'Follow my orders well and I'll arrange for your wish to come true. Now is there somewhere more private that we can discuss the details?'

Rochester let his arms fall down to his side as he nodded towards another door down the hall. 'We can go to my study.' He led the way and for a brief second, he wondered, *Will I regret this deal, but considering the end result, I have decided anything is worth it to finally conquer Acacia Tempest.*

Young Love

That night Mary dined with Ethan and Acacia, and while Acacia fed the dogs and cats outside on the verandah, Mary and Ethan were doing the dishes. With Mary's concentration on scrubbing a pot, Ethan placed his arms around her waist from behind and tenderly kissed her neck. Mary giggled and tried to shrug him off.

'Not here Ethan! What if Acacia was to walk back in?'

'Ace's not a prude!' Ethan chuckled, refusing to release her. 'If she found us kissing, she wouldn't have a heart attack.'

Mary turned around and with her back pressed against the sink she wrapped her soapy hands around his neck. 'I don't suppose Acacia would have a heart attack unless we started to make love on the kitchen table.'

Ethan's eyes danced wickedly. 'Only if we hadn't finished the dishes.' Mary's laughter was smothered by Ethan's mouth covering hers.

At that moment Acacia silently entered the kitchen. Upon seeing the embracing young lovers, she slipped her cloak off the hook beside the door before retreating from the house again. It was already dark outside, the rain had cleared for the moment but a cool wind was blowing, causing Acacia to wrap her cape closely about her.

Ethan is right, the sight of them kissing doesn't faze me, but it does depress me a little. All of a sudden I feel very much alone and I must forcefully stop myself from wondering what it would've been like if Michael had not been a priest or can he only show how he truly feels in our dreams?

These deliberations were broken by the sound of the side gate squeaking open. By the light of the three-quarter moon, Acacia found her heart racing as the man of her recent thoughts approached her. Involuntarily, she smiled and her smile was returned.

'I hope I'm not intruding. Thomas sent me out for some fresh air.'

Acacia shook her head. 'It's funny though, I was just thinking of…' She broke off not wishing to reveal her deepest feelings. Michael Casey closed the gap between them.

'Don't be embarrassed, Acacia. I haven't been able to stop thinking of you since we first met. Your bewitching eyes have taken possession of my soul.'

Before Acacia had the opportunity to reply, Michael had drawn Acacia into his arms and lowered his head to kiss her. Not a gentle kiss, but one that was as soul searching and commanding as his words had been. Acacia was about to wrap her arms about his neck when a massive warning signal went off in her head.

There is something so familiar about the way he kisses. An image flashed before her eyes from the scene the day before in the Rectory garden and the vision of Jordan appeared before her. Horrified Acacia pulled violently out of the man's arms.

'How dare you trifle with my personal heart ache?'

Michael reached out his hand to her, but Acacia stepped back out of his reach. 'I don't understand. I thought that you wanted this?'

Acacia moved forward suddenly and slapped his face. 'With him, Jordan, not with you! I want no substitute! I need no alternative!'

Having heard Acacia's voice raised in anger, Ethan and Mary came running out of the house. Surprise was written all over their faces as they recognised Michael.

'Ace? Michael? What's wrong?' Even as Ethan's words were spoken, Michael's face began to disintegrate.

'Ask your Mentor!' demanded Acacia as Jordan's face and figure were revealed as the image of the priest slipped away like a mist.

'Is this your idea of a joke? Are you trying to deliberately hurt me?' Acacia fumed.

Jordan waved an airy hand. 'I thought I was being helpful. I doubt there is any other way that Acacia would get her shining knight into her bed.'

Ethan screwed up his nose in disgust. 'That's despicable! How dare you…' A sudden flash zooming across the sky, turning the dark skies red in colour, cut off his words.

What Have You Done?

The mischievous glint was back in Jordan's eyes as the wind dropped completely, no noise could be heard as if they had entered the eye of a hurricane. This lasted only a few brief seconds to be shattered by a horrendous screech that was so loud and high pitched that it threatened to burst their ear drums and forced them, except Jordan, to cover their ears. Like the silence, this too passed, travelling up through the village. Acacia turned smouldering eyes upon Jordan.

'What do you think you're playing at?'

The Elder sighed. 'Why do you naturally assume that I have anything to do with this?' No one was convinced by this appeal of innocence.

'Oh please!' Interjected Ethan. 'No one else is capable of creating such illusions as these except one of our kind!'

A harsh laugh answered him, a sound that sent a chill of foreboding down Acacia's spine. 'Aren't we having fun yet? You care too much what these mortals think about you.' drawled Jordan.

'We do have to live amongst them Jordan!' Acacia demanded, 'What do you think this will achieve?'

A wicked, sardonic laugh came from Jordan. 'For too long Samhain has been trivialised and commercialised. It is time that the mere mortals realise the true meaning of Samhain and I intend that it will be a lesson they will never forget!'

To prove Jordan's point, screams could be heard from the village. Rushing through the side gate to the front of the cottage, at least three of the four people were surprised to see villagers running out of their homes chased by a variety of animals ranging from bats, reptiles and other creatures that most people fear or dislike. Jordan laughed heartily.

I'm disquieted by what tickles his sense of humour. Acacia sighed. *I fear for Ethan under Jordan's guidance and a glance across at Ethan's face is enough to inform me that he shares my fears.*

Mary was simply not impressed. 'Don't you think that you're being just a little bit juvenile? Acacia has worked hard to make this community understand the truth and peaceful nature of witchcraft. In one night you may have destroyed all that hard work for the sake of infantile pleasure. Or is this your idea of reconciliation?'

Hastily Ethan stepped forward to place himself between Mary and Jordan, fearing an outbreak of Jordan's anger upon Mary. Jordan surprised them all by laughing.

'Mortals must never be allowed to forget the power that we possess. Not that we'll ever forget the years of persecution that our kind and innocent people have been made to suffer.'

Mary shook her head. 'This is not the way, just as war and violence are not the way. We're supposed to be better than animals, but at times we're no more than the waste that they excrete.'

The sky changed colour, making it look like the stars were on fire. Jordan smiled ruefully. 'Ah Mary! Such a quaint turn of phrase. How wise and noble art thee!'

With a flippant wave of his hand, Jordan left the stunned trio as he sauntered back up to the village. Acacia pulled herself together and led the teenagers back into the house and sat them down at the kitchen table.

'You'd better stay here tonight, Mary, it may not be safe for you outside. Call your father so that he won't worry about you.'

Rising to her feet to obey, Mary disagreed with Acacia's last statement. 'Dad never worries when he knows that I'm with you or Ethan. But it is only courtesy to call him.'

Ethan waited until Mary had left the room to use her mobile phone in the hall, before he spoke. 'Shall I make up the spare bed?'

'Unless…' The look Acacia cast him was quite intent.

'No,' Ethan cut her off, 'not yet Ace.' The usually cynical teen was actually blushing.

Acacia smiled understanding. 'The sheets and extra pillows are in the linen cupboard. I'll just go and check the Protector to see how he is holding up under Jordan's juvenile assault upon the village.' Although he laughed, Ethan was privately concerned about the future activities of Jordan.

A Moment Of Smugness

Whistling cheerfully, Jordan wandered up the main village street wading through the chaos of distressed villagers; his hands were tucked into his jacket pockets and he wore a general air of satisfaction. *I'm pleased with what I've been able to achieve in less than two days and,* Jordan realised smugly, *that it won't be too many more days before the village will be under my complete control. That will naturally include Acacia. Failure to succeed in this direction twice, has momentarily darkened my mood, but I always enjoy a good hunt. I only hope that the prize at the end will be as exquisite as I imagine it will be.* Casting Acacia for the moment from his mind, Jordan turned his attention to finding gratification of the sexual kind elsewhere.

The Home Care Nurse

Before the sky show had begun, Michael was trying to quietly rummage around in the kitchen preparing a cup of tea and a couple of muffins for supper. A chuckle came from the doorway, causing Michael to spin around to face Daniel Hamilton, the Home Care Nurse who had joined the Rectory that morning to assist in looking after Thomas. With Friday afternoon, Saturday and Sunday being

Marjorie's days off, the boys were forced to fend for themselves. They were her allotted days helping out at the homeless shelter.

Michael considered the new arrival. Daniel was about Acacia's age and his youthful and handsome face made him look even younger, especially with his slim build. Daniel stepped further into the kitchen.

'You don't have to worry about sneaking around, Father Michael, Father Thomas agreed to a light sedative, so a Brass Band couldn't wake him.' His accent held a soft Irish twang, which was pleasant to listen to. Laughing Michael gestured towards a kitchen chair.

'Would you like a hot drink? If we get no further rain tonight, then the temperature will drop pretty quickly.'

Daniel nodded his acceptance, sprawling himself gracelessly into a chair at the table. 'Coffee please, and I'd love a muffin, if there's plenty.'

Michael returned to the fridge and grinned. 'No problem there, as Marjorie keeps us well stocked when she's not here.' He placed two small plates on the table with the container of muffins, jam and butter, and sat down opposite Daniel to wait for the kettle to boil.

'Tell me about yourself, Daniel.'

Being a person who did not mind talking about himself, the young nurse leant back in his chair and started on his life story.

They were working their way through their second cup and Daniel's third muffin when the sky erupted in colour and that horrific scream swept through the village. Michael bounded to his feet and was heading for Father Thomas' room before Daniel could even gather his bearings. By the soft light shed from the bedside lamp, Michael could see as he rushed into the older man's room, that true to Daniel's word, Thomas was still fast asleep. Returning to the kitchen, Daniel was obviously quite shaken by the scream and looked at Michael in wonder.

'Doesn't anything rattle you, Michael?'

The priest managed a crooked grin. 'The last three days have been so bizarre that I suppose I've been expecting something to occur tonight.' He moved through the house to the front door and threw it open. The red sky was an impressive sight, although Michael placed his hands on his hips and looked grim, Daniel was suitably impressed.

'Cool!'

Michael grunted in deep thought, stepping through the doorway to stand upon the top step. From above him a drop of liquid fell upon his forehead, and absently he wiped it away, before turning back to speak to Daniel. Doing so, Michael came under the porch light.

'Jesus!'

Frowning, Michael forgot what he was about to say. 'I don't approve of blasphemy, this is a house of God!'

Daniel shook his head. 'No, I mean… Look at your hands.'

Impatiently Michael raised his hands, gasping as blood flowed from his wrists and dripped down his fingers. Glancing down he found that there was also blood pouring out of his shoes as well as staining the sides of his jumper.

'How on earth?'

Daniel didn't answer; he simply grasped Michael's arm and dragged him into the kitchen. Holding Michael's hands under the running water, the young nurse found that blood continued to flow even though there were no obvious wounds.

'This isn't working. Something happened as soon as I stepped outside. Perhaps we missed something.' Michael strode back to the front door, dripping blood along the way. Daniel followed, completely bemused. Michael stepped out onto the step, but this time he looked straight up at the doorframe.

'By all that's holy!'

Daniel looked over Michael's shoulder and gasped at the sight of a fresh heart nailed into the top of the doorframe. 'Is it human?'

Michael shook his head. 'I don't know. I think we need to call the police.' Blood dripped out of Michael's shoes making puddles across the ground. As the villagers came running and screaming out of their homes, Daniel shook his head.

'I think they'll be pretty busy, don't you?'

Officialdom

It was less than half an hour later that Sergeant Alfred Boyd entered the Rectory by the side door. He left a forensic officer out the front, to photograph and dust for prints before removing the heart for examination and place a barrier around the path so that they could look for footprints and other evidence in the morning. Daniel showed the Sergeant into the kitchen, where Michael sat with towels wrapped around him to soak up the blood that continued to pour from his non-existent wounds.

'I'm sorry to disturb you so late at night, Sergeant but there is something devilish going on in the village.'

Boyd scratched his balding head as he rocked gently on his feet. 'No need to apologise, Father. Have you spoken to Acacia about what has occurred here tonight?' The policeman gratefully took the seat that was offered to him as Michael shook his head.

'I suppose I should have, considering Wednesday night...' Michael broke off recalling his present company. Boyd chose to ignore his unconsciously spoken words.

'Don't tell her, not tonight. Acacia is a sweet girl but I want her to remain safe in her home tonight. The last thing I want is a witch hunt.'

Michael wasn't given the opportunity to inquire as to what he meant, as the policeman's mobile began to ring. Boyd's face became a stone mask as he listened to the report of one of his officers.

'I'll be there as soon as I can. Seal off the area.' Hanging up, Boyd turned back to address Michael. 'You'd best come with me, Father, this may well have something to do with your unwelcome present.'

The police officer strode towards the door, but suddenly halted and looked around. 'You'd best bring a towel or two with you Father Michael. Blood is so hard to clean off the car upholstery.'

Surprise At The Crossroads

They drove down past Acacia's farm and out to the main road that joined the village roads to the motorways leading south to Tunbridge Wells. The crossroad trees looked eerie under the illumination of the powerful police spotlights.

Even before we pull off the road to descend into the woods, I know that something horrific is waiting for us as my non-existent wounds have begun to throb, mused Michael. A Constable emerged from the trees as they approached; he hid any surprise he may have felt at the sight of blood pouring forth from the priest's body.

'I've sealed the area around the body, Boss, but after I called you, I found something else.'

A shiver of dread ran through Michael as he followed the police officers further into the trees. The light from the high powered lamp was blinding and Michael nearly walked into the police tape that separated the crime scene. Constable Matthew Kane led them around so that they were behind the light and able to see more clearly.

Michael gagged. *I wish for blindness again, as the sight before us is so shocking by its horrific nature.* Having a good understanding of what Michael's next reaction might be, Kane grasped him by the shoulders and led him to a slight clearing where Michael promptly threw up.

Sergeant Boyd stepped up to the crime scene tape, ignoring Michael's dilemma as he examined the surrounding ground. 'Have you searched the area, Kane?'

The Police Constable looked away from Michael's heaving body. 'Yes Boss, as well as I could in this light. Funny thing, though, none of the grass is at all trampled down.'

'Hum!'

Michael rose shakily to his feet, wiping a tissue across his mouth. Kane sympathetically handed him a mint before they rejoined the Sergeant. A second glance did not make the vision any easier, but this time, Michael managed to keep from being sick. Before them, embedded in the ground was a six foot wooden cross with an overweight, naked woman nailed to it, with a shining medieval sword thrust through her side, and a knife wound running down the valley between her breasts.

'Do you know who she was?' Michael managed to ask without being sick again.

Boyd nodded. 'Jenny Connors from the Freedom Inn. What was she doing out here?'

Kane cleared his throat. 'I may be able to answer that Boss.' He led them to a clearing to the left of the cross as he continued to explain, 'Farmer Green reported this, as he'd been out looking for his missing prize winning goat. Although he found his goat, he got more than he bargained for.'

A large five-pointed star surrounded by a circle was burnt into the ground. In the middle, the grass was well compacted and each point of the star possessed a black candle, which was no longer lit. Behind the star was a crude rock formation which was waist high with a flat top and laid upon it was Farmer Green's prized goat. Its throat had been slit, as well as a clean cut straight down the middle of its belly.

'Where is George Green now, Kane?'

The young police officer looked away from the dead animal and back to his boss. 'I sent him home after I took his statement. He was pretty shaken up.'

Michael had only briefly glanced at the dead animal, and could understand the farmer's reaction. *There is something about the scorched star that draws my attention back to it. I can almost hear the hard heavy breathing of two people, not present with us now.*

Kneeling down, Michael laid one hand, palm down upon the grass inside the star. He couldn't even hear the warning issued by both police officers that he should not touch anything at the crime scene. The blood that still poured from him spread quickly within the star and sent a pulsing sensation through Michael's arm to resound throughout his whole body.

The sounds that I'd been straining to hear have now increased in volume, making them more identifiable. The heavy breathing and the occasional cries of ecstasy are that of a man and woman having raw, passionate sex. Michael was knocked on his back as a scream surged through him as the woman was murdered in the throes of her orgasm.

Constable Kane bent down to assist Michael to his feet, but it was several minutes before Michael could verbally express what he had experienced. A look of serious scepticism crossed Kane's features but a shake of Boyd's head told him to keep his tongue between his teeth.

The Message

'I must offer Jenny Connors her last rites.' This was a statement and not a question as Michael headed back to the cross. The officers followed but Kane finally had his chance to have his say.

'Boss, what if Father Michael is the killer? We shouldn't let him touch anything. I mean, the bleeding hands, the so called sound impressions, how do we know that he didn't do this all along?'

Sergeant Boyd glanced across to ensure that Michael couldn't hear their conversation before replying, 'That was genuine horror upon his face when he saw Jenny and throwing up like that was an even clearer indication to his revulsion.'

'What about a Dr Jekyll and Mr Hyde scenario?' Kane wasn't satisfied.

Boyd shook his head. 'You're going to have to start reading something a little less dark, Kane.'

Michael had already slipped under the crime scene tape by the time the others joined him, but so far he hadn't as yet approached the body.

'Please place one foot carefully in front of the other, Father Michael that way it will be easier to identify your footprints compared to any others in the morning,' instructed Sergeant Boyd.

The blank look that Michael cast at him made him wonder if the priest had actually understood his words. Finally Michael nodded before moving as instructed towards the inert body. There was a startled look frozen on Jenny's face causing Michael to swallow hard to keep the bile from rising up his throat. There was no blood from any of the wounds on the body, not even from the knife wound to the chest.

'Deum Patrem nostrum: Uis colligat partu Minore providentia tua animabus nostris, mandato tuo et in pulverem reverteris.'

While extolling the prayer for the dead, Michael placed his hand opposite Jenny's forehead, as close as possible without actually touching her. His hand then lowered to hover over her heartless chest before moving to one hand. At that particular moment a strong gust of wind tore through the trees sending the Constable's cap flying and knocking Michael off balance, pushing him against the corpse. The blood from his hand came in contact with Jenny's cold lifeless fingers and without warning that hand grasped hold of Michael's.

'By all that's holy!' His attempts to pull away were unsuccessful as his hand was held in a death grip. The blood that had once flowed from him was suddenly sucked back into the inert body. Kane vaulted over the crime scene tape but even with his assistance, Jenny's hand refused to release Michael.

Jenny's head snapped up, her eyes were wide open and blazing red, the expression on her face was not at all like her. Kane stumbled back in terror, swearing in his confusion, but Michael was still captured.

'What are you?' demanded Sergeant Boyd.

The creature, for it was no longer Jenny, turned its red eyes to stare at Boyd. 'I am a messenger. You must prepare for the coming of the Lord of Destruction. Prepare your sacrifice and know that HE will destroy all that stand in his way.' The eyes returned to Michael. 'Not even you, holy man, can withstand the power of my Master. Prepare for the coming!' The head dropped down again, but the hand did not release Michael. Horror was written across the faces of the officers as Michael suddenly convulsed violently and the body holding him began to drain the life force out of the priest and draw it into itself.

This Is Going To Hurt

Michael beat his free hand against the one that imprisoned his, but he was growing weaker as his energy was being torn away from him. Standing like a stone, Kane watched on helplessly as his boss picked up a large club like branch and slipped under the crime scene tape.

'I'm sorry, Father, but this is going to hurt,' warned Boyd as he smashed the branch down upon the dead woman's hand. Indeed it did hurt Michael, in fact it broke his hand. But the goal was achieved as the blows of the branch also destroyed what little muscle control was left in the deceased's hand and Michael was finally released. Boyd was ready to support Michael as he began to collapse and the Sergeant motioned for Kane to stir himself and give him a hand.

'Take the Father to my car, then I want you to stand guard over the crime scene until I can send Forensics.'

Slipping his arm around Michael, Kane nodded. 'Yes Boss. What are we dealing with here? It can't be witchcraft as nothing like this has ever happened before while Elizabeth or Acacia have lived here.'

Sergeant Boyd wiped a weary hand over his face. 'Acacia's not involved, as no person who has such healing power in her hands could be capable of this sort of destruction. God only knows what that leaves us with!'

Not Tonight

Acacia deliberately held her arm against her side so that she could not reach out to touch Michael's shoulder as he slept and before she had gone to bed, had placed a spell on her tongue so that she could not speak.

Tonight is not the night for an intimate conversation. I don't know how to explain what happened when I thought Jordan was Michael and fell into his arms. I don't want to burden him with my breaking heart as I now know without a shadow of a doubt that I cannot love any other man but Michael. Will never love any other man but Michael!

Acacia sniffed inelegantly as she tried to ignore the tears that streamed down her cheeks and deliberately pinched her own arm to wake up. And to leave Michael to sleep in peace.

Saturday 26 October

Thomas' Request

Michael Casey woke up late the next morning after getting very little sleep. Sergeant Boyd had assisted Michael into the Rectory after seeing the emergency Doctor at the local clinic, who set Michael's broken hand in plaster. Boyd had left Daniel to help Michael in to bed, while he continued to investigate the strange events in the village. So drained of energy was Michael, that Daniel was surprised to find the priest dressing himself later that morning when he took a cup of tea into him.

'Don't you think that you should rest, Father?'

Michael shook his head as he sat on the edge of his made bed to put on his shoes. 'I must see Acacia. She and Ethan must leave the village immediately! They're in grave danger.' Michael struggled to use his damaged hand and in the end gave into Daniel's silent insistence to help. Daniel studied Michael's face carefully before he spoke.

'She must mean a great deal to you, Michael, several times last night you called out her name.'

Looking up startled at the young nurse, Michael was spared the need to reply by a weak call from Father Thomas. Both men raced to his room, fearing something was dreadfully wrong, and were relieved to find Thomas sitting up in bed looking a little stronger, even though his eyes were troubled.

'I want to go and see Acacia.'

Michael was stunned by the forceful nature of Thomas' words. 'Won't it be best if I brought her to you?'

'No,' Thomas shook his head. 'I want to get out for a while. There's no harm is there Daniel?'

Glancing briefly at Michael, who simply raised his eyebrows in question, Daniel agreed so long as Thomas rested when he got to the farm.

So Michael drove Thomas down to the Tempest farm, Daniel having ensured that Thomas was well wrapped up in warm clothes and a blanket. Thomas' car was an automatic so that it wasn't at all difficult for Michael to drive with only the use of one hand. Acacia was delighted to see them and refrained from making a comment about the unwise nature of Thomas venturing out of doors, as she showed them into the parlour.

Upon seeing Father Thomas; Mary arranged some pillows on the sofa for him to lie down. Glancing over her, Michael noted, *Mary looks very cute in one of Acacia's wiccan dresses and how more flattering that style of clothing becomes her, rather than her usual jumper and jeans.*

With a wave of her hand, Mary went off to her part time job in the village supermarket, and Acacia settled into a chair beside Thomas, who appeared reluctant to speak. Wondering if he was a hindrance to what Thomas wished to discuss with Acacia, Michael decided to make himself scarce, especially as Benny trotted down the hall to greet him.

'How about a cup of tea?' Michael suggested.

'That would be nice.' Thomas smiled gratefully up at him.

Michael was heading through the doorway, with Benny, the old German Shepherd at his side, when he heard the words, *'What happened to your hand?"*

Michael spun round; he had heard the question even though it hadn't been verbally uttered. A cautious look at Thomas meant that Acacia knew that Michael didn't wish to worry Thomas, thus the question being mental rather than verbal.

'It's a long and complicated story. I'll explain in private.' Michael thought and understood that she had received his reply when she slightly inclined her head.

An Impressive Trick!

The kitchen wasn't empty, as Michael had presumed it would be and he halted, fearing to break Ethan's concentration upon a small ball that was hovering mid-air in front of him. Jordan leant back against the kitchen bench, his arms folded across his chest as he watched Ethan. Benny, catching sight of Jordan, put his tail between his legs and headed back to the parlour.

'It's all right Michael, you can breathe. You won't disturb me,' Ethan drawled. Michael proceeded into the room, interested in the simple levitation trick.

'I was sent to make a cup of tea. I hope I'm not intruding?'

Ethan laughed. 'Of course not, I've been practicing this simple trick since I was three. Come and hold this while I put on the kettle.' Ethan cast Michael a quick searching look, to which Michael immediately responded and stepping forward, he held out his hands.

Although Ethan had noticed Michael's hand in plaster, he didn't mention it. He gently took Michael's hands between his own and held them upon either side of the ball, but not touching it so that it hovered between Michael's palms. Ethan turned away to fill the kettle and put it on to boil before he got the cups down out of the cupboard. Michael experimented moving his hands around the ball, which remained perfectly still in the air. Jordan roared with laughter as he clapped his hands together.

'Very good, little cub! You had me fooled for a moment. I was unaware of Michael's ability for non-verbal communication. Due to the speed in which you had communicated your orders to the priest, I didn't pick it up. So you're still in control of the ball?'

There was a distinctive gleam in Ethan's eyes as he turned to look at Jordan. 'I could possibly do this in my sleep. I was half expecting you to test me upon more complex spells and rituals.' Ethan glanced back at Michael, not waiting for Jordan to reply and thus missed the spark of anger in Jordan's eyes.

'What'll you have to drink, Michael?'

Looking away from the ball, Michael caught the deadly look in Jordan's face and wondered, *Does Ethan know what he is dealing with?* 'Not for me, thank you.'

Stretching his arms above his head, Jordan gave a slight grunt. 'If this is going to be morning tea, then I'm going out to smoke a cigar. Seeing as Acacia won't let me smoke in the house! When I return, I'll make the tests as complex as you like.' Not quite storming out, Jordan left through the front door, leaving the impression that he was displeased. Michael sighed deeply.

'I don't see Jordan fitting into these surroundings very well.'

Ethan shrugged. 'I don't think he intends upon us staying. He gave the impression that we would have to leave soon.' This thought depressed them both, perhaps more so, Michael as the thought suddenly popped into his head, *'Perhaps sooner than you realise, Ethan.'* But he would not elaborate, fearing to put a voice, even a non-verbal one to his concerns.

Thomas Seeks Answers

Now that he had Acacia alone, Thomas didn't immediately speak about what was troubling him. Instead he studied Acacia, who wore a white elaborate lace dress, very much in the gypsy style especially with her hair hanging down loose.

'You're looking very pretty today, child. It's a deep shame that you have no special loved one. Perhaps you shouldn't wait for Mr Perfect who may never come?' Acacia was surprised by such a personal question, but knew that it was made out of genuine concern.

'He has come, Father Thomas, but there are major reasons why we can't be more than friends.'

Thomas digested this before nodding and relapsed into silence. Acacia leant forward in her seat, her hands clasped lightly together.

'What troubles you, Thomas?'

'I know that there is grave danger descending upon our peaceful village and I'm afraid that I can do nothing to prevent it. Last night I wasn't as heavily drugged as Daniel perhaps thought and Michael screaming in his sleep woke me. Several times he cried out your name.

Somehow I managed to get out of bed, but only reached the kitchen. The floor was covered with blood and the sky was purple. Michael appeared this morning with a broken hand but won't explain how it happened. I know I don't have much time left and there is nothing left in me to withstand alone whatever evil that is descending upon us.'

Thomas tried to sit up but as he became more agitated, he collapsed back against the pillows. Acacia lay a calming, cool hand against Thomas' forehead.

'Ease yourself, Thomas. This panic attack will only bring you further pain. Yes, there is something going on, but it's not yet beyond my control. Michael doesn't wish to worry you needlessly. Things are not as bad as they may appear to you. I understand that the drugs that Daniel is administering to you can cause hallucinations and confusion.'

Thomas smiled and patted Acacia's hand. 'Dear child, you lie beautifully. I know that there will be a time soon that I must make a final stand against evil. I don't fear death; I only wish that my dying had been a little less painful. Promise me that you'll not hinder me when I am called upon to act?'

For a brief moment, Acacia saw the graveyard, at midnight, with Father Thomas walking steadily towards a misty vortex. *I know that I cannot prevent him from fulfilling his destiny.* With a sigh, she nodded. 'I will not hinder.'

Michael knocked before entering the parlour with two hot and steaming cups balanced in his good hand. Thomas managed a weary smile as Acacia drew up a side table that Thomas could reach.

'I hope I'm not intruding?' Michael asked, placing both cups on the table.

'Not at all,' reassured Thomas. 'You have rescued Acacia from me boring her to death. I'm feeling rather tired, so why don't you go and help Acacia for a while and I'll have a little sleep.'

In The Way

Taking this as a dismissal, Acacia rose to her feet and gently tucked the blanket tighter around Thomas before she picked up her cup and linking her arm through Michael's, led him back down the hall. In the kitchen, Ethan was sipping a cup of tea as Jordan absently shuffled a pack of cards. Upon Acacia's and Michael's entrance, Jordan looked up and a sneer quickly covered his face.

'What an enchanting couple you make! I thought we had agreed, Acacia that you would stay away while I tested Ethan?'

Ethan opened his mouth to retort, but a commanding glance from Acacia meant that his words went unspoken.

Michael sighed. 'I'm getting the feeling that I should have stayed in bed today. Everywhere I turn I'm always in the way.'

Glaring at Jordan, Acacia squeezed Michael's arm as she placed her cup onto the kitchen table. 'Nonsense! Jordan can move his testing to my meditation room where no one will disturb them, and you are going to help me with spreading some straw upon the gardens.'

Michael looked down at his broken hand and wondered, *what possible use can I be in hauling bales of straw?* He decided not to say anything and obediently followed Acacia out the back door. Sitting with his elbows on the table, Ethan studied Jordan. Their eyes locked and Ethan did not flinch under his Elder's glare.

'Do you have to work at being a bastard or does it come naturally?'

Jordan's eyes sparked with fire but the simple lifting of an eyebrow by Ethan quelled any retribution.

'I'm not so easily intimidated, and leave Michael alone. Ace is having enough trouble coming to grips with him being a priest. I don't want to see either of them hurt.'

Slowly, Jordan nodded. 'Shall we return to your testing?' He headed for the meditation room, and Ethan followed without an argument.

What Has Happened?

The day was surprisingly warm for autumn but there was still a cool breeze blowing. Nell and Jack immediately ran up for a pat before Acacia shooed them off. Wherever there was sunshine heating the concrete porch, there were cats stretched out, sunning themselves. Michael felt the breeze run through him, and he rocked slightly on his feet in a wave of fatigue. Acacia placed a supportive hand through Michael's arm and led him towards the stables.

'Come and sit down. We won't be moving straw, but I thought this would be a private place for us to talk.'

There were bales of hay stacked in the stable, which was empty, as the horses were out with the other animals. Michael gratefully hoisted himself up onto the straw stacks and with a deep sigh, laid back as Acacia sat down beside him.

'What has happened Michael?' Acacia spoke softly and waited patiently until Michael explained the events of the night before.

A silence followed Michael's words and he made the mistake of glancing up at Acacia as she contemplated his revelations. Sunlight streamed in through the stable doors, highlighting Acacia's voluptuous figure, which the heavy lace barely concealed from Michael's eyes.

'Holy Father! How is any mortal man meant to resist against temptation like that?' Michael's words were barely a whisper but so deep were Acacia's thoughts that she didn't hear him.

'I know what you're thinking.' Acacia's words made Michael start out of his skin as a deep flush rushed up his cheeks. 'It can't be Jordan, except for one thing, I would agree with you.'

Michael brought his thoughts back to the subject on hand, 'The fact that he bled?'

A nod answered him. 'There is only one way that he could've bled… but no previous deaths have been reported.' Wiping her hand across her eyes Acacia sighed. *Finding an answer is not going to be easy.*

Renewing Energy

Closing his eyes, Michael placed his good hand over Acacia's. His cold fingers surprised Acacia but she found that she could not move her hand away.

'Acacia, do you have anything to rejuvenate my energy?'

Her lips trembled in excitement. 'I know of a couple of ways that I can restore some of your energy levels, but I doubt that you would approve of the best way.'

Michael's eyes flew open and by the colour that covered Acacia's cheeks, he got the gist of her meaning. He swallowed hard. 'Do you have anything that I'd disapprove of the least?'

Gently sweeping her hair to one side, Acacia ensured that she touched no other part of him, lowered her head to kiss him. He immediately resisted and Acacia drew back.

'You must relax to be able to become a receiving channel.'

Acacia waited until he took a deep breath before trying again. This time Michael remained passive as her tongue gently parted his lips so that the kiss intensified. A tingling sensation swept over Michael's body, building to a gradual pulsating as Acacia's energy passed through him.

So absorbed was Acacia in the transfer of her energy, she did not immediately perceive when Michael began to respond and was kissing her back. His arms slid around her waist and drew Acacia down to him so that they lay chest to chest. Acacia broke off the kiss and tried to pull away but Michael's hold was strong, a surprise considering his broken hand and his previously weakened condition.

'Michael, don't do anything that you may later regret. Please think about what you are doing.'

With little effort, Michael flipped Acacia onto her back, still pressed hard against her. His eyes hungrily scanned her face, travelling down the supple body in his arms.

'How can I think straight when I have tasted the sweet nectar of forbidden fruit? I know that it's wrong, but I can't resist against this need.'

Acacia wished to rebel, but as soon as his lips touched hers, she found it impossible to resist against her own need for him. Her hands swept up his shoulders to entwine in his golden hair, as their kisses became more urgent and passionate. *I can feel the physical evidence of his arousing desire and I know that I should stop this now, but the temptation to give into the pleasure of Michael's good hand caressing along my body is too great.*

With nimble fingers, Michael undid the laces that held together the front of Acacia's dress and soon had exposed the delicate lace bra that attempted to cover the supple swell of breasts that lay beneath. A delft finger slid down one of the bra straps to further expose the desirable flesh beneath.

Michael's lips left hers to travel along her jaw and slowly, very slowly down her throat towards his intended goal. Acacia whimpered, as Michael was purposely slow in his seductive exploration. His lips caressed every inch of her chest except for the exposed, taut nipple that was puckered and throbbing for his touch.

To elevate some of the torment building up inside of Acacia, Michael cupped her breast, his fingers gently kneading her soft skin as his leg slid between hers to arrange a more comfortable position. Acacia cried in delight as Michael finally replaced his hand upon her breast with his lips.

'Michael! Oh Michael! You are worth the wait!'

As Michael's hand moved down to caress across her waist and along her curvaceous thigh, Acacia felt drops of moisture falling against her sensitive breasts. It took her a moment to realise that Michael was actually crying in his inability to control his own actions. *This realisation is a cold, wet slap in the face as I know that I must withdraw from Michael's embrace before our passion destroys us both.*

'Michael, you mustn't give into the demon that is trying to possess you. Fight it with the power of your faith and it will release you.'

Michael raised his head, his teeth clenched together. 'I… can… not! Help me, my Lord!' The sweat on his brow spoke of his struggle to regain control. Having no wish to hurt Michael, Acacia saw that his struggle would be easier if she was removed from his immediate personal space, so with only good intentions in mind, she kneed

Michael in the groin. His cry was more animal than human, but it achieved the desired goal as Michael rolled onto his back, clutching his groin. Acacia scampered to her knees, quickly readjusted her bra before laying a slightly trembling hand over Michael's heart.

He tried to speak, but Acacia whispered, '*Hush!*' Which silenced any possibility of speech.

'*Sleep, rejuvenate and restore the equilibrium of the mind, the body and the soul. Awake afresh and renewed, control will once more be yours. Sleep deep and calm and remember only, that I love you.*'

This time the tears were Acacia's as Michael's eyes closed and his body relaxed into an untroubled sleep. Acacia slid off the straw bales and in a melancholy mood limped out of the stables, unaware that the front laces of her dress were still undone.

That's Not Possible!

There was a bench outside the stables, where Tiger was enjoying the morning sun. Acacia moved the cat's back feet and tail to sit down beside him. The big cat opened his eyes, yawned as he uttered a protest at having been disturbed. But when Acacia's fingers found a particular itchy spot behind his ears, he closed his eyes again and began to purr. Having pacified Tiger, Acacia's thoughts returned to the matter at hand.

The possession of Michael must have taken place when Jenny's corpse had tried to drain his life force, thought Acacia. *If Lucifer, the Master of Evil is coming, then he must intend that Michael is put out of action as soon as possible so that there is less resistance to his taking over the village. But if the Evil One is coming, then was Jordan mistaken?*

'*Or lying?*' The intrusion of Michael's thoughts made Acacia jump to her feet and turn swiftly around. Michael stood in the stable doorway, looking pale and dishevelled but once more in control of himself.

'How could you possibly be standing there awake? You should've slept for several hours.' Acacia took Michael's hand and seated him onto the bench beside Tiger before sitting on the grass at his feet.

'Perhaps when you passed on your energy you passed on some of your power. What may have had control over me has now gone but I have not forgotten and I must beg your forgiveness.' His hand moved lightly and fleetingly across Acacia's cheek.

'There is nothing to forgive, Michael, but I'm still puzzled. Only Ethan has had the power to break any of my spells, and only in the last six months. How can a novice, uninitiated in our ways, gain so much power so quickly? I could only transfer my energy to you. It could be possible that Claudia's summons to the Evil One has actually unleashed other magical entities which we must also prepare for.'

Nodding slowly, Michael ran a shaky hand through his windswept hair. 'That brings us back to Jordan, was he mistaken, or was he lying?'

I Need Your Help

That question was to remain momentarily unanswered as footsteps approached from the house. Acacia rose calmly to her feet, with her hand extended to welcome Sergeant Boyd.

'Forgive me for barging on in, Acacia, but when no one answered my knock, I came on through.'

'Merry Meet Sergeant Boyd. Our house is always open to our friends. I presume you've come to discuss the events of last night? Michael has been filling me in on some of the details as he knows them.'

Boyd shook Acacia's hand; his quick eyes noticed her undone dress but refrained from comment.

'Forensics have been over the scene first thing this morning, and I'd like you to accompany me out there to see if there is any additional information you could supply us about what happened.'

Acacia felt Michael now standing close behind her, his hand lying against the small of her back as a warning.

'Of course, Sergeant. I would be glad to assist you in any way possible, but Thomas is here at present and I can't leave before he returns home.'

Boyd nodded. 'When you're ready, give the station a call and someone will see you out to the cross roads.' Turning to leave Acacia's voice arrested his progress.

'How much damage was done last night, in the village?'

The Sergeant looked back. 'Mainly broken furniture and scared out of their wits residents. The old folk's home seems to have been excluded from the chaos. Can you explain that?'

A gentle sigh answered him. 'The people in the home are usually close to crossing over. It is not wise for any spiritual force to harm or make mischief with ones so close to the end of this journey. Severe punishment would be issued out.' With a nod, Sergeant Boyd continued on his way, leaving via the side gate rather than through the house.

What Must He Think?

While waiting until she heard the Sergeant's car drive off, Acacia realised that Michael's hand was still lying against her back. She took a step forward before turning to face the priest. *Too close a proximity to him is not healthy for my already shaken self-control.*

'I wasn't going to mention Jordan to the Sergeant,' she reassured.

Michael shook his head with a look of bewilderment. 'I did wonder briefly, but my main reason for deterring you was that having been to the cross roads myself, I know what awaits you and I don't wish you to go alone. If the effect upon you is even a fraction of what it was for me, then I want to be with you for support.' The look of concern in Michael's eyes was genuine as his gaze travelled from Acacia's head to her feet.

'Damnation!' Michael's sudden exclamation startled Acacia. 'What must Sergeant Boyd have thought of us?' He gestured to the undone laces at the front of her dress and they both went scarlet as they couldn't help but remember how they came to be untied. Acacia retied the laces, her fingers trembling slightly. Michael reached out to take Acacia's hand and she would have pulled away but Michael tightened his grip.

'Acacia… under any other circumstances…' She smiled, grateful but refused to comment as something else caught her attention.

'Thomas is awake. We'd best go back in.' Acacia drew away from Michael and headed back into the house, not giving him the opportunity to reply.

Thomas' Warning

Michael decided that Acacia should accompany them back to the Rectory so that she could meet Daniel. Father Thomas waited until Acacia had left the room to gather up her cloak before speaking.

'I'm worried about Acacia. Such a lovely, young woman like her shouldn't be alone.'

Michael shook his head. 'I can't change what I am Uncle Thomas.'

'Ah! So you were the one she'd been waiting for! Actually I was thinking of Daniel. He might be able to bring her out from behind the walls she erects around her. What do you think?'

Michael shrugged, attempting to hide the unreasonable jealousy that was rising within him. 'Wouldn't hurt to promote a friendship, I suppose.'

Having caught sight of the tiniest trace of Acacia's lipstick upon the corner of Michael's mouth, Thomas frowned. 'No harm at all, my boy. But if you are to succeed in this parish, then you must be more careful about falling under the spell of the beautiful Acacia. You have a position to uphold in this community and I'll be greatly saddened if the church is cast under a disreputable shadow.' He stated, promptly dropping the matter as Acacia rejoined them.

Not A Good Time

The Rectory appeared eerily quiet as Michael and Acacia assisted Thomas to his room. Michael was surprised when he received no answer when he called out to Daniel that they were returned. So while Acacia set up the television for Father Thomas to watch, Michael went in search of the young nurse. Paranoia and concern began to flood through Michael as he went from empty room to empty room.

Just as he was about to call out to Acacia for assistance, Michael heard a voice from the smallest room in the house.

'Sorry Michael, I'm a little tied up at the moment,' came Daniel's voice from the toilet.

'Are you all right?'

Came a laugh. 'I really must learn to stay away from spicy foods.'

'I've brought someone to meet you, but we can't stay long.'

'Maybe another time, I'm not really good company at present.'

Michael could not help chuckling. 'All right. I'll see you later.' Ensuring that Thomas had all that he needed, Michael and Acacia headed back out to the car.

As soon as the front door had closed shut behind them, Daniel emerged cautiously from his hiding place in the toilet. *I feel bad about lying to Michael but I can't afford too many questions to be asked about why I feel the need to hide from Acacia.* Pushing back the curtains in the front window, Daniel watched the car drive away. *I know that Acacia would have but to set eyes upon me to know who I truly am. That would be dangerous for all concerned especially myself.* Absently, Daniel ran his hand along the windowsill and picked up a shard of glass in his forefinger.

'Blast!' He used a fingernail to flick the glass out but from the small gash where it would be normal to expect blood to pour forth; nothing came. Daniel lifted the injured finger to his lips for a moment, and when he lowered his finger, the wound was almost completely healed.

'Oh yes, Acacia Tempest, you would indeed be extremely dangerous to me and my purpose.'

Hostile Reception

The wooded area around the cross roads had been sealed off at the edge of the road, but that didn't stop curious on-lookers from pulling their cars off the road or walking down from the village to have a sticky beak at what was going on. The news of Jenny's death and the events that had led up to it had spread through the village like wildfire, but it couldn't be determined from where the original information came.

Michael slowed the car down due to the people who moved across the road like Brown's cows. There were several harassed police officers trying to maintain control over the curious crowd and as Michael tried to pull off the road, one Constable approached the car. Michael obligingly wound down his window.

'I'm sorry Father, but you can't park here. We're trying to move people on as there is nothing to see.'

Michael shook his head. 'Sergeant Boyd sent for Acacia to gauge her impression of the crime scene,' he explained.

Glancing across to where Acacia sat beside Michael, the Constable lost some of his anxiety. 'In that case, follow me. There is a clearing up ahead that's restricted for official vehicles.'

Due to the milling crowd, it was difficult for Michael to keep up with the Constable, so by the time his car reached the clearing mentioned, the Constable had already pulled back the security tape for them to drive through. As Acacia and Michael alighted from the car, the policeman put the tape back into place before joining them. His eyes swept quickly over Acacia and the sexual comment that Michael was half expecting never came.

'I hope you'll excuse me, Miss Acacia, but it might be best if you pull the hood of your cloak on so that it covers your face. This crowd is howling for blood and seeing you here might make them jump to the wrong conclusion.'

Acacia nodded and complied with his request. 'Perhaps for your reputation's sake, Michael, you shouldn't be seen with me.' The quiet, sad note in Acacia's words was like a sharp knife wound to Michael.

'It might just improve my reputation!'

Acacia managed a tight smile and allowed Michael to link her arm through his as they followed the Constable to the crime scene.

It wasn't possible for their progress through the trees to be completely invisible to the roadside crowd, for although Acacia's face was covered, her style of cloak was well known in the village and an uproar of angry voices occurred.

'Burn the witch!'

'Have you brought her to confess to her handiwork?'

'Deceiver!'

'Temptress!'

'Devil worshipper!'

That last accusation saw Acacia's head snap around as her eyes blazed with anger. 'How dare you cast such aspersions upon me?' Although her words were not shouted, they were clearly enough heard by all. Michael moved subtly to place himself between Acacia and the crowd.

'That won't help, Acacia. Let me deal with this, you need to focus your energy on assisting Sergeant Boyd.' Michael looked up and nodded to the Constable, who led Acacia deeper into the trees away from prying eyes and deliver her to his boss. As Michael approached the police barricade, his face was set in grim disapproving lines and the crowd before him fell silent. He stood with his arms folded across his chest, maintaining the silence for a moment.

'That is the worst display of Christian behaviour that I have ever seen! I could almost believe that we were back in the Dark Ages.'

A murmur broke out but one woman's voice was heard above the others. 'But Father Michael, what about the safety of our homes and our children? How can we protect them against the powers that we all know that the Tempests possess?'

Words of agreement were uttered, but Michael remained unmoved.

'Silence!' The force of his word surprised even Michael. 'Where has your common sense gone? In all the time they've been here, has anything like this ever happened before? What about when Elizabeth Tempest lived here?'

There was a general murmured, 'No.'

'Have you ever known Acacia to be unkind to either human or animal?'

'No.'

'How many of you have been helped by Acacia? Healed, counselled, a helping hand when it was needed, a sympathetic ear when it was required, or other assistance throughout the years?'

There was a shame-faced show of nearly all the hands of those gathered.

'But Halloween is approaching!'

Michael's eyebrows rose. 'As it had done so many times since Acacia arrived in the village. As it had done so since Elizabeth Tempest lived amongst you. Acacia is only here to assist Sergeant Boyd in his search for clues. I suggest that you all spend some time researching the difference between witchcraft and Satanism and I expect to see all of you in church tomorrow. Perhaps an hour of prayer will clear your minds of paranoia.'

There were murmurs of agreement and disagreement throughout the group as Michael turned away to head into the woods to join Acacia. *I don't, for the first time in my life, care if they dislike my words. This is a matter of honour as well as being my way of showing my support for Acacia and Ethan.* Michael's thoughts were redirected back to the issue at hand as he passed the cross, which now stood empty as Jenny's body and that of the goat had been taken away for an autopsy.

A policeman tried to stop Michael, but Sergeant Boyd waved for Michael to join them. Acacia sat down cross-legged, upon the ground, with her back to the altar and the star formation in front of her. When Acacia closed her eyes, a silence fell over the Officers.

Boyd motioned for a Constable to kneel down beside Acacia with his mobile phone to record whatever she said. Taking a deep breath, Acacia exhaled slowly as she opened her eyes. She drew in power and focused it around her hands. She made two small psi energy balls in each hand before slamming both hands together while shouting, '*Verum Fulsi! The Truth Shines!*'

Acacia's Vision

Darkness surrounded her and Acacia rose to find she was standing in a reflection of the night before. The Police Officers were replaced by twelve men and women dressed in flowing black robes and masks that completely covered their faces, and thus their identity. Acacia moved freely through the gathered group, a ghostly figure that could have no effect upon the event around her. Upon the altar, lay a jagged knife, a medieval style goblet as well as a much smaller, almost surgical knife.

There was general chatter among the group until there was a flash of lightning and a large puff of smoke emanating from above and around the altar. The masked group became silent as they dropped to their knees as the smoke cleared to reveal a tall, naked man, wearing a mask of the horned goat. The Stanger's purpose was to represent Satan as they performed a Black Mass. The Stranger came from behind the altar to stand with his back to the group and each shuffled forward on their knees to kiss the Stranger's buttocks.

Tied to a tree was George Green's prized goat. Acacia walked across to gently scratch his head and attempted to slip the rope from around the goat's neck, but her ghostly fingers were unable to grasp it properly and she was forced to feel the frustration of being able to only watch. The Stranger returned to his position behind the altar and led his kneeling followers through the ritual of the Black Mass.

The Stranger blessed the congregation by urinating over them before the goat was brought forth for sacrifice. The chanting began as the group swayed from side to side and the Stranger raised a jagged knife high above the bleating goat upon the altar. Acacia turned away as the knife was plunged in, and said a prayer to the Goddess that the goat's suffering would not be long.

Acacia turned around to find the Stranger draining the goat completely of its blood into a medieval goblet. Acacia wondered, *when will it overflow?* But the goblet kept accepting the blood until there was no more to be drained. The Stranger drank deeply from the goblet before holding it high above his head. The group surged forward to each in turn take the goblet and drink as much as they could before passing it on. The blood had an intoxicating effect and the group began to dance around, causing Acacia to laugh as the flowing robed people attempted to dance erotically. And mainly looked silly.

Clothing began to fly everywhere and it wasn't long before people were pairing off and flinging themselves into sex on the ground, or the more adventurous tried standing up. The Stranger was not happy enough with only one partner and was being pleasured by a young man and a middle aged woman.

Acacia was no prude but was sickened by the sight before her, and she wandered away from the main scene towards the area where

Jenny was found crucified. There were torches of fire lighting the area, allowing Acacia to clearly see why there had been no footprints in the grass around the cross. The cross was being erected by a band of ugly, little demons, which hovered over the ground by the use of tiny wings that flapped vigorously to keep them in the air.

The commencement of chanting drew back Acacia to the altar. In the middle of the star lay Jenny Connors, she didn't wear a mask like the others, and a quick head count meant that Jenny wasn't one of the original twelve. Jenny's wrists and ankles were tied with rope and held apart by stakes driven into the ground. Twelve naked and masked people circled the star as the Stranger stood over Jenny. She wore a full length white Victorian style nightgown, and appeared to be drugged but awake.

Twelve pairs of hands reached down to tear the nightgown away from Jenny's body as she lay giggling up at them. The followers returned to their circle as the Stranger mounted Jenny. The young woman's giggling altered to exclamations of desire and passion as his powerful penis bore deep inside of her.

Acacia forced herself to watch, as she knew that the slightest clue was essential in bringing these demonic acts to an end. *For a very, very brief moment, I envy Jenny as the Stranger's technique and prowess is obviously incredible.* Although slightly stimulated by the display of carnal pleasure, this came to a hard, cold stop as a knife was placed into the Stranger's hand and Acacia screamed, 'No!' as he plunged the knife deep into Jenny's chest. Acacia's scream mingled with Jenny's mixed cry of ecstasy and pain, before they both blacked out.

Kane's Disbelief

'Acacia? Acacia, can you hear me?' Michael's concerned face as he knelt over Acacia's inert body brought a sob of joy to her lips as her eyes flew open. Tears streamed down her face, as she managed to sit up. Without thinking, Michael took her into his arms, as he tried to sooth her.

'It's all right. You don't have to ever go back there.'

Boyd waited patiently until Acacia's sobbing had ceased before he delicately cleared his throat. 'When you are able, Acacia, I'd like to know what you experienced.'

Acacia wiped her fingers across her cheeks to wipe away the tears as she nodded. 'I'll be fine in a moment.' She took the tissue that Michael handed her and blew her nose and took several deep breaths to regain control.

Listening on the sidelines, with his arms folded across his chest was an unimpressed Matthew Kane. 'You don't honestly believe all this malarkey, do you Boss?'

Acacia's eyes blazed in anger but refrained from turning Kane into a mass of pain. Sergeant Boyd chuckled as Acacia rose to her feet with Michael's assistance.

'You like to live dangerously Kane. I trust Acacia to never play upon my ignorance. If she tells me that she experienced something in particular then I'm more inclined to believe her. Why don't you go home and get some sleep?'

Kane hesitated. 'I'm just waiting to see what we're up against, Boss.'

'All right Acacia, when you're ready.'

Casting a warning glance at Kane, Acacia recounted her brief walk into the past. 'They were preparing the way for the Master of Evil. The sacrifice is an invitation.'

Kane remained unimpressed and even more sceptical. 'Is that all?' he demanded.

'I beg your pardon!' Acacia's eyes opened wide in surprise.

'Come on sweetheart. You haven't told us anything we couldn't work out for ourselves! Convenient they were wearing masks, or were you saying that to protect your colleagues? How fine is the line between Satanism and witchcraft? Is there one?'

Acacia lunged forward to wipe the sneer from Kane's features but Michael pre-empting this action held her fast about the waist.

'*He's just trying to bait you!*'

'*And succeeding!*'

'Witchcraft has nothing to do with the one you call the Devil!

The White Witch will perform magic for the purpose of connecting with spiritual forces in the universe, in order to gain enlightenment. The Black Witch performs magic to cause harm or manipulate others. Between these lies the Grey Witch. Ethan and I believe in living in harmony with Gaia, Mother Earth and her fellow creatures. Our spells are rarely harmful, except in situations where it is essential to protect ourselves.'

'If we can return to last night, I could describe to you the physical characteristics of each person involved, their physique, their hair colour, age, at a rough estimate, as well as any unusual features that they may possess. But you can hardly round up all the villagers and demand that they strip off all their clothes! Your forensic officers should have been able to collect a nice range of samples of semen from the orgy. If you could supply me with pen and paper.'

Kane handed the items requested to Acacia with a mock bow, and Michael realising that Kane wasn't in immediate danger of being clawed to death, released Acacia's waist. There was a moment of silence as Acacia wrote and Kane locked his gaze upon Michael.

'You don't honestly believe in all this magic, witchcraft nonsense, do you Father Michael?'

Michael hesitated, waiting for Acacia to react, but she chose to ignore Kane. 'What you must remember, Constable is that everything is real to those who believe. What I have seen this past week has changed my perspective of life.'

Kane snorted in disbelief. 'So if I believe that it is literally raining cats and dogs, then it must do so!'

A mischievous laugh came from Acacia. 'Be careful what you wish for, Constable Kane,' she warned, returning the paper and pen to him, 'for it might just come true!'

Kane bristled defensively. 'Is that a threat, Witch?'

'Oh no! That is a promise!'

The Tree Dryad

Kane's eyes suddenly changed colour, first to a fluorescent green and then to a pink. Acacia took a hasty step back against Michael as she gasped in horror.

'Sacred Mother!' whispered Acacia, expecting to have to defend herself when she came to realise that everyone else was frozen in position. From behind her, Acacia heard a giggle and side stepping Michael; she turned to gaze up into the trees. The flickering colour that had reflected in the Constable's eyes was visible only to Acacia and with a sigh of relief she managed to laugh.

'Blessed be Sylph! I give you good morrow! What can this humble mortal do for you?'

The sparkling light descended from the trees and the brightness of colour dimmed so that Acacia could make out the features of a blonde, female fairy. Hovering at Acacia's face level, the Dryad or Sylph swept into a curtsy.

'Blessed be Acacia of the Tempest. It is perhaps I who can assist you. The man these mortals seek is not a man. You're in grave danger from this creature, you and your protégé. But you're not alone, he will take this village down with him given half a chance, maybe even…'

Acacia felt a chill down her spine. 'Do you have any advice or words of wisdom to impart?'

The fairy nodded sadly. 'Indeed I do, Acacia. There will come a time when you will be forced to submit to the designs of the Stranger.'

'Never!'

The fairy was patient with Acacia's outburst. 'I understand your disbelief, but you will find that you are forced to, in order to protect others. In a short period of time, his influence will take you over unless you find a means of purifying yourself. The dark seeds of evil must be replaced by the purity of light.'

Acacia swallowed hard at the thought of what she was yet to face. 'Ethan?'

Inclining her head, the dryad began to rise back up to the branches. 'Virginity is not the only source of purity, Acacia of the Tempest. Good luck to you.'

Movement returned to normal around her, as the sparkling light vanished altogether. For the others it was as if no time had lapsed, but it took a moment for Sergeant Boyd to penetrate the deep contemplation, which Acacia had fallen into. She finally turned back to face him, smiling apologetically.

'I'm sorry, you were saying?'

Boyd smiled sympathetically. 'It is obvious that this morning has been difficult for you. I was suggesting that Father Michael take you home, and if you remember anything else, to give me a call.'

'Of course I will. I just hope that I have been of some assistance.'

Kane huffed in disgust but they all chose to ignore him. Boyd offered them an escort back to Michael's car, but this was politely refused as Michael had a question for Acacia burning on his tongue.

'Acacia…' Even though his voice was quite low, she would not allow him to continue.

'Not here Michael, too many ears.'

Patiently, Michael waited as they walked passed the road side onlookers, who this time made no comments to Acacia; removed his car from the authorised vehicle area and were once more on the main road heading back into town.

'If that fairy is correct, then there is danger, not only to Ethan but also yourself. Isn't there?'

'How?' Acacia's jaw dropped in amazement.

Michael's expression was rather grim. 'My body may have been frozen but my mind was not. I heard everything that was said. What if you and Ethan left the village?'

Acacia shook her head. 'It wouldn't work as it would only increase the area under threat by the Stranger. We must make our stand here and fight.' She jumped, startled when Michael hit the steering wheel.

'I don't like feeling helpless! Is there nothing we can do to prepare ourselves?'

A sad nod answered him. 'Pray!'

A Strange Interlude

Just after midday, Mary left the supermarket where she worked to wander up the street to the café to wait for Ethan. He had called her earlier, telling her that he would take her to lunch. While she waited, Mary ordered a cup of hot chocolate before heading outside to find a table in the sunshine while it lasted. There were others, though, who had also had this intention, and every table had at least two people at it, except for one table, which was occupied by a stranger to the village. Taking a deep breath, Mary plucked up the courage and approached the young man.

'Excuse me, do you mind if I join you?'

Daniel Hamilton looked up, an easy smile forming as he gestured towards an empty chair. 'Tell me about yourself, Mary.' He leant back in his chair as Mary choked on her drink.

'How did you know my name?'

A chuckle answered her. 'I heard the girl at the counter call you by name. I'm Daniel Hamilton, I'm staying at the Rectory for a while.'

Mary nodded. 'You're here to look after Father Thomas. The good Father has done so much for this community, it's sad that the people hear the word 'cancer' and they'll run a mile thinking that if they visit such a terminally ill person, the disease will leap across the room and attack them.'

Daniel stared at Mary blankly for a moment. 'Such words of wisdom from such a young lady! Tell me, do you often visit Father Thomas?' He had half expected Mary to blush, but wasn't to be gratified.

'When I can, which I'm afraid to say is not as often as Acacia does. What with school, a part time job, as well as taking over all the household duties since my mother died two years ago; there never seems to be enough time for all the things you wish to do.'

With a sigh, Daniel nodded. 'Too true! Tell me about Acacia. What is she like?'

Mary heard herself hailed, and glanced over her shoulder before returning her attention to Daniel. 'No need, the boy approaching is

Ethan, Acacia's brother. He'd be more than happy to talk to you about her.'

Daniel took one hard look at Ethan before glancing down at his watch. 'Will you look at the time? I promised Father Michael that I'd be back already!' Daniel rose to his feet. 'Nice to have met you, Mary.' With a brief nod, he was gone, leaving Mary feeling quite stunned.

Not being the jealous, or possessive type, Ethan watched Daniel leave with only mild curiosity. Ethan was carrying a large picnic basket in one hand and had a tartan blanket thrown over the other.

'I hope your friend didn't leave on my account?' Ethan stated calmly, bending down to kiss Mary briefly. She was frowning as he sat down opposite.

'It seems illogical, Ethan, but I think that is exactly what it was. One minute he was asking about Acacia, then seeing you, he was suddenly off.'

'Acacia?' Ethan's eyebrows contracted into a frown as Mary finished her drink.

'So where are we going for a picnic?' Mary finally asked. Ethan's mood immediately lifted.

'However did you guess? I wanted it to be a surprise!'

'Teaser!' Mary playfully punched his arm.

He laughed. 'I thought we'd go down to the river. Some place quiet, just the two of us and we can forget about our cares and responsibilities for an hour.'

'Only an hour?' Mary pouted.

Rising to his feet, Ethan assisted Mary to hers before picking up the basket again. They headed up the hill towards the church.

'Only an hour, Mary, a wasted morning with Jordan means that I have work to catch up with on the farm.'

Sensing the anger inside him, Mary slipped her hand through his arm. 'Can I help?'

Ethan smiled. 'And what of your own responsibilities? But let's not think of that, this hour will be ours, time is precious.'

Mary nodded sadly. 'You don't know how true that is Ethan.' The wistful tone in her voice was not lost to Ethan.

'Meaning?'

Mary took a deep breath. 'There is something very important that I must tell you.'

'Mary…'

She immediately cut him off, smiling. 'No, not yet. On the way home, I'll tell you. As you said, this hour is ours alone.' Snuggling against Ethan as they walked, Mary ensured that they spoke of inconsequential and happy matters.

Claudia's Lesson

Standing in the shadows of the pagan temple, keen eyes watched as Ethan and Mary passed unaware of being observed. Curls of smoke formed lazy patterns above the watcher's head as he debated about following the young lovers. His cigar gleamed brightly in the semi-darkness as another young couple approaching from the village momentarily distracted the watcher. Nathaniel and Claudia were for once without their entourage and were also heading towards the river, minus a picnic basket but with a blanket. Glancing quickly back at the first couple, the watcher decided to focus his attention upon Nathaniel and Claudia.

Acting upon this decision, he stubbed out his cigar and stepped silently through the temple doorway. Claudia was the first to see Jordan emerge from the temple and was momentarily startled by his sudden appearance. Nathaniel was less disturbed, so as Jordan approached them, Nathaniel willingly held out his hand to the older man.

'It's Mr Jordan, isn't it? Ethan's new tutor? This is Claudia and I'm Nathaniel, we're in a couple of Ethan's classes.'

Jordan took the hand offered as he studied the boy. *There is a quiet confidence that is often overshadowed by the dynamic power of Claudia's personality.* 'I'm pleased to meet you both. In fact I've been wanting to have a word with you.'

Claudia's eyebrows rose in a disinterested manner. 'Really? Well perhaps we'll see you again soon. Right now we have something important to do.'

A deep, wicked chuckle escaped from Jordan as he moved between them and taking an arm of each led them in the direction away from Ethan and Mary. 'Oh I know exactly what you were going to do!'

Colour raced up Claudia's face as she attempted to pull her arm away from Jordan's, but although he wasn't hurting her, she was unable to break free.

'What's it to do with you anyway? We're of legal age!'

Jordan chose to ignore the acid in Claudia's voice, knowing that he had other means of melting ice. He laughed. 'I can teach you both the joys and raptures of this earthly world.'

Flushing up to his hairline, Nathaniel stared down at his feet as he mumbled, 'We do very nicely, thank you!'

The laughter that followed caused Nathaniel's colour to deepen. Jordan took the blanket from under Nathaniel's arm and laid it upon the ground.

'My dear boy, "very nicely" is not what I had in mind! You do well enough considering your inexperience and limited imagination but what I offer you can only be achieved through a lifetime of studying and practicing the art. For example…' Jordan drew them down to sit on the blanket with him. 'Claudia is too much in control, nearly always receiving and hardly ever giving. You're too passive all the time, Nathaniel.' Jordan had their complete attention, and he felt the adrenalin and excitement begin to flow through him.

'Let's begin with how you kiss. It illustrates your passive nature Nathaniel. There is no driving passion behind it. There are times when a kiss can intensify to the point you can give something of your own life force.'

Frowning, Nathaniel shook his head. 'I don't understand.'

Before Nathaniel could protest, Jordan drew the boy against himself, with one arm about his waist as his other hand cupped Nathaniel's face. Slowly Jordan lowered his head and claimed Nathaniel's mouth in a determined manner. Nathaniel's instinctive reaction was to push forcefully against Jordan's chest, but when Jordan's tongue slipped sensuously passed Nathaniel's lips, his resistance suddenly dissolved. The slow, lazy exploration of

Nathaniel's mouth, held a force, a power that left him with no disillusion that Jordan was in command. In several minutes Nathaniel would have given Jordan anything that he asked for, even himself.

A whimper escaped from the boy as Jordan drew away, but by the sardonic lift of one of Claudia's well plucked eyebrows, Jordan knew she would be harder to bend to his will.

'Does Acacia know that you like boys? Didn't think she would approve of a child molester?'

A laugh answered her. 'Hardly a child, Claudia, you are both bordering upon the edge of adulthood. Nor is it Acacia's place to condemn what I do or whom I like. I am her superior, my behaviour is beyond her criticism.'

Both Claudia's eyebrows rose this time as his words interested her. 'A man of power then? I like that!'

Jordan leant closer to her, his eyes staring intently into hers, his sexual appeal radiated from him. 'But you also fear power, don't you? You fantasise about being tied up in bed and being absolutely helpless as a man does what he wishes with your body. Then the fear rises that once out of bed, he may try to continue to dominate you. You don't like that idea. You like to have power too much yourself. But it does not need to be that way. Not if you define the parameters of the game.'

'Sex is not a game!' protested Claudia.

'Of course it is! Sex is the ultimate game. For when the pinnacle is reached, there are no losers; only winners!'

Claudia caught her breath as she fell mesmerised into Jordan's eyes. 'So what are the parameters?'

Jordan hid a triumphant smile as he felt Claudia give up the struggle to break free from his web.

'Someone like me would dominate you in bed and out; but Nathaniel, given a little power in bed, would become your absolute devoted slave out of it. The other thing is to use your imagination. A little play-acting never goes astray. It takes the simple, sometimes dull act of fucking and transforms it into the most erotic pleasure that you may ever experience. Try experimenting with different scenarios or doing it in different places. Increase the thrill by going to places where there is a chance you might get caught.'

Nathaniel squirmed restlessly in excitement. 'Can you show us?'

The Elder smiled; his web had captured two more followers. 'Of course!' He snapped his fingers and the trees suddenly disappeared, to be replaced by the image of an old-fashioned schoolroom. Nathaniel was dressed as a prim school Head Master, and Claudia was wearing the tightest and shortest school uniform that she had ever seen, it barely covered her knickers.

With his arms folded across his chest, Jordan surveyed them both before pronouncing, 'Delicious! Now here's a basic outline. Claudia has been a very bad girl and is forced to remain after school for punishment. The misdemeanour can be of your choice, as will be her punishment. Attempt to stay in character, and remember Nathaniel you are in charge!'

Looking up from examining himself in an old fashioned suit, Nathaniel frowned. 'What sort of punishment?'

Jordan moved across to caress Claudia's semi-clad bottom. 'Perhaps this delightful bottom needs spanking, or express your complete dominance by having her suck your cock before you lift her onto the desk and use her to satisfy your own needs.'

Jordan's mobile beeped and he reluctantly released Claudia's soft, delectable bottom. *I'd like to stay but I still have so much to do.*

'If you remain in character, you'll find it all the more enjoyable. Come Claudia, take your seat in class, the last bell is about to ring.'

Claudia sedately did as she was told, already falling into the role of a scared student, who had been caught in trouble. Jordan surveyed the scene with satisfaction and when the school bell rang, he vanished. Nathaniel took up a cane from the desk and slapped it lightly against the palm of his hand. He looked at Claudia quite forbidding and a chill of excitement ran down her spine. Jordan smiled as he walked out of the trees, the lovers oblivious to the real world around them as they lost themselves in the world of erotic fantasy.

Stormy Weather Ahead

By the time that Ethan and Mary returned to the farm, the fine weather, that had lasted all morning, had disappeared. Black, angry clouds covered the sky, winds rose up in the promise of an approaching storm, and the rain that began to fall appeared as if it was going to be endless. The source of this sudden weather change, Ethan found in the vegetable garden. Oblivious to the rain and the wind, Acacia was continuing to harvest the fruit and vegetables, as well as prepare the already empty beds for winter. When Ethan saw Acacia, he swore violently and ran forward to embrace her.

'Ace? What is it? What's wrong?'

Acacia looked at him in surprise as she smiled. 'Should anything be wrong?'

Ethan shook his head. 'You tell me! Look at yourself!' Using Ethan's eyes as a mirror, Acacia saw what had rattled him. An angry aura surrounded her whole body.

'Oh! You could say that I was rather pissed off. What with the villagers daring to accuse me of murder this morning, and Jordan leaving me a letter ordering me to run a commission for him this evening. Ordering me as if I'm some servant or second rate novice! I've been my own mistress for too long to submit quietly to such arrogance and uncivil demands.'

There followed a laugh from Mary. 'You can cause all this weather turbulence just by being pissed off?'

Acacia raised her eyes to the sky as if seeing the furious weather for the first time. 'I'm good, but not that good. I can lessen the effect though.' She closed her eyes and took a deep cleansing breath; a mischievous smile lingered upon Ethan's lips as he waited for her to impress Mary.

The wind rose considerably before it suddenly dropped almost completely. The rain continued to fall but the angry, black clouds became less threatening. With a deep sigh, Acacia opened her eyes again. Her angry aura was beginning to fade away.

'Anything else is beyond my control. So what's up with you two?' A silent, but speaking glance was exchanged between the teenagers and filled Acacia with a sense of apprehension. 'What has happened?' The anxiety in her voice urged Mary to reassure her.

'We're not in trouble. It's just that I have a problem and I need to talk to someone about it.'

Acacia slowly nodded, as her look of concern didn't disappear. 'Let's go inside then, I think I'll need to be sitting down for this.' Acacia left her gardening tools outside as she intended to return later to her work and followed the teenagers back into the house.

Mary's Future

With Ethan sitting on the lounge beside her, and her hands wrapped around a steaming cup of coffee, Mary found the courage to speak her mind.

'Dad was a long distance truck driver before Mum was diagnosed with a brain tumour, and although the majority of the nursing at home was left to me, Dad was finally forced to get a local job after Mum died. He's never liked being tied to one spot and is now looking to return to the road.'

Ethan placed a supportive arm about Mary's shoulders. 'Where does that leave you and your brother Davey?'

Mary sighed. 'That's the problem. Dad wants to arrange it so that we go to live with his sister and family in Liverpool. Another option he suggested was to live with Gran in London, on one of the estates. Thing is though, neither Davey nor I want to leave here.'

Ethan threw a quick glance across at Acacia, opened his mouth to speak but thinking better of it, and closed his mouth again. Acacia stared meditatively into space, her fingers steepled in front of her. This was a good sign not to disturb her.

'Have you considered, Mary, that Ethan may also be leaving the village soon, as Jordan has no intention of sticking around.'

Mary cast Ethan a concerned look, but he shook his head. 'Don't worry, I'm not going anywhere. My place is here.'

A chuckle escaped from Acacia. 'Do you plan to remain here forever?'

An understanding gleam entered Ethan's eyes. 'You know that is not what I mean, Ace! But I feel that when I move on and where to will be my decision to make and no one else's. We've always discussed what we both wanted.'

Acacia smiled and nodded. 'All right then but I fear we've digressed. Mary, you and your brother are more than welcome to live with us if that is what you wish and your father approves.'

Surprising them both, Mary shook her head. 'I knew that you'd offer, but it's not right. You both work hard to make ends meet, the last thing you need is two more mouths to feed.'

Laughter was the last thing that Mary had expected from Acacia. 'Dear Mary, we don't exactly wander around in rags! With two extra mouths come two extra pairs of hands. Anyway the offer still stands. Speak to your father and brother and give yourself time to consider your options. If your father wishes to start his old job immediately then you and your brother can move in here temporarily until a final decision has been made.'

Rising to her feet, Acacia left the young couple as she pulled on her overcoat and headed back out into the rain to continue working on the vegetable garden. In the parlour, Mary snuggled against Ethan as he took the cup out of her hands and wrapped his arms around her waist.

'What do you think?' Mary was still uncertain.

Ethan chuckled. 'I'll be able to see you anytime day or night! What do you think?'

Thumping his shoulder, Mary could not help but smile. 'Will it work though?'

'We'll make it work. Come on Mary, I'll take you home.'

Party Time

By the time night fell, the rain had settled in for the evening and promised to continue for several days. This, though, did not affect the party mode that surrounded the village. Jordan took over the

Freedom Inn, causing Mac to not only call in his entire staff, but also open up all available rooms as nearly all the village was drawn into Jordan's magnetism.

Rochester's Reward

Rochester would have gone down to the Inn, but Jordan had given him orders to stay in his study. Rochester grumbled as he was financing Jordan's little party but knew better than to make a fuss. *The final reward will be worth a few days of subordination to Jordan.*

Rochester had just finished his instructions from Jordan when there was a timid knock on the door. Displeased at being delayed further, Rochester snarled a demand for them to enter. The words of sarcasm that sprang to Rochester's lips vanished as the door opened and the last person he ever expected, stepped into his study.

With her hair flowing freely down her back, Acacia looked like a wood nymph in an emerald green chiffon fitted, A-line, below the knee dress. The dress had long sleeves with overlays, a shaped hemline with alternating overlays and a plunging neckline. Rochester's jaw dropped in stunned surprise. Acacia bore the air of a passive nature, but her eyes were blazing with defiance.

'Well, well, well! So the great Master keeps his promises. Please, please tell me you're here to pay Jordan's debt?'

Acacia moved forward to place a finger against his lips before leading him towards the sofa and gestured for Rochester to sit down.

Acacia undid the zipper of her dress and slowly, teasingly she slid the dress to the ground. Her hands reached back to undo her bra catches, but as Rochester's eyes burned with desire, and he licked his lips in lust, she lowered her hands again to increase his frustration.

He gave a strangled cry and would have risen to his feet, had Acacia not knelt suddenly before him, to remove his shoes and socks. His shirt and jacket were soon to join the pile of clothing developing upon the floor, but when Acacia reached out to undo his trousers, Rochester lost what little control he had left.

With an animal growl, Rochester threw Acacia across the sofa before tearing off the rest of his clothes. With lust filled eyes, he scanned Acacia from top to toe.

'You've no idea how long I've been waiting for this. I only regret that this moment can't last forever.'

Acacia's smile mocked him, as she knew his endurance would make forever an impossibility. Her smile chaffed his ego. 'So, still won't talk, huh? Well maybe there is another way to get sound out of you.' He tore away Acacia's underwear and without initiating any form of foreplay, he thrust straight into her. Acacia's lips parted in a scream but no sound came. Acacia's silent subordination filled Rochester with a sense of power and control that would ensure that there was not going to any pleasure in this encounter for Acacia. All that she could do was endure it.

The Mask Slips

Nearly an hour later, a bruised and sore Acacia slipped out of the de Bere mansion, leaving a sleeping Rochester stretched naked across his study floor. The street was nearly completely empty; even so Acacia glanced carefully around to ensure that no one was watching her. A mischievous laugh from her sounded extremely masculine as her face began to fade away into the mist. By the light of the moon, Acacia's image peeled away to reveal Jordan as he stretched himself once more to his normal size. He glanced back at the de Bere mansion and his laughter rang out through the street.

'You're mine, Rochester de Bere! You and all these weak minded fools are now mine! How easy it has been.' With a flash of lightning and a puff of smoke, Jordan vanished, leaving behind only the echo of his laughter.

A Mission For Mac

Despite the rain, the main street of Stirling village was alive with laughter and music, people talking or singing, flirting or dancing. The party at the Freedom Inn had spread out onto the surrounding streets. Daniel had left Michael to watch over Thomas so that he could slip down for what he called a quiet drink. Daniel's eyes opened wide in surprise when he saw people, often with someone else's wife or husband, or both, being openly affectionate and promiscuous.

Most of them didn't even notice Daniel as he slipped quietly into the pub via a side entrance. The spectacle inside took Daniel's breath away. The drink was flowing merry as not only were people being over familiar with each other, couples were stripped naked and openly fornicating on the floor, chairs, even on the tables. Glancing around, Daniel found no one else shared his disgust and with a small shake of his head, turned to the business he had come there for.

Having ascertained that Jordan was not currently in the main bar Daniel approached Allan Macbeth. 'I need to speak with you, Allan.'

Mac appeared a little surprised by Daniel's seriousness and managed only an uncertain smile. 'Sure laddie. Come and see me tomorrow. We're a wee bit busy now.'

Daniel shook his head. 'If you value the life of your wife and unborn child, then you'll find a minute now.'

'Have ye been talking to the Tempests?' The smile was completely wiped from Mac's face.

Again Daniel shook his head. 'I have my own sources of information.'

Mac stared at Daniel under bushy eyebrows before finally nodding his head. 'We can talk upstairs.'

Eleanor Macbeth looked up surprised as Mac and Daniel entered their bedroom. She sat in a deep armchair knitting a baby's jacket. Daniel bowed his head courteously.

'You and your unborn child are in danger if you remain in the village. Time is running out and soon it'll be impossible for anyone to leave here. You must leave now, tonight, if you wish to escape the fate suffered by Jenny Connors.'

Eleanor rose swiftly to her feet; her hands lay protectively over her abdomen as her eyes flew to her husband's face for reassurance.

'Can't ye stop this?' demanded Mac of Daniel.

His answer was negative. 'The sequence of events now being played out was set in motion before I even arrived. I can give you no reason to believe me, but if you ignore my warning, then it will result in your death.'

That was enough for Mac, from the top of the wardrobe he pulled down a suitcase and threw it onto the bed. 'You can go to your Ma's for a while,' he ordered.

'Make it at least till after All Saints day,' added Daniel.

'Don't I have any say in this?' Eleanor was not used to being ordered about.

Mac looked at the seriousness in Daniel's eyes and shook his head. 'No!'

Assault On Daniel

Leaving the pub, Daniel wasn't as cautious as he had been entering, and failed to notice Jordan in the opposite corner with his arms around two semi-naked women. Jordan watched Daniel exit, not once breaking the kiss with one young lady. Jordan had already noted the absence of Mac but until he saw Daniel, he hadn't considered it significant.

Closing his eyes, and taking a deep breath, Jordan allowed his inner spirit to float free of his body and leave the building. Looking one way, Jordan saw Daniel heading back up to the Rectory. Turning his attention to the rear of the pub, Jordan watched Mac put two suitcases into the back of their station wagon as his wife got behind the wheel. Retreating once more to his body, Jordan was displeased.

Daniel is going to be a hindrance to my plans and needs to be dealt with swiftly. Bursting out laughing, Jordan knew exactly how to do just that.

Like the night before, the wind rose to a howling scream before dropping away again, the sky alternated a myriad of colours as lightning danced majestically across the clouds. This, though, didn't even raise a murmur of interest in Daniel as he wrapped his jacket closer around him against the wind and the rain. His human reaction the night before had been purely for Michael's benefit. Out of the corner of his eye, Daniel observed what he feared would occur if Jordan discovered his identity.

Dark shadows, almost invisible in the night, moved stealthily around Daniel, closing in upon him. Several pairs of invisible hands reached out for him but Daniel slipped easily out of their grasp. A scream in anger emanated from the surrounding dark shadows and Daniel was not given the opportunity to escape again. Hands grabbed him from all around, even around his legs, with the intent to drag him to the ground, but this was not a mere mortal these demons were dealing with.

Daniel took a deep breath and let it out slowly. His whole body changed into a blinding mass of light and heat. The burning was so intense that it immediately shrivelled up the invisible demons as fire swept over them, consuming them completely. The smell of burning flesh filled the air and Daniel screwed up his nose as he returned to his natural state.

The smell of charred flesh is something that I'm not used to, even after all these eons. I hope that by the time I leave on Samhain, I'll not have too many more opportunities to experience that smell again. Brushing ash off his jacket, he continued his way back to the Rectory.

How Could You?

It was well after midnight when Acacia returned home with a basket overflowing with unusual herbs and fungi. Entering the kitchen, she was startled to find Ethan sitting at the table, his arms folded across his chest and his face a mask of cold fury.

'What the fucking hell do you think you were doing?'

Acacia's jaw dropped in surprise at the coldness of his tone of voice. She placed the basket carefully upon the table. 'I beg your pardon!'

'I thought we had no secrets Ace? So why didn't you tell me that you were going to fuck Rochester de Bere?'

Acacia's eyes blazed with anger. 'Ethan, your language! How could I tell you something which I did not do? And would never ever consider doing!'

His arms relaxed as he rose and approached Acacia. 'Then why has word spread throughout the village that Rochester has finally conquered your resistance?'

'I honestly don't know. Jordan sent me on a trek twenty miles south for these ingredients. I've been nowhere near the mansion or Rochester. Why would he spread such a lie?'

Considering this, a frown formed upon Ethan's brow, before he finally shook his head. 'He can't gain anything from such a trick. Shall I deal with him?'

'Perhaps you should show him that it's not nice to piss off a witch. How could you even think that I would so demean myself anyway?'

Colour swept up Ethan's cheeks. 'I didn't want to Ace, but when you consider Jordan's note and how angry you were about it, I thought that was what he had demanded of you.'

Acacia cast him a look of horror. 'If he had, there would not have been a mild storm, but a raging disaster!'

Ethan's laughter was cut short by the shaking of the house foundations. 'By all that's sacred!'

A Test For Ethan

The cats fled the house, and as Acacia and Ethan headed for the front door, they were nearly bowled over by the dogs that also fled out the back. Tiger was the only one brave enough to stay by his mistress' side.

'Wow!' stated Ethan as all the animals disappeared. 'That must have been some tremor!'

Acacia flung the door open and her cry of alarm sped Ethan on to join her. Outside of the property perimeter flew the demons that Acacia had seen in the woods at the crossroads. They were throwing rocks and other missiles, which battered against the protecting force around their property but did not pierce through it.

'How long can the Protector stand up to such abuse?'

Acacia put up her hand as if feeling the invisible force. 'Against them, maybe a week, but I won't force her to be subjected to such annoyance. Here is a real test for you Ethan. Do you feel up to it?'

He took a deep breath before nodding his head and exited the property. The demons stopped pounding the force field to stare dumbfounded at Ethan who ignored them completely as he sat cross-legged on the ground. At a very low pitch, Ethan began to chant softly and white smoke began to rise from around him. It swirled and curled, increasing in volume as it rose.

'In the shadows, evil may hide, Banish all that attempt to attack the protector. Show them the light of love and let their intentions be reversed.'

Demons, being curious creatures, came forward to take a closer look at the rising mist. Closer and closer, they flew to the harmless smoke, mingling around and through it. In a flash, tentacles of the white essence reached out and grabbed each of the demons, drawing them deeper into its centre. The demons struggled and screeched in anger but the smoke refused to release them until they became completely limp and dropped harmlessly to the ground. Only when all the demons were grounded, did Ethan's chanting stop and the essence receded back within him.

With Ethan once more on his feet, Acacia finally stepped out of the Protector's influence.

'Did you kill them?' Her question was one of professional interest.

'Nah! Something better, Ace, when they come round, until the break of dawn they'll be unable to do harm, only good deeds.'

Hugging him, Acacia joined in with his laughter. 'Excellent! They'll think twice about trying to attack us again!' She pressed a tender kiss against Ethan's cheek. 'Now, what are we going to do about Rochester?' Arm in arm, they walked back into the house, Acacia put on the kettle as they had much to plan.

Shattered Dreams

'Michael?' The soft female voice and the gentle touch to his shoulder caused his eyes to fly open and sit up abruptly in bed.

'I'm surprised to see you here tonight!' There was a hard tone to his voice and anger radiated from his eyes. 'I would've thought you'd be too busy fornicating and carousing with your new lovers! Why torment me if you wish to fuck the likes of Jordan and Rochester?'

Acacia winced at the ugliness of his words. 'That wasn't me! Last night I didn't visit your dreams as I was ashamed of what happened between Jordan and myself.' She reached out to lay her hand over his but he wrenched it away in disgust.

'So you have succumbed to your Elder's charms? How long was it before you took him into your bed?'

'Please listen!' Acacia begged. 'Last night after dinner but before that sky show began, you came to me in the garden and we kissed.'

'I never left the Rectory until Sergeant Boyd took me down to the crossroads!' Michael tossed back his bedding and springing to his feet he began to pace up and down his bedroom. Anger, disappointment and jealousy exuded from his every pore.

Acacia grabbed him firmly by the shoulders and forced him to look at her. 'You're not listening! I thought it was you until you kissed me and I realised that it was in fact Jordan who had assumed your image. I told him I wanted no substitute! No alternative lover! That I only wanted… you.'

Michael paused to consider her words before he finally spoke, 'Are you telling me that Jordan is a shape shifter? Is metamorphosis possible amongst your people?'

'Possible yes, but it is rare. Tonight I was nowhere near Rochester or the village. Jordan had sent me on an expedition to collect an array of rare and hard to find herbs and mushrooms. He wanted me to have no alibi to refute Rochester's claims that I visited him.' A shudder ran through Acacia. 'That I slept with him!'

'Jordan took on your form and fucked Rochester? Why?'

'To discredit me! To finalise the deal he made with Rochester to finance him. Jordan knew that if I wouldn't sleep with him, I would certainly not sleep with Rochester.'

Michael cupped her face between his hands and looked down into the truth in her eyes. 'I have no right to feel jealous! No right to ask you to wait for me to make a decision. No right to...' Unable to finish the train of thought that was exposing his tortured soul, he lowered his head to kiss her. A gentle, soft, giving kiss so unlike Jordan who took in demanding, aggressive desire. A kiss that could lead them on a slow journey towards ecstasy if they allowed it.

'Michael!' The hand that shook his shoulder and voice in his ear was definitely male. As he awoke from his dream, a curse rose immediately to his lips which surprised his waker who gasped and then chuckled. 'Sorry Michael. Naughty dreams huh? I thought you were having a nightmare the way you were thrashing about and muttering to yourself,' apologised Daniel as he released his shoulder. 'I thought you men of the cloth were supposed to be beyond the weaknesses of the flesh?'

'Even in our dreams?' Michael's lips twisted in wry amusement as he tried to regain control over his anger at Daniel. 'Do you want anything else?' *I'm trying to keep the annoyance out of my voice but the sight of the young nurse smiling cheekily down at me is exasperating.*

'Just trying to stop you from hurting yourself! Try to think purer thoughts and have better dreams Michael.' Heading towards the door, Daniel was surprised when the priest threw a pillow at his head.

Sunday 27 October

Sunday Mass

The reverent sounds of Bach filled and resounded throughout the church. *Its quality and magnificence make the emptiness of the church even more noticeable,* mused Father Thomas as he sat in a padded wheelchair, well rugged up. He looked around, disappointed at the lack of attendance for the morning mass. *Never have numbers been so low in the history of our little parish.*

Daniel sat in the pew beside him, staring meditatively into space. Stepping out of the sacristy, Michael straightened his cassock before looking up to find no more than five people apart from Thomas and Daniel in the whole church. *Disappointment is not the adjective that I'd have used, but as they say, the show must go on.*

The organ basically drowned out the half a dozen people present as they sang the first hymn. As the last note died away, Michael heard the unexpected sound of a vehicle horn. All heads in the church turned to stare in disbelief at the double entrance doors as Acacia breezed into the building. She looked as fresh and as lovely as a spring day, in a light, silky dress of a maroon colour that was more suitable for summer than a day approaching winter.

'Sorry we're late, but one of the buses had a flat tire. Assistance from able bodies will be appreciated.'

'Assistance for what?' Michael looked at Acacia stunned.

A roar of laughter came from behind Acacia as a very big man, still muscular despite his snow-white hair and walking stick entered the church. 'We ancients need a helping hand, my boy, so jump to it!'

The congregation immediately sprang to their feet to obey the man used to having his orders obeyed after 35 years as a naval Captain. Leading the way down the aisle, Michael glanced across at

Thomas, to find that Daniel had vanished. He was not given a chance to consider Daniel's defection as school students, the residents of the retirement village and nursing home descended from the buses and filled his church by tenfold.

Into Michael's tender care was placed Mrs Carpenter, a ninety-year-old woman who was rather frail and rarely left her room. *The fact that she has come to church, when I am to perform a service at the retirement village later this afternoon, means that Mrs Carpenter has bestowed upon me an incredible honour.*

'Was that the hymn "How great thou art" you were singing as we arrived, Father?'

Michael had to bend his head to catch Mrs Carpenter's softly spoken words. 'Indeed it was.'

Mrs Carpenter sighed. 'That was always one of my particular favourites. Half a dozen people can barely do it justice.'

Michael gently patted her hand as he led her to sit in a comfortable chair beside Father Thomas. 'Then we shall try again now that you're here to lead us.' Michael turned to see the church swell in congregation and his heart was overwhelmingly full of gratitude and brotherly love for this simple act that Acacia and Ethan had done.

It's as if they've had some forewarning of my predicament, they have done their best to prevent it. Having ensured that their entire bus loads were comfortably seated, Acacia and Ethan headed for the doors.

'Will you not stay?' Michael didn't know where his words came from and immediately wished them unsaid. A mischievous look was exchanged between the Tempests as they turned back to face Michael.

'We thank you, Father Michael, but we must decline.' Acacia smiled as she looked quickly around the packed church. 'Blessed be!' With this blessing she and Ethan departed and Michael regaining his equilibrium, again began his service.

Which One Is It?

The bus drivers stood behind one of the buses to shelter from the wind as they enjoyed a cigarette together. They tipped their caps as Acacia and Ethan passed them on their way to the cemetery. Acacia's timely rescue plan had puzzled Ethan but since it was instigated, to its conclusion, he hadn't had the opportunity to question her about it. Even in her haste to execute her plan, Acacia had found the time to pick a basket of flowers for the small cemetery for the coming of Samhain. So as Acacia pulled on gardening gloves, Ethan waited until they were alone in the cemetery before asking the question on his mind.

'What's going on Ace? What haven't you been telling me?'

Acacia had knelt down beside a grave and had begun to tidy and weed the site before pausing to look up at Ethan as he stood in front of her, his hands upon his hips.

'Sit down please Ethan. I didn't tell you what happened at the cross roads as I didn't wish to worry you.' Acacia waited until Ethan was seated beside her before continuing to speak, 'The Stranger is amongst us. The village is falling under his corrupt powers. It looks like we'll have to go through this torment after all.'

Ethan took this announcement rather calmly considering his own uncertain future. 'But which one is it, Ace? Jordan or Daniel?'

Her eyebrows rose in surprise. 'Daniel? Thomas' nurse? Why do you suspect him?'

Stabbing a stick into the ground, Ethan screwed up his nose as he considered his reasons. 'It's hard to say, but he's taken great care not to be seen by either of us. He was asking all manner of questions about you to Mary, but ran a mile when I appeared.'

'He could simply be fearful of witches.' *Even to me that suggestion doesn't sound feasible.* Acacia returned to arranging flowers upon the grave beside her.

Ethan frowned. 'Or fearful of being recognised for what he truly is.' Following Acacia's example, he began to work on the graves around him, not realising how close to the truth he actually was.

'So how do we go about discovering which is the Stranger?'

The question surprised Ethan as Acacia was deferring to him as she would with an Elder rather than her student. He scratched his head in thought. 'It might help if we actually met this Daniel.'

Nodding Acacia stated, 'I'll see if Michael can help us pin him down. In the meantime Ethan…' She looked up, her eyes sparkled with unshed tears. 'Please be careful!'

Mac's Anguish

While Michael preached to a more reasonably sized congregation, Ethan and Acacia worked quietly but industriously upon tidying the graveyard. This serene calm was shattered by a four-wheel drive vehicle speeding up the hill and screeching to a halt not far from Acacia, in a spray of gravel. An agitated Allan Macbeth leapt out of the vehicle and would have strode purposefully into the church had Acacia not called out his name.

'Wither away Mac? I hope you're not intending to disturb Father Michael's sermon with such a sad countenance as yours?' A snarl and look of contempt met her jovial words.

'It be one of y'r kind I'm looking for! He said 'twas safer out of the village that Eleanor was in danger here! It was all a plot to murder her!'

Acacia ripped off her gardening gloves as she hastily rose to her feet to place a calming hand upon Mac's shoulder. 'Slowly Allan! Who are we talking about? What has happened to Eleanor?'

Taking a deep breath, Mac managed to pull himself together. 'Last night Daniel Hamilton came to the Inn and told me to get Eleanor out of the village for her own safety. This morning her car was found smashed against a tree and no sign of her.'

Frowning as he dusted the dirt from his knees, Ethan ambled forward. 'Have they found any trace of where she went?'

'She has simply vanished and I wanna know what that bastard intends to do with my wife!'

As Macbeth headed full force towards the church, Acacia still had hold of his shoulder and was dragged off balance, sending her crashing to her knees.

'Halt!' The commanding tone used by Ethan was one, which neither Mac nor Acacia had heard before, and resulted in freezing Mac in his tracks, unable to move or control his own legs.

'There's no point disturbing the church, Mac, Daniel isn't there,' Acacia explained.

'Then I must continue to hunt him down!' Mac turned towards the Rectory but his feet refused to move, acting like they were glued to the ground. Frustrated, Mac glared at Ethan.

'Damn ye laddie! Release me from y'r sorcery. Ye can't deter me finding Eleanor.'

Ethan shook his head. 'Your search is pointless Mac, if she was taken by the person we think did it, you won't find her in this world.'

'Oh God No!' Macbeth completely lost it. 'She's dead!'

Acacia, having risen to her feet consoled him. 'What Ethan means is that you may not be able to go physically where Eleanor is being held. Not that she is actually dead. You must trust us, Mac, to return your wife safely but make too much noise and they may kill her immediately. Give us time to discover in which dimension Eleanor is being kept.'

Macbeth scratched his chin, thoughtfully. 'This has something to do with ye both hasn't it? And all these strange events?'

Acacia nodded. 'We didn't cause those events to occur, we're simply caught in the middle of them like everyone else. Go home and search no more today. We'll contact you soon.'

With a snap of his fingers, Ethan released Macbeth's feet but when the Innkeeper turned his attention to the Rectory, Ethan issued a warning, 'Don't do it Mac! You don't understand what we're dealing with here!'

Macbeth looked back at Ethan; his lips thinned in disapproval and his eyes gleamed dangerously. 'Ye wouldn't be threatening me now laddie?'

Ethan laughed. 'Never Mac! I could kill you without moving from this spot. I have no need to threaten you.'

The big ex-navy man stared at the slim teenager and would have laughed had the truth not been evident in the seriousness of Ethan's eyes. It was Macbeth who looked away first, before getting back into his Land Rover without another word and headed back into the village.

'Should we examine the crash site?' asked Ethan.

Acacia inclined her head in agreement. 'It would be advisable.'

Linking his arm through hers, Ethan added, 'and on the way you can tell me exactly what happened at the cross roads.'

Glancing into Ethan's determined eyes, Acacia realised that he would be satisfied with no less than the complete truth, so she took a deep breath before beginning her story.

Ethan's Revenge

Rochester de Bere woke up that morning feeling rather seedy and well hung over. *I don't remember coming home from the Inn, let alone managing to get into bed.* Scratching his chin, he realised that he was in desperate need for a shave and staggered across to the mirror. The reflection caused him to scream in horror, for not only was there on his face a five o'clock stubble, but also whiskers of an animal, large pointed hairy ears and the buck teeth of a rat.

Whirling around in disbelief, Rochester felt something moving on his back. Looking around, he caught sight of a huge hairless tail attached to his lower back. His scream echoed throughout the mansion as he cursed all witches and their kin. Ethan had ensured that all that saw Rochester that day would know him for the rat that he was, unfortunately it would last only a day.

Searching For Clues

By the time Ethan and Acacia reached the crash site, Eleanor's car had been towed away, and although crime scene tape still surrounded the area, the site was deserted.

'Tell me what you feel?' Acacia spoke softly to avoid breaking the atmosphere around them.

Ethan screwed up his nose as he glanced around, high jumping easily over the police security tape. 'Claustrophobic. As if walls are closing in on me.'

Acacia nodded, slipping elegantly under the tape to join him. 'That is the Stranger's wall erecting itself around the village. According to the book of the Nephilim soon no one will be able to leave or enter through it. What images do you receive about Eleanor?'

'I'd like to know the answer to that too!' The masculine voice from the trees made them both jump. Constable Matthew Kane emerged from behind the tree he had been sitting under.

Acacia's eyebrows rose in astonishment. 'I didn't think you believed in anything that witches had to say?'

Kane surprised them by laughing. 'I don't like what you do but I've learnt a lot in the last forty eight hours and I concede the need to be a little more open minded. A woman does not simply run off a clear and straight stretch of road, crash into a tree and completely vanish. And from what I just heard you say, something extremely supernatural is going on here.'

A significant glance was exchanged between the Tempests and Ethan shrugged. It was Acacia who answered the Constable.

'We're entering a time of uncertainty and chaos. Until Samhain, Halloween to you, has passed, this village is in extreme danger.' She moved towards the trees and Kane, clearing the way for Ethan to examine the crash site on his own. Grasping Acacia's purpose, they wandered into the woods.

'Death?' It was obvious that Kane was thinking of Jenny's murder.

'I don't know. Jenny was sacrificed to pay homage to his Master. Others may have already died, but I can't tell you how many more will lose their life before this is over.'

For a moment Kane chewed on his bottom lip. 'Who then is the Stranger?'

Acacia shook her head. 'I don't know.'

He cast her a shrewd look as his eyebrows rose. 'Don't you? Or are you trying to protect someone? If we take the term stranger as being literal then we have three obvious options. Jordan, Daniel Hamilton and Michael Casey. What do you say to that?'

Surprise flittered across Acacia's face at the mention of the last name. 'You honestly suspect Michael?'

'Why not? He certainly doesn't act like any Catholic Priest that I've ever met! He has also been hanging a lot around you two. I mean Father Thomas was friendly with you but I saw the way Father Michael held you yesterday at the crossroads. There is a connection between you that is not normal. One might even suggest that your unconscious actions are those of lovers rather than two people who have only recently met.'

A deep flush of colour swept across Acacia's cheeks. 'Well then you're wrong, Constable! Dead wrong! I trust you keep such an opinion to yourself. Such an allegation would completely ruin Michael's reputation. I can assure you that the Stranger was called forth after Michael arrived in the village. Anything else is just none of your business!'

'Oh ho! So there is something going on between you two! Or is that just wishful thinking?'

Memories of Saturday morning in the stables came back to Acacia causing a smile to flit briefly across her face. It was quickly replaced by a look of regret for what should never happen again. Kane didn't miss this change of expression and he regretted his teasing.

'I'm sorry. I've touched a raw nerve haven't I?'

'Never mind.' Acacia shrugged. 'We can't always have what we want.'

'Ace, I've found something!' Ethan's voice called them back to the crash site, where they found him lying flat on the ground, with his nose close to the grass.

'With all the feet that have trampled over this area it's a miracle that this could be seen at all!' He pointed to an area of sand with a pocket knife, forcing Kane to drop to the ground beside him to see what he was pointing at.

'Is that some sort of hoof print? It's almost like a pig's trotter. Is that significant?'

Acacia almost smiled at the sight of the two young men lying on the grass side by side, heads close together. *I'm surprised by how human Kane appears for a change.*

'Very significant,' answered Ethan sitting up. 'What you're looking at is the footprint of a demon. That makes finding Eleanor a little more difficult, and a lot more dangerous.'

Kane's eyebrows rose in question as he got back onto his feet and dusted himself off. 'Why?'

'It means that she's no longer in this dimension.'

Kane burst into laughter. 'Oh no, no! Now you've gone too far! Another dimension? This is not the television shows "Supernatural" or the "X-files", this is real life! Try again!'

Ethan's eyes flashed with indignation but Acacia sent him a telepathic message to be silent.

'You have a stable, logical head on your shoulders, we may need you as an anchor to this world, so keep away from the disruptive influence of Jordan and Daniel.'

'I still don't understand any of this.' Kane shook his head.

Acacia pressed his hand reassuringly. 'Don't worry about understanding, Matt, just believe that we know what we're doing.'

Michael Seeks Answers

The service had concluded by the time Ethan and Acacia returned to St Andrews, and the students and the Senior Citizens were being loaded back on to the buses. This was a lengthy process as many of the elderly paused to have a word with Michael or Acacia. So it was quite some time before Michael had the opportunity to speak privately to Acacia. Ethan reading the unspoken message in Michael's eyes had volunteered to escort Thomas to the Rectory and see him settled back into bed. Still attired in cassock and stole, Michael walked with Acacia through the graveyard.

'How did you know?'

Acacia frowned, as she had to bring her thoughts back from contemplating Eleanor's disappearance. 'About what? Oh, that your church would be empty?' Michael nodded.

Acacia smiled. 'I used logic. With nearly all the adults in the village attending Jordan's all night party, people with massive head aches and the memory of unbridled fornication would hardly be fronting to church the next morning.'

'Tell me… tell me about Halloween.'

'Samhain is so much more than most people perceive. It is the celebration of the end of harvest, and the end of the witches' year. The God is dead, his seed harvested and the Goddess, now hag like, goes into mourning, to await for her mate to re-join her in the spring.' Acacia sighed, 'It's also a time to remember those who have departed and bless those unborn yet to come. Your doors should be thrown open in welcome and a feast prepared to invite in old friends and family.'

There's a sparkle in Acacia's eyes and a breathlessness in her voice that makes me realise what a religious experience a true witches' Halloween is. I thought that I'd be more sceptical about the ways of the Craft but nothing said by Acacia seems to be unnatural, and I wonder what is happening to my long held beliefs and faith? The magical glow surrounding Acacia began to dim as she came back to reality.

'It's important that I meet Daniel.'

Michael frowned in thought. 'You don't think he's the Stranger, do you?'

Acacia shrugged her beautiful shoulders. 'I don't know, but if Allan Macbeth catches up with him first he may be a dead man.' Acacia explained about Eleanor's disappearance.

'What can we do?' Michael finally asked.

Acacia shook her head. 'At the moment, there is nothing we can do. Tonight, I'll seek guidance from the ultimate source of knowledge.'

A spark of interest lit up Michael's eyes. 'Can I come too?' His curiosity increased as a deep flush of colour swept across her face.

'I think not, Michael. This is something that I don't think you're ready for. Nor am I ready to share it with you. It… It is a little too personal.'

'More personal than almost making love in your barn?' Michael's eyebrows rose in surprise.

A gasp of astonishment escaped from Acacia. 'That is a low blow, Michael! I had not expected that from you!' She turned to walk away from him but Michael firmly grasped her arm with his good hand.

'I'm sorry, Acacia, it was wrong of me to throw that in your face. Is there nothing that I can do to help?'

Acacia looked at Michael with very serious eyes. 'Father Thomas has a special task to perform as Samhain ends, please ensure that he does not meet his God before then.'

Confused, Michael shook his head as he released her arm. 'I can't prevent the inevitable.'

'No! But you may just be able to prevent murder!'

The Waterfall

As night fell, Acacia dressed warmly against the chilling winds and headed deep into the woods that backed onto her farm. *Although I am tired, Ethan and I had put in a full day's work on the farm, but I know that I have to concentrate upon the task ahead of me.* Thus with her energy resources low, it was possible for Acacia to be followed without her knowing it.

The dark figure kept back well hidden by the trees but ensured that Acacia was never let out of their sight. The moon wasn't yet full; even so Acacia's follower heard the waterfall before it became visible.

As waterfalls go, this one wasn't extensive by any means, being no more than ten feet high. Even so, the water cascading down, shimmered silver in the moonlight and possessed a magical aura about it. Acacia halted by the edge of the pool that resulted from the waterfall. For a moment she stood staring up at the cascading water, so still that the only movement was that of her loose hair and cape in the crisp breeze.

When Acacia looked around to ensure that she was alone, her follower moved quickly back into the protective darkness of the trees. He did not wish her to know of his presence. Satisfied Acacia stripped completely out of her clothes and without even pausing to consider how cold the water would be, she waded in towards the base of the waterfall.

'*Cleansing waters of wisdom, I embrace you within myself, I am a seeker of knowledge, and courage in the face of darkness. While my heart sings your melody may my spirit be protected from harm.*'

A sympathetic chill ran down Michael Casey's back as he watched Acacia step under the curtain of falling water. *I know that it was wrong to follow Acacia here, but my instinct to know had overridden my morals. Now, though, my morals are again rising as from my position in the trees, every curve and every seductive line of Acacia's naked body is visible in the moonlight and it awakens a desire in me that I'd thought had been long suppressed.*

For a quarter of an hour, Acacia stood still beneath the waterfall, the water pounding down on top of her and when she stepped out instead of looking battered and worn, she looked refreshed and even younger. Despite the danger of being dragged under, Acacia floated on her back amidst the foaming, bubbling water that should have swept her away with its flow and force, but she remained perfectly still in one position as she became one with the water around her.

I suddenly feel the desire to join Acacia, to feel just as free and to be just as harmonious with nature. He was undoing the buttons of his overcoat when he heard the soft tread of footsteps behind him. Fearing for Acacia's safety and her modesty, Michael picked up a sturdy stick off the ground and turned to confront whoever approached. As Michael's eyes opened wider, his jaw dropped in surprise and the stick fell from his hands. Before him stood a man-beast, the head and torso of a man, the lower forequarters of a small horse and the antlers of a great stag. Instinctively Michael crossed himself.

'The Devil!' He whispered in fright.

The Horned God smiled. 'No Michael, in fact the opposite. To the witches I am simply the God. To others I am Pan, or Herne, the Sun or any other deity that has a beneficial hand in the lives of mankind.' His voice was deep and rich. Glancing fleetingly back to where Acacia was still floating in the foaming water, Michael asked, 'Did Acacia summon you here?'

'No, I am not one to be summoned or ordered about. Acacia has asked us for guidance and assistance, I could have left it up to the

Goddess to communicate with Acacia, but I decided to see her myself.'

Michael went quite pale. 'Is the news about Eleanor Macbeth bad then?'

'It's not good, but it is not hopeless. The dimension the expecting mother was taken to is heavily guarded by demons and other magical deterrents which makes it difficult for any deity to intercede in this matter. Your best option is to seize her the instant she is brought back to this dimension, the evening of Samhain.'

'If we can't?'

'Then mother and child will be sacrificed. Evil will walk freely upon this earth.' The God began to fade into the shadows.

'Wait! Didn't you wish to see Acacia?'

A mischievous gleam entered the God's eyes as he had barely taken his gaze off Acacia's floating body since he arrived.

'I have, my son, and what a beautiful creature she is! Such a vision of her young and supple body shall sustain me through my months of death or winter as you call it. But don't tell the Goddess that! By the end of the season, I shall be more than ready to be reunited with my beloved Goddess. Perhaps it is time to consider the end of your own winter, Michael.' The God waved his hand towards Acacia; 'Your Goddess awaits you.'

Michael sadly shook his head. 'No! I will not violate my vows of celibacy. While I am still a Catholic Priest I must continue to act like one!'

The God grinned as he continued to fade. 'You've hardly been acting like one since your arrival in Stirling. Let me know if you ever change your mind, Michael. Give Acacia my message, and good luck to you both. You're not alone, my protection will never be far away. Blessed be.' The last words came out of the darkness and were touched with a sadness that Michael found difficult to shrug off.

Breaking A Spell

Pulling himself together, Michael realised he had a problem, what to do about Acacia, who was still floating in the cold, foaming water, completely naked. Taking a deep breath for courage, Michael approached the riverbank.

'Acacia!' Michael spoke firmly, but his voice was lost in the sound of the pounding water cascading down. He tried hard not to look at the way the moonlight danced over Acacia's voluptuous breasts and down her stomach to her shapely legs.

'Acacia.' This time Michael yelled, and managed to pierce the trance like state that Acacia had submerged into. So startled at being addressed by a human voice, Acacia lost her concentration and was swept under the water.

'Bloody hell!' Michael ripped off his overcoat before he ran into the river when Acacia did not reappear and dived in to rescue her. This wasn't an easy task for when Acacia had broken her trance, she was unable to remain in the same place so that the current had carried her a few feet away before Michael finally found her floating face down.

Using a lifesaving hold, Michael dragged Acacia to the bank before picking her up in his arms to carry her to the grass. Without thinking, he placed her into the coma position and went through his first aid training, checking her breathing and pulse. Although her heart was still beating, Acacia had stopped breathing.

'Damn you, Acacia, you're not leaving me that easily!' Michael rolled her onto her back and began mouth to mouth resuscitation. In the most harrowing minutes of his life, up to that point, Michael prayed as he frantically tried to breathe life back into her.

Tears of joy shone in Michael's eyes when Acacia finally gasped for breath and he quickly rolled her back onto her side so that she could purge her system of any water that she may have taken in. Picking up his overcoat, Michael wrapped Acacia up in it as he said a prayer of thanks for her safe return.

'Next time… I'll let you come so that I can teach you… how to release a person from a trance properly.' Acacia's voice was barely a whisper and Michael had to lean over her to hear.

'Which is?'

Acacia's chuckle turned into a watery cough as she attempted to sit up. 'Go back to your fairy tales, Michael, do you remember Sleeping Beauty?'

'Oh!' Michael did not know what else to say.

'Could you find my clothes please, this breeze is a little chilly.'

Michael willingly complied, knowing that the sooner Acacia was fully clothed again the better it would be for him. He turned his back on her as she slipped back into her clothing.

'I have seen him!' Michael could no longer keep the information to himself. Acacia paused in doing up her cape, her eyes resting thoughtfully upon the back of Michael's head.

'The Stranger?'

'No, your God.' Michael turned around, his eyes glowing with excitement.

A look of astonishment flittered across Acacia's face as she did up her cloak before handing Michael his overcoat to put on over his saturated clothing.

'How did he appear to you?'

Michael frowned, wondering if that was at all relevant considering the information he had imparted. 'I heard footsteps behind me, when I turned there was this man-beast.'

'Was he solid or ghost like?'

'Solid.'

'Did the Mighty One speak to you?'

'Of course! I'd tell you what he said if you stopped plying me with questions! What does it matter what I saw?' He was a little irritated by the irrelevance of her questions.

Acacia laughed in delight. 'You don't understand the honour that has been bestowed upon you. Some of the Family have only ever heard footsteps, others a ghostly apparition, very few actually see the physical God and converse with him. Did he bring news of Eleanor?'

Michael nodded. 'But it's not good news.' He continued to explain all that the God had told him. Acacia didn't seem surprised that Eleanor was momentarily out of their reach.

I'm Not So Sure

As the clouds swept across the night sky, threatening rain, Michael decided it was time to escort Acacia home. She agreed and as they retraced their steps through the woods, Michael asked a question that was puzzling him.

'What is so special about Eleanor Macbeth?'

Acacia didn't immediately answer, hoping that she may be wrong and was hesitant to speak her fears. 'Eleanor is three month pregnant. It isn't widely known because she's had several miscarriages over the past few years and they didn't wish to see a rise of false hope this time. She may have been taken to a dimension that has a different concept of time so that when Samhain arrives, Eleanor could be due to give birth.'

'Then?'

'She would be forced into labour, and as the baby is born, it would be sacrificed. The purest life form is that of the newborn. Tap into its power and anything is possible.'

'Do you have a plan of rescue?'

Acacia shook her head. 'Not yet. I'll want to discuss our options with Ethan.'

'When you do come up with a plan, include me in them. I'll try not to let you down.'

Acacia halted and placed a hand upon his shoulder. 'You never have let me down Michael, and to be honest with you, I don't think that you ever will.'

'What about your expectations of me when I first arrived? What about those shared dreams?'

Her hand dropped away as colour flooded Acacia's cheeks. 'It's not your fault that I had those expectations. Besides which, we've resolved all that haven't we?'

There was a pause before Michael answered, 'I'm not too sure that we have.' Acacia looked puzzled but didn't resist when he placed his hand through her arm and continued their footsteps towards the Tempest farm.

'Meaning what Michael?' Although she was frightened of what his answer might be, she had to know.

He took a deep breath and let it out slowly. 'I don't rightly know. Something has happened to me since I arrived here. I'm changing and I don't know if I'm comfortable with that. I thought I had a clear vision of what I needed in my life and where I was heading.' Michael sighed before he continued, 'God, a Christian God was to be my life and I was content with that decision until I met you. I'm confused; I no longer know what to think, what to believe. The most perplexing thing is that the more that I hear about the ways of the Craft, I begin to realise that it is a very natural way to live. How can I sustain two beliefs?'

A sheep trotted up to greet them as they entered a small gate at the back of the property. Acacia paused to scratch the sheep's head before they continued on to the house.

'You can't sustain two faiths, you must have one belief that is solid and true to you, but you can be open to the knowledge that other beliefs do exist and must be accepted for what they are and not dismissed entirely as being wrong. They're not wrong, none of them are wrong, they're merely different.'

Michael shook his head. 'That's not quite true, what about some of these fanatical cults?'

'I see your point, some of them are downright nasty. I'll have to reconsider that concept.' Acacia fell silent as she contemplated this change in philosophy.

The dogs raced down from the house to see who had entered the property and upon determining that it was only Michael and Acacia, the dogs danced around them, yapping happily in greeting.

'But how do I know which is the right one for me?' His attention returned to the question burning in his brain.

Acacia shook her head sadly. 'Only your heart can answer that question.'

They parted company at her side gate, with Michael refusing Acacia's offer of an escort home. *As I walk through the streets, I notice how quiet the village is, perhaps too quiet compared to the previous evening. There are no little demons flying around, no lights streaking across the sky and no street drinking or debauchery. In fact there is no one around at all. The calm before the storm*, thought Michael, not realising how true that was going to be.

Why Are We Meeting Like This?

'Michael?' The soft female voice and the gentle touch to his shoulder caused his eyes to fly open and sit up abruptly in bed.

'I thought we'd said everything we had to say on the way home from the waterfall?' Michael scrubbed a weary hand across his eyes.

Acacia shook her head as she sat down on the edge of Michael's bed. 'I am not the one who has created this dream connection between us. Someone very powerful wants us to get to the bottom of our feelings and we obviously haven't got the message yet.'

'Is this dream weaver trying to help or hinder us? I feel guilty every time I see you in reality due to what we've done or almost done in our dreams. Is someone trying to bring us together or create awkwardness between us or… distract us from the real issues that are going on around us?' His fingers travelled across the top of his blanket towards Acacia's but stopped short of actually touching her when he realised what he was doing. Acacia didn't immediately reply as she considered all the options.

'Actually, I'm not certain that we are dealing with one person but at least two. One wants us to give in to our desires in our dreams and another is forcing us awake before we can fulfil that need. Is either method supposed to force us to satisfy our lusts in the real world and why the rush? I would've thought that all the chaos that we're currently combating is more important than our feelings.' As those words came out of her mouth Acacia had a sudden insight as to their meetings.

'Unless someone wants us distracted so that we're not as alert to the danger as we need to be or… both of us have been celibate for the past seven years… maybe that purity is what they wish to destroy. Maybe it will be essential to use that purity in order to save Ethan and without it…' A shudder ran through Acacia as she was unable to finish that train of thought. *It could be that not just our faiths are being tested but our very souls as well?*

This time Michael allowed his fingers to cover and entwine with Acacia's. 'Then perhaps it is time to wake up!' *It's not what I want but it is what we need to do. Damn! Why is it so hard to be an adult?* Together Acacia and Michael pinched each other's arms and returned to their own rooms in the real world.

Monday 28 October

Beware Of Greeks Bearing Gifts

The birds had barely begun to sing when Ethan burst into Acacia's bedroom the next morning. She was already up, half naked with a pair of jeans and a black skivvy lying on the made bed waiting for her to put on. Ethan was fully dressed.

'Ace, you've got to come see!'

Acacia laughed, not in the least embarrassed about him bursting in while she was semi naked. 'And Blessed Meet to you too, Ethan.'

Ethan flushed, remembering his manners. 'Blessed Meet Acacia, but do hurry!'

No sooner had Acacia pulled on her clothes, Ethan was dragging her downstairs and out of the back door. The sheep were happily grazing, the horses had been groomed, the cows milked, the eggs collected and the day's pickings of fruit and vegetables had been harvested. Not only that, the dogs and cats had all been fed.

'How long did it take you Ethan?'

The teenager emphatically shook his head. 'I didn't do it. Do you think we might have acquired what the Christians call a Guardian Angel?'

Frowning in thought, Acacia gave an ambiguous answer. 'Hum! I wonder!'

The sky appeared clear of the clouds that they had been experiencing the last couple of days, giving cause for Acacia to wonder, *Are we in for an unusually warm day?* Still suspicious, her eyes scanned the landscape.

'We thank you Jordan, but what must we do in return for such an honour?'

Ethan looked at her as if she had lost her mind, but a deep masculine laugh appeared out of nowhere, as Jordan materialised in front of them. His appearance was startling to say the least, as he was dressed in leather pants and an open necked shirt, his glasses were gone and his hair hanging loose down his back. He looked like he had just stepped off the set of the television programme "Hercules".

'I detect a note of suspicion, Sweet Angel. I didn't wish for you to be slaving away when you could be enjoying the village's Medieval Faire with me.'

'But why the funny clothes?' Ethan shook his head in disbelief.

An elaborate smile spread across Jordan's features. 'I have turned back time in the village, to an era where mysticism was an accepted way of life. Come, your costumes await you in your rooms, and our journey into the past begins.' Jordan led the way into the house, carrying the goods that he had harvested, but Ethan had one more question.

'What about school?'

Jordan waved away this problem. 'Today no one works. It is a time for celebration.'

As Acacia and Ethan ran upstairs to change their clothes, one thought disturbed Acacia, *What exactly are we celebrating?*

The Medieval Faire

As light flittered through the village, it altered its appearance to take on the look of an ancient settlement. The Faire was to be held on the cricket ground just behind the large square that was commonly used for market day.

The weather is promising to be much warmer than it should be for autumn, and I put this down to Jordan's handiwork, decided Acacia. *Which is just as well for the costume Jordan has given me is scarcely designed to keep me warm.*

The dress was above the knee, silk, white with a plunging V-neck line and a gold metallic belt. *With the soft silky material swirling around my legs, I'm positive that this was not the average wear of the common ancient Grecian. Especially when I notice that Jordan's eyes continue to drop to my exposed thighs, I know that my costume is more for his benefit than being realistic.*

As they walked up the street, Ethan also noticed the direction of Jordan's wandering attention and his lips thinned in disapproval. His eyes met Acacia's but she only smiled and shook her head. Even though it was still early in the morning, there were already plenty of people around.

Stalls and children's games were being set up as Mac was establishing a beer tent. He did not look happy, but managed a wave in their direction. Jordan left them at that moment to supervise the musicians and seeing Mary similarly attired to Acacia in a blue dress, Ethan headed off leaving Acacia alone. Not that Acacia was alone for long as she was soon surrounded by a group of children who dragged her off to a grassy area to play games with them.

Still On Duty

Several hours later Matthew Kane, dressed like an ancient warrior and looking very uncomfortable about the whole thing, found Acacia in Mac's makeshift Inn, drinking a goblet of apple cider. She grinned at how awkward he looked in his leather and armour attire.

'We need to talk.' His tone was hardly friendly.

Acacia's smile disappeared immediately. 'Oh dear, what have I done now?' Her tone was light but wary.

'Outside please!'

They had attracted a bit of attention from the other patrons and Acacia rose obediently to her feet. As she followed Kane out, whispers began among the patrons about the hostility evident between Kane and Acacia.

I don't actually feel the animosity I portray, but I don't wish for Acacia to be seen as working too closely with the police. They walked through the crowd together, Kane's hand under her elbow.

'Are you ever off duty Constable?'

Kane's eyes were constantly scanning the crowd. 'Not when murder is involved! There is something I want you to see, but we can't leave here together. Meet me where Eleanor Macbeth had her accident.'

Kane released her arm and walked off in the opposite direction. Acacia watched him, bemused about his protective nature towards her, and was curious to know why.

A Patient Vigil

Since early morning, Michael had been sitting beside Father Thomas' bed, reading aloud from David Kossoff's Bible Stories. Thomas was under a light sedation but Michael believed that his uncle could still be aware of his presence. An intravenous drip fed into Thomas saline fluids and morphine and there was equipment to automatically drain away any waste. Michael put the book down and checked the bag that contained urine to see if it required emptying.

The colour of the liquid worries me, being orange brown, and a clear indication of the start of renal failure. The end for Uncle Thomas is near, but I wish that there wasn't a deadline hanging over all our actions. The bedroom door opened a fraction and Marjorie peeked in, fearful of disturbing the dying man.

'Cup of tea, Father Michael?'

Michael rose to his feet, stretching. 'No, thank you, Marjorie. I'll be in the church for a while if anyone wants me.'

Marjorie opened the door a little wider to allow him to pass by. 'Shall I find Daniel to sit with Father Thomas?'

'No!' His command was a little too sharp, and Michael managed to say in a softer tone, 'No, that won't be necessary. I'd be grateful though if you would just check up on him every once and a while. And don't let anyone into the Rectory without my knowledge.'

'Of course, Father Michael.' Marjorie looked perplexed but didn't press him for further answers, which was just as well for he was not about to give any.

What Are You?

Entering the church through the sacristy, Michael was surprised to hear a soft humming coming from the altar. Coming to a sudden stop, Michael's jaw dropped in wonder as seated cross-legged in a yoga position and levitating about four feet off the ground was Daniel Hamilton. His eyes were closed and he continued to hum a monotone sound.

'What are you?' Michael demanded.

Daniel's eyes suddenly opened and Michael was forced to take a step back in horror. The eyes that stared at him were a luminescent brilliant blue.

'Holy Mother of God!' Instinctively Michael crossed himself and glanced around for a means of escape. The glow began to fade as Daniel chuckled, returning his feet to terra firma.

'An interesting question, Michael. You ask what I am, and not who am I. You're therefore in Acacia's complete confidence then?'

Nodding warily, Michael sat down upon one of the pews. 'Are you human?' He realised that he was treading upon uncertain ground if Daniel was as powerful or as dangerous as Acacia feared, he could be in serious trouble.

'Not in the true sense.' The honesty of the answer puzzled Michael.

'Is Father Thomas in danger from you?'

'No. Tell me Michael what do you fear?'

It's impossible to put all of my fears into words, many of them I've been so stringently denying, that to speak them would force me to accept their existence. Daniel waited patiently, as Michael's head remained lowered, his hands clasping firmly together between his knees.

'I fear for the safety of the people in this community, especially Acacia and Ethan. They have the most to lose from the Stranger.'

Daniel smiled gently as he laid a hand upon Michael's shoulder, causing him to look up and meet his eyes.

'You love her, don't you?' An unemotional mask covered Michael's face as he stood up and brushed Daniel's hand off. In an agitated manner, he paced the floor.

'It is not my... my duty to love one person more than another. I am a servant of God, first and foremost!'

Daniel shook his head. 'No, Michael. You're a man, first and foremost. But we have digressed, at this point in time, it isn't possible for me to fully explain my purpose in this village, except to say that no one will come to harm from my hands.'

With this Michael had to be content, for Daniel, with a nod, walked out of the church with no intention of revealing anything further.

Even so, I am uneasy about Daniel's explanation and confused as to the true nature of my feelings for Acacia. To put all thoughts of the beautiful Witch out of his mind, Michael decided to scrub all the pews, in the hope that his mind could be occupied in more virtuous thoughts.

This Won't Be Pleasant

Having met Kane along the roadside, away from prying eyes, he led Acacia towards the very edge of the village perimeter. The further they went from the village centre the colder it became, and Acacia wished that she had brought a cloak with her. Kane assisted Acacia over a low fence so that they could cross a field full of sheep, but not one word was spoken until they entered a wooded area on the opposite side of the field.

'What you're about to see is not a pretty sight, but it has all the markings of the murder of Jenny Connors.'

In the quietness of the woods, a shiver ran down Acacia's spine, as it was too quiet. *There's no sound of birds or any other animals at all to be heard and that worries me.*

As they approached their intended destination, the smell of death wafted up to meet them, momentarily gagging Acacia. Kane glanced at her sympathetically, pausing but she waved him on, determined not to throw up. He handed her a cloth facial mask and upon donning one himself, he nodded in the direction ahead of him.

'Let's get this over with.' And they moved on towards the increasing putrid smell.

A small circular clearing appeared amidst the trees, in the middle of which, lay two open graves. The bodies inside were neither in coffins, nor upward facing. Acacia was surprised to see not the faces of a man and woman, but the backs of their heads. Kneeling beside the graves was a small, unassuming man, who was the Police Medical Officer.

'Does that mean something, Acacia?' Kane's words broke in upon Acacia's observation. She looked up at him in deep thought, before kneeling down beside one grave and placing her hand across the top of it.

'Some believe that how you're laid in a grave is the direction that you will take in the afterlife. The killer has tried to force their souls into hell.'

The Doctor rose to his feet and gestured for Kane to move with him to one side, so that Acacia couldn't overhear them.

'Matt, these corpse are very different from what I'm used to dealing with. I mean they're completely…'

'Bloodless?' Interjected Acacia, proving that she had excellent hearing.

Kane nodded solemnly. 'All right Shamus, get them back to the morgue. I not only want to know what killed them, but also who they are.' He turned to address the still kneeling Acacia, 'Unless you wish to make any examination?'

Acacia shook her head as she rose to her feet. 'No, but I do have one request. When the autopsy is concluded, incinerate their bodies immediately, just in case.'

The Doctor looked from Acacia to Kane in disbelief. 'You're not going to accept this nonsense are you Matt?'

Kane stared silently at Acacia's serious face for a moment before nodding. 'Do as the lady says, Shamus, we're no longer dealing in a realm of logic that I can understand.' The Constable's tone was a dismissal for the Doctor as Kane gestured for Acacia to join him.

'I have some questions you may be able to answer, Acacia, but first, some fresh air I think.'

What Does It Mean?

They headed out of the circle, back towards the village as Shamus called up his team to remove the bodies. Kane waited until they had walked out of earshot and were able to remove their masks and breathe fresh air again before he began his questions.

'It wasn't necessary for you to go into that trance you used at the cross roads was it? You already knew what had happened to those people.' Acacia nodded, her hand unconsciously scrunching up the face mask. 'Totally drained of blood, so what are we dealing with here? Vampires?'

This time Acacia shook her head. 'Not in the true sense. Vampires drain their victims of blood for sustenance; these people were drained so that one with no blood in his veins could easily pretend to be like us. The Stranger is an eternal being, as the Servant of Evil, it has no need for the life force that drives us, as evil power provides it all the sustenance that it needs.'

'This blood, though when stolen and used by the Stranger, does not regenerate itself and therefore must be replaced at regular intervals if proof is continued to be needed that they are supposedly human.'

With the exception of the sound of their footsteps through the grass, there was for a considerable period of time no other noise as Kane considered Acacia's words.

'Will he kill again?' The look of sadness upon Acacia's face was enough to answer him, but Kane waited patiently for her to speak.

'Now that we're isolated and the village is falling swiftly under the Stranger's control, there is every chance that he will try to take as many souls as possible with him when he returns to his Master. Or he may be satisfied to leave with only the sacrifice that was promised to him.'

'Which is?'

Acacia choked back a sob and Kane did something out of character and immediately placed his arm around her shoulder. 'You?'

'No,' she shook her head. 'Ethan.'

'Perhaps we could…' Acacia was never to learn what Kane was about to suggest as the ground trembled violently beneath their feet.

A Fiery Display

A mushroom cloud of dirt and smoke rose from the middle of the village cricket pitch and screams ascended in fear. They both broke into a run as the screams continued to fill the air.

Flames blazed in a circle in the middle of the pitch, with the villagers gathered around it mesmerised by its brilliance. Kane arrived out of breath and Acacia made her way to Ethan's side. Jordan was dancing around the circle of fire, chanting an incantation that although no one but Acacia and Ethan could understand, the others were moved by Jordan's performance.

'He's out to destroy all that we've worked to achieve in this community,' bemoaned Acacia.

Ethan shook his head. 'He's out to control the village and make it more difficult for us to fight him alone. He is the Stranger, isn't he?'

'Yes. Why was there screaming?'

A shrug of his shoulders indicated that Ethan didn't know what the fuss had been about. Mary, who was standing quietly beside him, was more attuned to the hysteria.

'It's not every day that you feel the earth open up around you and explode like a volcano.' Mary hesitated as a frown descended upon her brow. 'Acacia, is hell really going to break loose?'

A glance at Jordan, who had been joined in his dance by several of the villagers, caused Acacia to tighten her jaw in determination.

'Not if I can help it!'

Gather Up The Children

The Faire went well into the day, not that Acacia, Ethan and Mary stayed there long. As more people joined in Jordan's dance of fire, the general standard of morality of the villagers rapidly decreased. Before leaving, Acacia ensured that Karen Greeves, the High School Principal and a few of the other teachers herded the younger members of the community away from the scene of depravity and to a place of safety. As night fell, some parents remembered their responsibilities and headed home to their children, but many people remained with Jordan, their partying promising to go well into the night.

The Attacks Begin

Sometime after midnight and after Acacia and Ethan had retired to their beds, there was a thumping upon their front door. Throwing back her blankets, Acacia found that it was warm enough to not pull on a dressing gown over the sloppy jumper she was wearing. Padding barefoot out of her room, Acacia checked on Ethan, who still slept, before slipping down the stairs to the darkness below. With a click of her fingers, the lights in the kitchen turned on automatically. Entering the hall, a second flick of her fingers turned on the lights above her.

The rhythmic thumping on the door had continued all this time, pushing Acacia's patience to the limit. *I notice that none of the dogs have come to see what I am doing which is unusual. I wonder where is my fearless Tiger?* Ripping open the front door, Acacia's jaw dropped as she was rooted to the spot in shock.

Standing on the doorstep was the body of Michael Casey, using his severed head in his hand to knock on her door. Blood oozed from the head, splashing all over Acacia, as it mumbled, 'The Lord is my shepherd, I shall not want, for he layth me down in green pastures…' As the hideous apparition approached her, with its arms extended, Acacia screamed.

With a heart-stopping jolt, Acacia sat up awake in her own bed. With a sigh of relief she began to realise that it had all been a nightmare. Taking a deep breath, Acacia threw back her bed covers and breathed another sigh to see that she was not stained with blood. Not wishing to disturb Ethan or worry him, Acacia slipped out of her bed and crept down the passage to the bathroom, intending to splash cool water upon her face. She hesitated before entering, hearing the sound of dripping, like a leaking tap.

Her latest dream had shaken Acacia so it's with considerable apprehension that she finally opened the door and reached across to manually switch on the light. A quick glance around, the bathroom appeared to be normal, it was in fact a leaking hand basin tap that she had heard. Relieved that it was as simple as that, Acacia stepped into the room and turned on the cold tap to splash her arms and face. Doing so, her eyes were closed and she didn't see the water suddenly turn blood red. It felt warmer too, which made Acacia look up into the mirror in front of her to find her face and arms dripping with blood.

'Sacred Mother! What's going on?'

The bathroom door slammed shut behind her and two figures materialised to block her exit. It was difficult to recognise the two corpses from the graves that morning, as their flesh was dripping away from its bones as if fire was eating away at them.

Acacia sighed. 'Let me guess, they haven't incinerated your bodies yet?'

For an answer, the creatures let out a hideous screech and began to close in on her. Acacia adopted a defensive mode.

'I'll take that as a yes!' Pressed against the hand basin, Acacia happened to glance down at the mess upon the bathroom floor from peeling flesh and she screwed up her nose.

'Gross! This could get pretty messy!' Absently she wiped the dripping blood from her face as she raised her other hand to the ceiling.

'*Gone be now this hex, broken be this curse, let the evil power, threefold be reversed!*' As Acacia spoke this spell three times, the creatures, for they were no longer human, exploded into thousands of little pieces.

Acacia's arms dropped wearily back to her sides. 'What a mess.' *I certainly don't feel like cleaning the bathroom at the moment.* So finding a lipstick in the cupboard under the basin, she wrote upon the mirror, 'Use other bathroom.' Although that was what she wrote, that was not what appeared on the mirror, as the words were reversed.

'I must be going mad!' Acacia frowned, until the truth hit her, 'Or dreaming again! The Protector would never have allowed those creatures into the house without a fight!'

Closing her eyes, Acacia took a deep breath before screaming with all her lung capacity. 'Jordan! Stay out of my mind!'

With a jolt Acacia found herself once more in her own bed, the door flying open as Ethan came running in.

'Ace? I heard you scream. What's wrong?'

Managing to sit up, Acacia studied him doubtfully. 'Is that really you, or am I dreaming again?'

In reply Ethan slapped her across the face. Her cheek stung where a red mark was already beginning to appear as Acacia sat momentarily stunned. Ethan sat on the bed, watching her, deeply concerned.

'Well that felt real enough!' Ethan laughed at Acacia's casual acceptance of being struck.

'It's not like you to have nightmares, Ace!' Acacia agreed, taking a long drink of water from the glass on the bedside table.

'Not without assistance, anyway. I think… I believe that Jordan is trying to control me through the dream world. Blur the lines of reality. To weaken my resistance against him. To stop me meeting Michael in our dreams.'

The morning air was quite cool so as Acacia briefly detailed her dreams to him, Ethan slipped under the bed covers beside her. With a brother's love, Ethan drew Acacia down into his arms and held her protectively.

'So how do we keep him out of our heads?'

A sigh shuddered through Acacia's body. 'Sleep as little as possible? No, we must learn to guard our minds against external control. You must be especially careful, Ethan, he may attempt to seduce you into believing that what he is doing is right.'

Instinctively, Ethan's arms tightened around Acacia. 'Once our chores here are done, I think we need to see Michael. It's time we set up a council of war.'

Acacia agreed. 'We might even be able to pin down this elusive Daniel. Until then, perhaps I should mediate to clear Jordan's influence from my mind.' She would have risen but Ethan refused to release her.

'We will win this battle you know!'

A tired smile answered him. 'Pure thoughts. Pure faith. Pure love!' Acacia just prayed that it was true.

Tuesday 29 October

Endless Night

Lightning flashed and thunder rolled as dark menacing clouds turned day into virtual night. Howling winds tore through the village from one direction and then another, but none of these climatic manifestations stopped the followers of Jordan from carrying out his orders. There were many preparations to take place as Halloween was but two days away. The cemetery had to be decorated, and a huge bonfire built on top of the hill and in general the village had to be prepared for the coming of their salvation. Or damnation as Acacia saw it.

Matthew Kane witnessed many of the preparations as he wandered through the village. *My fear for the future grows with a disgust of the animal behaviour being exhibited by the villagers.* Very few businesses were open and operating as many people were openly drinking, gambling or having sex wherever and whenever it took their fancy.

There are no children around, which I'd have expected to see as Jordan had announced that this week is to be a holiday for all to enjoy. Parents, though, were too preoccupied to properly care for their offspring so they'd readily agreed when Karen Greeves had suggested a sleep over at the high school gymnasium for all the children.

That had been Acacia's idea, of course, in the desperate hope to keep the innocence of the children free from the evil that was freely walking through their village. The older teenagers, especially Claudia and her friends had been more difficult to persuade and many remain in the village determined to enjoy all the depravity that was consuming their world.

Without displaying any particular emotion, Kane had accepted the strange events going on around him, but as Sergeant Boyd came up the street with a group of villagers in tow, the Constable's eyebrows rose in surprise. They all looked like they had slept in their clothes and several were carrying firearms.

The Sergeant drew Kane to one side to speak to him privately. 'Where do you stand, Matt?'

Kane looked left, then right, before he stated in a dead pan voice. 'At the moment, Sir, in the middle of High Street.'

There was a moment's hesitation as it looked like the Sergeant would explode but suddenly the older man began to laugh. 'You like living dangerously. Who are you answerable to?'

Kane's quick, searching eyes noted his boss's dishevelled appearance and the citizens carrying guns and he made a quick decision.

'I am loyal to my country, and my colleagues but I'm prepared to be neutral. If the Evil One is truly coming, then I'm hardly going to be able to stand in his way.'

Boyd studied him for a moment, the crowd behind him was getting restless, but the Sergeant ignored them. Finally he smiled, reassured. 'You're a strange one, Matt. What if we'd been a posse out to kill Jordan?'

Kane shrugged. 'Educated guess, Sir. It's pretty hard to resist the charm of the man.' There was general agreement about that.

'Well we're rounding up all who refuse to conform to Jordan's message and locking them safely in the cells. Their time of judgement will come, but we can't have them getting in the way in the meantime.'

Personally, Kane thought, *the cells might actually be a safe haven for the stronger willed villagers.* Making no attempt to stop his boss, Kane continued his walk through the village streets.

Panic Arises

A crisis was evident when Ethan and Acacia entered the Rectory. Villagers, who hadn't succumbed to Jordan's power were confused, scared and angry by the immorality that was befalling their loved ones, friends and neighbours, now surrounded Michael.

'What can we do to escape this fate?'

'What can we do to save our friends?'

'How can we stop the evil that is descending upon us?'

Michael was bombarded by question after question and actually looked relieved when Acacia came to his assistance. She had a very soothing nature and with the use of carefully chosen words, sympathetic noises and attentive listening, she managed to quieten the group to listen to her.

'Once Samhain has passed, the spell over your friends and family will be lifted. Your children are safe with Karen, and it is advisable that you either join them at the school or take refuge in the church. Do not attempt to confront Jordan, you'll only get hurt.'

Michael supported Acacia. 'We must all remain strong and remember that what eventuates in the end will be the will of God.'

At least the note of hysteria has eased. Michael sighed in relief. Some accepted the sanctuary of the church, whereas others decided to be with their children.

As the mass filed out of the building, Ethan had already headed over to the church and was helping to move the pews so that they could lay upon the floor blankets, mattresses, rugs and sleeping bags for those who wished to remain. It wasn't long after Acacia's speech that others joined Ethan to help. Acacia sighed wearily. *I didn't think that it would've been handled so easily.*

Marjorie, who had remained out of the way when the hysterical and angry mob had descended upon Michael, now appeared with an armful of blankets. Her face was alight with energy and purpose, as the crisis was the life's blood to her sense of duty as a Christian.

'I'll assist Ethan in setting up the church before I begin upon a substantial dinner that will feed all who seek our protection. Do you have any orders for me, Father?' Michael was overcome by the woman's obvious delight at being useful in a crisis and managed to shake his head.

'No, indeed, you must do as you see fit, Marjorie. I'll keep watch over Thomas until Daniel returns from the village. I think you'd better be prepared for many lost sheep.'

Marjorie refrained from clapping her hands in delight. 'Of course, Father, you can rely upon me.'

The woman waddled away and for a moment Michael and Acacia just looked at each other before they burst into laughter.

'We really shouldn't laugh,' stated Michael, 'her heart is in the right place, but it's just that her enthusiasm in a crisis does seem a little odd.'

Acacia smiled kindly. 'I think it is an enthusiasm for organisation and being in charge that drives Marjorie. Is there anything that I can do to help?'

Michael shook his head. 'Marjorie will let us know when she needs us. Meanwhile, we should talk to Daniel. Oh why didn't I see you last night in my dreams?'

'Jordan is bombarding my sleep with nightmares. I might not be able to sleep again until this is all over.' Acacia collected her cloak and promising to return soon, she headed back down to the village to find Daniel. *Not an easy task as I've never met him before but I have a feeling that this won't be a problem.*

Acacia's Strange Reaction

In preparation for feeding a large number of people, Marjorie had sent Daniel to the village to buy as much food as he could manage with the church kitty. Daniel was packing the last box of groceries into the back of Father Thomas' car when he saw Acacia heading down the street towards him.

There's no way that I can escape meeting her, but it's her reaction when she sees me that I'm worried about. Not that Acacia looks particularly frightening; in fact she looks quite adorable in a black skivvy, a wool tartan skirt and knee high boots.

'Oh my God!' The exclamation from Acacia was not said lightly and she began to sink to her knees in homage before Daniel.

'Wait!' Daniel's voice vibrated with authority as the single word froze Acacia's position. Daniel strode forward to grasp her shoulders and whispered urgently in her ear. 'Don't betray me, my child, we're not safe here! Protect my secret.'

'Anything, oh Cernunnos! You have but to command!' Acacia was unfrozen and fell into Daniel's arms. For a moment she closed her eyes and breathed in his scent. 'Oh how I have waited for this moment!'

A deep chuckle answered her as Daniel gently put her at arm's length. 'My child, you know that I'm a one Goddess man. Please don't offer me temptations that will destroy sweet harmony.'

Acacia looked at him wistfully. 'It wouldn't be the first time that a God mated with a mortal.'

Daniel shook his head. 'No Acacia, I foresee another man in your future.'

'No one could take the place of you!'

He laughed in delight as he gestured for Acacia to get into the car. 'I'm flattered, my child, but I think we should return to the Rectory. We have much to discuss.' Getting into the passenger's side Acacia couldn't argue with that.

Daniel's Identity Revealed

While Michael and the other villagers who had opted to stay were being organised by Marjorie, Ethan had slipped away to sit with Father Thomas. Mary was already there, entertaining Thomas with the results of the last school soccer match, which was an interest of the Priest's. He was awake, but utterly zoned out at times, even so he was glad to see the young couple.

Having assisted Daniel to bring in the boxes of food, Acacia quietly entered Thomas' room. 'Well! Did someone host a party and not invite me?' The room did seem quite crowded.

Smiling wearily Thomas held his hand out to Acacia. 'Dear Acacia, these children have been diverting an old and tired man.'

Acacia returned his smile, pressing the shaking hand that reached for her. 'Would you like to know a secret, Thomas? Or perhaps you already knew?'

Thomas slowly nodded his head. 'Daniel? Oh yes. I know. I saw it at once. It must be because I'm close to the end now.'

Daniel entered the room, and the result was instantaneous. Ethan dropped to his knees on the floor in front of Daniel, bowing down to the ground. Mary looked from Daniel to Ethan in surprise, as she was at a loss to understand Ethan's reaction until she squinted and stared very hard at Daniel. His image began to alter and blur around the edges; an aura of liquid gold surrounded him as huge fluffy white wings adorned his back.

'Oh my…' Mary also dropped to her knees and placed her hands together in prayer.

Daniel chuckled. 'So you still cling to your Christian beliefs? Otherwise you would have seen me as a horned God and not as an Angel.'

Mary squinted again, Daniel's image changing slightly again. This time, for a brief moment, Mary saw the Horned God.

Daniel touched Ethan's shoulder and ordered him to rise. 'As you see, I had to avoid you, for I knew my secret would be revealed the moment you or Acacia saw me. That would have been disastrous to my plans.'

Ethan offered Daniel, who was once more in human form, the chair, asking, 'Are you here to deal with Jordan?'

Daniel sitting down, crossed his legs at the ankles and shook his head. 'No.' His glance transferred to Thomas and his expression softened. 'My assignment is to see Thomas safely to his next life. He has a little task to perform and I'm here to assist him. There are those whom it would benefit to see Thomas ascend to his next destination before it is time for him to do so.'

Thomas nodded wisely. 'I've known this for some time. One final service to mankind.'

Acacia squeezed his hand. 'A grand finale?'

Thomas smiled. 'Now I think I'll sleep. You have much to plan and I must reserve my energy.' Obedient to the old man's wishes, the group filed out of the bedroom, and headed to the study.

Theological Explanation

Mary wore a puzzled frown. 'There is something I don't understand. How can you be an Angel and the Horned God? For one thing they're different religions, and they have a different standing within those religions.'

All eyes turned to Daniel as they settled down in the chairs in the study and Michael put away his sermon notes. The answer was to surprise them all. Daniel cleared his throat, his eyes meeting each of theirs in turn before he answered.

'Within all religions there is a belief that their God is the only true God. They are correct, all of them. There is one entity that we call, in one way or another, God, but it is the same entity, it just appears different to different people. It was easier for me to appear as an Angel, because many people have no idea what God does look like, so I adopted a form that you could easily associate with.'

'The Supreme Entity has two sides, a positive and a negative, good and evil if you like. Most of the time the positive can keep the negative under control but if the negative is called forth as it has been here, it must be humans who right the balance again. That is why I can only hold Jordan back rather than vanquish him. I must stop him from killing Thomas before he has a chance to fulfil his destiny. Jordan and I are each like an arm; we're a part of the Entity but not the whole of it. Does that make sense?'

There was a general look of bewilderment, but slowly each of them nodded. A twinkle entered Daniel's eyes as he read the varying degrees of satisfaction. *I'd known that the truth would be difficult to accept but they had asked for it.* Daniel allowed his words to sink in for a moment before he leant forward and drew their attention back to the business at hand. The Council of War had been called.

Task Force

The Council of War could do nothing to prevent the events that were going to happen from happening, but there were several strategies that they could employ when the events did occur. Michael was to spend the rest of the day rounding up others in the village who hadn't fallen under Jordan's spell and bring them up to the church. Marjorie would ensure that all had a bed and food.

It was essential that Daniel continued his vigilance over Thomas to protect him from harm. Acacia needed to discuss the autopsy with Matthew Kane, before she, Ethan and Mary attempted to contact the Family for any assistance that they could offer.

Seeing Matthew was as easy as walking into the police station. He was the only one there, as his Sergeant and the rest of his colleagues were still out on the streets ensuring that no one hindered Jordan's plans. Kane wasn't surprised when Acacia walked in with Mary and Ethan.

'I suppose you're here for the so called non-believers?' He led them down to the cells where a dozen people had been locked away. Acacia looked at the fear in these people's eyes and wondered, *Do they really know the trouble that is about to descend upon us?*

Acacia nodded. 'They'll be more comfortable at the church. Ethan and Mary can take them, I had something else to ask you.' Kane unlocked the cells and the villagers gratefully filed out.

'Follow Ethan and you'll be all right,' ordered the police officer. Like lambs, the villagers followed the teenagers out of the police station.

A quick glance around the cells assured Kane that no one was left inside before he led Acacia back to his desk.

'You want to know about the bodies I suppose.' He pulled up a chair for her as he sat down and sorted through a pile of papers.

'Not the gory details, just the highlights.'

'I do have a question I want answering Acacia,' Kane stated as he continued to hunt for the information Acacia wanted.

'Yes?'

'Why aren't we all raving lunatics by now? There shouldn't be this calm acceptance from believers and non-believers with the coming of the Devil, should there?'

Acacia shook her head as she sighed, suddenly feeling very tired. 'There has been hysteria, but nothing like you'd expect. That is the effect that Jordan will have over all people. It comes down to a matter of faith and how strong it presides in some people more than it does in others. Your non-believers have a stronger belief in their God than those who are following Jordan do. It is their belief in God that will give them the strength to see this through without becoming a complete fruit cake.' The relevant papers were finally found.

'As you said, their bodies were completely devoid of blood. The male body had been dead since last Thursday, the woman, only Monday. If the pattern holds, then it will be tomorrow that he'll need to kill again for blood.'

Acacia shook her head. 'It's not necessary for Jordan to place blood in his veins, he no longer needs to maintain the facade of being human. Was there anything else about the male victim, anything that may have been unusual?'

Kane flipped through his papers once more. 'Now that you mention it, there was something about the man. Now what was it…? '

Acacia gave a delicate cough. 'Was it something to do with his skin or determining his age?'

'That was it exactly! Determining the exact time of death was apparently a little difficult. According to the autopsy, the man should have been a couple of hundred years old, but he barely looked forty.'

'Thank you.' Acacia nodded solemnly and let out a sad little sigh.

'Does that mean something to you?' The Constable escorted Acacia to the front door.

She sighed again. 'Oh yes, that man was supposed to be Ethan's next Mentor. He should have possessed even greater powers than Ethan and myself combined.'

Kane looked horrified. 'Yet Jordan was able to kill him?'

'Yes.'

Kane took a deep breath and let it out very slowly. 'Then we could be in serious trouble?'

'Yes!'

A Distress Call

It is painfully obvious, now, Acacia mused, *that there is little that I and Ethan can do alone. We need guidance to our future actions and I realise that I'll have to risk possible death by attempting to contact the Family.* With the invisible and impenetrable wall now completely surrounding the village, it had been impossible to contact Family members while inside their home. *I'll have to risk an outside meditation, away from our protective force field, which will expose me to Jordan and his followers.* That was a risk Acacia was going to have to take but Ethan was not prepared to let her face that danger alone.

As soon as it was dark, well darker than it had been during the day, Acacia, Ethan and Mary, who went along as look out, left the farm by the back gate and headed down to the waterfall. The Tempests were dressed in white kaftans, and they lay a circle of blue candles in a small clearing. Once the candles were lit both Acacia and Ethan sat down, cross-legged within the circle. Their hands linked, their eyes were closed and with a low chant, they entered into a state of meditation while Mary watched over them.

'Sisters of Night, hear my plea, break through this evil barrier and come to me. Brothers of Cloak, send us your power, do not desert us in this desperate hour,' called Acacia.

For about an hour, Mary roamed restlessly around the circle, her eyes constantly alert and scanning the surrounding trees for any danger.

'Howl! How! How! Howl!' When the dog bayed, Mary half jumped out of her skin. The single dog howling was followed by other canines and appeared to be getting louder. Remembering her instructions, Mary extinguished all the candles and carefully removed Ethan's hands from Acacia's. She quickly knelt down and kissed Ethan hard upon the mouth. His eyes immediately opened.

'What is it?'

'Howl! How! How! Howl!' The dog's baying coming closer answered his question.

'Damn!' Ethan sprang to his feet, reaching out to touch Acacia's shoulder, but Acacia spoke before he managed to make contact.

'Run, both of you! Get back to the farm now!' Her eyes remained closed.

'I'm not leaving you!'

Acacia opened her eyes, so ablaze with power that it brought Ethan to his knees.

'I'm nothing, Ethan, I'll distract them while you escape. If something happens to me, if the protective barrier around our home fails, seek refuge with Michael.'

'Ace!' Ethan shook his head, trying to fight against Acacia's power.

'No! Just Go!'

Mary tugged upon Ethan's sleeve, as the sounds of the dogs grew closer. 'Acacia must know what she's doing.'

At the sound of human voices mingling with the dogs, Ethan suddenly turned on his heels and hitching up his kaftan, he and Mary ran back to the house. With a sigh of relief, Acacia closed her eyes again and waited.

Naughty Witch

A little shiver of fear ran down Acacia's spine as half a dozen men with rifles, blazing torches of fire and hounds, straining at their leashes surrounded her. Their rifles covered her, but none attempted to touch her, they were obviously waiting for orders. There was a flash of light and a puff of smoke, which announced Jordan's arrival. The mob impressed by his appearance moved aside and bowed their heads respectfully. Acacia, opening her eyes, remained calmly detached as she stood up.

'Naughty, naughty, Sweet Angel! I thought you would've realised the futility of defying me by now? No one can save you. You and this village are mine to do with as I see fit.'

Acacia dusted the grass off her kaftan. 'You're wrong, Jordan, give us time, we'll not only manage to withstand you, but we'll also defeat you!'

Jordan threw his head back and roared with laughter, a response that Acacia had not expected. 'Innocent one, you have no time! These simple morons are hankering for a hunt, so I'm going to give them one. A Witch Hunt!' Jordan checked the watch on his wrist. 'You have a ten minute head start.'

'You must be joking!' Acacia's jaw dropped in surprise.

Jordan did not look up from his watch. 'Nine and a half minutes.'

Acacia swallowed hard, picked up the hem of her kaftan and ran for her life.

The Hunt

Ten minutes did not get Acacia far, as she ran away from the farm, knowing that the Protector would be unable to withstand any assault made by Jordan and his men. She wanted to lead them away from Ethan and Mary. She ditched the kaftan, because unlike Claudia and her friends, Acacia was dressed underneath. The howl of the dogs was never far behind as Acacia weaved frantically through the trees.

The moon shone down sympathetically upon her, but granted her no assistance, as it's almost full form made it easier for the hunters to track her. Her heart pounded wildly in her chest, her lungs felt like they were about to burst, her damaged ankle screamed at the strain she was putting on it and even though she would never give up, there was no chance for escape, while those men fed off Jordan's immensely growing power.

'Howl! How! How! Howl!' *They're so close, too close for comfort. There's no time to cast any spells, not that I'm even certain that they would work with Jordan's influence over these men.* The pain in her ankle was unbearable, but Acacia ignored the pain and ran on.

An explosion erupted in front of her, spitting up dirt and branches, causing Acacia to be thrown backwards by the force of the blast. She struggled to sit up but the wind had been knocked out of her and she was unable to get to her feet before the dogs were upon her. Snapping, snarling jaws of teeth descended as one canine latched onto Acacia's leg.

'Get off Hound from Hell!' Acacia kicked the dog with her other foot, forcing it to release her but not before its teeth had sunk deep into her flesh causing a wound that made it impossible for Acacia to use that leg even if she could have stood.

The hunters finally caught up with the dogs and Acacia found herself looking up at the barrels of death. The men were breathing hard, a lot harder than she was; as they were definitely more out of shape.

'Well then? Get on with it! Or can't you pull the trigger without Jordan holding your hand?' Acacia sneered.

A hesitant glance was exchanged amongst the men; they had never killed another human being before. Acacia staggered painfully to her feet.

'Well?' Her chin went up in defiance, she would meet death bravely. Almost as one, they raised their rifles, so that it wouldn't be one particular man who actually killed her. Her confident smile put them off, but they aimed and simultaneously fired. Acacia took a deep breath and prepared herself for death, but it never came.

The bullets never hit her, stopping an inch away from her as if she was protected by an invisible force field. Acacia closed her eyes for a moment as she breathed a sigh of relief. The hunters looked at each other in confusion.

'Thank you, Cernunnos!' whispered Acacia.

A moonbeam shone down in front of Acacia, causing her to collapse to her knees as Daniel materialised before them. The men took a hasty step backwards but didn't immediately run, as Daniel reached out to touch Acacia's cheek with the tenderness of a father.

'You took a great risk, my child.'

'I had to know if the Family could be contacted, my Lord.'

Daniel nodded, assisting Acacia to her feet. 'I know. Go now, I'll deal with this.'

Evenly Matched

Turning to head back to the farm, leaning on a sturdy branch to support her weight Acacia limped straight into Jordan, his arms folded across his chest and looking very forbidding. The hunters quaked in their failure to kill Acacia. Jordan cast them only a brief glance.

'You can't get good help these days!' He waved them away, and the men and their dogs made good their escape to leave Daniel and Acacia alone with Jordan.

'Acacia, go home!' ordered Daniel, never taking his eyes off Jordan's face. Acacia moved around Jordan but he was not prepared to allow her to get away so easily and grabbed her arm.

'No! She is very much a part of this!'

Daniel reached out to force Jordan to release Acacia, but she had reacted just a little quicker, sinking her teeth into the arm that imprisoned her wrist. Instinctively Jordan released her as he cried out in surprise. Finally free, Acacia ran for safety, leaving Daniel to settle matters with Jordan, knowing that she would only be in his way.

In the woods, two great beings circled each other, assessing each other's strengths and weaknesses.

'You can't possibly hope to win against the likes of me?'

Daniel smiled at Jordan's arrogance. 'Funny, that's what I was thinking about you. You failed to turn Acacia; she was too powerful for you. That must have wounded your pride, bruised your male ego.'

'Damn you! No one can withstand my power for long!' With a snarl, Jordan launched himself at Daniel, taking him in a bear like grasp. Light erupted from both of them, flooding the area with brilliant illumination until it was so intense that they exploded out of their human forms and took their battle to the skies.

Thunder roared and lightning flashed like it had never done before. They were evenly matched; one being as powerful as the other, such a fight would be difficult to win. As if realising this, Jordan suddenly pulled away from Daniel and descended once more to earth to resume his human form. Daniel slowly followed suit.

'Very good! I'm impressed!' sneered Jordan. 'Trying to make me waste valuable energy in a pointless battle. But it won't work. We will succeed! No one can stop us now!' He turned and headed back to the village. Daniel shook his head as he watched him leave.

'We'll see! Time will tell!'

An Expensive Lesson

Ethan and Mary had been waiting for Acacia to return and were very concerned when she staggered into the house, in terrible pain. She patiently submitted to Ethan bathing and dressing her leg where the dog bit her before re-bandaging the sprained ankle. Deciding that it wasn't safe for Mary to go outside she stayed the night, in the spare bedroom, but Acacia would not allow herself to sleep.

Until daylight, she would sit motionless in her bedroom, in deep meditation. *I can't allow Jordan the opportunity to again take over my dreams. The fact that we've failed to reach the Family is a dreadful blow, but worse is the fact that Jordan will crucify us the first chance he gets.*

Ethan had tried to make light of their tense situation. *Actually I wish the hour of reckoning to come, as the waiting is interminable!* These reflections he kept to himself, Acacia had enough to worry about.

Wednesday 30 October

Eternal Darkness

It was about seven a.m. when Acacia became aware of the scent of hot tea and toast. Slowly opening her eyes, Acacia was confused by the lack of light in the room. *The sun should have risen but outside it is as dark as if it is the middle of the night.* Acacia stood up, stretched out her aching limbs and picking up the steaming cup of tea, she limped downstairs to the kitchen. Mary was drying the dishes and Ethan had just entered from outside.

'Ethan?' At the sound of Acacia's voice, he immediately assisted her into a chair.

'It's been like this since I got up.' He nodded towards the darkness outside.

Mary turned, wiping her hands on the tea towel. 'What does it all mean?'

Placing her cup on the table in front of her, Acacia sighed. 'I think it's the beginning of the Eternal Night. We may not see sunlight again until Sunday morning. If ever!'

Ethan sat down opposite Acacia, his hands tightly clasped together to prevent displaying his anxiety. 'What must we do, Ace?'

Looking from Mary to Ethan, Acacia shook her head. 'I don't know. I feel you'll be safer if you remain in the house. But you may be of service up at the church, helping Michael and Marjorie. I must seek an alternative source of assistance.' Making this decision, Acacia rose wearily to her feet.

Ethan's eyebrows rose. 'You're going to tap the Well of Experience?'

'Yes.' Acacia returned upstairs to her room to shower and dress.

Mary looked at Ethan with an obvious question in her eyes. 'What does that mean?' Ethan stood and took Mary into his arms.

'Where would you find the largest number of people with the most experience?'

'The retirement village, of course!'

Ethan kissed the top of her head. 'Exactly! Shall we go and give Michael a hand?'

Mary nodded; clinging to Ethan's hand. *I'm amazed by how brave he appears in the face of all that is yet to come.*

Man To Man Chat

Despite the darkness, the church was buzzing with activity. Marjorie had it all under control, the refugees had been fed and bathed and the breakfast dishes were being washed and put away until they were needed for lunch. Marjorie waved Ethan and Mary up to the Rectory, as she had more than enough people to organise and order about without needing their assistance.

The teenagers entered the Rectory via the kitchen door, to be welcomed by the melodious sound of a Welsh male choir. Ethan halted in his tracks, his eyes closed as he allowed the music to sweep over him, until every note sang through his veins. With a blissful sigh, Ethan opened his eyes again.

'Now that is music!'

Mary shrugged. 'I didn't know you liked that sort of thing.'

Ethan laughed. 'Music transcends all religion. Come on, let's find Michael.'

While Daniel watched over the sleeping Thomas, Michael was in the study, working upon Sunday's sermon. He worked industriously as his topic was about giving in to the wiles and temptations of the Devil and the perverted pleasures that he offers.

I only hope that we'll all live long enough for me to deliver the sermon on Sunday. Michael looked up pleased when Mary and Ethan knocked and entered the room.

'Come to shed some light in this darkness?' Michael's cheerfulness was a surprise considering their future.

Ethan smiled. 'Come to do what Acacia calls a good deed in a wicked world.'

That caused Michael to laugh. 'But when you got here, you found that Marjorie had everything under control? Yes, that's why I'm here, keeping out of harm's way.' He gestured for them to sit down in the straight-backed chairs opposite him.

'Actually,' Ethan began, a slight flush rising across his pale cheeks. 'I'd like to have a chat with you, you know, man to man.'

'Shall I go elsewhere?' Mary half rose again from her seat.

Ethan reached out and took her hand, lowering her back into her seat. 'No, no. It's about what we discussed this morning.'

'Oh!' This time Mary blushed which wasn't easy for someone of her colouring. 'In that case, I think I will leave and you can tell me the answer later.' This time she stood up and left the room before Ethan could persuade her to change her mind.

Pre-empting Ethan's question, Michael got in first. 'If you're after tips upon performance and prowess, then you've come to the wrong man. It's been way too long!'

'No, no,' reassured Ethan, feeling embarrassed about the whole subject. 'More a moral dilemma. I don't want to discuss how to, but should we. Mary and I… I mean. I know that we're legally of age and we hadn't planned on getting physical just yet in our relationship, but tonight might just be the last night for me here.'

Michael tried to protest but Ethan hadn't finished. 'I'm not being negative or giving up without a fight, but there is a chance that when all is said and done to protect the ones I love, I may have to go with Jordan. I just don't want to have any regrets about things that I never got to do.'

Michael leant back in his chair, pressed his fingers together as he considered what Ethan had said.

'Perhaps what you need to ask yourself is, will you regret pushing your relationship beyond what it is ready for, if we do succeed in foiling Jordan's plans? You're both becoming responsible young adults, but if you have any doubts, it is best not to do something that cannot be undone later.'

Slowly Ethan nodded his head. 'And if we decide to go through with it?'

As grave as a Judge, Michael looked sternly at Ethan. 'Then remember to satisfy her needs and desires first!'

Mary Is A Little Lamb

While Ethan was talking to Michael, Mary slipped out of the house into the garden. *The air is still and silent, as if the birds don't know what to make of the darkness.* As she considered this, Mary moved around the garden till she was opposite the bench. About to sit down, a deep masculine voice startled her.

'Mary, Mary, quite contrary, how does your garden grow…'

Mary spun around, her breath catching in her throat as Jordan suddenly materialised out of the darkness. 'What do you want Jordan?'

Jordan was dressed in a black suit and polo shirt. With the exception of his gleaming white teeth and glowing bright eyes, he was almost invisible in the false night.

'I've been waiting for you.'

Mary's eyebrows rose in surprise. 'Why?'

There was his deep chuckle. 'Can't you guess what I want you for?'

As her cheeks blazed, Mary was glad for the darkness. 'Well, you are blunt, aren't you? You're too old for me, even if I did find you the least bit attractive!'

Jordan drew in a quick breath. 'Here's honesty! You know your future don't you, little lamb?'

'I don't understand you!' Mary frowned.

Taking her hand, Jordan sat her on the bench and perched beside her. 'You're to be a famous mother, dear Mary, like the other Mary, your first born will be a Saviour. What sort of Christ or Antichrist will depend upon the man chosen to father that child?'

Mary inched away from Jordan as much as the bench would allow her. 'If you dare violate me, I shall not allow a child of your making to be born!'

'Your Christian values won't allow you to abort a child, a living being.'

Mary raised her chin in defiance. 'I will not support evil, or a child that is designed to destroy lives. I don't believe in abortion, but I do believe that there are sometimes mitigating circumstances, and rape is one of them!' She rose promptly to her feet and would have marched straight back into the Rectory, but Jordan grasped her wrist in a hold that wasn't only inescapable, but also painful.

'Brave words, little lamb, but could you suit action to words, I wonder? Are you prepared to die for a cause?' Into Mary's captured hand, Jordan pressed a jagged blade; similar to the one used on Jenny at the crossroads. Mary looked down at the dagger, so cold in her hand and yet so ornate and beautiful. Jordan released Mary's hand.

'Would my death at this moment gain anything?' She asked, returning her gaze to Jordan's face. A thought popped into her head, making her eyes gleam as she tightened her grip upon the dagger.

'Unless I was capable of taking something evil with me!' With a lightning movement, Mary's hand was raised and the dagger plunged directly through Jordan's heart.

Surprised by her own actions, Mary took a step backwards, her hands raised to cover her mouth in horror at what she had done. She looked up at Jordan stunned as he laughed and pulled the dagger out of his chest with little trouble and no blood loss. Within seconds the wound was healed.

'Good, quick reflexes, Mary, but as you see, I'm not that easy to kill. Now it's your turn.' Jordan placed the dagger back into Mary's hand. 'How indestructible are you, little lamb?' He guided Mary's hand, so that the dagger was pressed lightly against her left breast.

'Kill me within you!' He demanded.

Blood dripped from the point of the dagger as Mary fought against Jordan's power urging her to kill herself. Her hand shook violently as she could not stop herself from slowly driving the knife into her chest. The pain was excruciating and in despair, Mary screamed.

'You have... no power... over me!'

Jordan chuckled. 'Then why are you sinking a blade into your own breast?'

Mary took a deep breath, closed her eyes and she began to pray, '*To you, O Lord, I lift up my soul; in you I trust, O my God. Do not let me be put to shame, nor let my enemies triumph over me. No one whose hope is in you will ever be put to shame, but they will be put to shame who are treacherous without excuse.*' As her self-control began to return, she threw the dagger to the ground, pressing her hand against the half-inch wound that had resulted above her left breast.

'I think that you should leave now, Jordan.' Although still defiant, her words were little more than a whisper. Taking a step back as Jordan reached out for her, Mary held out a forbidding hand to hold him off.

'Don't come any closer! Touch me and I'll scream.' This threat did little to deter Jordan, but a protest from behind Mary had more effect.

'Don't be so sure of your welcome, Jordan. When Mary says no she means no. You'll have me to answer to if you distress her further.' A serious Ethan strode across the lawn to join Mary. Although Jordan smiled, he refrained from laughing, as Ethan was deadly serious.

'Are you threatening me, little man? I don't advise it. Your powers can hardly match mine and you will be sadly at a disadvantage.'

'Don't bet on it, Jordan!' Ethan folded his arms across his chest. 'You've yet to see the full extent of my powers.'

Jordan held up one of his hands in a mock submissive manner. 'Maybe I'll get a chance to see just what you can do tonight. Till then!' With a theatrical flash of smoke, Jordan vanished, leaving a feeling of dread behind him.

Tenderly, Ethan checked Mary's wound and was satisfied that it was not too serious.

'You did well, Mary. I'll ensure that you're not left alone again.' He removed a clean handkerchief from his jeans pocket and pressed it firmly against the bleeding wound. 'The wound isn't deep, but I think we'll see a doctor any way, before we head home.'

Mary didn't protest, but she did have one question as they left the Rectory garden. 'What will happen tonight, Ethan?' For a moment, he did not answer and they walked on in silence.

'I don't exactly know, but according to what Ace read in that Book of the Nephilim, Eleanor's baby will be sacrificed for the coming of the Master of Evil. If we fail to prevent his arrival, then Hell could be unleashed upon the earth. If we do succeed, I may still be forced to go with Jordan. I don't know whether he'll leave the rest of the village or take them with him. Anyway, this may be my last…' Ethan found that he could not finish his sentence.

'It won't happen Ethan!' Mary wrapped her arms around Ethan's waist. 'I won't let them take you away!'

Ethan tightened his hold on her. 'We may not have a choice. Acacia is working on a plan, we just have to be patient.' No more would Ethan speak upon the subject as he led Mary into the Doctor's surgery.

Insurance

When Ethan and Mary had left the Rectory garden, a figure moved cautiously through the darkness to where the blood stained dagger lay upon the grass. The figure silently examined the dagger before carefully wrapping it in a handkerchief without wiping any of the blood off and carrying it away.

Well Of Knowledge

Far from working confidently upon a plan, Acacia was feeling very low and depressed. Usually when she visited the retirement village, she experienced an exchange that wasn't only pleasurable but also profitable. From the elderly, Acacia received their knowledge, experiences and wisdom; and in return they received her youthful energy and ability to heal and ease pain. Today, though, due to the lack of sleep and excessive worry, her energy levels were seriously depleted. The usual sunshine that she added to the place was not evident, and was more noticeable with the eternal darkness outside.

So used to helping others, Acacia was surprised when her elders flocked supportively around her. Captain James Ashworth organised a cup of tea and saw that Acacia was seated in a comfortable chair in their common room as the other residents gathered around her, the possibility of being useful again stirred their aging blood. The Naval Captain pressed a steaming cup of tea into her hands before sitting down beside her.

'Now, my girl, open the budget! We know that something has been going on in the village and you and Father Michael have been pretty quiet about the whole thing. Now you've got yourself into a bind and have come to us for advice. So what has been going on, and what can we do?' Acacia looked around at the wisdom that surrounded her and with a deep sigh, knew that she had done the right thing by coming here.

With as few words as possible, Acacia explained the events of the past two weeks, glossing over certain details that were highly embarrassing and personal such as her Saturday encounter with Michael and their intimate dreams. When she was finished, a pin drop could have been heard, the silence was so overwhelming. Not a word was said as Acacia's story was sinking in, and the vast storage of wisdom was being put to use.

Mrs Carpenter had a question. 'Why haven't we been affected by these demonic carry-ons?'

Acacia took a drink of her tea before answering, wondering, *how do I word it tactfully?* 'All here are in a stage of life called the Blessed. When you reach a certain age, you gain a special protective coating, if you like, from anything paranormal. Any non-mortal interference of the Blessed just doesn't work. This is the Goddess's way of protecting those who may be about to join her in a new life.'

There was a murmur of confusion throughout the group.

'Does that mean that we're all going to die?'

Acacia smiled gently. 'We're all going to die sooner or later, but being a Blessed can last up to thirty years or so, especially with the greatly increased ability these days to live longer. Usually it begins about seventy, and remains with you until it is time to pass over into the next life.'

Captain Ashworth quelled the idle chatter. 'Very interesting, but what can we do to help you, Acacia?'

She covered her eyes with one hand in weariness and gave a tiny sob. 'I don't know what to do! Ethan must be protected, but I must rescue Eleanor and send the Master back to where he belongs. Even if he is sent back, there is still Jordan to be dealt with and I just don't think that I can do this on my own.'

'What you need, my girl, is a plan of action!' The others agreed with the Captain's suggestion. 'Firstly, you must decide what is going to occur first, and deal with that, then deal with the next thing. There is no point jumping from one job to the next as nothing will get completed, you'll just exhaust your energy and you will certainly lose. Now tell us again what is going to occur and in what sequence do you expect them to occur.'

Acacia put down her cup and concentrated on the task ahead of her. Slowly and concisely they went through the problems that Acacia faced and how they could be handled.

Show Time

The only distinction between day and night was the fact that the full moon became almost as bright as a beacon to cast an illumination across the village as the wind died and everyday noises became non-existent. From the sanctuary of the Rectory, Acacia, Ethan, Mary and Michael watched as the villagers, dressed in black cloaks, and walked mesmerised up to the graveyard.

Amongst the tombstones, Jordan had set up an altar for the ritual sacrifice, as Claudia and her entourage arranged their circle of black candles nearby. The girls were once more attired in their black kaftans and were very excited about being a part of such an event.

A large, muscular figure, also dressed entirely in black, slipped almost invisible between the buildings, silently following the villagers, stalking them, waiting patiently as he crept closer for the right moment to strike. A couple of stragglers were caught lagging behind, the large pursuer slamming their heads together, knocking them unconscious before dragging them into a dark secluded area. Emerging, he had their cloaks thrown over his shoulder as he sought more prey.

This is the sort of action that I've been waiting for. This afternoon, Acacia had come to me, promising I could be a part of Eleanor's rescue, so long as I didn't mind a little fighting and more importantly, that I followed her orders to the letter. Mac had agreed readily, *what man with Scot's blood and the Navy in his veins would've said 'no'?* Right now, he was to take out a couple of villagers so that they could have their cloaks and thus they could all move undetected through the followers of Jordan.

With enough cloaks for everyone, Mac stealthily but reluctantly rejoined the team in the Rectory sitting room. *I would've liked to have knocked a few more of Jordan's followers unconscious.* There was a glow to his cheeks and a gleam in his eyes, a clear indication that Mac had enjoyed himself more than he perhaps should have done.

'Och lass! If ye be pulling off this caper, I'll be calling the baird after ye!' Mac handed out the cloaks; his attitude was predisposed that they would succeed.

'Even if the child is a boy?' Michael grinned mischievously.

Mac looked at the priest as if he had lost his mind. 'Of course not Father! What a daft name for a boy, think on! It'd have to be Ace if it was a boy!'

The cloaks were slipped on and the hoods pulled down to cover their faces. Acacia looked at them each in turn.

'You all know what to do?' There was a general nod.

'Daniel will remain here to protect Father Thomas until it's time for them to join us. Good luck!' They slipped out through the side door and joined the massing people in the graveyard. Acacia's group split up, each had a different job to do, and the most important of all was to get as close to the front as possible without being recognised or discovered.

Claudia and her girlfriends stood in a circle around the ring of candles, their hands joined, chanting the previously unknown second half of the spell that Jordan had given them, that would call forth the

Master of Evil. Nathaniel was nowhere to be seen, as he had been emphatic that he did not want to be involved.

Jordan was to perform his own ceremony. Standing over his makeshift altar, Jordan raised both hands causing the sky to rumble and lightning to flash. Out of the clouds, demons descended, carrying between them the sleeping body of Eleanor Macbeth. She was now no longer only three months pregnant but ready to give birth.

Mac would have immediately rushed to his wife's side but one look from Acacia quelled his rash thought. There was a time and a place for everything and Mac pulled himself together, remembering that he had a job to do. Ethan and Mary edged through the crowd towards Claudia's circle. It had been thought best to keep Ethan as far away from Jordan as possible and he was more than capable of dealing with Claudia without assistance.

The demons holding Eleanor pinched her several times to wake her. Opening her eyes to find Jordan standing over her, a large dagger in his hand held over her stomach, Eleanor did what any woman would do… she screamed.

The sound was a knife through Mac's heart and only with extreme effort did he stop himself from leaping into action. *Acacia had been very specific about what I could and could not do as my actions were a vital key to the successful rescue of my wife.* The villagers mindless chanting rose over Eleanor's scream and yet it was burnt into Michael's brain.

I've never heard such terror before and pray to God that I never will again. Acacia gently nudged Michael out of his momentary loss of concentration as they edged their way towards the altar.

'*Try to block it out Michael!*' thought Acacia, her own face showed the strain she was under, although she appeared outwardly remarkably in control. Once in position, Acacia glanced across at Mac and nodded her head. Jordan, unfazed by Eleanor's screaming, called for his Master.

'*Come Master, Take the energy from the unborn, Privilege your humble servants with your presence, Bring chaos to the unworthy!*'

Michael laid his hand upon Acacia's arm as she dragged in a deep unsteady breath. '*Ready?*'

Michael nodded and pushed forward to the front of the crowd with Acacia by his side.

The Rescue

'Look! He's coming!' The cry from the crowd caused all heads to turn to where the finger was being pointed. Against the backdrop of the trees, a vertical vortex appeared that opened up to another dimension.

On cue, Mac burst through the crowd, throwing off his cloak in a fit of madness. With a warrior's cry, Mac began attacking the people around him as they tried to keep him from reaching the altar. Jordan turned, angry at having been disturbed, his knife changing direction to aim purposefully at Mac as a half a dozen men wrestled him to a standstill.

'Futile Macbeth! You shall join your wife and child in death!'

Mac only laughed. 'Go To Hell!'

During the distraction, Ethan and Mary had jumped upon Claudia and her girlfriends, breaking their circle in the hope to weaken the vortex and prevent the Devil from coming through. Although the vortex flickered for a moment, it was too late to stop it retaining its form. The demons were also distracted by Mac's performance long enough for Acacia and Michael to get close to Eleanor.

Acacia threw a smoke bomb to cover their actions as Michael punched a demon in the face forcing it to release Eleanor. The other demons shrunk away, screaming, from the altar as Acacia threw a spell of righteousness at them. Between them Acacia and Michael got Eleanor to her feet before Jordan became aware of their actions. With a roar, Jordan swung around, the blade in his hand glistening wickedly in the moonlight. Acacia placed herself between him and Eleanor.

'How dare you interfere in my ceremony? You'll pay for this Sweet Angel!' His approach was full of menace.

'Not if I can help it!' Mac broke free from his captors and a flying kick landed squarely in the middle of Jordan's back. Seizing the moment of confusion as Jordan collapsed to the ground, Acacia turned her head to instruct Michael.

'Get Eleanor to the church!' Mac ran up to hug his wife but didn't leave with them to seek sanctuary in the church.

'Your job is done Mac.' Acacia was surprised when he remained beside her. The big Navy man shook his head.

'I'm done when this devil's spawn is back where he belongs!'

Jordan rose slowly to his feet, his anger evident in the look that he cast around him. Only when his eyes lighten upon Ethan did his expression ease.

'So the protégé has come to meet his new Master! Shall you join him tonight, little man?'

'Not tonight, Jordan. Not if I can help it!' Out of the darkness, stepped Constable Matthew Kane, a gun held in either hand. He looked like a gun fighter out of a Western movie, but no one was laughing for Kane was deadly serious.

'Get behind me, Ethan.' Kane ordered.

Glancing across at Acacia, who simply nodded, Ethan obeyed the policeman, taking Mary with him. Not at all pleased, Sergeant Boyd pushed back the hood of his cape as he made his way to the front of the crowd.

'You promised not to interfere!'

Kane shook his head. 'Devil worship is one thing, killing an innocent child is another! If you want to go to hell, then be my guest, but don't take the innocent with you.'

Jordan strode purposefully towards the Constable, not at all worried by his weapons. 'You have no jurisdiction here. You can't hurt me, but I can make your life a misery.'

Although he swallowed hard on a moment of fear, Matthew Kane did not back down. *There are just some things that I cannot condone.* Their eyes locked and held, Kane refusing to submit. Acacia moved cautiously forward, wondering, *Are we in for a major staring competition?* The ground beneath their feet began to tremble. Smoke poured forth from the vortex as it began to spin violently in an anticlockwise pattern.

The Battel Between Good And Evil

'Oh no!' cried Acacia, her eyes flying to where Ethan stood protecting Mary. *Here's trouble! Mega trouble!* With a triumphant cry, Jordan turned to the vortex, his hands thrown up into the air.

'Father! I welcome you!' A tall, slender man, in his mid-forties stepped out of the smoke.

'My son, it is good to once more be free to walk this earth! My appetite has increased tenfold, I hope you have some worthy disciples for me to sample?'

Kneeling down in front of his Master, Jordan pressed the older man's hand against his lips. 'You'll have a choice of some very pretty women, Father.' With a wicked laugh, Jordan rose to his feet. 'Some of the young men aren't bad either! I promise you that you'll enjoy what has been prepared for your entertainment.'

'That's disgusting!' Matthew's protest caught them all by surprise. 'Hey, I'm all for freedom of choice, but half these people have been brainwashed into believing that you're some kind of Saviour. They wouldn't know if their arses were on fire unless Jordan told them! We don't need you, or what you offer, so just fuck off back to where you came from!'

Acacia groaned in disbelief. *Kane has as good as sealed his own death sentence.* The Master of Evil looked at Kane in disapproval before raising his eyes to Jordan's face.

'I thought you had everything under control? Never mind, he won't worry us for long. Kill him!' A stunned silence followed the Devil's words as Jordan turned to obey his command. Kane swallowed hard but stood his ground, and Acacia was about to step forward when Mac grabbed her arm and pulled her back. His attention had been caught by the sudden appearance of a light from behind the assembled group.

'Acacia, look!' She wasn't the only one to follow the direction of Mac's finger, the whole crowd turned to see what was causing such brilliant illumination. Even Jordan paused in placing his hands around Matthew Kane's throat.

The light grew stronger and the crowd parted to allow it to move through the middle of those gathered without hindrance. Tears glistened in Acacia's eyes as the illuminating figure of Daniel Hamilton escorted the newly dead spirit of Father Thomas O'Brian towards the vortex. The power of Daniel's radiance brought those gathered to their knees and a groan to Jordan's lips.

'I had hoped that we would've been further established by the time you arrived. Even so, I don't see what you can do alone against our combined power.' Jordan stepped back to join his Master. Acacia removed her arm from Mac's grip and moved to join Thomas.

'They're not alone.'

'Ace, no!' Ethan tried to rush out to pull Acacia away, but Mary held him back.

Jordan smiled. 'Sweet Angel, you're always a constant amusement to me. But even you are not beyond my influence.'

'But we are, my boy!' The commanding voice of Captain Ashworth boomed through the cemetery as he and a dozen other elders from the retirement village made their slow and painful progress to join Acacia.

'You shouldn't be here, it's too dangerous! Please, I don't want your lives upon my conscience.'

The Captain kindly took one of her hands. 'Dear child, we've lived full lives, one way or another, and many of us will be grateful to be finally free from pain and an undignified life that age has forced upon some of us.'

'Besides which, my dear,' Mrs Carpenter took Acacia's other hand in her frail grip. 'Even if we're a little premature, you promised us youth, health and beauty once more when we cross over.'

'But…'

The Captain did not allow her to finish. 'Let us be heroes one more time, Acacia. Let us go out in a blaze of glory and not completely broken by pain and suffering.'

'I can't stop you.' Nor could Acacia stop her tears but managed to nod.

'There was never any chance of that!' Captain Ashworth grinned like a schoolboy. 'Macbeth, hold her until we're gone!'

'Aye, Aye Captain!' Mac saluted the retired Naval Officer, firmly grasping Acacia's arms to keep her from joining the group of elders.

A smile of indulgence had played about the Master's mouth while this had been going on. *I'm amused by the presumptive beliefs that I'll be so easy to get rid of, but I've dealt with mortals many times before in the previous eons.*

'So you intend to send me back, do you? Well I'm afraid even the Blessed cannot achieve that miracle.'

Despite this warning the elders began to surround the Master of Evil. For the first time since arriving in the cemetery, Father Thomas spoke, 'I am more a threat to you than you realise, Satan. The Lord teaches us that there is good and evil in all of us, and that it is a constant battle for good to dominate, sometimes it does not succeed. As a representative of God, of goodness, I am your other half; together we make a whole. To defeat these people you must first defeat me.'

Jordan laughed. *For eons, men like Thomas have come up against my Master and always lost.* The Master was not worried.

'A lifetime ago, before my descent in disgrace, I sat beside God in Heaven. Before our Father created you mortals I was his favourite. Despite my fall I am still an Archangel. Are you an Archangel Thomas? Daniel may or may not be a match for Jordan but he has no power to vanquish me. I have no need to defeat the people in this village, Thomas, as they're already mine to command. Neither Jordan nor I can touch the Blessed, but they can. Have you considered that?'

Thomas obviously had not, nor had the other elders who looked at the Captain a little alarmed. Thomas, strong in his faith, only smiled.

'I do have something that might interest you.' He slipped his hand under his cassock and withdrew a blood stained dagger. Jordan thought he recognised it from his earlier encounter with Mary in the Rectory garden. The blood was Mary's, and as Thomas calmly pointed out, that was the blood of a virgin.

Daniel grinned mischievously. 'Your little show down with Mary and the dagger in the garden gave me an idea. So I asked our brother Michael to borrow one of his toys.' Involuntarily everyone looked at

Michael but Daniel kept his gaze tauntingly upon Jordan's face. 'No, no, not Michael the priest, but Michael the Archangel. Mary kindly donated some more of her blood. You do remember Brother Michael don't you Lucifer? He was the one who cast you out of Heaven. He or his appointed champion can send you straight back to Hell.'

The confidence that Satan had portrayed up until that moment crumbled a little as he took a hasty step backwards. Jordan attempted to jump between his Master and Thomas, but found Daniel efficiently blocking his way. As they struggled, so evenly matched, Thomas drove the dagger through Satan's heart, murmuring, 'God forgive me for what I do, and welcome me into your embrace.'

With intent purpose, Thomas' spirit stepped into the Master's body, becoming one with him. Then the struggle began. Good battled Evil as one tried to dominate over the other. The figure, Satan/Thomas thrashed about, arms flinging everywhere and the elders looked at each other, uncertain what they should do. Acacia came to their rescue.

'Form a circle around them, join hands and sing.' The first part was easily arranged, but what to sing. Acacia shook her head. 'Something religious with a good beat.'

There was another moment's pause before Captain Ashworth cleared his throat and began to sing. 'Onward Christian soldiers, marching as to war. With the Cross of Jesus going on before.'

By this stage the rest of the Blessed had joined him. Jordan cried out as if in agony.

'That is torturous!'

Daniel still battling Jordan, only grinned. 'A bit off key, but it's not that bad!'

Jordan refrained from answering as the Satan/Thomas figure suddenly went very still. The singing stopped and the assembled crowd held its breath, waiting to see who had finally won. Even Jordan and Daniel ceased to wrestle. Acacia was the only one who dared to speak.

'God speed you on your new journey, Thomas.'

Satan/Thomas smiled across at her. 'You never doubted me?'

She returned the smile. 'No, only myself.'

'Forgive me my child as I am the one responsible for you and Michael meeting in your dreams. I knew neither of you could speak openly about your feelings in the real world. And I just knew that you needed to give any relationship a fight chance.'

'Thank you Thomas… we'll see…' Even in the moonlight Acacia could not hide how her cheeks flamed. 'Unfortunately the ring surrounding you cannot be broken before you enter the vortex.'

The Blessed understood exactly what she meant and began to move towards the vortex, still surrounding Satan/Thomas. Kane couldn't believe that Acacia would let these people walk away to their deaths.

'Is there nothing you can do?' He demanded.

Her eyes met his and with tears in her eyes she shook her head. 'The Blessed are beyond my powers if it is refused. I must allow them to take the road that they have chosen.'

Silence followed the departure of the Blessed and Satan/Thomas and not until the vortex closed and vanished completely did Daniel finally release Jordan. He joined Acacia, embracing her as Mac finally released her arms.

'It's also time for me to leave you. I too must apologise as I have been the one preventing you and Michael from getting physical in your dreams. In time you'll come to understand why. You've done well, Acacia of the Tempest, and you will succeed if you follow your heart.'

With a wave of his hand to Mary and Ethan, Daniel began to ascend into the sky and in a flash of light returned to his heavenly home.

Thwarted Again

A feeling of apprehension came over Acacia as she turned to face Jordan, waiting for him to pass sentence for her interference. To say that Jordan was angry would be an understatement of the century, but Acacia kept her chin up, prepared to face her punishment with a brave countenance.

'You've become an annoyance, Sweet Angel. I cannot afford to allow you to stand in my way again.' Jordan's hands reached out and encircled Acacia's throat. With a simple twist of his fingers, Jordan would break her neck, cleanly and swiftly. Jordan dragged in a shuddering breath as if he was preparing for the ultimate sexual experience for him.

'This I'm going to enjoy!'

Mac attempted to push Jordan away from Acacia, but the Devil's servant was not prepared to play games any more. He hit out at Mac, sending him flying half way across the cemetery. Jordan's hands returned to Acacia's throat, she made no attempt to fight as Jordan's fingers tightened and then hardened into immobility. Surprise swept across Jordan's face as he found that his hands were frozen and beyond his control.

'You don't have the power to do this!' Jordan yelled into Acacia's face causing her to flinch.

'No, I don't.' She whispered.

Laughter came from an unexpected source. Mary held her hands in the air in the exact same position that Jordan held around Acacia's throat, her fingers were as rigid as Jordan's. With a wicked smile, Jordan found himself actually amused by the situation.

'So the little lamb has unsuspected talents! But for how long do you think you can keep up the concentration? As soon as you relax, I will kill her.'

'Not tonight!' Ethan was suddenly standing right behind Jordan. He reached one hand up to Jordan's neck and locating certain important pressure points; Ethan eased Jordan down to the ground, unconscious. Acacia drew herself out of Jordan's grasp and tenderly rubbed her throat.

'He'll be out for a couple of hours,' stated Ethan, looking casually at the still assembled crowd. 'Shall we send them off home?' He added.

Acacia agreed. 'Good idea. I think Eleanor will need my assistance, so why don't you go back to the farm and try to sleep? With Jordan still here, tomorrow may still be a nightmare.'

Like obedient sheep, the crowd wandered home. Matthew Kane followed them to ensure that they all got to where they were supposed to be. Ethan was reluctant to leave Jordan unrestrained, but as Acacia pointed out, there was nothing that they could do about him until midnight of Samhain. Resigned to the fact, Ethan took Mary's hand and they headed down to the farm. An excited Mac was already at the church door and Acacia had to run to catch up with him.

A New Life

From the Sacristy came the sounds of heavy breathing punctured by the occasional cry of pain. On a mattress on the floor, Mac found his wife propped up by a bank of pillows, Michael's hand being crushed by Eleanor's as Marjorie prepared a towel under Eleanor's bent and spread legs and spoke gentle words of reassurance.

'Mac! Acacia!' At Eleanor's cry, they both dropped to the floor either side of Eleanor and Mac took the hand that Michael had been holding while Acacia took the other.

'We're here, love. All will be grand!'

Marjorie, a mother of five adult children, nodded in a professional manner. 'In a minute, Eleanor, I want you to push as hard as you can.'

Tears streamed down Eleanor's face. 'I can't! I don't have the strength.'

Marjorie glanced up at Acacia for assistance but she was already unbuttoning the first couple of buttons of her own dress. Acacia pressed Eleanor's hand against her heart and took a deep breath.

'Take strength from me, Eleanor, and give me your pain. Remove this pain and give Eleanor strength, for this child's sake I will go to any length.'

Michael watched in awe as a glow surrounded Acacia, growing brighter for a minute before beginning to travel down Eleanor's hand and then her arm before completely embracing Eleanor's whole body. Eleanor's tears ceased as Acacia gave a sharp, sudden gasp as she eased Eleanor of her pain by taking it upon herself. It was the only sign that Acacia gave of the strain that it was taking on her body and Michael prayed that she would not take on more than she could handle.

'Now, my dear, push!' Instructed Marjorie. 'Breathe now, that's it! Push again.'

Before my very eyes a life is being born, mused Michael, *and I am humbled by the experience.* With one last push came the cry of the new born, tears of joy this time adorned Eleanor's face as Marjorie tied and severed the umbilical cord and cleaned the blood away from the child before handing the precious bundle to her mother.

'A little girl! Congratulations Mr Macbeth!'

Eleanor looked up at her husband in doubt. 'You don't mind that she's not a boy?'

Mac looked down adoringly at the two women in his life and knew himself to be the luckiest man in the world. 'Don't be daft, love! You're both here, alive, that's all that matters.' He gently kissed his wife's forehead and tenderly touched the tiny hand of his child.

As soon as the little girl had begun to breathe on her own, Acacia had released Eleanor's hand and her body slouched in exhaustion. While the Macbeth family enjoyed the first minutes of their daughter's life, Acacia staggered to her feet and headed for the external door. Michael met her half way and giving her a supportive hand, assisted her out into the fresh night air.

'Are you all right?' His concern deeply touched Acacia and she managed to smile wearily.

'Nothing a week of sleep wouldn't cure! Marjorie will keep watch over mother and child until proper medical care can be guaranteed. Get some rest, Michael, we may have won this battle but we have not yet won the war.' Acacia started in the direction of home, but Michael retained a firm grasp of her hand.

'Is it safe for you to go alone?'

Her shoulders shrugged. 'You're needed here. I'll be all right. Blessed Part Michael.' The words seemed so final but obediently Michael turned back into the church as Acacia made her weary way home.

Time For Punishment

A sudden chilling breeze brushed across Acacia's cheeks and stirred her hair from her shoulders. Acacia stopped walking, she wasn't far from the cemetery, but she didn't turn around as the air swept across the nape of her neck.

'Is it now time to die, Jordan?' Acacia remained quite calm as a pair of hands descended around her throat. As Jordan laughed harshly, he removed his hands again.

'I've decided on a different punishment for you, Sweet Angel. I've got a taste for male virgin flesh but I'm prepared to compromise…'

Acacia spun around in disgust. 'You bastard! You couldn't get me any other way, so you're going to use Ethan against me! I know you're not bluffing, but damn it all, no, I won't let you get what you want!'

The wicked laughter that rang out as Jordan wrapped his arms about her waist was like a slap in the face. 'My Sweet Angel, I could take you both! You'd have no means of stopping me but I did half promise the boy to the Master. Right now, though, I'm seriously pissed off, and as they say, I want my pound of flesh one way or another.'

'No! I can't do it! Not even to save Ethan! I'll fight you if you attempt to touch me!'

'So be it!' Jordan shrugged in indifference.

As he grabbed hold of her arms Acacia scratched her nails down his cheek to make him release her and tried a spell.

'Great Goddess protect me from this evil with your shield, Give me the strength I need to defeat the wicked powers that he does wield.'

With one hand Jordan wiped the blood from his cheek while still retaining a painful grasp on Acacia's arm.

'No effect, my sweet one. Try again.'

Swallowing hard, Acacia began to fight against him with both her hands and feet as she recited, *'Send this demon back to Hell. Make sure he can no longer dwell, in this place of love and joy. To defeat what evil he may deploy.'*

A kick to his groin actually hurt him, causing him to lose the last of his patience. 'Enough woman! Your spells are useless against me! So just be quiet.'

Acacia opened her mouth to speak but found that she had no voice at all. *I don't need to be able to say the spells aloud!'*

'*Spells be Gone!*' Jordan temporarily wiped all knowledge of her Craft from Acacia's mind. And now that she couldn't even scream for help, all she could do was fight. Which she did with what little strength she had left.

Painful Lesson

In no mood to be gentle, Jordan swept Acacia's feet from under her so that she fell on her back amidst the gravestones. The breath was knocked out of her, giving Jordan the opportunity to pin her down with his own body before she could regain her fight. The front of Acacia's dress was torn away in his impatience and her bra straps were yanked down to reveal her desirable breasts. Having managed to easily restrain her pounding hands in one big hand, Jordan's mouth covering Acacia's in one of his soul-searing kisses, as she could not help groaning silently in disgust and attempted to bite his lips to cause him pain.

As Acacia continued to thrash wildly beneath him, trying to throw him off, trying to get her hands free so that she could fight him and to knee him again in the groin, his blistering lips trailed regardless down her throat and across her shoulder. One of his hands lowered to tear away her knickers. In a moment of savagery, Jordan's teeth sank deeply into Acacia's shoulder, not a gentle nip but a flesh tearing bite that had Acacia throwing her head back and silently screaming in agony. A hungry, self-satisfied smile covered Jordan's face as his fingernails tore into Acacia's flesh, her arms, her stomach and across her back.

In preparation, Jordan only undid the zipper of his trousers to release his massive erection before he thrust deep into her. Once again Acacia screamed in silence, as more than seven years of abstinence meant that she was not prepared for the savagery of Jordan's possession, especially with no preparation or foreplay. As blood dripped from her shoulder, and tears fell down her face, Jordan was ensuring only his own pleasure as he thrust harder and faster and more ruthlessly into her. *I am going to ensure that Acacia will remember this lesson for a very long time.*

Jordan's anger meant that his endurance was going to be short. When Acacia felt that he was about to shoot his load, she fought even more frantically against him to get him to withdraw, but Jordan only laughed, crushing her struggles beneath him.

'Do you think that I don't realise that my seed will make you mine? By saving Ethan tonight from me, you've just handed him to me tomorrow. You won't be able to stand against me! Ah, Yes!' Jordan buried his head into Acacia's breasts as he came, his pleasure heightened by the knowledge of his success. *I've finally conquered Acacia's resistance, even if it had to be done with extreme force.*

This time when Acacia pushed him away, Jordan rolled off and came easily to his feet, fixing his trousers as he looked down appreciatively at Acacia, sobbing silently as she attempted to straighten her torn clothes.

'Perhaps we can do this again some time? Like in an hour maybe?'

Acacia glared up at Jordan as she pressed her hand against her bleeding shoulder. 'Go To Hell!' Her voice had returned.
Jordan laughed in delight. 'All in good time, my Sweet Angel! And now that you're mine, I'd say Ethan's descent is also inevitable. La bella ironia! The beautiful irony!' With a click of his fingers, Jordan had vanished and Acacia finally burst into tears.

All we had worked so hard to achieve is undone in five minutes of savage rape. The words of warning from the Sylphs fairy returned to her.

'The dark seeds of evil must be replaced by the purity of light.'

Determination saw Acacia rise unsteadily to her feet and look hesitantly down the hill towards the Tempest farm. *In my condition there's no possibility of making it on my own.* So Acacia turned towards the Rectory. *I'll need Michael's help to get home to Ethan.* This decided, Acacia drew the fragments of her dress together and staggered towards the house.

Your Bed Or Mine?

Sitting at the kitchen table, a steaming cup of chocolate in his hands, Ethan once again looked up at the clock on the wall. Mary had just completed making up the spare bed and sank into a chair opposite him.

'Acacia could be a couple of hours, Ethan. It depends upon how long Eleanor Macbeth is in labour. The best thing we can do is try to get some sleep.' She reached across the table and took his hands into hers. Mary's sensible words did little to comfort Ethan.

'I shouldn't have left her! Jordan will now be carrying a major grudge against her. If only…'

Mary's hands tightened in response to the longing in Ethan's voice. 'We must deal with the probable and not the impossible. About what you discussed with Father Michael… Your bed or mine?' There was a slight tremor in Mary's voice as she tried to sound as casual as possible. For a moment, Ethan just stared at her, and she feared that she had said the wrong thing. Finally Ethan smiled tenderly, rose to his feet and led Mary up to his room.

Acacia's Desperate Need

Having only just changed into his pyjama's Michael was startled by an impatient knocking on the front door. Fearing that more trouble was already brewing, Michael threw on his dressing gown and virtually ran to the door. The sight of Acacia leaning against the doorframe for support, half naked and looking like death, robbed Michael momentarily of speech.

'Please! You must help me!' Acacia took a step forward and collapsed into his arms. Carrying Acacia inside, Michael used his foot to slam the door shut behind him before taking Acacia to his room and laying her down on his bed. Switching on the top light, and drawing apart the torn material of Acacia's dress that she had been trying to hold together, Michael discovered the extent of her injuries.

'Holy Mother of God! Acacia, did Jordan do this to you?'

Finding it difficult to speak, Acacia nodded. 'Ethan! Must get to him quickly.'

'Then Jordan managed to rape you?' Michael's teeth ground together in suppressed anger. 'Ethan may not be able to help you. He asked me if he should spend tonight with Mary.'

A sob broke from Acacia. 'Then I am lost! I can no longer help him.'

Michael frowned in thought as he tried to remember what the Sylphs had instructed Acacia but it wouldn't immediately come to him. Eventually he shook his head, deciding it was action that was immediately needed.

'Come on, into the shower. You're going to wash that animal's touch off you!' He assisted Acacia to sit up and placing an arm around her waist got her to her feet.

'That won't be enough!'

I know that damn it! 'One thing at a time. Shower first, then your wounds. In the meantime, I'll think of something.' Supporting her, Michael helped Acacia out of what little clothing she had left on, started the shower, and got it to a reasonable temperature before thrusting Acacia under it. Only when he was certain that she could stand on her own feet, did he leave her to find the first aid kit in the kitchen... and something else.

Returning to the bathroom, Michael tried to not stare at the beautiful but ravaged naked body that stood in his shower, and handed her a cooking implement with a blush.

'Fill it with water and use it to flush any remnants of Jordan out of inside of you.' *I know using the turkey baster won't be enough but we have to try everything to save Acacia from falling victim to Jordan's wicked plans.*

Back in his bedroom, Michael opened the first aid kit and arranged the supplies of dressing and antiseptic that he would need, all the time trying to think desperately what else he could do. On impulse he slipped into Thomas' room and picking up a packet of his pain killers before slipping back into his own bathroom to press two tablets into Acacia's hand.

'Michael!' The voice startled him and looking up as he left the bathroom, he found an old woman standing in the doorway.

'Oh my…' Instinctively Michael fell to his knees, the glow that surrounded the woman was not normal.

'Only you can save Acacia now. Virginity is not the only form of purity. But you must be careful, my son, very careful. You must engage not only your body but also your mind and your heart. Your very soul must love her and ensure that it is more than just a physical act but a spiritual experience.'

I desperately want so much to satisfy Acacia's and my own burning need, but a small voice of conscious is screaming at me! 'I took a vow of celibacy when proclaiming my belief. I can't break that, not even for Acacia.'

The old woman sighed as she moved forward slowly to lay a wrinkled hand upon his shoulder. 'God will understand the need for this one sacrifice. With every passing minute, Jordan's influence is spreading, beyond the village and will begin to destroy the gentle fabric that binds our worlds together. Love her, not because you have to, but because you want to. When light returns to this world, all sins will be forgiven. That I promise you.'

Her message given, the old woman began to fade away. Michael pinched his own arm as he rose to his feet to ensure that he wasn't dreaming and the pain reassured him. *I have doubts, so many doubts, but there's no time to address any of these. Now is a time for action, and I'll have to bear whatever the consequences are later.*

Looking young and vulnerable, Acacia stepped out of the bathroom, wrapped in a fluffy green towel. Michael snapped out of his reflections and taking one of Acacia's hands, he sat her on the edge of his bed. In silence, he applied antiseptic to her shoulder wound, amazed at Acacia's self-control as the liquid stung like fury. Michael pressed a heavy padding over the wound, securing it with surgical tape. Hesitating, Michael's eyes locked with Acacia's as his hand reached out to remove the towel that kept her decent.

'Michael?' Doubt, fear, confusion, they were all there in her voice and he smiled reassuringly.

'Please trust me!' His hand moved up to lightly caress her cheek. She closed her eyes, sighed and slowly nodded.

Michael undid the towel and as it fell down to surround Acacia on the bed, Michael swore under his breath. Not only were there some serious scratches over her body, Acacia was already developing some large bruises.

'That bastard shall pay for this!' promised Michael, wiping the minor wounds with the antiseptic liquid. When this was completed, Michael took off his dressing gown and wrapped Acacia in it. He moved the medical kit off the bed to the chair he usually used when reading late at night. Only when Michael finally sat down on the bed beside her, did Acacia open her eyes.

'Michael…what am I going to do? All is lost.'

He placed his forefinger against her lips. 'Don't say that Acacia. There is still hope. Tonight I've been given a reprieve from my vows and I can love you, as I cannot normally do. As I have many times wanted to. As I have fantasied about ever since I first met you. This may be our only chance to express how we truly feel. Please, don't turn away from my love!'

Acacia scanned his face intently, looking for any sign of insincerity. There wasn't any to be found. 'What about after tonight?'

Michael shrugged. 'None of us may be alive come Sunday morning! We'll face our judgement one way or another then.'

Acacia shook her head and sighed, she tried to sit up. 'I can't let you make such a sacrifice!'

In a fit of uncharacteristic anger, Michael grasped Acacia's arms and forced her to look deep into his eyes. 'Damn your sacrifice! Can't you see that for one night only, I'm being permitted to be just a man? Not a servant of God, or a Holy man to the community, but a man, who can feel, act and love like all normal men! Do you not still feel a little something for me anymore?' The desperation in his voice brought a sob in response.

'How can you ask me that question, Michael? I love you more now than I ever did!'

Tenderly cupping her face, Michael let out a sigh of relief. 'That I all I needed to know!'

No Longer Dreaming

His kiss was tender and loving; such a contrast to the savage, demanding nature of Jordan, and Michael made no attempt to immediately touch any other part of Acacia's body. *I'll try to restore Acacia's confidence before ensuring that she is completely pleasured.* Acacia, though, hungered for the touch of the man she had been waiting for, for seven long years.

If tonight is going to be all that we have, then I want it to be unforgettable. Her fingers worked swiftly to undo the buttons of Michael's pyjama top and pushed it ruthlessly off his shoulders before pulling him against her, ensuring that their kiss intensified as her hands moved sensuously against the warmth of his solid chest. With a shaky laugh, Michael managed to place Acacia at arm's length for a moment.

'Acacia, I must know… how badly did he hurt you… when… well…' *I cannot put it into words what that animal has done.* Smiling Acacia moved so that she could lie down properly across the bed and undid the belt of the dressing gown that she wore.

'There'll be no pain, Michael. Our love will ensure that!' *That and Father Thomas' pain tablets.* Slowly she allowed the gown to fall apart to reveal despite her wounds the voluptuous and desirable body. Michael was about to lie down beside her when he recalled that the top light was still on. He was about to get up when Acacia grasped his hand.

'No, I want to see as well as feel every moment we have together. Something to remember in the future. Something to hold on to if we must be apart.'

Michael understood, as their future was so precarious. Slowly, very slowly, Michael began to explore Acacia's body with his fingers and his lips, He watched with interest as Acacia's eyes glazed over and her breathing deepened. *I know that Acacia is impatient, but it has also been a long time for me and being too hasty will only be disastrous for us both.*

With a deep contented sigh, Acacia wrapped her arms around Michael's neck, her fingers entwining through his hair causing him to deepen the kiss and increase the intensity of the passion that was building between them. Michael's own hand was doing some exploring of its own. For a long time, he teased and caressed Acacia's breasts.

It is finally a relief to give into the feelings that I've been trying so valiantly to suppress. Michael smiled as Acacia squirmed in delight beside him and when he lowered his mouth to suckle upon the other breast, Acacia's sigh of pleasure sent a tremor of excitement through Michael. *Here, finally is the woman who has invaded my dreams and I'm now capable of satisfying my own mental and physical need for her. The only thing I regret is the ability to only use one hand as the other is still broken and in a cast.*

His good hand now travelled down Acacia's waist, across her stomach and as his fingers gently slid between her thighs, Michael's mouth once again claimed Acacia's in a kiss that was to leave them both completely breathless. Acacia's hips bucked as Michael's thumb gently circled her clitoris and his forefinger traced a sensuous pattern around her melting flesh before he slowly used his finger to enter her.

'Oh Michael! Time has made you forget nothing!'

He smiled bashfully as her impatient hands tugged ruthlessly at his pyjama pants. *I'd thought that I'd feel guiltier about making love to Acacia, but it's actually a relief.* Michael assisted Acacia in the removal of the last of his clothing. His cheeks reddened as Acacia gave a gasp of surprise at the size and girth of Michael's erection.

Lovingly, her fingers closed around and caressed him as her lips sought his to cover the groan that rose from his throat as Acacia repaid his loving touch.

'Acacia, please! I don't want to…'

She released him, understanding how Michael's control would be weakening. Acacia wrapped her arms around Michael's waist and with a reassuring smile; she drew him on top of her, and wrapped her legs around his hips.

As Acacia took a deep satisfying breath, Michael propped himself on his elbows to ensure that he didn't crush her. This gave him the opportunity to watch Acacia's face and the changing emotions that fluttered across it. Michael dragged in a shuddering breath as he prepared himself for the experience of a lifetime. For a moment, Acacia read doubt in Michael's eyes and she raised one hand to caress his cheek.

'I'll understand if you can't go through with it.'

Michael turned his head so that his lips brushed against the palm of her hand. 'And lose you forever? No! I must know if the reality is as good as the dream.' His mouth locked onto Acacia's as he slowly entered her. Inch by inch he descended, which was too slow for Acacia's liking and she thrust up her hips to speed their joining, but Michael was not going to be rushed, he had waited a long time for this moment. He laughed gently at Acacia's impatience.

'Patience, my love, or it'll be over too soon!' Acacia took a deep breath, trying to control the frantic need for satisfaction and to allow Michael to set his own pace.

Only when Michael was fully embedded within her, did he relax and allow his head to drop against Acacia's undamaged shoulder as his breathing quickened. He remained perfectly still for so long that Acacia touched his face with tenderness.

'Michael?'

He raised his head and laughed in delight. 'Perhaps this is the time to end my winter!'

'I don't understand.' Acacia shook her head.

Michael finally moved inside her, one slow, long lunge. 'The Horned God said that you were my spring. Shall we see if he was correct?'

A shaft of pleasure surged through Acacia with each of his movements and the ability to think logically was quickly vanishing.

'Oh yes please!' She sighed and lifted her hips to meet his next thrust.

Acacia closed her eyes and allowed the developing feeling of fulfilment and pleasure sweep over her as their bodies fell into a gentle rhythm as old as time itself.

I wish it could last forever but realistically I know that Michael will be unable to control himself for very long. Opening her eyes again, she concentrated on increasing his pleasure. Tightening her inner muscles around him, squeezing him from the inside as his thrusts became faster, deeper.

So intent upon making Michael come first, Acacia was caught by surprise when Michael's hand slid between their bodies to lightly caress her clitoris as he suckled upon her breasts. Acacia clasped him to her, crying out his name as exquisite pleasure burst throughout her body. His iron control was finally gone as Michael began to thrust faster, deeper in search of his own release. His own cry of pleasure as he spasmed deep within her, sent a second wave of delight through Acacia.

They were breathing in shuddering gasps as Michael laid his head against Acacia's breasts and she stroked the soft thickness of his hair. *I want to thank him, but I'm too tired for words.* Attempting to leave the protection of Michael's arms, he raised his head in protest.

'No! Stay please! Let me enjoy this moment while I can!'

Acacia settled back down, drawing his quilt over them. Michael's head once more lay against Acacia's breasts as their breathing began to slow to normal. Acacia clicked her fingers and the light was extinguished. Soon Michael's regular breathing told Acacia that he was on the verge of sleep. Closing her own eyes, Acacia was settling her own mind for meditation when she thought she heard Michael whisper, 'I love you!'

Thursday 31 October

Something I Need To Know...

Michael knew that he must be dreaming. Acacia lay still pinned against him, their arms entwined and his naked body already responding to the closeness of her. She was awake, watching him, her eyes filled with her love for him.

'Are you who you should be?' The question sounded stupid even as he said it, but Acacia obviously understood because she smiled.

'Oh yes! Good has triumphed this time over evil!' She moved sensuously against him, her fingers dancing lightly across his bare back.

'Are you in terrible pain?' His eyes did little to conceal his concern from her.

Acacia shrugged. 'A little stiff and sore. It's mainly my shoulder that hurts. I read the instructions before taking another couple of Father Thomas' tablets.' Michael hesitated, as Acacia's fingers travelled down his arms and across his chest.

'I have no right to ask this of you...' He paused; the words unnecessary as Acacia reached down to caress him intimately.

'You need to know if last night was just a fluke?'

Michael nodded, his hand already moving to cup her breasts. Acacia laughed gently as she rolled onto her back and Michael settled himself once more between her legs. For a moment Michael continued to study Acacia's face before he slowly sank deep into her receptive body.

By the first thrust, Michael realised that this was not a dream. He suddenly stopped, his face burying into Acacia's shoulder as he fought to control his own overwhelming desires. Acacia tenderly stroked his hair.

'Oh my Lord! What am I doing? How could I take advantage of you like this?' Michael tried to withdraw but Acacia kept her legs locked around his hips. 'Acacia please let me go! I shouldn't be inflicting this pain upon you!'

Three days without sleep was finally taking its toll upon her and tears fell uncontrollably from her eyes.

'Acacia? Please, my love, don't cry! Let me get off you so that I'm not hurting you.'

She released him and turned her face away as the tears continued to fall. 'If you truly don't love me, then I suggest that we leave it there!'

Michael did not immediately move. *Her words are like a knife thrust through my heart. I suddenly realise that I care for Acacia, care deeply for her. But is that love?* 'Acacia… tell me please… what do you want?'

She bit her lip as she attempted to suppress a sob. 'I don't know! I want what is best for us both, but… I want… I need…'

Michael dragged in a sharp breath due to the look of desire in Acacia's eyes. Slowly he raised his good hand to caress her breast as he took one slow, long stroke inside of her. She let out a sigh of ecstasy.

'Is that what you want?' His own voice was quite husky and had to be forced from his throat.

A cry escaped from Acacia. 'Yes! Oh, Yes!' Her arms slid up his chest to join behind his neck. She hesitated in doubt. 'But you?'

A gentle smile touched Michael's lips. 'I'm fighting the need to see what it takes to send you beyond ecstasy!'

'That seems fair enough!' Acacia's eyes lit up in delight as she returned his smile.

She drew him down into a kiss that left Michael in no doubt about Acacia's feelings. Her body moved against his, coaxing him into action and Acacia gasped at the thrill of him moving again so expertly inside of her. Michael rocked gently into her, intending to make their love making last as long as was possible this time, but Acacia had other ideas as she wrapped her legs around his hips and used her heels to push him harder into her.

Understanding her need for intensity rather than longevity, Michael drove himself harder and faster into her receptive and willing body as his lips teased and suckled upon her breasts. Her fingernails scrapped lightly down his back as she thrust up her hips to meet each of his powerful possessions.

A gasp of surprise escaped from Michael, as he looked into Acacia's eyes. The blue had deepened to the colour of sapphires and glowed as gems do under a spotlight. Michael wasn't given time to consider this phenomenon as Acacia's nails dug into his shoulders, indicating how close she was to climaxing. His thrusts became wild, powerful and possessive as his own need for satisfaction could no longer be denied.

'Michael! Oh my beloved! You have no equal!' Acacia's praise sent him over the edge and they climaxed together. Their breathing was ragged as pleasure flooded over them and Michael collapsed in satisfaction. His thumb teased across Acacia's nipples as his body continued to pulsate inside her and she stroked his shoulders as they fought to bring their breathing back to normal.

Michael groaned, burying his head into her breasts. 'Is such pleasure sinful?'

Acacia's eyes were filled with concern. 'Hush Michael! Don't spoil the moment! Sleep now; you'll need all your energy today.'

He disengaged himself from Acacia as he rolled onto his side and gently drew Acacia against him as he yawned sleepily. 'Sunday, when this is all over, we'll discuss our future.'

Acacia smiled sadly at his optimism that they would survive the night and gently kissed his brow as his eyes closed. 'Of course, Michael!'

Heading Home

Remaining only until she heard the deep, regular breathing of Michael sleeping, Acacia reluctantly removed herself from his arms and rising from the bed, stretched her aching limbs. She was in quite a bit of pain from her fight with Jordan and although her time with Michael had been enjoyable, it had only added to the discomfort she was now suffering. When the pain killers kicked in, it dropped the pain level to a steady ache.

She borrowed a tracksuit from Michael's chest of drawers, bundled her ruined dress under her arm as it was not fit to be worn, and once dressed, Acacia pressed a tender kiss against Michael's lips before she slipped silently out of the Rectory. Heading home, the streets were still silent in sleep and she thankfully met no one.

The farmhouse was also silent as Acacia entered. She glanced briefly into the spare bedroom and seeing the unslept bed, she believed that Michael had been right about Ethan and Mary spending the night together.

Returning downstairs to the kitchen, Acacia was immediately surrounded by cats all begging to be fed. The dogs, woken by the cats' meows, were not be outdone and joined in the chorus. With a sigh, Acacia turned on the light and looked up at the clock on the wall. She was surprised to see that it was already 6.30 am. Acknowledging the animals, Acacia fed them all before heading upstairs to run an aroma-therapeutic bubble bath.

Ethan's Indignation

Half an hour of soaking in the soothing, hot herb filled water, saw Acacia's body begin to relax and start the healing process upon her aches and pain. With her eyes closed as she breathed in deeply the fragrances that emanated from the bath, Acacia found herself falling asleep. She was just pleasantly drifting between the land of the consciousness and dreams when the bathroom door was flung forcefully open. Acacia started awake, alert for danger, fearing an appearance of Jordan but relaxed again when it turned out to be only Ethan who strode into the room.

'And what have you been up to, Sister mine?' Ethan's tone was teasing rather than serious. Acacia's eyebrows rose in mockery.

'I might ask you the same question Ethan. Mary didn't sleep in the spare room did she?'

Ethan's countenance turned bright red and looked guiltily behind him to where Mary stood outside the bathroom, not wishing to also barge in. Ethan opened his mouth to retort but the words died upon his lips as Acacia rose out of the water. He had seen her naked before, which was not the problem, for the first time since he had entered the room he realised that Acacia was injured.

'By all that is sacred! What's been going on?'

Wrapping a towel around herself, Acacia smiled reassuringly and took out of the cupboard a first aid kit. 'It's not as bad as it looks, Ethan. I'll explain what happened while I dress, and then I'll need you to look at my shoulder.'

Ethan followed her out of the bathroom, down the hall to her bedroom and would have entered had Mary not laid her hand upon his arm.

'Shall I make breakfast?' Ethan's concerned expression softened at Mary's willingness to always be of assistance.

'Thank you. A full breakfast may be necessary as we can't tell when we might be able to eat again.'

Mary nodded and headed down to the kitchen as Ethan continued into Acacia's room.

Acacia's story didn't take long to tell as she slipped into a white, silk slip dress that reached down in a flare to her ankles. Ethan was silent until Acacia removed the dressing that covered her shoulder and he looked upon the skin that had been torn by Jordan's teeth.

'Bloody Hell! You shouldn't have sacrificed so much for me!'

Tears shone in her eyes as Acacia sat down on the edge of her bed. 'What else could I do? Jordan had every intention of raping you! I couldn't let that happen! I tried to fight him, I even tried to curse him but he was too strong for me.'

Silent once more, Ethan concentrated upon cleaning and redressing Acacia's shoulder as he considered her words.

'Why didn't you come to me? Afterwards?' His words were little more than a whisper. Acacia reached out to run a tender finger down his cheek.

'Michael thought that you might be spending the night with Mary. Besides…' Colour swept across Acacia's face as she broke off in embarrassment.

Ethan's eyebrows rose as he smiled wickedly. 'Was he any good?'

Acacia couldn't help laughing at the impertinence of his question. 'Oh Yes! A truly memorable and glorious act!' With a thoughtful look at her younger relative, she added, 'Et tu?'

Ethan looked away as he chewed upon his bottom lip as he carefully considered his answer. 'We didn't, Ace! Oh yes, we both had thought about it, even got into bed together, but it just wasn't right. The right moment that is. So we didn't do it. Michael was right; we would've regretted rushing our relationship.'

Embracing Ethan, Acacia kissed his forehead. 'Your time will come! We'll need to discuss today's plan but that can wait until after breakfast.' Placing her arm around his waist, Acacia led Ethan out of her room as the smell of cooking bacon, eggs and toast wafted up to entice them downstairs.

Nathaniel Makes A Stand

Although the sun was again blacked out, this didn't deter Claudia de Bere from continuing with the planned Halloween party. *In fact due to the darkness, I've decided to start the party early. I was disappointed by the result of Jordan's ceremony last night, but I'm not about to let that stop my party mood.* A troop of teenagers was under orders from Claudia setting up chairs and tables, the sound system and decorations. The food was being organised and overseen by Cheryl, Kym and Merelda in the de Bere kitchen.

Claudia, escorted by Nathaniel flittered between her home and the temple, throwing her orders left and right, supervising and thoroughly enjoying herself, so long as she did not have to do any of the work. Nathaniel was worried, and as Claudia threw her commands around, he remained in a thoughtful silence. That was until Claudia ordered a couple of older teenage boys to borrow a couple of dead bodies from the funeral parlour for decoration.

'Really Claudia! You can't go around using the bodies of dead people as ornaments! It's just not done! Besides being disrespectful.'

Claudia swung around her eyes glaring daggers at him. 'Your choir boy morality is going to stop you from ever having any fun. It's about time that you realise that I'm in charge here and if you don't like that then you can take a hike!'

Not for the first time, I see Claudia for what she truly is. Normally I can ignore this image, but this time it refuses to vanish from my mind. 'Is that your final word?' His tone was quite cold and distant.

Claudia threw up her hands in despair. 'Are you really that thick? Whatever did I see in you anyway? Nothing you say or do will make the slightest bit of difference! With someone like Jordan around, what possible use would I have for you?'

Nathaniel's face was now a mask of stone. *I'm not prepared to allow Claudia the satisfaction of knowing how much she has hurt me.* 'Fine! I wish you joy with him, Claudia!' He turned away and began to walk back to the village.

'Nate! Where are you going? I haven't finished with you yet!' Nathaniel kept walking, not looking back or turning around again, but kept walking as Claudia screamed after him.

Constable Kane Keeps Watch

From where he sat on a bench outside of the Chemist shop, Kane had an excellent view of the main street and the people who went happily about the preparation of the biggest Halloween that they had ever seen. Teenagers and adults were industriously working under either Claudia's or Jordan's instructions.

Do any of them realise the full extent of what had taken place last night? That we had been only minutes away from releasing Hell upon the earth and yet here they are planning a childish party without a care in the world. The streetlights had remained on since they had lost the sun, and lazily Kane wondered, *What will that do to their village's electricity bill?*

Nathaniel's depressed countenance and slouched shoulders as he passed Kane set him immediately apart from the happy, brain washed workers. Casting his mind back to the night before, Kane realised that Nathaniel hadn't been present at the gathering. *I wonder if Nathaniel can be rescued?* This caused Matthew Kane to spring to his feet and join the teenager.

'Problems Nathaniel?'

Nathaniel jumped; he hadn't heard the Constable fall into step beside him. 'I've lost Claudia, and I think I'm glad.'

Kane hesitated, then put his arm around Nathaniel's shoulders. 'Work is the best remedy! Would you be prepared to do a job for me?'

The teenager looked up at him doubtfully. 'Is it illegal?'

Kane chuckled. 'No, it isn't. When Acacia arranged for Karen Greeves to take most of the kids to the school, it wasn't possible to arrange a great deal of food. What I want you to do is go to the grocery store and get as much supplies as you can with the money I give you. Then take it over to the school. I don't dare leave the village myself.' Kane removed his wallet from his back trouser pocket and handed Nathaniel all the cash that he had.

'But what if Mr Abraham doesn't open his shop?' Nathaniel hesitated in putting the money into his own pocket.

'He'll open up if you knock on the door and explain your purpose.'

Nathaniel was about to comply when a horrific thought arose. 'Will Jordan try to harm the other kids?'

Kane sighed. 'I really don't know! I hope not but…'

Solemnly Nathaniel nodded his head. 'Should I stay with them to help protect them?'

A smile of delight swept across Kane's face. *I had not been wrong about the boy.* 'That is a good idea! Tonight anything could happen!'

Nathaniel nodded, forgetting his own problems as he headed for the grocery store, a new sense of purpose giving him a feeling of usefulness and a means to forget his own troubles.

Matthew Kane received a fright of his own as Jordan materialised behind him.

'You're not thinking of interfering are you Matthew?' Jordan's lazy, mocking tone made the Constable spin around in surprise.

'That depends upon what you mean by interference. I won't let you harm the children! The adults should have more sense but the innocence of youth will not be scarred by your hand.'

A gentle amused laugh came from Jordan. 'Is that a challenge? Do you honestly believe that you have any possible means of stopping me from doing anything that I wish to do?'

In honesty, Kane shrugged. 'I don't know, but I'll give it a damn good try! I'm not afraid to die for a cause.' The last thing Kane expected was for Jordan to smile at his show of defiance.

'There are worse things than dying, you know! And I promise you I know them all!'

With a flash of smoke, Jordan vanished and Kane dragged in an unsteady breath. *I don't want to know or even consider what Jordan had meant. If my fate is to be horrific, then I'd rather not think about it before it happens.* Kane returned to his seat of observation to wait for the time he would be called upon to act.

Are You Decent?

There was a knock on the bedroom door, and a cautious call of 'Father?' which awoke Michael later that morning.

'Father Michael? Are you decent?' He realised that he was naked, lying on top of his sheets, entwined with his quilt. Hastily he drew the quilt over himself.

'What time is it, Marjorie?'

The housekeeper opened the door to look at him, concerned. 'It's almost midday! I wouldn't have disturbed you, but Mr and Mrs Macbeth would like their baby christened as soon as possible. Just in case anything happens today.'

Michael nodded, running a hand over his face as he attempted to wake up as Marjorie retreated. *One thing that strikes me as odd is that Marjorie has never asked if I was decent before.* Slipping off the bed, Michael wondered, *How much does she know, and how am I to continue my duties as a man of God?* Heading for the shower, these thoughts were momentarily cast aside as Michael prepared for what could possibly be the worst day in his entire life.

In the kitchen, Marjorie had prepared Michael an early lunch and although she looked at him keenly as he sat down at the table, the housekeeper made no mention of the previous night.

'I've tidied Father Thomas' room and arranged his bedclothes so that it looks just as if he was sleeping. Arrangements can be made for a burial on Monday morning, if we don't have too many difficulties today. There will be someone to see you from the Retirement Village tomorrow about the twelve souls they lost last night. Shall I press your cassock for the Christening?'

Michael stared at Marjorie in amazement at her calm acceptance of so many deaths. 'About last night…'

Marjorie cut him off immediately, swallowing hard upon her Christian morals. 'I don't want to know, Father Michael. Acacia is a good girl; she would never compromise you if it weren't important. Mr Macbeth wishes to see you as soon as you've finished your meal.' Marjorie left the room, intending to iron Michael's cassock, leaving him no opportunity to reply.

Which is just as well as I have no idea what to say!

A Christening

The Sacristy had been transformed into a mini nursery by the time Michael entered that afternoon. Mac had snuck down to the Inn for the few things that he and Eleanor had already bought for the baby. There was no shortage of advisers for the new parents, or baby sitters, as the people bunking out in the church were a mixture of experienced parents and grandparents. Seeing Michael dressed in his complete priest's garb, Mac gave a sigh of relief as Michael approached him.

'I know I'm being foolish, Father, but I'd rather the bairn was christened before this frightful night begins,' explained Mac.

Michael laid a comforting hand on the big man's shoulder. 'Not at all Mac. Who can guarantee what will happen today? To make things easier, I'll bring the ceremony to your wife, so that she doesn't have to be moved. Excuse me a moment.'

Michael found that he had plenty of assistants setting up the christening bowl, finding the appropriate text and the anointing oil. There was a moment of embarrassment for Michael when he came face to face with Acacia, Ethan and Mary who had brought Eleanor a small christening gown for the baby. Acacia gave him a shy, embarrassed smile, obviously as unsure of what to say as he was.

Michael returned her smile and turned to initiate the Christening of Acacia Kaitlyn Macbeth.

Proving Himself

The main doors of the church burst open and a yell of a madman tore through the building. 'I've come for you, boy! Prepare for your punishment!'

For a moment, I thought, that it was Jordan, but the hysterical note in the voice is wrong, considered Acacia. Instead a still whiskered and pointy ears Rochester de Bere pointed a rifle at the assembled group. One woman screamed and passed out at the sight of the rat/man, but no one paid attention to her as Michael stepped forward to address Rochester.

'This is the House of God, Sir! Step outside and let us discuss this in a rational manner!' There was a hysterical laugh as Rochester turned around to show the tail that was attached to his lower back.

'Rational? I'm a fucking rat, for Christ's sake! How am I supposed to be fucking rational about anything?'

Acacia had attempted to keep Ethan back, but he moved around his Mentor to join Michael. Ethan glanced over his handiwork with a wicked grin.

'That's amazing! The spell shouldn't have lasted more than a day. My powers must be increasing! This is between you and me Rochester, let's step outside.'

Ethan walked calmly out of the church, not at all concerned about the rifle being pointed at him. Acacia would have followed them out, but Mac grasped her arm.

'Don't love, he has to prove himself.'

'But that's a real bullet he has in his rifle!' Acacia pulled violently against his hold for a moment, and then she stopped fighting. 'All right.' A mischievous smile lit up her face. *'A toad or a frog, Ethan.'* She sent the message telepathically and waited patiently for the results.

With his arms crossed, a wicked gleam in his eyes, Ethan waited as the rat/man circled him with his rifle pointed purposefully at the teenager.

'Well?' Ethan's calm taunt brought a snarl to Rochester's lips.

'You must consider this your last party trick, heathen! I won't be made a mockery of! Prepare to die!'

Ethan laughed. 'Take your best shot!'

Rochester levelled the rifle to aim at Ethan's heart. The boy waited patiently, with no sign of being scared. Rochester de Bere hesitated and then catching the mocking gleam in Ethan's eyes, he pulled the trigger. The bullet whizzed through the air towards Ethan, but it never touched him. The bullet stopped mid-air, frozen in mid-flight about an inch from Ethan's chest.

'What kind of devilry is this?' Rochester demanded.

Ethan reached out and plucked the bullet out of the force field that surrounded him. He looked at the bullet carefully before slipping it into his pocket.

'Now what shall you do?'

Rochester swore violently. 'Damn you to hell, boy! You'll be less cocky when I tell exactly what I did to your lovely sister.'

The teenager's lips thinned in disapproval as his eyes hardened to take on a deadly glow. 'Watch your mouth! Speak one foul word against Acacia and I'll cut your lying tongue out!'

Rochester laughed, a diabolical sound. 'Jealous boy, that I had her first? Shall I tell you exactly what we did? All the depraved acts I made her do to me?'

Ethan's hands clenched tightly into fists by his side. 'A rat wasn't good enough for you! Let's see how you enjoy being a toad!' Ethan swept his hand across Rochester. '*It is time for this rat to learn some respect, turn him into a form that he will regret.*'

The rat/man screamed as he began to shrink, turn a brownish green colour and become an ugly amphibian. Ethan bent down and picking up the rifle and the toad by a back leg, he carried it back into the church.

There was a round of applause as Ethan threw the toad onto the floor at Acacia's feet. She beamed in pride.

'You didn't even break into a sweat! Was the transformation at all difficult?'

Ethan scowled 'Not really, he made it easier by pissing me off!' His brow lightened. 'What shall I do with the toad?'

Mary giggled. 'How about your jacket pocket, Ethan? I mean you wouldn't want Mr de Bere hopping away!'

The tension flowed away from Ethan as he laughed. The toad hopped towards the door, but escape was impossible. Ethan locked his eyes upon the amphibian, and it began to levitate off the ground.

'*Make this toad as light as air, and bring him forth into my care.*' The toad floated towards him and Ethan opened his pocket and the toad floated in. The applause that followed brought a tinge of embarrassed colour to Ethan's cheeks.

Come For The Child

BOOM! The earth seemed to tremble beneath their feet, shaking the very foundations of the church. BOOM! BOOM! BOOM! BOOM!

'What on earth?' asked Michael, as the vibrations surged through the floor.

Ethan, still a teenager, knew exactly what it was. 'Claudia must have already started her little party as that is the bass of a powerful sound system or sub-woofer turned right up.' Faintly they could hear music actually accompanying the Booms.

Mac shook his head. 'Those kids will be deaf before the night is over!'

Acacia cast him a look of pity. 'You obviously don't know teenagers, Mac. That's one of the joys you've to look forward to in the future.'

The Innkeeper grunted, 'Thanks for nothing!'

The thumping of the music suddenly stopped, and the silence that followed held such an ominous note that Acacia turned concerned eyes to Ethan.

'What do you think?' she whispered, as if fearing to break the silence that surrounded them. Ethan's eyes rose to the ceiling as his ears strained for something that was obviously inaudible to the normal human, returning his gaze to his Mentor's face, he slowly nodded his head.

'They're coming.'

'Whom? Jordan?' Michael looked intently from one to the other.

Acacia glanced across at him and managed a tight smile. 'No, not yet! The dead are now rising for their one day of freedom. Most of the time there is no trouble, but with Jordan at hand he might try to turn them against us. The possessed villagers cannot enter this church as I have sealed all entrances with a spell to keep them out, but ghosts don't need doors!'

A murmur of confusion and fear arose from the assembled villagers.

'Are we going to die?'

'How do we protect ourselves?'

'What about the children?'

Ethan held up his hands to stop the barrage of questions. 'The children are safe so long as they remain with Karen Greeves at the school. Remember that basically these are your ancestors, who under normal circumstances wouldn't wish to harm you. You must be calm and welcoming. Marjorie what we need is salt and lots of it. We need to place everyone in a circle of salt.'

Chewing on her thumbnail, Acacia had been staring thoughtfully at Eleanor and her tiny daughter. Making a quick decision, she touched Ethan's arm. 'Prepare them, there is something I must do!'

Acacia grasped Michael's hand and motioned for Mac to follow, and led them into the Sacristy, shutting the door behind them.

As Ethan and the others lit all the candles they could find and scattered salt on the floor, Acacia was kneeling down beside Eleanor on her mattress.

'Do you trust me, Eleanor?'

The new mother looked at Acacia is disbelief. 'You have to even ask? We are in your hands!'

Acacia nodded. 'Remove the baby's clothing for a moment.' She looked back up at Michael. 'Could you light me a new candle please? White preferably. And can you bless it?'

Mac sat down on the mattress to assist his wife in undressing their only child. Opening a cupboard, Michael removed a candle from a packet, said a prayer and lit it before handing it to Acacia. She absently thanked him; her eyes locked with Eleanor who held in her arms her baby girl, now naked except for a nappy.

'She will cry, but there will be no lasting damage. Her life is in danger!'

Glancing down at the candle, Eleanor began to understand. Swallowing hard, she nodded. 'Let's get on with it then!'

'Now wait a minute!' Mac's protest was cut off by a furious look in his wife's eyes.

'Trust and believe, Allan! I will not lose my child now!' Eleanor glanced back at Acacia. 'Go ahead!'

Acacia held the candle on a slant so that it began to drip wax, when it was constant; she held it over the baby's chest. *'Protect this child, from all whom mean her harm. Let all who enter, know that she is a protected one!'*

With a careful movement Acacia dripped the wax to make a sign of the cross over the baby's skin. Baby Acacia screwed up her face, the burning unpleasant, and although the little child whimpered, she didn't scream. Anxiously wringing his hands, the father was glad when Acacia handed the candle back to Michael.

'Is that it?' Mac asked.

Acacia shook her head. 'No, one last thing.' She smiled reassuringly at Eleanor. 'Turn the baby over please.' She glanced back up at Michael. 'Do you still have your pocket knife?'

'Holy Mother of God! No!' Mac lost all control.

Acacia laid a calming hand on his arm. 'Relax; the blood will be mine, not the baby's.' She took the knife silently offered and without a pause, ran the blade across her wrist. Michael was finally moved to protest.

'Be careful Acacia. We can't do without you! I can't do without you!'

Acacia tenderly touched his cheek before holding her bleeding arm over the child. This time the pattern made was that of a pentagram within a circle. As soon as it was complete, Acacia pressed her hand over the wound.

'No one will dare touch her now! Wait until the blood is dry, then you can dress her again.'

Michael dragged Acacia to her feet, and managed to get her to stand still long enough for him to bandage her bleeding arm. The windows began to rattle as the wind rose to loudly sweep around the church.

'There's someone at the door!' Acacia's words sounded foreboding, yet strangely familiar and suddenly Michael was truly afraid.

Michael didn't know what to expect. *I've never seen a ghost before, and the typical stereotypes from Casper to Freddy Kruger are running through my mind.* A white mist seeped through the exterior wall, separating into individual forms before becoming solid, recognisable figures.

The group of ghosts looked like ordinary people with the exception that they were dressed in the costume of their own period, and everything about them was white. There was a mixture of men and women from various periods in time and for a moment the living and the dead just stared at each other.

Acacia swept into a deep curtsy. 'Blessed be, ancient ones! We welcome you to your day of being earth bound once more.'

A 17th Century male ghost stepped forward to stare hard at Acacia. 'You're a witch, aye? I've killed enough of thy kind in my time! Well, I admit thee have pretty manners, so I have a message for thee.' Suddenly the ghost's face disintegrated into a savage animal. 'Burn in Hell!'

Acacia took a hasty step back, although her eyes opened wider in surprise, she did not react to this sudden attack. 'What did Jordan offer you? Mortality? Immortality? You should be warned, Jordan's deals are always a two edged sword.'

A late 19th century teenage girl touched the older ghost's arm. 'Shall we just get what we came for, George?'

Michael's eyebrows lowered into a deep frown. 'Which is what?'

The sight of the silver Cross around Michael's neck made the ghosts step back a little, fearfully. It was the girl who answered, much to the disapproval of the other ghosts.

'Jordan wants the child. If we take her to him, he'll let us live again.'

For some time Eleanor had been watching Acacia. Now, finally her mind was made up, and looking across to the gathered ghosts, Eleanor held up the baby. 'Take her then!'

Mac gave a cry of disbelief. 'Have ye gone mad, love?'

Eleanor did not take her eyes off the ghosts. 'No, I just trust Acacia.'

The Victorian teenage ghost took the newborn baby and cradled her in her arms as she looked down into the angelic face. The teenager looked up and her eyes met and held with Acacia's. A gentle smile touched the lips of the ghost as she undid the child's clothes. She suddenly turned, faced the child towards her colleagues as a light from the baby's eyes pierced through each of them, causing them to fall to their knees in humble homage. Cradling the child once more the teenager redressed the baby as she turned back to smile at Acacia.

'Did I do well, sister?'

Tears shone in her eyes as Acacia returned her smile. 'Yes beloved! You've finally earned the release you deserved all those years ago!'

The ghost lowered the baby back into her mother's arms. 'You have a beautiful child, Eleanor. Tonight, she inherits my own gifts and powers. Trust in Acacia, she will teach you how to train the little one.'

Before their eyes the Victorian girl changed to an all over golden colour, as baby Acacia's eyes changed from brown to the deep blue that was characteristic of the Tempests. Acacia embraced the ghost girl in a manner that indicated that they had known each other very well.

'I must go now, Acacia. I'm glad that we had this chance to meet again. Believe and you will succeed. Blessed Part.' The ghost held Acacia at arm's length as she began to fade.

'I shall miss our annual talks, sister. Enjoy your spring.' Acacia unashamedly allowed the tears to fall as the girl vanished.

Michael came up behind Acacia and placed his arm around her. 'What of these others?'

Acacia smiled gently, at where the other ghosts still knelt. 'They are free of course. They should seek out their own kith and kin as it might be the only time mere mortals will actually be able to see them.'

The ghosts rose doubtfully to their feet. The 17th century gentleman expressed all their feelings. 'Aren't thee going to punish us?'

Acacia shook her head. 'If you want freedom, you must stop punishing yourselves. Let go of the past. It'll never occur again. You must embrace what will be your future beyond this earthly confines.'

'That is what frightens us!'

Acacia sighed. 'While you cling to these physical forms, you will never be free. You should be no more than an entity of past memories and wisdom that can transcend between this life and the next at will.'

The old gentleman took Acacia's hand and pressed it against his lips. 'Thou art wise beyond thy years, child. Please forgive my earlier outburst.'

Acacia smiled. 'Of course!'

'Good-bye fair Witch. May thy Gods help and protect thee.'

The ghosts reformed into the general mist and seeped back out through the wall.

A Different Battleground

A scream of terror came from the church, an obvious indication that the other ghosts were not as easy to pacify as the ones who had just left. Acacia threw open the door, urging Mac to stay with his wife as she and Michael headed out into the war zone.

Ethan and Mary were attempting to keep everyone calm, but as the angry ghosts surged on the group, they had simply freaked out, which only added fuel to the fire. Acacia placed her hands upon her hips and shook her head in disbelief.

'Honestly! You're worse than children!'

As with the ghosts in the sacristy, there was an assortment of centuries represented, and although Acacia would normally enjoy discovering their personal stories, these ghosts were in no mood for talk. There was no way of beating these apparitions on a physical level; control had to be gained through the mind. Acacia sighed as Ethan pushed his way through the mixture of living and dead to stand beside her.

'Reasoning with them didn't work, Ace! They're only in the mood for a fight.'

The ghosts were floating around the room, some were moaning, others rattling chains, some shouting words of abuse as they rushed at and through the living.

'We'll just have to take their anger away then.'

'How?' Puzzled, Michael wished that he wasn't so ignorant of their ways.

Ethan answered, 'You can draw the battlefield onto the cerebral level. It can be very dangerous, especially if you lose.'

'I don't intend to lose, Ethan.' Acacia patted his shoulder. 'Once their fight has gone, you'll be able to reason with the ghosts.'

Slowly he nodded his head. 'Be careful, Ace! Please!'

Acacia drew Michael aside for a private word. 'I might be out of it for a while, so you'll need to keep an eye on Ethan. If…. if anything does happen to me, I want you to temporarily take over Ethan's guardianship. Until the Family can finally reach us. Will you promise me that?'

Michael smiled reassuringly. 'I promise, but it will never happen. We'll be here waiting for you when you return. Never doubt that.'

Acacia nodded. 'I believe you!' Briefly she kissed him on the mouth before turning to enter the middle of the mingling ghosts.

With Ethan's assistance to begin with, Acacia began to spin upon the spot.

'Take away the hate they feel. Restore their emotions and heal their scars. Take away their anger, this I ask.'

Light radiated from Acacia as she continued to spin, and the ghosts were drawn reluctantly towards the light. Each in turn entered

Acacia's body and was spun out again, renewed as all anger had left them. The ghosts in fact looked quite dazed, as some became almost transparent in form. When the last ghost had passed through Acacia, she suddenly stopped spinning and collapsed unconscious to the floor. Michael pushed others aside as he knelt down to cradle Acacia in his arms. Ethan laid a reassuring hand on Michael's shoulder.

'Ace will now fight, or try to reason with the anger on another dimension. She'll be like this for a while. Perhaps moving her to a quiet place would be a good idea.'

Michael nodded. 'Would my bedroom do?'

'Perfect!' A hint of a mischievous smile flittered across Ethan's features. 'I'll sort this lot out if you'll see that Ace is comfortable.'

People made way as Michael easily, despite his broken hand, lifted Acacia up into his arms and carried her through the back of the church to the Rectory. Ethan shared a secret smile with Mary before gathering ghosts and humans together for reconciliation.

What's Cooking?

The sizzling, succulent smell of a barbecue finally dragged Matthew Kane away from his bench on the high street and up to the temple and the Halloween party. *The music, if that's what it is, I can tune out, the debauchery out in the open I can ignore, and although the appearance of the ghosts startled me, I accepted that in my stride. It's the BBQ though, that has me puzzled. Many of the adults standing around the BBQ aren't waiting for the meat to be cooked properly before tearing the flesh away from the bone.* Kane nodded amicably at the group.

'I usually like my steaks well done. What exactly is that? It smells a little like pork.'

A man grinned at him, blood dripping down his chin. 'It's Mrs Shaw.'

Kane suspected them of joking until he saw a chopping block behind the group with a blooded axe, a pile of woman's clothing and an odd assortment of body parts. *I thought I'd seen and heard everything, but I was wrong.*

'Want some? Jordan's getting us some tenderer cuts.'

Kane didn't even hear the man's question as he turned and ran as fast as he could away from the scene of mutilation. Kane only paused upon the other side of the cemetery to throw up.

Mankind has finally achieved to sicken me in disgust. I want to be done with them all, but something that man had said, needs acting upon immediately. Kane straightened, pulled himself together and went to the church in search of Ethan and Acacia. *The children hiding at the school are in mortal danger!*

Cannibalism

When Kane burst through the church front doors, the ghosts were just departing. One ghost, a reasonably modern male, paused and glanced back at Ethan. 'Is this the one?'

Ethan shook his head. 'No, he's with us. See if any of you can talk some sense into the others out there.'

The ghost nodded his head and vanished along with his fellow spirits. Mary took one look at the stricken features of Matthew Kane, and the grey colour of his face, so she quickly poured him a large brandy, (used by Marjorie for shock) placing it firmly into his hand and urging him to drink. The Constable gulped down the alcohol, and coughed violently as the fiery liquid hit the back of his throat.

'Where's Acacia?' He demanded in a harsh voice.

A silent look was exchanged between the teenagers, as Ethan sighed. 'She's not available at the moment. What's happened?'

Matthew looked at the sea of faces watching him. *The news of cannibalism is not something I wish to spread around!*

Ethan sensed something of Matthew's dilemma as he suggested, 'We'll find Michael in the Rectory.'

They slipped out through the backdoor to the Rectory and found Michael seated in a chair, pulled up beside his bed upon which lay Acacia, so peaceful did she look that it was hard to believe that a battle was going on inside her head. For a moment Matthew was distracted.

'Is she all right?'

Ethan nodded. 'Ace, is fighting a private war.'

'They're beginning to eat each other!' Matthew Kane blurted out. 'I think Jordan is going to kill a couple of children for them to also BBQ. We must do something to stop this insanity!'

Mary agreed. 'Can we borrow Father Thomas' car, Father Michael?'

'Of course! What do you plan to do Ethan?'

The young wizard chewed on his bottom lip. 'I think we need to provide the school with some serious back up. Stay here Michael and watch over Ace. Are you up to this Constable?'

Matthew took a deep breath and nodded.

Michael blessed them; 'May God be with you!' The trio raced out of the Rectory, everyone praying that they would not be too late.

Desperate Dash

The speed limit was well and truly broken as Kane sped them through the village streets in Thomas' car. The school was deserted as they roared in for a skidding stop. Ethan was out of the car before the engine had even been switched off, and Mary and Matthew had to run after him. He headed for the gymnasium where the children, and the more responsible parents were camped out, but Matthew was shocked to find a rifle rammed into his chest by a determined Karen Greeves.

'For God's sake, we're friends!' cried out the Constable, not too happy about the idea of having his heart blown out. Karen caught sight of Mary and Ethan and immediately lowered the gun.

'I'm sorry, but we've had to be so careful.'

Kane nodded as he regained his equilibrium. 'Well the worst is yet to come. Jordan is on his way, but protection will soon be at hand.' He glanced across at Ethan before quietly adding, 'I hope!'

Mary, though, had no doubts that Ethan had a plan. 'This building must be secured. All possible means of entry must be blocked!' she added.

Karen agreed. 'I've checked, but I'll get some of the parents to double check the doors and windows.' Turning to the main body of the group, Karen put out the order.

Ethan glanced around the gym as he stroked his chin deep in thought. 'I need four strong willed volunteers,' he finally said.

'If you want us to guard the doors,' said one father, 'I hope the Constable has brought an arsenal of weapons.'

Ethan grinned mischievously. 'No we're not using guns. I have something more effective in mind. Your bodies will remain in the gym but I'll be sending your spirit outside in the form of an animal.'

To show Ethan support Matthew said, 'Count me in.'

Nathaniel strode through the group to stand in front of Ethan. 'I want to help.'

Ethan placed his hand on his peer's shoulder. 'Nice to see you finally broke the shackles Nate.'

A mother and a father came forward. 'What do you want us to do?'

Karen was amazed at this simple acceptance of whatever magic Ethan was about to pull off. 'Can I be of use?' she asked.

'Most definitely.' Ethan drew these select few away from the rest of the group as he didn't want his next words to cause a panic in the children. 'Jordan's followers have reached a level of depravity that I didn't think possible. They've killed and eaten another human and are probably on their way here for… more tender meat as they put it.'

'That's impossible!' said Graham, the father.

Matthew shook his head. 'I saw and heard their boast myself otherwise I wouldn't have believed it either.'

'What do you need us to do?' Julie asked calmly, Graham's wife laid her hand on his arm.

'Your animal spirit will stand guard outside the gym's four entrances. You will be able to communicate with each other in here in English but outside all they'll hear is the animal's natural noises so the mob won't know what you're saying.' Ethan took a deep breath and lightly pressed his hand against the pentagram around his neck. 'Now you might want to sit on the floor for when your spirit leaves your body you may be a little dizzy.' As the volunteers obeyed Ethan continued, 'Take a deep cleansing breath and let it out slowly. Do this three times. Then I want you to think of the biggest most ferocious animal that you can imagine.'

Ethan turned to Mary. 'This might freak out the children so get the other parents to turn any little ones away. Thanks.' He gave his girlfriend a reassuring smile before turning back to the volunteers.

Matthew was the first to be able to release his spirit animal as something big, black and menacing emerged from the policeman as mist and slowly took a solid form. Karen exclaimed and looked up at Ethan in surprise. 'That's a bear!'

'Very good!' A sardonic look crossed Ethan's features. 'Give the Principal an A for Zoology!'

From Nathaniel emerged a tiger, Graham's animal came out trumpeting his entrance as a large elephant filled the room and Julie surprised the others by thinking of a hippopotamus.

'Hey,' Julie defended her choice, 'I heard on an episode of "QI" that the hippo kill more people than any other animal.'

Ethan turned to the Principal, 'We need aerial support. Eyes in the sky rather than a defender.' Karen closed her eyes and an eagle formed from her spirit. 'Nice,' said Ethan. 'Now remember don't be afraid to defend yourself but don't attack first. We don't want to kill anyone unless it is absolutely necessary. They may be under Jordan's spell but they are still our neighbours.' Ethan opened the front doors of the gym and the animal spirits left to surround the gym. As they took up their positions they became solid and formidable.

Animal Protectors

Outside, Karen the eagle circling high in the sky screeched alerting the people in the building that someone was approaching. Mary was ordered to remain inside as Ethan and Matthew slipped outside, and Mary locked the door behind them. Mathew's bear stood outside the front door. Three cars had pulled up and a dozen men jumped out. Some had rifles, others axes or hunting knives.

'Bloody hell!' whispered Kane, pulling out his own guns, 'Has the whole world gone completely mad?'

Ethan shook his head. 'If Jordan has anything to do with it; the world soon will be completely immoral and insane.' His hand travelled down the bear's head and neck, caressing his fur as he growled at the intruders who sauntered up to them.

'Give us the children!' demanded one gunman.

'Go Fuck Yourselves!' Ethan laughed, 'Oh sorry, you probably already have!'

Kane rolled his eyes. *Antagonising maniacs is hardly going to get us anywhere.* 'Do what you will to each other, but the children will not be harmed! Leave now before you get hurt!'

There was general laughter from the armed men. 'We have weapons!'

Ethan shook his head. 'We have animal protection.' There was a roar from the bear, tiger, and hippo as the elephant trumpeted. The men seemed to only notice the bear for the first time. There was a nervous look exchanged, but they did not back down.

'Jordan promised us young tender meat!'

That was too much for Matthew. 'Isn't there anything you can do to stop this insanity, Ethan?'

'Bear, these men are the enemy! If they try to harm us, kill them!'

Ethan's bluff was called as the men moved closer. A low growl emerged from the bear as he bounded into action, putting himself between Ethan and the gunmen. Some of them ran away, but others remained determined. Rifles were raised but before a shot could be fired, the bear was leaping at them.

Matthew could not believe how easy it was to allow his spirit animal to attack. A couple of men were knocked to the ground, and another fled in terror. There was a terrified scream as the bear lowered his massive jaw to the throat of one man, pinned beneath him.

'Bear you have done well!' Ethan's voice made the animal look up at him. 'Come, we've made our point.'

The bear obediently joined Ethan's side. Ethan paused long enough to give the bear a good scratch behind the ear before he issued a warning to the gunmen.

'The animals will be here to protect these innocents until the sun rises again. Next time I mightn't be here to call them off from a kill. Remember that, or be prepared to face the consequences of having your throat ripped out!' Those still standing helped up the men on the ground, and headed back to their cars.

One gunman shouted out, 'They can't stay in there forever! Nor will Jordan be pleased when he learns of your interference!'

Ethan shrugged. 'Go To Hell! Don't tell me how to fight this war. You've already lost!'

'You haven't heard the end of this!' was the gunman's final parting shot.

Matthew looked at Ethan in admiration as the cars drove away. 'Are you as brave as you appear to be?'

A look of surprise entered Ethan's face as he sighed. 'No, Matthew, I'm actually scared shitless! But that's not going to get the job done. Come on, I'm hungry. Maybe they've saved a hot dog or something for us.' With his mask of control firmly back in place, they were let back into the gymnasium and left the bear and the other animals to guard them.

Just One Will Do

KABOOM! The windows in the gymnasium rattled violently but they didn't shatter. KABOOM! With a flash of lightening, the gymnasium was suddenly filled with smoke. Ethan glanced around in professional interest.

'We're in big trouble!'

A deep laugh answered him. 'Oh my dear boy, you have no idea how much trouble you're in!' As the smoke cleared, Jordan became visible inside the gym.

'Still after your pound of flesh, Stranger?' asked the teenage wizard.

Jordan inclined his head in agreement. 'You like a joke don't you Ethan! But when I make a promise I keep it. One child will do!'

Ethan shook his head. 'Where will it end? One child won't go far when they all get a taste for human flesh. They'll only want more and more! One child will not do!'

Jordan grasped Ethan by the throat and lifted him bodily off the ground. 'Are you defying me?'

'Must be a slow news day!' Ethan croaked, making no attempt to tear at the fist around his throat. 'I thought that was obvious!'

'Don't push my patience boy, I have so little left.'

'You surprise me!' Ethan chuckled.

Help came an unexpected quarter as Nathaniel stepped bravely forward. 'Leave the others alone and I'll go with you.'

Ethan was released and dropped back onto the ground as Jordan looked over Nathaniel in interest. Matthew Kane laid his hand upon Nathaniel's shoulder.

'Do you understand what you're letting yourself in for?' asked the policeman.

Nathaniel nodded, a look of grim determination on his face. 'I can guess! Will that satisfy you Jordan?'

Jordan didn't immediately reply as he was looking around the gym at all the young people. 'Do you know what I would find entertaining?' When no one answered Jordan's question he continued, 'To watch the good folk of this village carve up and BBQ their own children! It's only a pity that I won't be around tomorrow when they begin to realise what they have done.'

A hysterical cry went through the room.

'You're Sick!'

'Insane!'

'Barbarian!'

Matthew held up his hands for quiet. 'They'd have to get in first, and that's no easy feat. They were sent packing last time.'

Jordan airily waved his hand. 'Then you only faced a dozen, this time I'll send the whole village down. An army of crazed, insane people are a little harder to scare off, even for your spirit animals.'

With a sigh, Mary shook her head. 'When are you going to end this madness? What do you gain from all of this?'

A wicked, wicked smile spread across Jordan's face. 'Immense pleasure, my dear little lamb! This is far from over, Ethan. The villagers will come!' With this parting shot, Jordan vanished.

Nathaniel looked from Matthew to Ethan. 'We're in trouble, aren't we?'

Ethan let out a deep sigh. 'Oh yeah! The very deepest!'

Internal War

Noise seemed to be attacking Acacia from all sides as she ran through a maze of people all screaming, crying or shouting out their anger and frustration. The noise was deafening, crowding in on Acacia as a physical pressure, as she tried to keep the anger from consuming her soul.

As the maze twists and turns, I realise that running is useless, as only more and more angry people seem to press around me. So I'm going to do something that will either save me or kill me!

She stopped running and stood perfectly still as she looked at the sea of faces around her. The abuse, language, complaints and tears continued to pour out of these people and Acacia began to see them as being quite pathetic.

Quite unexpectedly, Acacia started to laugh. The more their noise continued, the more she laughed. This was a sound that some of these people had not heard in a long time, as they had heard nothing but their own anger and the complaints from the others. Acacia's laughter stunned them into eventual silence, and only when her laughter was the only sound to be heard, Acacia finally stopped. She now had their complete attention.

'How long have you been doing this to yourselves? For how long have you allowed this anger to prevent you from crossing over to a new life?' Acacia received dumb expressions from those assembled, and she shook her head sadly. 'It's your unresolved issues, anger or grief that is holding you to this earth-bound half existence. That can only be making you angrier. Let it go, and allow the healing process to begin.'

The voices rose again.

'What do you know of my problems?'

'You don't understand!'

'The mistakes I have made!'

'Revenge will be mine!'

'Anger is all we have known for so long.'

The noise level increased as the people began again with their complaints. Acacia sighed; *reasoning is obviously not going to work with them.* She pressed her hands against her ears, but the noise kept coming at her like a wave constantly washing, battering against the shore. Somewhere over all of the angry voices, Acacia heard the soft, mesmerising sound of a gothic rock singer.

I'm so tired of being here,
Suppressed by all my childish fears.
And if you have to leave,
I wish that you would just leave.
Cause your presence still lingers here
And it won't leave me alone,
These wounds won't seem to heal,
This pain is just too real,
There's just too much that time cannot erase.''

Acacia sighed, falling deep into relaxation; as the magical lyrics of Amy Lee and Evanescence's "My Immortal" had always had a calming effect upon her. Now, as the voice continued to sing, Acacia raised up her own voice in song.

When you cried I'd wipe away all of your tears,
When you'd scream I'd fight away all of your fears,
And I held your hand through all of these years,
But you still have all of me.'

The noise around her no longer existed as the purity of song filled her with the love and power to block out their hatred. As Acacia and the gothic voice continued the song, the angry people started to become less angry, some of them even stopped talking so that they could listen to the singing and the emotions that the words represented. The magic and mystic of the song was destroying their anger, and very soon all had stopped speaking to listen to her message of hope and love.

'You used to captivate me by your resonating light,
Now I'm bound by the life you left behind,
Your face, it haunts my once pleasant dreams,
Your voice, it chased away all the sanity in me.
These wounds won't seem to heal,

This pain is just too real,
There's just too much that time cannot erase.
When you cried I'd wipe away all of your tears,
When you'd scream I'd fight away all of your fears,
And I held your hand through all of these years,
But you still have all of me.
I've tried so hard to tell myself that you're gone,
But though you're still with me,
I've been alone all along.
When you cried I'd wipe away all of your tears,
When you'd scream I'd fight away all of your fears,
And I held your hand through all of these years,
But you still have all of me.
All of me... me... me...'

Slowly as their anger diminished, the people began to disappear. They had finally found it possible to let go and cross over. Acacia continued to sing as the people around her became transparent and then vanished. It was not until she and her musical mentor had completed a second song that Acacia found that she was completely alone. The voice disappeared as Acacia fell to her knees and sent a prayer of thanks to the God and Goddess, and the musical talents of Amy Lee and Evanescence.

Entrapped

The sound of slowly clapping hands made Acacia jump, rise quickly to her feet and turn to face Jordan. She was still trapped in the dream realm. Her breathing quickened as she realised the danger she was in. Jordan smiled like a wolf would smile at a lamb he was about to make his dinner.

'Very good, Sweet Angel! I did not think that you could handle so much hostility. Perhaps I've made it all too easy for you.' Even though she knew there was nowhere to go, Acacia backed away from him.

'Do you enjoy what you do?' she demanded.

Jordan shrugged. 'Who wouldn't? A life of morals is very boring, my dear. Just look at your pathetic Michael.'

'But you destroy people's lives. Their souls!'

'So?'

'That is wrong, Jordan. It's not what life is all about.'

He chuckled, taking a step closer to her, his eyes half closing in a seductive manner. 'Innocent one! Life is a game of chance, some will live, and others will die! Your seven deadly sins are the greatest joys of the Master.'

Acacia folded her arms across her chest, determined to bring this interview to a close. 'What do you want from me?'

Jordan looked surprised as he scanned her from top to toe. 'What do I ever want?' He laughed as Acacia defensively stepped away from him. 'But I must ensure that you're with me, if not, well then I must keep you out of my way.'

Acacia nervously licked her lips. 'Why would you consider me a danger? You'll attempt to take Ethan with you tonight, whether I'm there to stop you or not. So who else is in danger from you?' She received no reply except the raising of his sardonic eyebrow. 'Who?' There was now an edge of urgency to her voice.

'*Acacia? Wake up Acacia! Ethan needs you!*' Michael's voice broke through into Acacia's thoughts. With blazing eyes Acacia glared at Jordan.

'What have you done?'

'Nothing!' A flash of white teeth was displayed as Jordan smiled. 'Yet! But trapped in here, you cannot hinder my plans!'

Acacia shook her head, a look of determination in her eyes. 'Don't bet on it!' Removing from her cleavage, Acacia drew out her necklace to reveal the pentagram amulet that had lain hidden.

'*With Pentagram and magic verse, I must escape this wicked curse. As these words of freedom are spoken, Let this evil spell be broken.*' As she spoke the spell, Acacia felt herself return to her physical form, but Jordan wasn't going to allow her to escape so easily.

'You may run, Acacia, but you can't hide forever. If you choose to cross me, be afraid, be very afraid!'

With these final words ringing in her ears, Acacia suddenly sat up, her chest heaving as she gasped for breath, as if she'd been actually running. Michael was kneeling beside her, one of her hands being held in his, wearing a look of deep concern he never took his eyes off her face.

'Acacia! Did you understand me? Did I manage to reach you?'

For a moment all Acacia could do was nod her head as she came to grips with being back in the physical world. 'Ethan! Where is he?'

Michael had the grace to look a little guilty because Acacia had left Ethan in his charge.

'Well, he, Mary and Matthew Kane are at the school. Mary called me. Apparently Jordan is sending down all the villagers to have a BBQ with their children.'

Acacia frowned as she tried to understand what was so desperate about that. 'And the problem is…?'

'It's the menu choice really. The villagers intend to BBQ their own offspring!'

Acacia's eyes opened wide in surprise. 'Sacred Mother preserve us all! Will nothing be left untouched by this madness?' She managed to swing her legs over the side of the bed and stand up without swaying too much. Michael was already on his feet and heading for the door.

'We'll need a car.' He said and Acacia agreed with that.

'And a plan!' Acacia also agreed with that. *But the latter needs more thought as I'm fast running out of ideas.*

Mass Blood Lust

Bloodthirsty, flesh hungry villagers armed with rifles and sharp and deadly gardening implements, in fact anything they could get their hands on, made their way upon foot towards the school. They moved as one mass down the roads making Michael glad he and Acacia had borrowed Mac's four-wheel drive, as they were forced to go over countryside to get around the mob and to the school first. One group of villagers was already outside the school, surrounding the gym, banging occasionally on doors or windows. The massive animal spirits remained an effective defence against the siege.

There were too many people milling around for it to be safe for Michael to drive any closer, their only alternative was to get through on foot. Acacia wrapped her cloak firmly around her and placed a hand upon Michael's arm to stop him surging forward.

'*Dark and Shadows, Make us disappear from view, invisibility we need from you.*' Acacia whispered her spell and she and Michael began to disappear from view.

'Are we still here?' whispered Michael as Acacia led him towards the angry crowd.

'Hush! We must not be heard!' Acacia retained possession of his hand as they slid silently and unseen through the people. No one suspected who passed by them, but there was still a problem of the doors all being locked. Although invisible, they could not walk through walls.

'*Ethan? I'm here! Michael and I have come to help you.*' Acacia sent the message telepathically. People were still too close to the doors for Ethan to safely let them in; so Acacia threw up one hand so that sparks flew up into the sky, and went off like fireworks. The people gathered outside, turned to watch the display giving Ethan half a minute to open the door so that two invisible figures could sneak secretly in.

Once safely inside and the doors locked again, Michael and Acacia slowly became visible again. There was a murmur of astonishment and surprise from the parents and children assembled inside, and there was a round of applause as Acacia and Michael materialised. Sadly Acacia shook her head.

'Magic is still a stage act to them!'

Ethan lost some of his composure and hugged Acacia, grateful for her safe arrival. 'I honestly didn't know what to do, Ace! As strong as these people are, their animal spirits can't handle an entire village! I don't think I can either!'

Acacia surprised everyone by slapping Ethan's arm. 'Have I taught you nothing? When you take away reality, what remains?'

'Insanity?' drawled Matthew Kane. He managed to look rueful as Acacia cast him a speaking glance.

'Ethan?'

'What you have left is imagination. I see what you're driving at, but it's one thing to make a couple of people invisible. It is something else when it comes to nearly a hundred or more.'

Mary frowned thoughtfully as she listened to their conversation. 'What you need is to be able to do is make the people inside invisible and make the people outside think that the people inside are fleeing, to draw them away from the school.'

Looks of astonishment were centred upon Mary as they attempted to make her suggestion feasible theoretically.

'Can you do that?' demanded Kane, still very unsure of the powers of the Craft.

Acacia nodded. 'It can be done, but it would take a powerful source of energy. I don't have that much strength left.'

'But I have!' Ethan's eyes locked with Acacia's.

Again Acacia nodded, her eyes quite sad. 'It'll leave you vulnerable to an attack from Jordan though.'

This problem Ethan waved away with a gesture of his hand. 'He'll come for me anyway. If I can save these children, then it will be worth the risk!' His mind was obviously made up.

Michael looked around the room at the people waiting for them to save their lives. *This may be the greatest challenge we'll ever face.* 'So what do we need to do?' *There is so little time left as midnight will soon be upon us.*

Ethan removed his necklace and silver pentagram that he always wore, and looked down at it as he spoke deliberately. 'What we need is someone very sane, who can keep their cool in an emergency.' Slowly he looked up, his eyes going straight to Matthew Kane.

'What do I have to do?' The Constable swallowed hard.

Ethan smiled reassuringly, as he placed his necklace around Matthew's neck. 'You'll be my channel. As Acacia and I lead the blood thirsty villagers outside away from the school, with a phantom image of the children, you'll be able to make yourself and the others here invisible.'

'There is one problem, though,' added Acacia. 'The children must be kept as quiet as possible. To be truly invisible you cannot be seen or heard!'

Michael had a question that worried him. 'Would the villagers return here once they realise that they've been duped?'

Ethan shrugged. 'Possibly, but it should give Matthew enough time to get everyone up to the sanctuary of the church. It'll be crowded, but it'll only be till midnight.' He glanced anxiously across at Acacia, before adding, 'We hope!'

The lights in the gymnasium were deliberately dimmed as Ethan prepared Matthew who sat on the floor meditation fashion with his legs crossed and his hands palms upwards upon his knees.

'Try not to think too much. Just imagine what it would be like to be invisible. The wind blowing felt, unseen, but for its effect. The villagers may burst in, but you must remain calm. Once they see us fleeing the building, they'll come after us,' instructed Ethan.

Matthew wriggled for a moment until he got comfortable. 'I am the wind! I am the Phantom! I am the Shadow!' The bear, Matthew's spirit animal began to vanish outside.

Ethan nodded his approval. 'Very good.' Turning back to Acacia he added, 'It is time we left.'

Both Michael and Mary had no intention of being left behind and stated almost simultaneously. 'I'm coming too!'

Ethan cast a questioning look at Acacia, but she only shrugged.

'They must be allowed to choose their own destiny. The farm is closer, I think. Are you ready Ethan?'

The Phantom Chase

They crept out of one of the doors of a changing room, which wasn't being guarded outside. All attention was focused on the front doors. Nathaniel's tiger spirit had come round to protect the front doors as the bear disappeared. Ethan closed his eyes and took a deep, deep breath.

'*Through this man take them out of sight, and make their reflection appear to flight.*' As he did so all colour and visibility began to vanish from the people inside the gym, and a three dimensional image of each of them appeared outside. When this was completed, Ethan opened his eyes again.

'Let's go!' There was power now in his voice as he was in charge.

The villagers outside witnessed Ethan lead his false army across the playground. There was a universal cry at the sight of the escaping images, and the chase was on. The time for sneaking around was over, and now it was time to run, and run hard.

'*Take the blood lust from these men and protect the children from their kin.*' Acacia chanted as she ran beside Michael. The savagery and blood lust left the mob, but the need to follow Jordan's orders still consumed them. So the chase continued.

Once the area was finally clear of all villagers as Matthew Kane led the children and their parents out of the gym the phantom images following Ethan vanished.

I hoped we would've led the mob further away from the school by the time they vanished, mused Ethan, *and that the villagers won't turn back for the children. Acacia's spell has seen to it that their lust for human flesh has been vanquished.* Ethan glanced across at Acacia; her sheer will to survive was all that was keeping her going.

'We've got to slow them down further, Ethan.'

He nodded. '*Spirit of light, make them see that they cannot fight gravity. Make their feet as heavy as lead, as they become light in the head.*'

The spell worked almost instantly. The mob of villagers taking on a vacant expression as their footsteps slowed to a heavy walk. They would continue to follow, but it gave Michael, Mary, Acacia and Ethan the opportunity for a head start. As they approached the farmhouse, Acacia felt relief and pain. Her damaged leg and ankle were killing her. *Although we'll momentarily know sanctuary, Jordan will now come for us. The hour of Samhain midnight is close at hand!*

Last Line Of Defence

Entering the house, Michael securely locked the door behind them, Ethan and Mary raced upstairs to close and lock all the windows as Acacia attended to the downstairs doors and windows. The wind howled loudly around the house and the dogs cowered under the lounge suite, a feeling of foreboding swept over Acacia. *I know this time there can be no escape from Jordan. His power has become too strong to match, even for Ethan. The Protector will stand no chance against him.*

'Ace! Come and see this!' Ethan's command from upstairs saw Michael and Acacia bound up the stairs two at a time. They found Ethan and Mary standing in front of the front bedroom window. Acacia pushed the curtains to one side and surprised Michael by swearing. Towards the house approached the villagers in a zombie like fashion and many were now carrying torches of fire.

'That bastard is just not going to play fair! They'll burn down the house. This insanity will take us all with him!'

Ethan frowned, deep in thought. 'Will the Protector keep them out?'

Acacia shook her head. 'Them, yes but against the likes of him? No, I must try something else now. Stay up here and on no account should you leave this house till morning.'

The lights went out as Acacia descended the stairs and she quickly flashed a telepathic message to Ethan.

'Do not leave the room you're in and lock the door!' As she sensed her way through the hall, Acacia heard the external French doors in her meditation room rattle in the strong wind. With the intention of completely securing the door, Acacia entered the dark room. The rattling stopped immediately but that had more to do with the fact that the wind had suddenly died outside than anything Acacia could do.

A mischievous, wicked laugh from behind her sent a chill down Acacia's spine. Even before she turned around, she already knew that she was in trouble.

'I don't suppose you would be prepared to make a deal?' She said to the dark, seemingly empty room. A second laugh directed Acacia's eyes to the corner of the room behind the door. The only thing that Acacia could see was the white of Jordan's teeth and the strange glow that emanated from his eyes.

'Are you offering yourself, Sweet Angel? Yesterday, I may have actually accepted your offer, but now that I've seen the power that Ethan possesses, I'd be a fool not to take such a prize of a pupil under my control.'

Acacia attempted to contact Ethan, but Jordan was blocking her reception.

'Naughty, naughty, Sweet Angel. You must know by now that you're no match for me? The boy is too young yet to be able to control all of his powers. I was surprised, though, that you felt the need to cleanse yourself after I left you last night!' Jordan moved forward to place his hand under her chin and forced her eyes to lock with his.

'And end up like those people outside? Someone must stand against you!'

His laugh resounded through her whole body. 'What I meant was that I had expected you to turn to the boy and not the priest. Why did you choose a less pure vessel?'

Acacia tried to pull away from Jordan, but his grip tightened as his arm slid around her waist and he held her against him. 'Ethan's first time should have been for him and not for duty. I could not ask that of him, and you knew it!'

At the edge of her consciousness, Acacia felt Michael's presence outside the room, and knew that she would have to distract Jordan's attention to give Michael a chance to escape.

'What was I then? Business or pleasure?' demanded Jordan.

Managing to smile, Acacia moved slightly against him. 'A bit of both.' She lied. 'You know your own attraction, I feared submission, but it doesn't mean that I couldn't have enjoyed you if you'd been a little more giving. You may be evil itself, but you certainly know how to use that body your Master encased you in!'

Jordan's eyes sparkled. 'Come with me then! Together we can mould Ethan into the new Demonic Saviour! I can see to it that you will live forever.'

Acacia hesitated, wondering, *How much power do I possess over him?* 'My soul for Ethan's?'

She was answered by a sigh. 'Ah, so we're back to business. You do realise that I could take you with me anyway, don't you? Every second you hesitate, you lose your will to resist me. You have nothing left to bargain with, Sweet Angel, the boy belongs to me!'

They both heard the back door creak as Michael opened it. Jordan swore as he slapped Acacia hard across the face. 'You cunning little jade! But he's not important to me; the priest's fate was sealed when he succumbed to your bewitching charms. The boy will come with me now, Acacia. You can come or stay, it matters not, just don't get in my way! Bring the boy to me, or do I have to tear this house apart?'

'That won't be necessary.' The lights flicked on as Ethan entered the room. 'Michael has taken Mary to the safety of the church. You cannot hurt them now. I'll go with you but you must liberate the village from your spell.'

Jordan released Acacia to turn and face Ethan. 'You're mastering your powers very quickly Ethan. Under my guidance, you'll soon be ready for world domination.'

Acacia moved around Jordan and grasped Ethan by the shoulders. 'No! Oh, Ethan, you can't! The Family will ensure that you're taken care of, but I'm a minor player, I mean nothing compared to you!'

Ethan smiled tenderly at her as he shook his head. 'You once told me, Ace, that when the time comes, I'll know what my destiny will be. The time has come. If I leave with Jordan, this nightmare will end.'

A laugh came from Jordan. 'Don't bet on it, protégé! The Master has many plans for you. Frankly I had expected to have had much more fun before you submitted. Never mind, the circle of fire, our entrance to Hell, awaits us.' He gestured towards the door but Acacia refused to release Ethan.

'Don't do this! Please!' Tears sprang to Acacia's eyes as Ethan gently removed her hands.

'Trust me, Ace! This is the best way!' Kissing Acacia on both cheeks, Ethan turned to address Jordan. 'I'm ready.' Ethan led the way out of the front door. The zombie like crowd surged forward but was controlled by a gesture from Jordan, who followed a deeply distressed Acacia out of the house.

'Go, my moronic followers! Go and finish preparing the circle of fire for our departure!'

The people turned and headed in a slow march, up to the cemetery and the church on the hill. As they followed the crowd, Acacia laid an insistent hand on Jordan's arm. 'You promised that you would leave the village as you found it!'

Jordan's eyebrows rose in surprise as he tucked her hand into his arm. 'I don't remember any such promise, Sweet Angel. But if you ask nicely…'

Ethan frowned in disapproval. 'Don't push it, Jordan! I'm coming to the end of my patience!'

'Oohh! So the child protégé has a temper! Good, perhaps there is hope for you yet!'

Ethan glared at him. 'I doubt it! And keep your hands off Acacia. If I have anything to do with it, you won't get a chance for second course! You wouldn't ever have had first course if Acacia hadn't felt that it was her duty to protect me from your depravity.'

Jordan's laughter brought angry colour to Ethan's cheeks, 'Oh, how noble, man cub! The only problem is the fact that your virtuous Acacia actually enjoyed her first course. She just doesn't want to give in to complete freedom.'

With the cemetery in sight, Ethan stopped and turned to face Acacia, horror written across his young face, 'Ace?'

She felt the accusation in his eyes and Acacia flinched as she reached out to take one of his hands. 'It's not like that, Ethan! Of course I didn't enjoy being raped. I did fight but I had to lie to him just now to see if he would take me instead of you.'

Ethan frowned in thought and Acacia began to tremble, fearing that she had incurred his displeasure.

'What about Michael?' Ethan demanded.

The bonfire was lit and it illuminated Acacia's eyes and without being able to stop herself, she smiled dreamily. 'Michael was able to touch something deep inside of me that no one else has ever been able to reach. If I ever had the chance to live my life with one man, it would be with him.' Acacia gave a startled cry as Jordan roughly grasped Acacia's arms and pulled her against him.

'Let us settle this once and for all! No priest is better than I am! You shall spend an eternity realising your mistake!' Jordan headed towards the circle of fire, his grip on Acacia unrelenting as he now intended to take her with him. Around them, the villagers stood in a large circle around the flames; their vacant eyes looked deep into the mesmerising flames.as they danced and leapt into the air.

'No!' The command came not from Ethan, but Michael as he arrived from the direction of the church. The large metallic cross around his neck caught the light of the flames and caused the villagers to cry out and shield their eyes as they collapsed to their knees and pressed their faces into the grass.

Jordan shook his head as he looked at the villagers tremble at the sight of an icon of God.

'You really can't get good help now a days! Well Priest? I don't cower to a religious symbol, so I hope you have something more productive to add to this performance?'

As Jordan had loosened his grip upon Acacia, Ethan drew her away from him and the flames. Michael would not look at them, keeping his attention solely upon Jordan.

'How much fun will you really get breaking the boy? A day, maybe a week, but not much longer. Someone like me would take you years of torture to break.'

Laughing, Jordan clapped his hands together, 'Very impressive, Priest! With Acacia it was sex, with you its torture. Nice try, but no cigar! I am taking what I came here for.'

Ethan stepped calmly towards Jordan; his face set in determination. 'And no one else! Only me!' His words were a clear warning to all, but as Jordan stepped into the circle of fire, Acacia could not help herself.

'Ethan, No!' She reached out to him, but as he turned to face her, his eyes radiated white heat as he filled her with pain.

'I'm sorry Ace!' It brought a lump to his throat as he watched Acacia fall to her knees in intense agony. As he stepped into the circle,

Acacia collapsed completely. The flames leapt higher, as Jordan and Ethan were swept up in a vortex of wind. In a flash of lightning, the fire died and they were gone.

Aftermath

The town hall clock chimed midnight as Michael knelt down beside Acacia. When they looked out of the church doors and seeing the villagers return to their normal selves and rise to their feet; Mary and Matthew Kane came down to join Michael.

'Ethan! How I failed you!' Acacia's cry of anguish brought tears to Mary's eyes.

Matthew, not liking to see Acacia so distraught, kept his attention on Michael. 'Shall I see the villagers in the church returned to their homes?' Michael nodded in agreement, and Matthew went back into the church to get everyone organised.

'What is going on, Father Michael?' This came from Mrs Catherine de Bere.

Michael took a deep breath and looked at his dishevelled parishioners. 'It's a long story, Mrs de Bere. Go home, everyone, and I'll see all of you at Mass tomorrow. Regardless of whether you're Catholic or not! All your souls need to be cleansed. '

Mary laid her hand on Michael's shoulder. 'Take Acacia home and care for her. I'll round up these lost sheep before I join you.'

Sighing, Michael glanced at the bewildered expressions on the faces around him. 'They might not even remember what has passed this week.' Looking back down at Acacia, who quietly wept, he added, 'We shall never have that luxury.' Mary walked back up to the church without replying, as they all knew that there was no reply suitable.

Michael assisted Acacia to her feet and tried to guide her steps back to her home, but she was reluctant to leave the cemetery.

'I have destroyed everything! Your life, Ethan's, even Mary's. I must remain here! I must wait for Ethan's return.'

Michael placed his arm firmly around Acacia's waist and forced her to start down the hill. 'You can't stay here Acacia! Ethan won't be coming back. You haven't slept in four days and you're exhausted.'

Although Acacia's feet moved down the hill, she continued to look over her shoulder at the area of scorched grass where the circle of fire had recently been. 'I can't leave, I must be with Ethan!'

Finally, Michael lost his patience and scooped Acacia up and over his shoulder. Although Acacia protested, Michael kept walking even as she pounded her fists against his back.

The farmhouse was eerily silent as Michael carried Acacia inside and up to her bedroom. Throwing her onto the bed, Michael captured Acacia's hands in his own as she attempted to scratch his face.

'Sheath your claws, Tigress! I'm too tired to fight and so are you. Ethan is not coming back; you just have to accept that!'

Suddenly Acacia gave up the fight and went limp, collapsing into the softness of her bed. 'I should have gone with him. The Family expected me to protect him. Ethan was our future.'

Shaking his head, Michael sat down on the bed beside Acacia cradling her in his arms. 'Perhaps this was Ethan's destiny, for he has indeed saved mankind from the prospect of the Eternal Night. Ethan will never be dead so long as you always hold a place for him in your heart.'

'Or at least a room in your home!' This drawled statement from the doorway surprised them both as they exclaimed simultaneously, 'Ethan!'

Greek Mythology

Wicked laughter danced in the boy's eyes, his arm around Mary, who was beaming, as Acacia and Michael sprang up from the bed to embrace them. Laughing but also crying, Acacia held Ethan at arms length, her hands cupping his face. Mary held onto the Book of the Nephilim.

'Oh, you wicked boy! How did you escape from Jordan?'

Ethan eased Acacia and Mary down on to the bed, before throwing himself onto the pillows. 'I never thought that I would ever be grateful to you for forcing me to read Greek mythology. With our own wealth of history, I had never seen the point. But as I entered the circle of flames, a little story came back to me.'

Michael sat down beside Acacia as Mary grasped one of Ethan's hands and begged, 'Which one?'

Michael smiled; *Our curiosity is exactly what Ethan wants.*

'Orpheus and the Underworld. He loses his lover, Eurydice and journeys to the underworld to bring her back. He was told not to look behind him until he was on the other side of the underworld, but he did look and thus lost Eurydice forever.'

Michael frowned in deep thought. 'Did Jordan lose you because he looked back?'

A wicked chuckle answered him. 'No, Jordan lost me because he didn't look behind him! That is why I couldn't let you come with me, Ace, vanishing would not have been possible if there had been two of us.'

'Oh wicked, wicked boy! How you scared me!' laughed Acacia, through her tears.

Mary, though, was frowning. 'Won't Jordan return once he realises that you didn't go with him?'

Ethan shook his head; again the mischievous smile appeared. 'He went back voluntarily, midnight has now passed, besides which Jordan has his sacrifice.' He paused to give his words time to sink in for effect.

'Whom?' Michael had little patience left.

Ethan laughed. 'I put Rochester de Bere, the toad, in his coat pocket!'

Laughter filled the room and Mary hugged Ethan in delight, but Ethan hadn't finished. Yet!

'There is something else that I wish to discuss with you, Ace; now that Jordan is fading into a memory.' Ethan's seriousness surprised them as they waited impatiently for his revelation.

'The Family will send me a new Mentor, but I don't want to leave you and the farm. Not yet any way. He'll have to adapt to our way of life here, unless you want to get rid of me?'

Acacia pressed his hand reassuringly. 'Of course I don't want you to leave but your Mentor…'

Ethan would not let her finish. 'He'll have to adjust and that is final. Wherever I go, I want it to be possible for you and Mary to be with me.' He then gestured to the Book of the Nephilim. 'We'll hold on to this here until the appropriate authorities come to relieve us of its presence. Another thing, sister, I think that it's time that you gave me a brother-in-law!' Ethan's eyes rested upon Michael, his message very clear to all.

Acacia glanced nervously up at Michael's sudden unemotional mask. 'Ethan, it's not as easy as that. I forced Michael to break his vow of celibacy. That was a major sacrifice! I... we cannot ask Michael to give up all that he believes in. We belong to two different worlds; our way is not for everyone.'

'That is very true,' agreed Michael. 'I'll have a lot to learn in my new way of life.' Ethan and Mary laughed as Acacia's jaw dropped in surprise.

'I don't understand! What about St Andrews?' demanded Acacia.

Michael tenderly cupped Acacia's chin in his hands as he smiled. 'Having tasted heaven, how can I possibly return to that previous life and be content?'

'You need time to consider such a quantum leap in lifestyles,' argued Acacia.

Michael shook his head. 'I have considered. Every waking and sleeping moment you're not far from my thoughts. I've come to realise that I can't live without you!'

Ethan nodded his head wisely and whispered to Mary, 'That sounded like a marriage proposal if I ever heard one!'

Acacia threw a pillow at his head. 'Be quiet, brat! This isn't the time for such a discussion. I think we all need time to sleep on this before we continue this conversation any further.' The two men accepted this statement as they exchanged a speaking glance and Mary wondered, *How soon can we get a replacement pastor for St Andrew's church?*